I0658930

Family Shadows

Jeanne Moon Farmer

Word Light Press, Maitland, FL

Family Shadows
Jeanne Moon Farmer
Book One of the Family Shadows Series

© 2013 by Jeanne Moon Farmer
ISBN: 978-1-938643-00-2

AUTHOR'S NOTE: Family Shadows is a work of fiction. Names, characters, events and incidents are either the products of the author's imagination or used in a fictitious manner. Any resemblance to actual persons, living or dead, or actual events is purely coincidental.

WORDLIGHT
PRESS

Word Light Press
P O Box 94-8636
Maitland, Florida 32794-8636
theshadowbooks@gmail.com

Cover design: Rik Feeney / **www.PublishingSuccessOnline.com**
Photograph: © OSTILL | Bigstockphoto.com

Acknowledgements

God put some extraordinary people in my life who helped me create this novel - people with talent, grace, warmth, and wisdom. The generosity of their time and talent poured forth as a priceless gift once I uttered the words, "I have an idea." They believed I could do it before I did.

I would like to thank my two critique groups. First, my friends and business partners, Beverly Haskins and Diane Mullen, who lived the journey with me from the first words on the page. This special team read, reread, edited, suggested, and helped me keep the events and characters of this book real. Their red pens were the first to correct my grammar and word usage, and I can still hear them asking, "Why is this relevant or necessary?" Their hard work turned my dream into a reality.

Second, fellow wordsmiths, Peggy Harris and Verta Sorenson, kept my writing in the 21st Century. They didn't hesitate to say, "you can do better than this," when they saw that I was going off track with a character or thought I needed some 'white space' on a page.

My Book Club 'sisters,' Marion Daley, Linda Fegan, Pam Foxman, Patty Fritch, Cindy Hennig, Marina Lombardo, Sherry O'Leary, and Leslie Reilly gave me the courage to begin writing. Once a month for twelve years these gals have devoured the written word searching for great stories, and every now and then they looked at me and said, "write us a good book."

My sons, Ty, Todd and Troy Moon, encouraged and contributed in their own special ways. Ty, an avid crime drama reader and war history buff, helped me through the court room scenes and guided me through the Korean Conflict - "get your facts right, Mom"; Todd reminded me that I had two minutes to grab his attention -"make those first words count, Mom, then keep my attention with some good dialogue"; and Troy wanted the characters to be real and very human -- "make me hate Mary Ann, make me want Carter to win, and help me understand why the characters do what they do." I'm so glad I taught these guys to read and they continue to share my love of books.

Buddy and Laurette Byram, my brother and sister-in-law, checked on my progress every week and kept reminding me to "go for it." Buddy helped me remember the Miami of our childhood and youth.

My story editor, Jennifer Gregory, guided and polished until this book became a finished product that is reader - worthy. Her honesty and skills made a difference.

And, publishing coach extraordinaire, Rik Feeney, helped me put all of the pieces of the puzzle together. His knowledge - and ability to communicate what he knows - is amazing.

Special thanks and hugs to the two who lived with me through this labor of love - my husband, Gary Farmer, and my mother, Billie Byram. Their patience, understanding, and encouragement are my anchor.

Dedication

Dedicated with love to Ty and Todd
and all children, adopted or otherwise,
who are raised by loving individuals
who are not their biological family.

Table of Contents

Family Shadows

Prologue

Miami, June 1956

The latest copy of Life Magazine had come in the mail and all day Gracie McDeal had looked forward to enjoying the photographs and articles. Sitting at the kitchen table after dinner, she sipped her cup of tea and leisurely flipped through the pages. Baltimore: Crossroad for Culture and Sports, she cringed as the title jumped off the page. Nothing good ever came from remembering Baltimore.

Years ago, she and Edgar had run away from that city to start a new life in Miami and they had never looked back. Tonight, the magazine article stirred it all up again and the image of a frightened young girl seeking comfort from the beautiful windows at St. Peter's Church flooded her mind. How familiar it felt to gaze at the stained glass faces of the Holy Family. How often Mary's face had renewed her and given her hope. She still carried in her heart a promise that she knew had been given to her by the Blessed Virgin. But hope and comfort were shattered as the years of darkness crashed into her and made her vulnerable. Squeezing her eyes shut, she tried to shake off the shadows of the past.

Startled by the front door bell, she let the magazine slip from her hand and hit the floor. Who in the world would come calling after 9:00 PM? Surely, her son Carter, who sat watching T.V. in the living room would take care of the caller. Picking up the magazine, she slowly made it into a fan and waved it back and forth in front of her damp face. The June air hung heavy inside the kitchen and the little bit of air stirred up by the fan made the room feel even warmer. If this was June, she hated to think how the rest of the summer might feel.

"Who rang the bell this late at night, Carter? Nobody comes to call at this hour."

Concerned when he didn't answer, she listened for any sound that might give her a hint of what was happening. It was a relief when she heard his footsteps coming closer to the kitchen. She dropped the magazine on the table and ran her fingers through her curls in case he was bringing someone to visit.

"Mom?" Carter stood in the doorway with a puzzled look on his face.

"What's the matter, son? You look like you've seen a ghost. What in the world is in that box?"

PART ONE

SHADOWS FORM

"There are men too gentle to live among wolves
Who toss them like a lost and wounded dove.
Such gentle men are lonely in a merchant's world
Unless they have a gentle one to love."
James Cavanaugh

Chapter One

Carter - The Early Years

From the day he was born, Carter McDeal had satisfied his mother's desire to be needed. She pampered him, worried over him, and molded him with a routine that would become as much a part of his personality as his love for the big city busses that carried people to all parts of the city. He loved to watch the busses go up and down the streets, he loved to ride the bus, and he dreamed that one day he would be able to drive the bus. His best Christmas gift was the model bus his father gave him when he was eight years old. In his mind this was not a toy to play with in the backyard; it was a symbol for his dream. It sat on the shelf in his bedroom to be admired and polished. Whenever he took it to school for 'show and tell,' he would brag to the other boys that one day he was going to drive a big bus for the transit company.

His parents, Gracie and Edgar, were pleased their son had a dream, but they always hoped he would aspire to something beyond driving a bus. Edgar, who dropped out of school after the eighth grade, had a list of priorities for his son, and decided early on to put aside money every month to help Carter go to college. He told Carter over and over that he wanted him to have the kind of education that would open doors for him. As soon as Carter was six years old, he was enrolled in the parish school where the nuns would make sure he had what he needed to make his dad's dreams come true. Edgar's dreams were big; Carter's dreams were the size of a city bus.

When Carter was ten years old, America entered the conflict against Japan and Germany. His dad was drafted into the army, was shipped to Europe to fight, and within the year was killed in battle in a far off town in Italy.

While his mother grieved in obvious ways, he did his grieving silently. He didn't have a name for his feelings, but sometimes he felt relieved that he would never again have to see the disappointment in his dad's eyes. Now the only dream that existed was his, and the competition between his dream and his dad's was wiped away by the bullets of someone neither he nor his dad ever met.

Fortunately, his dad's life insurance and military benefits made it possible for his life to move forward without too many financial obstacles. His mother could remain at home and he wasn't pressed to go to work before he completed high school.

For financial reasons, he left parochial school after he finished junior high, and enrolled in Miami Jackson High School. This was his awakening to girls, one girl in particular named Sharon Peterson. She was a perky blonde with curly hair and deep blue eyes that seemed to always reflect the summer sky. She would never look twice at him so he admired her from afar. They sat next to each other in English class, but he felt too shy to even look in her direction. She surprised him when she began to talk to him about homework assignments and class projects, and over the weeks he went from nodding his head to responding to her questions. Throughout the school year it got easier and easier to talk with her, but he never made any overtures beyond their English class assignments.

On the first day of his senior year, his spirits lifted when he walked into the chemistry lab and Sharon was sitting at one of the lab tables. Abandoning the usual calm and reserve that governed his life, he stepped out of his shadow and uncharacteristically took the seat next to her. For weeks, he made every effort to engage her in conversation and to take note of where she was and who she was friendly with during lunch time. He watched to see if she was walking in the hall with a boy or if a boy sat with her at the lunch table. When he was sure there wasn't a boyfriend in her life, he made up his mind to ask her to the homecoming dance in October.

This was a risk - I'll have to practice what I want to say or I'll mess it up. Standing in front of the mirror, he rehearsed asking her to the dance and tried out some small talk that might keep the conversation going during the dance. For days the practice went on and on before he had the nerve to tell his mother what he was about to do.

"Guess what I'm going to do, mom?"

"You'll have to give me a little hint, Carter, or I could go on guessing all night."

"I'm going to ask a girl to the homecoming dance. She's really special, mom, and I know you'd like her."

"Oh, Carter, that's wonderful news." She stopped what she was doing at the stove and sat down next to him at the kitchen table. "I've put aside a little bit of money, and I want you to go and buy yourself a new suit. Go to Sears Roebuck and see what's on sale. Then you'll have enough to buy your girl a corsage and pick her up in a taxi," she said and smiled timidly. "Carter, do you want me to teach you how to dance?"

Her offer touched him. The money didn't really surprise him because his mother was always making sacrifices for him. But her excitement made him see her with new eyes. He had never thought she might understand his loneliness or his dreams, or see him as someone other than her little boy. For the first time he wondered if she might have dreams, too, and he realized that there was more to her than being his mother. This moment of awareness was beyond the shadows of his own self-centered existence and he remembered all the times his father had told him to try and make her happy. As he looked at her, he saw how drained and tired she was and he felt ashamed he had never noticed it before. He wanted to hug her and tell her he loved her, but this was not their way. Instead, he nodded yes to her invitation and silently vowed that one day he would find a way for her to really smile again.

"Mom, did you and dad go dancing? You know, before I was born. I can't imagine dad dancing." Carter gave a little chuckle and shyly lowered his eyes. "Mom, what's it like to love somebody the way you loved my dad?"

Gracie's response was tender and wistful. "Carter, it's hard to put love into words. You'll know it when it happens. It's like being in a big bear hug that never ends."

Carter watched as a change came over his mother's face. He couldn't read her expressions, but he thought he saw joy and pain.

The past washed over her as she remembered Edgar and she whispered, "Oh, Carter, I pray you will have someone in your life who loves you the way your father loved me."

* * *

The place where God lived was old and dark and glorious to Gracie O'Brian. It was where she found safety and protection. St. Peter the Apostle Church, built in Baltimore in 1842, ministered to the growing Irish population who had immigrated to the city in large numbers to work for the B&O Railroad. Statues of angels and the Holy Family inhabited the imposing Greek revival style building where young Gracie spent many hours naming each statue, praying to each angel, and trying to decide which angel was her guardian. "Gabriel, today I'd like for you to watch over me. Yesterday was Michael's turn." She had her favorites, but the beautiful angel standing closest to the Holy Family was the one that most often sat on her shoulder when she needed comfort and help.

As she sat on the hard pew that was polished to a high sheen, she absorbed the quiet majesty of the church. She found delight in the beautiful icons and the light filtering through the rich, jeweled toned windows mesmerized her. The four imposing stained glass windows cast a rainbow of light across the worshipping parishioners. The glass depicted Christ and Biblical scenes that heightened the sense of mystery she always felt when she entered St. Peter's. Everything about the church told her this was the special dwelling place of God. One of the stained glass windows portrayed the Virgin Mary. The figure was tall and her face showed that she was unafraid of the grief she must have been experiencing. This was the window Gracie loved. Every time she looked at the sad face of the Virgin Mary, she felt the tears pool in her eyes and she wondered why God had let them take Mary's son away from her.

Even at her young age, she thought losing a child was probably the most tragic thing that could happen to a woman.

Every day, until she started school, Gracie walked to the church with her grandmother. She watched the old woman finger her rosary beads and listened as she asked for forgiveness and protection for her family. Her heavy Irish accent did not hide the passion in her words and her prayers were as mysterious to Gracie as everything in the church.

Once she started school, her grandmother walked her to the gates of St. Peter's School before continuing her own walk down the block to the entrance of the sanctuary. The routine was the same until Gracie was twelve years old. Then she learned first hand about grief and suffering. On a cold, icy day in January, she woke up to voices and anxious movement in her house. Her father was shouting to her brother to run for Dr. McInnis and her mother was crying and calling to her grandmother to please wake up. Gracie bounded out of bed and raced to the door of her grandmother's bedroom, but when she tried to enter, her mother told her to go downstairs and start the kettle.

In a short time, the doctor arrived. He stayed behind the closed door of the bedroom for only a few minutes before her mother's wailing announced her grandmother's death.

The next change occurred the day before St. Patrick's Day. Her father came home and told them he had been demoted at his job on the railroad. In her eyes her father was a giant man of few words who worked, went to the pub and never went to Mass. He was a proud man who knew the job he did for the railroad was important and now, that job was no longer his and he didn't know why.

Her father simmered and smoldered as the days and weeks went by and he struggled with his anger and helplessness. Without the presence of her grandmother, he soon exploded into an abusive, cruel man. He blamed everyone but himself when food for the table was scarce or when the bills couldn't be paid. He yelled at everyone, he took the strop to her brother in a rage over the slightest perceived misbehavior, and he chased her to her room whenever he saw her reading or doing homework. But his main target was her mother, and as his drinking increased, he often forced her mother to drink with him. The sounds that came from their bedroom after some of their drinking bouts embarrassed and shamed her. Why would her mother beg her father not to do something, then moan, "Yes, yes, yes?"

She couldn't imagine who this man was who felt no shame in hitting the woman he was supposed to love. Over the next few months, Gracie began to understand what the pleading and moaning meant as the nights of out-of-control sex became more frequent and the beatings became more intense. Whenever her brother tried to intervene and take the blows for his mother, her father's rage escalated. She lived in fear that her brother would be killed.

When Gracie turned fourteen, her mother's latest pregnancy became the catalyst for a horror she didn't think she would survive. Her father turned away from her mother and began to visit her in the night. When it first started, he walked into her room, knelt beside her bed and quietly called her name. As soon as she answered him, he put his fingers to her lips to silence her, and then awkwardly pushed her nightgown up around her neck. At first all he did was look at her, and when she tried to cover her body, he left the room. Soon looking at her no longer satisfied him and he began to explore her body with his hands and mouth. He fondled her breast and forced his fingers inside her. As she started to scream in pain, he clamped his hand over her mouth and held it there until she thought she would suffocate. When she struggled, it seemed to intensify his attack on her body. Night after night he returned and she came to expect that his groping would go on for hours. Her stomach turned at the smell of his sour, alcohol breath, and his rough hands pinching and pawing every part of her body frightened and disgusted her.

Three months into the pregnancy, her mother miscarried and Gracie prayed her father would return to his own bed and leave her alone. Instead his groping turned to brutality. She tried to defend herself as he forced her legs apart, and before he could stop her, she called loudly for her mother. For a moment, she thought he would leave, but when no one came to rescue her, his attack grew more forceful and determined. From that night on, both she and her father realized that her mother's fear had given him permission to continue and he relentlessly pursued Gracie. It seemed that his goal each night was to leave her body more bruised, torn and battered than the night before. Yet, every night before he left her room, he brushed the tears from her cheek and whispered in her ear, "I'm so glad you like this. You're such a good girl, Gracie. I'll come back tomorrow night. You make me so happy, but remember Gracie, this is our little secret." He looked her in the eyes and his voice became cruel, "You wouldn't want me to hurt you, would you?"

Do all men do this to their daughters, or was it just her? Why didn't her mother come when she called? What good were the questions when there were no answers? She must have done something to deserve this; this must be her punishment. Disgrace kept her submissive, and night after night, she endured.

Her refuge was the church. Her mother could not protect her, her brother had run away from home, and she was alone with her shame and her hatred. Dread and fear drove her into a world of silence that was soon noticed by the Sisters of Mercy who ran the school at St. Peter's.

One Monday morning she was called to the school's front office to meet with Sister Theresa. What had she done wrong? Why did the school principal want to see her? There was an awkward silence before the nun began to question her about her school work and the evident drop in her grades. Quietly, she assured Sister Theresa that she would do better. Just when she thought the interview was over, Sister Theresa asked her how she got the bruises on her arms and legs. She stuttered that she had fallen, but Sister Theresa was firing questions at her faster than she could answer. She couldn't think fast enough to invent a story that might be believable, and when Sister finally asked if her father had beaten her, she simply stood up and ran out of the room.

Gracie did not return to class that day. Instead she ran out the front door of the school and made her way to the church door. She ran down the aisle of the church, forgetting the Holy water, forgetting to genuflect, and flung herself face down on the floor beneath the stained glass window of the Virgin Mary. Hot tears ran down her cheeks and sobs welled up from her very soul. "Mother

Mary please intercede for me, give me strength, help me find a way to repent of my sins. Please, show me what I've done wrong and I'll change. I promise. Sister Theresa knows. She knows how sinful I am and I don't want to face her again. There's no way God will forgive me for what I've done. Beloved Mother of God, I need you more than I've ever needed you before. I can't go to confession. I can't be made clean. Please help me." When her tears were spent and her strength was gone, she pulled herself off the floor and eased onto the wooden pew.

As she lifted her head and opened her eyes, she was awed by the brilliance of the colors that radiated from Mary's beautiful, sad face. Mary's presence was all around her and she was embraced by a warmth that comforted her. In the glow of the jeweled light, Gracie asked the Mother of God to be her mother, to protect her, and lead her out of the home that no longer gave her refuge. As soon as the words were out of her mouth a peace came over her and she knew she would survive whatever was ahead.

When she left the church her thoughts were still with the Virgin Mary and she clumsily ran into a young man who was walking down the sidewalk. Looking up, she recognized her brother's friend, Edgar McDeal. He was older, so they had never said more than hello to each other.

"Hey, what's wrong with you? You just about knocked me over. Why don't you watch where you're going?" He was upset and she thought he might hit her, but then he regained his balance and looked at her. "Oh, sorry. I thought you must be some stupid kid looking for a fight. You're Danny O'Brian's sister aren't you?"

She nodded her head, said she was sorry and hurried on down the street. Half way down the block she felt him walking close to her. Why? What did he want? Could she out run him? When he began to whistle she realized she wasn't in danger. She wasn't used to boys paying attention to her and Edgar's actions were unnerving. She kept her eyes focused on the street ahead and tried not to look in his direction.

After an uncomfortable few minutes, Edgar stopped walking and said, "I'm going to come over to see you tonight. I'll meet you on your front porch." Her head cleared and she tried to tell him it wouldn't be possible for her to meet him, but he was already running back up the street toward the church. Edgar had the long legged gait of a track star and she liked watching him run. He had to be at least twenty since he was Danny's friend, and to her that seemed old. Why does he want to meet me tonight? I've already told him I don't know where Danny went. Then she smiled, could this good looking, older boy be interested in her?

It would not go well if her father discovered Edgar on the front porch. She had to find some way to keep him from coming over to her house.

After dinner, her father stood up from the table, grabbed his cap and grumbled that he was going to meet his pals. She knew she would have several hours before he returned and she prayed she could convince Edgar not to stay on the porch for more than a few minutes.

As she was finishing the dishes, there was a knock on the front door. She didn't wait to see if her mother would stop her, she simply turned and walked out of the house. Edgar stood in the shadows of the streetlight and startled her when he stepped forward.

"Hi, Gracie. Did I scare you?"

"Edgar, you've got to go. My dad will be here any minute. Please go."

"Wait, Gracie, don't leave. I won't stay long. You know when Danny ran away, I lost my best friend. Do you ever here from him?"

"No, Edgar, I don't even know where my brother is. I pray all the time that he's safe. Now, please go."

"Gracie, do you think if I'm really careful, you know, if I don't hang around your house, do you think we could be friends?"

She was flabbergasted. "Sure Edgar. I'll see you around." She turned to go back in the house, knowing this was some kind of joke.

"Gracie, meet me for ice cream at Duffy's on Sunday. I'll be there at 1:00. Don't forget."

21

There was no way she could say no and her face brightened as she nodded her head yes. She wanted to fall down on her knees and thank the Virgin Mary for answering her prayer. "I knew it. I knew you would find a way, Blessed Mother. You sent him to rescue me, didn't you?"

She counted the hours until Sunday afternoon. She planned to wear her new birthday sweater and grandmother's long black skirt that had been altered to fit her. She fretted over her hair. Should she wear it down or pulled back with a black ribbon? But in the middle of daydreaming reality crept in and she realized she'd never be allowed to go out after Mass to meet Edgar. She didn't have girlfriends she could pretend to meet and she couldn't think of any other reason to leave the house. The little bit of hope she experienced turned to despair as she whispered to the Virgin Mary, "Please don't let me down. I know you'll find a way."

During the week she thought she might see Edgar on the street or at the church, so she could back out of their date. But that didn't happen. She knew if she didn't show up at the ice cream parlor, Edgar would never ask her again.

On Wednesday during Mass, as she was kneeling to pray, the light reflected on the Virgin Mary, and Gracie saw compassion and kindness on the beautiful face. She knew the Virgin would help her find a way.

Saturday nights were always the worst. Her father would have been at the pub most of the afternoon and evening and he would be roaring drunk when he stumbled up to the house. She knew one of two things would happen, either he would come up the stairs in a rage and begin to beat her mother or he would creep up the stairs and silently let himself into her room. But tonight, neither of these happened. To her surprise, her father stumbled to the bathroom and she heard him vomiting as if his stomach was being torn from his body. The sound of his retching went on for what seemed like hours. Every time her mother tried to help him, he bellowed for her to get out and leave him alone.

When the house was finally quiet, she tiptoed to the hall and looked toward the bathroom. Her father was passed out on the floor.

His body was twisted in a grotesque manner and his breathing was very shallow. She had never seen him like this and she returned to her room hoping he was dying.

After Mass, Gracie returned home to find her mother sitting at the kitchen table sipping a glass of wine. She walked over and touched her gently on the arm. Her mother's eyes were red rimmed and puffy, and Grace thought her mother's hunched shoulders made her look older than forty-two.

"Are you all right, Mama? You don't look like you slept very much last night."

"I'm okay, Gracie. I just needed a little glass of wine to settle me down."

Gracie hated that her mother drank so much and often drank alone. Before her grandmother's death, her mother never drank. Now, she wondered if her mother was ever truly sober.

"Is dad going to be okay? He was really sick last night."

"Oh, he's got a touch of flu. He'll probably stay in bed all day."

She almost shouted hallelujah, but restrained herself. After she fixed lunch for her mother, she said she had forgotten her Missal and needed to go back to the church to see if it was still on the pew. Her mother raised her head and slowly smiled, "I don't believe you Gracie, but I'm not going to stop you."

Gracie ran down the walkway and arrived at the ice cream store just in time to see Edgar go inside. She opened the door and slowly walked over to the table where he was sitting. When he stood up and looked at her, she thought she saw the miracle she had prayed for. In her dreams Edgar would take her away from the house that had been slowly poisoning her body and spirit.

With her mother as a silent accomplice, she and Edgar continued to meet on Sunday afternoons for several months before Edgar told her that he was moving to Florida to find work. She sat stone-faced as she listened to the news. This was not the direction she thought their lives would go; she felt fear and dread returning. But Edgar reached across the table and took her hand. Startled, she looked up and saw his smile and realized he was asking her to come with him.

She did not hesitate, and within the week they were on a Greyhound bus headed to Miami. All of their belongings were in two drawstring laundry bags and their combined wealth added up to $245. But to Edgar and Gracie, that seemed like more than enough. They had never talked about a future and had only shared a few quick kisses. But she hoped they could forge a relationship that would help her heal her wounded soul.

Stepping off the bus, the first thing that hit them was the heat. The second was a realization that they were really alone. With some help from the ticket agent at the bus station they got directions to the downtown Catholic Church. The priest welcomed them and told them about a boarding house located near 7th Avenue where they could get a room and a daily meal for only $12 a week. But when Edgar told the priest they wanted to be married, the priest said that they could not live together until the ceremony had taken place. Gracie and Edgar arranged for that to happen at 3:00 the next afternoon. In the meantime, Edgar would stay overnight at the rectory and Gracie would go to the boarding house.

They walked to the boarding house and were able to rent a second floor room with a small bed, a dresser, two straight chairs, a tiny icebox, and a little table that held a hotplate. Their new life had begun.

That night, after Edgar had returned to the church, the reality of what she had committed herself to diminished her joy and renewed her fears and guilt. How would she explain to her new husband that she was not a virgin, and what would she do if he didn't want to stay with her?

She needed the comfort of St. Peter's stained glass window of the Virgin Mary. This new church was larger and more ornate and though she had found the face of Mary in many of the windows, the stained glass in this church told a different story. She had searched each depiction of Mary, hoping for one that she could connect to. But, nothing happened and the old feelings of unworthiness resurfaced.

As her husband, Edgar would be expecting certain things from her. She thought about what she was running away from and started to tremble. If he did stay with her after she confessed, what would he want her to do? Would he be brutal, like her father? How would she ever want his touch?

"Mother Mary, how can I get through this? What have I gotten myself into? I want to marry Edgar, but I'm so afraid. Please help me." She fell asleep with her rosary beads clutched in her hand. In the middle of the night, she thought she felt Edgar climb in bed with her and she sat up in fear. She wanted to run away, but she had no money and no place to go.

Getting up, she knelt beside the bed. "You've brought me this far, Mother Mary. Help me to face my new life unafraid."

☐ The next afternoon, when Gracie said, "I do," the love she saw in Edgar's eyes made her feel safe. As the priest continued with the ceremony, she began to realize that God lived in this place, too, and maybe everything would turn out all right.

"Gracie, my love, this is our special day and we are going to celebrate." Edgar's happiness was contagious and as they walked away from the church, Gracie gave him a little smile. "Keep your eyes open for the finest restaurant and start dreaming of what you want to eat at our wedding feast."

"I'll look for something we can afford, Edgar McDeal. You don't have a job and we don't have money to waste on a feast."

"Just this once, Mrs. McDeal, we are not going to worry about the cost of dinner. Today is our once in a lifetime day. I'm not planning to ever have another wedding day." Edgar laughed and twirled Gracie around. But all she could think about was whether the people on the street were staring at them.

They headed east toward Biscayne Bay and beautiful Bayfront Park. They strolled through the park, stopping often to admire the lush, tropical foliage that was so unfamiliar to them. The colors of the trees and flowers were bright against the blue of the bay and she promised to learn the names of every one of these botanical wonders. They bought a bag of peanuts, sat on a bench to feed the flocks of pigeons that seemed to be following them and watched the fishing boats returning to the harbor.

"Edgar, this is the most beautiful place I've ever seen. Promise me we can come here every now and then." Gracie let the beautiful scene wash over her and for a few minutes she was happy. They started to walk again, exploring the market stalls where they could purchase cold drinks, post cards, and fresh fish. There was so much to see and experience about this new city they were going to call home.

As they strolled along a path that led away from the water, they discovered the entrance to the Rock Garden. The pathways in this stunning garden led to a grotto and waterfall surrounded by benches where visitors could sit and enjoy the peace. The foliage in the garden was so thick it masked the sounds of the city and created an oasis of tranquility. Green was everywhere and Gracie was awed that so many variations of the color existed - from emerald to lime and everything in between - the colors in this garden seemed exaggerated and so full of life. Until this moment she had thought the colors in the stained glass windows were the most beautiful she had ever seen, but now she had found a place that rivaled those windows.

It was here in this beautiful garden that Edgar turned to her and told her for the first time that he loved her. He held her hand, looked deep into her eyes, and promised he would protect and take care of her. She held her breath and felt the blush of redness rising across her cheeks. In her sixteen years, no one had ever said these words to her, no one had ever offered her protection.

"It's okay Gracie, if you can't say you love me. I've got enough love for both of us." He moved closer to her and drew her to him in an embrace.

"Oh, Edgar, I don't want this moment to ever end."

They sat in the Rock Garden until the sun began to set and the noise from the Band Shell brought their attention back to real life. It sounded like the musicians were tuning their instruments for a concert. Edgar got up off the bench, stretched, "I don't know about you, but I'm starving. It's time to find someplace to eat." They walked out of the calm into the noise of the people who were walking toward the Band Shell and the shouts of the vendors who were hoping to make a sale before the concert began.

Edgar noticed a sign for a restaurant on a large ship moored at the north end of the park and he began to steer her in that direction. But as they approached, she became aware of the patrons dressed in their finery and knew that even if Edgar wanted to splurge, they would not be able to afford to eat aboard the Prinz Valdemar. She saw the disappointment on Edgar's face.

"Gracie someday we'll walk up that gangway and eat a dinner aboard this ship. But for tonight it looks like we'll have to settle for a hot dog and cold drink from one of the vendors." Their big splurge was a bag of popcorn they carried with them to the concert.

The bandleader, Caesar LaMonaca, led his musicians through an hour of music that included Sousa marches, lively show tunes, and some of the popular love ballads of the day, like "As Time Goes By" and "Dancing in the Dark." Gracie was the happiest she could ever remember as she held her new husband's hand and watched the silvery moon rise up out of the bay. The music and the breeze off the water held her captive and lulled her into forgetfulness. Edgar held her close as he danced her around the park. It was like a fairy tale.

The concert ended and they began the walk back to the boarding house. With every step she felt the fear return. She was married and the wedding night bed was waiting for her. Edgar would be expecting this evening to end in a way she knew she was not ready for. In her urgency to flee her father's house, she had not stopped to consider she might be moving from one bedroom of pain to perhaps another.

Edgar insisted on carrying her across the threshold and made a big commotion in the downstairs parlor when he announced to Mrs. Dillon that he and Gracie had just been married. Mrs. Dillon, the owner of the house, was all aflutter to think she was part of Edgar and Gracie's wedding day. She went to the kitchen to bring out a coconut cake she had baked that morning for everyone to share. The other boarders who lived in the house were called to the parlor to join in the celebration.

As Mrs. Dillon served her coconut cake and ginger ale, the boarders welcomed the couple and toasted their new marriage. There was a festive atmosphere in the room when Mrs. Dillon reminded the gathering the newlyweds probably would like to go to their own room. Everyone smiled a knowing smile, raised their glasses one more time, and wished them a long and prosperous life together.

As the door to their first home closed, Edgar took Gracie in his arms and gave her the first real kiss of their relationship. Mixed emotions coursed through her as she found herself responding to Edgar's passion. But, there were still secrets that had to be revealed before she could ever give herself to this man. Husband was a title that carried with it the memories of how her father had treated her mother and she felt herself wanting to withdraw from his embrace.

Edgar sensed her hesitation and stepped back. "Sorry, Gracie, here I am just thinking about myself. I keep forgetting how young you are. It's all right, honey, I'm not going to force you into something you're not ready for. We'll take it slow, okay?"

She didn't have any words. She let her eyes say thank you. But, her body was experiencing new sensations that excited and scared her. Could love making really be something wonderful? She liked the feel of Edgar's body, and his kisses had stirred something very deep within in her.

"I'll be waiting for you when you're ready." He dropped his arms from around her and began to pull his belongings out of the laundry bag.

Gracie was grateful and disappointed by Edgar's attitude and she turned to ready herself for bed. Maybe he can tell I'm not a virgin and really doesn't want me. Doubts filled her and she wondered if he didn't find her desirable. The sexual tension was confusing and she decided the best thing she could do was go to sleep. She grabbed her toothbrush and night clothes and went down the hall to the bathroom they shared with two other boarders.

Later she climbed into bed and pulled the covers tightly around her while she waited for Edgar to return from the bathroom and turn out the light. When he finally slipped in the bed beside her, she held her breathe. She was surprised when he leaned over and kissed her gently on the forehead. "We'll take it slow, Gracie. I don't want you to ever be afraid of me."

In the morning, they got up early, went downstairs to breakfast, and began talking with the other residents about finding work. Within the next two days, Edgar found work with the railroad as a baggage clerk and Gracie began to work behind the counter at the Home Dairy, serving ice cream and sodas. Their new combined income made them feel rich. But Edgar was a very frugal man and sat her down to help him work out their budget. They agreed they would live on his salary and begin a savings account with hers.

"I've got a plan, Gracie. If we can live on my salary, we'll have enough in savings from your paycheck for a down payment on a house. It'll take us a few years, but we can do it."

Although they could always go down to the parlor in the evenings and listen to the big radio Mrs. Dillon provided, their first purchase was a small radio they could enjoy in their room. Too often, the residents at the boarding house spent the evening arguing over which radio station to listen to, and Gracie knew Edgar wanted peace and quiet when he came in from work. Some nights, if they weren't too tired, Edgar turned on the radio and they danced around their small room. Joking, laughing, and acting like kids on a Saturday night date, Gracie was becoming more and more comfortable with Edgar's body next to hers.

Over the next few weeks they established a rhythm for their life and she felt her fears gradually becoming less and less overwhelming. She and Edgar were growing closer together as friends, and she was allowing herself to enjoy his nightly hugs and kisses. After dinner every evening when they returned to their room, Edgar would turn the radio on to a station that played beautiful music and he would encourage her to sit and talk with him about her day at work. Gradually she found herself sharing small details of her life in Baltimore, but she carefully avoided any discussion of her family. Since she had never had a friend, her attempts at conversation were awkward at first. Edgar put her at ease with his storytelling and humorous accounts of the strange baggage people took with them when they rode the trains. She loved the sound of his voice, his easy laughter, and the way he would sit and look at her whenever she talked to him. And, she loved to dance with him.

One evening, Edgar's mood and tone turned serious. He reached for her hand, looked at her with desire. "Gracie, I think I've waited long enough."

She trembled and slumped down in her chair.

"Give me some credit, Gracie. I told you we'd take it slow and I'd wait till you were ready. But you're driving me crazy. I can handle whatever you have to tell me."

"I'm not being fair to you. But I'm scared, Edgar." She didn't look at him.

"I want to know why you won't let me touch you. I need more than kisses from you, Gracie."

Her tears turned to sobs but he did not let go of her hand. He sat with her until the sobs ebbed, "I love you no matter what and I'll never leave you."

Silently she thanked the Virgin Mary for sending Edgar and prayed for the words she needed to tell him her story.

"Edgar I wasn't truthful with you when we got married." Her voice quivered and she whispered, "I'm not a virgin." When the words were out of her mouth, she looked over to see if she could read the reaction in his eyes.

He sat very still, but didn't let go of her hand. "That's not the end of the story, you owe me the truth."

"It's about my father," she hesitated, and then whispered, "and what he did to me." Edgar jumped up from his chair and knelt down in front of her. There were tears in his eyes.

"Oh, Gracie, I knew things at your house weren't good, but I never suspected this. My sweet Gracie, don't you know I'd never hurt you. Hush now, don't cry any more." Edgar pulled her up from the chair and wrapped his arms around her. He hugged her to him and began to gently caress her. "I'll show you that it can be good, Gracie. Please trust me. All I want to do is love you."

That night when the light had been turned out and Edgar reached for her, she rolled over in his arms and allowed herself to be loved.

* * *

Carter had never gone on a date before, but his instincts told him this could be one of the best nights of his life. After the awkwardness of meeting Sharon's parents, everything about the evening was better than he dreamed it would be. Sharon made him laugh; she stumbled through his self-conscious attempts at dancing; and she listened when he talked. Her enthusiasm and zest for life were different from what he was used to. She grabbed his hand and pulled him out of the shadows - and he let her.

Why would she want to spend time with me? He asked himself over and over, and waited for her to walk away from him. But the homecoming dance was the beginning of a relationship that carried them through senior year, and he dreamed it would carry them through a life together. As graduation approached, their relationship intensified.

"Do you ever think about our future?" Sharon whispered, as they sat in the swing on her back porch. "Do you ever dream about getting married and having a family?"

"Yeah, someday. But, I think more about how I'm going to be able to support a wife and kids. You know I've applied to drive for Miami Transit, but I still don't know if I'm going to get hired." He moved closer and put his arm around her. "I've been thinking I could drive during the day and take some classes at the community college at night. But, right now I don't have any answers."

"Do you love me, Carter?"

"Of course I do, Sharon. You're the best thing that's ever happened to me."

"You know I could get a job after graduation and save up some money. Then we could get married next year. Maybe we could live with your mom for a year or two, and save up to get our own place."

"Whoa, Sharon, you're way ahead of me! We can't rush into marriage like that. We need to wait until I have a job."

Sharon pouted as he tried to reason with her. "I'm ready to get married, and I thought you were, too. I don't want to wait a long time." She moved closer to him and her caresses became bolder. "You know you can do more than kiss me. Don't you want me as much as I want you?" That night she made herself more available and guided his touches. Reason gave way to passion and he didn't give a thought to her parents asleep in the room just beyond the porch. Touching, kissing, fondling every part of her body made him greedy for more.

"No, Carter." Whispering breathlessly, Sharon moved away. "We have to wait until we're married." Moving her hand from inside his jeans, she smiled. "Oh, Carter. It will be really great after we're married."

Days before graduation, the reality of life caught up with him when things happened that would alter his life in unexpected ways. First, his application to the Miami Transit Company was not accepted because of his age and lack of experience. Second, even though he didn't know it at the time, a conflict erupted in a country half way around the world.

Carter was more than a little concerned about his future prospects. He couldn't think of a job that he could apply for that would give him the kind of money he needed to support a wife, and he still had almost three years until he could be hired to drive a bus. Staying awake half the night, he traced the patterns the street light created on his ceiling and worried about what he would do. It had been a long time since he had thought about his dad, but tonight he wished he could ask him for advice.

The next morning he noticed a new sign posted in the school hallway and walked over to see what it said. Uncle Sam Wants You read the Army poster. A recruiter would be on campus the next day to talk to the young men who were graduating. At first, he wasn't interested because he knew what his mother's reaction would be if he told her he was joining the army. But, the more he thought about it, the stronger his interest became. After class the next day, he took a seat in the school auditorium along with 40 or 50 of his classmates. The recruiter made Army life sound almost glamorous as he pointed out opportunities like the GI Bill. Carter began to get excited when he learned the Army offered young men a chance to further their education and learn skills that would ensure them jobs once their enlistment was over. When he heard about this, he wondered if that could really make college an option for him. If he was going to give Sharon the kind of life she deserved, he was going to have to do more than drive a bus. As soon as the recruiter finished talking, Carter walked to the front of the auditorium and without really thinking about it, he enlisted. Now, all he had to worry about was telling his mother and Sharon.

He decided to tell his mother first. That night after dinner, he offered to help her with the dishes. While she washed and he dried, they talked about graduation and baseball. He loved the Yankees, and Mickey Mantle was fast becoming the home run king. His mother wasn't really interested in baseball, but she always listened. After a few minutes of conversation, he turned the subject to what he wanted to do after graduation.

"Mom, I've been thinking about going to college, maybe get a business degree, and I know we've had to use my college fund to pay for other things. But, today I heard all about the GI Bill and how the military would pay for my education." He paused and waited for a reaction. When his mother didn't respond, he plunged on. "So, I enlisted in the Army today."

"You did what?" Her voice broke, "How could you do that without my permission?"

"Mom, I'm 18. I can sign for myself. And, it's just for two years." He was pleading now. "I'll probably be sent to someplace like Ft. Benning, Georgia. By the time I get out, I'll be old enough to go to work for the transit company and the Army will pay for me to go to college at night."

"No, Carter," she began to cry. "You know what happened to your dad. How could you do this?" Gracie held on to the kitchen counter and let her tears continue to fall. She couldn't see the concerned look on her son's face.

33

"Mom, please don't cry. It'll be all right. There isn't a war going on. This is different. It's not like when dad was called up. You'll see, mom. It'll be all right."

He had known his mother was going to be upset, but he hadn't counted on her tears. It wasn't like his mother to cry, and it took him by surprise. Now he was worried. If telling his mother was this hard, how was Sharon going to react? This was not as easy as he thought it would be. After the dishes were put away and his mother calmed down, he told her he needed to go tell Sharon.

"Son, telling me was easy." Gracie's voice still reflected her hurt and anger. "I bet Sharon is going to give you more than a few tears."

When he got to Sharon's house they went for a walk. As they strolled toward the park, he told her what he had done. Surprisingly, there weren't any tears. Instead she let go of his hand and turned angry eyes toward him.

"Why did you do that, Carter? I thought we had plans."

"Sharon, I won't be gone long and I'll be able to come home on leave. You wanted to take that secretarial course and it's two years, right? We'll both finish up at the same time. Then you can get a good job, and so can I." He kept talking, trying to make her understand. "The GI Bill will give me the money to take night classes at the university, and I could get a really good job when I graduated. And, just think of the money I'll be able to save up while I'm in the Army."

"This isn't fair," her voice rose and her body stiffened. "What am I going to do for two years while you're gone? I thought, oh, never mind what I thought! You're ruining all our plans. If you really loved me you wouldn't do this." She ran ahead of him. "I'm so mad, I can't talk about this anymore."

Gracie became sullen and withdrawn when she learned a conflict had started in Korea. What if Carter was taken away from her like Edgar had been; what if he never returned from this war they weren't calling a war? At a time when she should be celebrating her son's graduation from high school, her fears were running rampant instead. She knew Carter loved Sharon, but she was afraid this new plan of his might destroy the relationship between them. From everything she observed, Sharon would need more than a promise if she was going to wait for Carter. She liked the girl well enough, but Sharon was pretty and lively and loved to have a good time. Gracie couldn't see her sitting at home for years waiting on Carter to come home from war. She knelt down beside her bed and prayed to the Virgin Mary for advice. After a few minutes, she knew what she had to do.

Carter was sitting at the kitchen table studying for his last high school exam when she walked in and sat down across from him. As soon as he looked up, she reached for his hand and placed her engagement ring in his palm. "Ask her right after graduation," she said, and then got up and left the room.

Her son's girl would have a ring on her finger when he went off to war and she prayed Sharon would be waiting for him when he returned.

The horror of war began for Carter as soon as his feet landed on Korean soil. As a member of the 45th Infantry Division, the months of training that started in Fort Polk, Louisiana ,and were completed on a base in Japan, did nothing to prepare him mentally and emotionally for the realities of combat. He knew the drill; he was a good soldier. But the idea of being a good warrior was outside his comfort zone. His sense of duty and his feelings of preparedness were soon shattered by the battles that raged on for days and weeks for the sole purpose of claiming land that did not seem to be strategically viable. General Douglas MacArthur, after the victory at Inchon, was more than determined to end the conflict quickly and gave orders for offensives others in command felt were needless and risky.

Dear Carter,

Nothing much is going on in Miami. I've got a job working as a receptionist in a lawyer's office downtown. The job is easy and I get to meet a lot of people, so that helps the time go by faster. My boss is a nice guy. He's married and has three teenage kids.

I had dinner with your mother last Sunday, and of course, all we did was talk about you. She can tell some funny stories about you! She's holding up okay, but she misses you. I miss you too, and I'm counting the days until you're home. I'm so lonely without you. I need your arms around me right now! A few kisses would be nice, too.

Love you, love you, love you, Sharon XOXOXOXO

In the late fall of 1952, the division received word they would be relinquishing command of Old Baldy Hill to the 2nd Infantry Division and they would be heading back to the States. A feeling of resolve fell over the 45th and every man in the division was determined he would leave Korea with his body intact even if his spirit and soul were in shambles. The count-down for returning home began and Carter marked off every day with a scratch on his canteen.

Hey Babe, Just a quick note to tell you I love you. This place is awful and I can't wait to get home. I've got a friend named Jack that I hope you can meet someday. I think you'd really like him. Sharon, all I do is think about getting home to you. Nobody should ever have to go to war -- you wouldn't believe some of the horrible things I've seen. But, I guess I'm here fighting so you will never have to see what happens in war.

Gotta' go. Remember I love you and as soon as I get home we will get married -- so keep making all those big wedding plans of yours.

Love, Carter

The morning of October 18th dawned with rain and silence. Everyone in camp was on edge as they listened for any sound that would give them a clue to the enemy's whereabouts. After hours of waiting, the commander decided to send out several small groups to reconnaissance the perimeter. Carter and Jack were assigned to move out to the right with three others and report any movement or activity. Each man carried his M1 Garand combat rifle at the ready and stealthily moved through the mud in the direction of the enemy lines.

After an hour of walking, with no movement detected, the leader of the group signaled for them to reverse their order and return to the base camp. Because of the intense rain, the mud seemed thicker and Carter's steps felt heavier. His vision was becoming increasingly blurry and he was losing a sense of his surroundings. But the walk went on with his sense of hearing heightened. He heard the distinct thud of the incoming mortar round before he heard the shrill whistling sound. As he was taking cover, he realized that Jack was behind him and seemed to be falling forward on top of him. He felt Jack's weight fall on his back and tried to move from beneath his body, but the pressure only increased. He felt trapped and immobile before he realized that the noise had stopped and all around him was eerily quiet. He wanted Jack to move off of him and was becoming agitated that his friend was so heavy. Still, he sensed that he should remain quiet for a while longer. He tried to slowly move his arms toward his face to keep the mud from oozing into his eyes and nose and mouth, but because of Jack's weight, he was losing the feeling in his arms.

After what seemed like hours, he heard a kind of moaning. It was the sound of pain too intense for screams and it frightened him. Where was the moaning coming from, and why was that the only sound he heard? Before he could make any determination, he heard the sing-song sound of Chinese words coming closer. The mud shifted under the footfall of several soldiers running in his direction. He stopped his struggle to move from under Jack's body and felt his breathing slow to an almost indiscernible level. He waited for death.

The Chinese soldiers moved quickly among the fallen bodies. When they came to the man who had been moaning, Carter listened in horror as one of them plunged a bayonet into his buddy's chest. Apparently, this satisfied the Chinese and he sensed their retreat. He lay still until he was sure he and Jack were alone before he quietly asked him to move. When there was no response, he began crawling from beneath Jack's body. When he had freed himself and could look around at the carnage, his mind could not grasp that he was the lone survivor. He sat in a daze trying to reconcile what he had experienced. He looked over to where Jack's lifeless body lay. It was then his mind registered that the back of Jack's head had been blown away by the exploding mortar.

Bile rising in his throat, he inwardly screamed in anguish to a God that had seemingly abandoned them all. He had to move away before the Chinese heard him and returned to kill him, too. With that thought, his adrenalin thrust him forward and he began running in the direction of his camp. Before he reached the area where he knew his division was based, he heard movement ahead of him and began to frantically look for a place to take cover. He was almost crazed when he finally saw that he was surrounded by American faces and English words. As he tried to make sense of their words and questions, he realized that this was a search party that had been sent out to find his team. He gave in to the protection that was being offered, shouldered his rifle and allowed them to escort him back to the base camp.

He went through the debriefing in a dream state, devoid of emotion, and told of the incident that had robbed the other four men of their lives. It was only in the retelling of his experience that he grasped the truth of this day. His friend Jack had sacrificed himself so he could live. He sensed a rawness coursing through his body and felt himself moving from the dim light of a rainy evening in Korea back into the shadows that were his safety.

Dear Carter, You are always in my thoughts and prayers. I don't want you to worry about me and things at home. I'm managing just fine and I'm learning that I can do more things than I thought - like mow the lawn and clip the hedges. You'd probably get a kick out of seeing me push that lawn mower, but our yard looks almost as nice as when you were here to take care of it. I hope you received the box of shortbread - I sent enough for you to share with your friends. I pray every day for the angels to watch over you. Take care of yourself, say your prayers, and come home safe. Love, Mother

PS - I haven't seen too much of Sharon lately, but I know she must be busy at work.

When the orders finally came down for his division to be returned to Louisiana, he received the final devastating blow of the war. He opened the letter all soldiers dread:

Dear Carter, I hope you're well. I know you're really getting anxious to come home, but I thought you should know before you get here that I've met someone and I'm going to marry him. I know that this is shocking news, but you've been gone so long and I've been so lonely.

I should have written long before this - but I just couldn't find the right words. You were my first love, Carter, and I'll never forget you. I know you probably won't forgive me, but please don't hate me.

Last night I worked up the nerve to give your mother back her ring. Take care of yourself.

Always, Sharon

That night, after he had burned all of Sharon's letters, he stopped thinking of college and vowed he would never let another woman cause him this kind of pain.

Finally back in Florida, Carter's application to the Miami Transit Company was accepted and he was enrolled in the bus driver training program. After the hell of war, becoming a bus driver gave him a sense of stability and safety.

The first day he walked into the bus yard and took his turn behind the wheel of the bus, he knew he had made a choice that would bring some purpose back in his life. The eight weeks of training passed slowly for him and there were times when he wondered if he would ever really be out on the road on his own. When that day finally came, to his amazement, he was assigned Route Six - the route that served his neighborhood, the route that he had traveled all his life.

There were no first day jitters and nerves for Carter. He knew his job and he knew he would do it well. As he watched the people board the bus, he wondered who they were and where they were going. I hope I won't always feel like I'm driving a busload of strangers.

Chapter Two

Carter, Miami 1955

Waking up at 4:00 AM, when the depth of night gave way to the palest hint of daylight, Carter forgot the horrors witnessed during his time in Korea. For a moment or two, it was possible to release some of the heartache that had been with him since the breakup with Sharon. He stretched out his body and rubbed the sleep from his eyes. For a few minutes he lingered in a dream-state. He imagined owning a fancy car or buying a speed boat. He pretended he had tickets to see the Yankees play in the World Series. He saw Sharon waiting for him just beyond the shadows. He was a realist who accepted the mundane nature of his average day, but for a few minutes, while 11th Avenue slept, he enjoyed his dreams. This was his time, before life and the bright sunlight of a Miami morning chased him back to the shadows.

Sliding his tall frame out of bed, he ran his fingers through the length of his thick, chestnut hair. It's the luck of the Irish to have a fine head of hair, so he'd been told. And, the curse of the Irish to have fair skin. The kind that meant a bad case of sunburn if he wasn't careful. He turned on the bathroom light and began lathering his face to shave. As he moved the razor across his chin, he squinted at the face in the mirror, at least you're not ugly.

He dressed in the crisp, freshly ironed uniform his mother had placed at the foot of the bed. Just yesterday, he had told her once again, "Mom, you work too hard. You don't have to stay up so late just to make sure my uniform is freshened up and pressed."

"Oh, honey, what else have I got to do?"

Every afternoon when he returned from his job as the driver of the Route Six bus, she greeted him at the door with the same words.

"Carter, hurry and get out of that uniform so I can hang it on the outside clothes line to freshen it. You want to look good for your passengers, don't you? And, I don't want to be up all night." While his mother took care of his uniform, he put the shine back on his shoes and polished the Miami Transit insignia on his cap. Their routine rarely changed.

"Carter, the little things make a difference. The little things bring you out of the shadows into the light. So, always take care of the little things and God will take care of the rest." Mimicking one of his mother's favorite sayings, he turned out the bathroom light.

Stealing quietly down the hall, he dodged the squeaky planks in the floor. It wasn't fair to rob his mother of the two hours she could sleep before her day began. He meant to fix those planks, but somehow that job kept getting pushed to the bottom of the list of things needing his attention.

His mother always referred to their home on 11th Avenue as the 'cottage.' The house, built in the 1930s, was painted white with gray trim, including the gray shingled roof. It's best feature was a front porch that ran the width of the house, with four gray pillars and a half wall made of Florida field stone. Sitting on the front porch in one of the rocking chairs, he could watch his mother working in the front yard flower beds that she laughingly called her gardens. He had lived in this house most of his life and couldn't imagine living anywhere else. Once he had dreamed of settling down with Sharon in a house just like this one, but that dream didn't matter any more.

The warm aroma of the biscuits, fresh baked the night before, filled his nostrils. His mother baked the biscuits every night just before she went to bed. When she took them out of the oven, she carefully covered two of them with a dishcloth to make sure they stayed fresh for his breakfast. She buttered them while they were still hot and placed a dab of strawberry jam inside each one. As he sat in the kitchen with the single light above the stove breaking the darkness, he saw himself as a little boy at that same pine plank table listening to his mother say, "Honey, I added the jam to sweeten you up for the day." And even as a grown man, he still thought that the strawberries helped him keep a smile on his face as he dealt with all the people who rode with him on the Route Six bus.

He got up from the table and turned on the gas burner under the coffee pot. As the coffee perked, he sat back down and began his morning prayers. His mother was over zealous about church and it bothered her that he didn't go to Mass every morning. But Father Sean helped him out by telling her, "Mrs. McDeal, God surely understands that the Route Six bus starts its journey before the church is open. I think the Almighty will hear Carter's prayers no matter where he says them." So, even when he didn't feel like praying, he thanked God for Father Sean.

Seven minutes later, biscuits and coffee devoured, Carter closed the kitchen door and stepped off the little stoop at the back of the house ready to start his day.

Sitting astride his bicycle, he headed down the street toward the bus barn. As a kid, he had worked hard to save the money for this bike and this morning he laughed when he tried to calculate how long it would take to buy a car. But, for now he was grateful the bike cut the time to work in half and gave him the exercise he needed to off-set all the hours he sat in the driver's seat of the bus. Staying fit was important.

Allappatah, his neighborhood, made up the heart of his Route Six bus run. The neighborhood was colorful most of the year because the yards were filled with beautiful sub-tropical plants. This morning, even though it was too dark to see the flowers, he smelled gardenias, frangipani, oleander, and jasmine - pungent, sweet fragrances so familiar in south Florida. It never occurred to him to be afraid of the dark streets. After all, Miami was a place where most of the people he knew didn't lock their doors.

Reaching the humid bus barn, Carter walked toward the Route Six bus amid the familiar revving of bus engines and men's voices competing with the roaring motors. In the far corner of the barn, his supervisor sat behind an old wooden desk going over the day's roster. "Morning, Sully, looks like a good day for bus riding," Carter called to him.

Jeanne Moon Farmer

"Git outa here, Carter. I ain't got time to waste on your yapping this morning. It ain't no picnic I'm having here."

Sully, more short-tempered than usual this morning, was trying to find someone to take an extra shift. The cigar perched at the corner of his mouth sent swirls of putrid smoke into the air, clouding up the room. Now would not be a time to talk to Sully about anything.

Carter went through his checklist and moved his bus to the fueling area. He was the only driver who had a checklist and the others made fun of him because of it. The army taught him that paying attention to details saved lives and he was going to do everything possible to keep his riders safe.

"Hey, Carter, did you get all your check marks this morning? Is Sully going to give you a gold star?"

"Carter, why do ya waste so much time with that stupid checklist of yours? Ha, you make driving this bus too hard."

"Let's see, I got four tires; check. Two windshield wipers; check. One steering wheel; check. How many checks does it take to make a bus, McDeal?"

He laughed at the good-natured barbs of his fellow drivers and welcomed this early morning banter. It mattered that when the Number Six rolled out of the barn it was clean, the windows were open an inch from the top, and the hold straps were not frayed. He took care of the little things. Five days a week he drove six round trips before his shift ended and he carried as many as 300 passengers on his run between Hialeah and the Burdines department store on Flagler Street in downtown Miami. The much maligned checklist had earned him several commendations; so let the others laugh!

He eased the bus out of the barn onto NW South River Drive and headed toward 36th Street. The industrial area around the bus barn looked shabby and neglected. The street was lined with junk yards and marine businesses, and the view of the Miami River was partially hidden. In this neighborhood, the river was all about work. There were no pleasure boats, no palm trees, no five star restaurants. Unless you liked to look at barges, there was no reason to gaze toward the river. He was glad the scenery got better toward Hialeah where he picked up his first fare of the day.

Mrs. Snyder was always the first person to step on the bus. She was there the first day he drove the route, and she was still there two years later. Every morning she stood at the curb with her tote bag and old pocketbook, waiting for the bus to pull up and the door to open. The bus stop has a nice bench, someday I'm going to ask her why she never sits on it. Her plain, blue house dress was always covered by a clean, starched yellow apron that he thought made her look top heavy. She rode with him all the way to Burdines and then got off to walk three blocks to the restaurant where she had been a waitress for ten years. She worked the breakfast and lunch shift, so she would be back on the bus at 2:00 that afternoon when he made his last run of the day.

Every morning she smiled at Carter and asked in her slow paced southern drawl, "How you doin' today, Sugar?"

"I'm fine, Mrs. Snyder. How 'bout yourself?"

"Mornin' always comes too early for me. I could probably use another couple hours of sleep."

Carter liked having regulars on his route. Knowing their names and parts of their stories kept him connected, and he even called some of them friends. Stop after stop the seats filled with people who worked the jobs that helped others start the day. On most mornings, by the time he arrived on the fringes of downtown, the bus would be full and people would have to stand and use the hold straps.

As the bus moved east on 36th Street, Miami began to wake up. The streets were busy with cars, and the noise of the city accelerated from a whisper to a shout. He loved the music and rhythm of this city. In fact, he loved everything about it.

At the stop on 12th Avenue and 36th Street, Rosanna waited for him. She was a young girl, 17 or 18 at the most, who went to Lindsey Hopkins, the vocational school downtown. She always looked neat and well groomed even though her clothes were well worn. She had one dress for Monday, Wednesday and Friday, and another for Tuesday and Thursday. When he first started driving the route, she was so skinny he thought her family must be struggling to make ends meet, but lately it looked like she was putting on some pounds. Maybe things are better at home and there is more food on the table.

Rosanna probably lived a few blocks from his house because he often saw her walking to the park. If he and his mother were out working in the yard, she would stop and talk with his mother about her flower beds and why the plants looked so healthy. Although she never stopped for long, she always took a few minutes to make polite conversation with them. Almost every day, when she got on the bus, she asked him, "How's your mother doing? I bet the roses in her garden must be in full bloom today."

Rosanna would graduate from her coursework at the end of May, and she had shared with him that she hoped to find a good job as a court reporter in a city like New York or Los Angeles. He liked to ask her questions about what she was studying at the school, so it didn't take long for them to develop an easy conversation pattern. She asked him about his mother, and he asked her about school. On Monday through Thursday, it always started with, "Rosanna, how's school going?" But, on Friday it changed to, "Rosanna, is today test day? Good luck. I bet you'll get an A." She smiled at his questions and on Monday through Thursday she answered, "It's real good, Carter, real good." And, on Friday, "I'll either be smiling or crying when I get back on the bus this afternoon; then you'll know if your good luck wish did me any good."

He liked her smile and hoped her dream wasn't too big to be realized. He wished her success, and liked that she was determined to work for it. He hoped a time would come when she would have a closet full of beautiful clothes, not just the two dresses she wore to school.

As the bus approached 7th Avenue, Miss Ruby got up off the bus bench and walked slowly to the curb. She was heavyset and moved her cumbersome body as though she was carrying the weight of the world with her. He wanted to know how old Miss Ruby was, but of course he never asked. In some ways she looked young, but in others she looked as old as Methuselah. It was a labor for Miss Ruby to climb the bus steps and he wished he could bend the rules so she could take a seat near the front of the bus, but that wasn't possible. It was the mid-1950's; Miami was part of the segregated South and Miss Ruby had to sit in the back of the bus.

"Miss Ruby, did you hear about what's going on in Alabama? Looks like things might be headed for a change. Some lady named Rosa Parks sat down at the front of a Montgomery city bus and refused to give up her seat to a white man."

"Mr. Carter, there ain't no way a colored lady in Alabama is gonna bring 'bout no change likes you is talkin' bout. I'll be sitting at the back of this bus 'til I die, and you knows it."

Every day when Miss Ruby got off the bus she thanked him for his help. "You is a good man, Mr. Carter. I shore do 'preciate you lookin' after me."

"No problem, Miss Ruby. No problem at all. You take care of yourself today."

Stop, go, stop, go. The bus continued down Biscayne Boulevard, but fewer people got on the bus in this part of town. The folks in the houses and apartments along this major Miami thoroughfare were not early risers. Their jobs probably didn't start until 9:00 and they most likely drove their own cars. But one gentleman was always waiting for him at the corner of 20th Street. The distinguished looking Mr. Fitz dressed like a successful businessman in a three-piece suit, a hat and polished shoes. He walked with a cane that appeared to be more for show than need. A distinct accent and impeccable manners reminded Carter of the stereotyped butler in a manor house. The gentleman carried a folded up Miami Herald under his arm and always made his way to an empty hand strap even when seats were available. He rode the twenty blocks to the center of Miami standing up. Carter never knew what Mr. Fitz did after he got to town but he could always count on him being back on the bus when he made his last afternoon run.

Carter pulled the bus up to the street where Rosanna got off. He could see the school building from Biscayne Boulevard, but she had to walk several blocks to the entrance. He wished her good luck on her test as he opened the door. Today, she turned and, instead of waving good-bye, she gave him a look that puzzled him. She looked him in the eyes and held his glance until he became uncomfortable and turned away. Then she smiled at him and hurried down the steps to the street. She didn't look back at the bus as she walked away. It was unusual when she didn't tell him good bye and he wondered if he had offended her in some way? Scratching his head, he watched the teenager until the bus began to roll again.

Chapter Three

Rosanna

"Come inside this minute. I can't have you going to church in a dirty dress," mother yelled. But Rosanna didn't want to come inside, she wanted to sit on the sidewalk and play with the little roly-poly bug. She had been told often enough that if she got it dirty, she would be in trouble. This was her Sunday dress, a hand-me-down from her older sister Nancy that was a soft lavender and when she wore it, dad would always sing a silly song about "Lavender blue dilly, dilly," that made her laugh. Her mother was usually quiet unless she was yelling at her about some rule she had broken. Mother was the keeper of the rules and Rosanna knew there were consequences for breaking them. They weren't written down anywhere, but she and Nancy knew they existed, because mother was always saying, "You know the rules."

Life in the house on 14th Avenue was very safe and Rosanna didn't know she was poor. She just thought her lack of certain things was another part of "the rules." There was always food on the table, even though she had never tasted roast beef or steak or cheesecake. As time went by, she discovered what it meant to be poor. From listening to other girls talk, it dawned on her she had never worn a store-bought dress, never been to a movie, never had a birthday party, and never been on a vacation. She began to be more aware of the things she didn't have. She loved her family, and life at home was bearable, but she didn't want to be poor forever. Rosanna knew she had to find a way to get beyond the narrow parameters of this life if she was going to have all the things she was missing.

Her parents were expecting her to follow in Nancy's footsteps, but her sister's path never interested her. Nancy was going into nurses training at Jackson Memorial Hospital and was going to marry her boyfriend, Matt Sanders, in June.

"Nancy, I don't think I can be a nurse; all that blood and gore and creepy stuff. Maybe you can handle it, but I'd throw-up." Rosanna made a retching noise that caused Nancy to laugh in mock disgust.

"You're right, sis, nursing would probably make you sick. But, Mom thinks we should both be nurses. You better come up with a good plan if you want to change her mind."

"I want to do something exciting and I'm leaving Miami. What do you think about New York or Los Angeles?"

"Doesn't matter what I think, but you're crazy to even think about moving away."

"You wait and see. I'm going to find a job that pays a bunch and then I'm out of here."

"Rosanna, get a grip. How are you going to do all that without going to college? You know there's no money for that. You might as well start dreaming about marrying some rich old guy who'll leave you all his money."

"Don't be stupid, Nancy. I'm serious."

Nancy opened her math book and started to work on the assignment that was due in the morning. "If you want my advice, you'll go talk to Sister Agnes. She'll help you find something and she'll give you ammunition to use when Mom starts saying "No."

"I'll think about it, but one way or another, I'm leaving here." She stuck her bottom lip out in a pout. Why wasn't Nancy taking her serious?

"Miami's not so bad, and you better not shoot off your mouth about leaving. Mom will go crazy on that one."

The next day, Rosanna went into the school office and made an appointment to talk to Sister Agnes. She was afraid the Sister would just tell her to go on to the Catholic high school and take a few typing classes, but the Sister talked about several different options that piqued her interest. There were college scholarships if she kept up her grades or there were new classes being offered at the vocational school downtown. As they continued to explore possibilities, Sister Agnes told her about a career in court reporting. Rosanna stopped her and asked what a court reporter did. After a brief explanation, Rosanna decided it sounded glamorous; it certainly sounded more exciting than anything else they had talked about and she decided to go to Lindsey Hopkins Vocational High School after she left Corpus Christi. Now all she had to do was convince her parents.

The deadline to register for the vocational school was the end of April and she needed her parent's signature. Her father wouldn't give her a hard time about her choice, but mother would not be so easily swayed. She hoped Nancy would support her, but she just laughed and said, "Let me know when you're going to tell Mom 'cause I want to be as far away as I can be."

Three days before the registration deadline, the family was gathered for dinner when her father asked, "Where are the papers I need to sign for Notre Dame Academy?"

"I don't have them, dad. But I have papers for the vocational school that I need you to sign."

"What in the world are you talking about, Rosanna? There is no way you're going downtown to school," said mother as she jumped up from the chair. "Absolutely not. You're going to Notre Dame and then into nursing like Nancy."

"Mom, that's not fair! I don't want to be a nurse. I want to be a court reporter." Rosanna's voice rose as she looked at her mother's rigid back.

"Rosanna, calm down. What in the world is a court reporter?" said her dad.

"Dad, it's a great job. Court reporters are stenographers. They have to type real fast so they can sit in court and record everything that people say. I'd be good at it, Dad."

"How did you find out about this 'great' job, Rosanna?" said her mother sarcastically.

"I talked to Sister Agnes. She's the one who suggested I go to the vocational school. I can get all the classes I need for high school, plus get certified as a stenographer,"

Her mother returned to the table and sat quietly while father asked question after question about court reporting, the vocational school, and how she planned to get downtown every day.

When he ran out of questions, he got up from the table, looked at his wife, shrugged and said, "We won't argue with Sister Agnes."

***

From the first day, Rosanna loved the vocational school. Luckily, her enthusiasm was matched by her achievement in class and she was a model student. She loved competing with herself and her classmates to see who could type the most words per minute. At first, 225 words seemed daunting, but over time she could meet that requirement and more.

As she prepared for her final year at the school, her plans were coming together better than she ever expected. Her teachers praised her work and told her she would be able to find a top job anywhere she wanted to go. Her focus and determination were paying off and she was counting the days until she could leave Miami. She began researching job opportunities in different cities and kept imagining a life of glamour for herself. She would have money, beautiful clothes, a swanky apartment, and important friends. Then she met Phillip.

It was on the Thursday of the first week of school. She was sitting in the school cafeteria finishing her sandwich when he pulled out the seat next to her and sat down. He was cute, in a goofy kind of way, with a crew cut and big blue eyes. I don't have time for boys right now. All I want to do is finish school and get on with my life.

After he introduced himself, he told her he had just moved to Miami and was at the school to register for some classes in mechanical drawing. She didn't like the way he was looking at her and his persistent attempts to make small talk made it hard for her to concentrate on her reading. She told him good-bye and left the table in a hurry.

Every day for the next few weeks, Phillip showed up at lunch time. If she went to the cafeteria, he was there. If she decided to eat at one of the benches outside, he would find her. He was always trying to engage her in conversation and didn't seem to mind her short answers to his questions. Rosanna didn't know what to make of his attention and couldn't imagine why he continued to seek her out.

Phillip was not easily deterred. For weeks, he continued to find her during the lunch period, talk her ear off for twenty minutes and then go on his way to class. On Halloween, he asked her to go with him to a friend's party. He told her it would be fun and she would have a chance to meet some of his friends. Rosanna had never been to a party and she was thrilled. He picked her up in his old jalopy of a car and they drove across town. When they crossed the bridge to the beach, Rosanna asked him where they were going. He told her the party was at Haulover Beach. This was a remote beach north of town and she couldn't imagine how they could have a party in the dark. By the time they arrived, the party-goers had built a bonfire and everyone was sitting around it drinking beer. She didn't like what she saw and asked Phillip to take her home. But he persuaded her to stay for a little while.

As the beer flowed, the party got wilder. Boys were stripping to their underwear, racing into the waves, and yelling for the girls to follow them. When several of the girls started taking off their clothes, she told Phillip she was leaving. He'd had five or six beers already and she was concerned about him driving. "Let's go, Phillip. I'll drive and you can stay at my house until you sober up." He had always treated her with respect, so she was unprepared when he told her she would have to walk because he wasn't leaving. "Don't be a prude, Rosanna. Lighten up and have some fun." The tone of his voice was cruel and his expression frightened her. She picked up her purse and the shoes she had taken off earlier and started walking down the beach. She was in trouble because this beach was so far away from town, but she was hopeful she could find a pay phone to call Nancy.

Rosanna had walked a long way from the bonfire when Phillip caught her by the arm and told her she couldn't leave. When she pushed him away, he grabbed her and threw her to the sand. Before she could catch her breath, he had fallen on top of her and was pulling her skirt above her waist. She screamed for help, but they were too far away from the party and the sound of the waves drowned out her voice. Phillip overpowered her. The more she struggled, the more persistent he became until he had torn her panties off and entered her. The pain was unbearable and she screamed so loud she was sure someone would hear her. But no one came and the assault continued until he was spent. When Phillip's body became still, she realized he had either fallen asleep or passed out, and she was able to roll away from him.

With purse and shoes in one hand, she brushed the sand out of her hair and clothes, and took off running as fast as she could down the beach. Tears streamed down her face and her heart pounded so hard she could feel each beat. How was she ever going to get home and what would she do if he woke up and came after her? There were only a few cars on the road and not one of them stopped to find out why a young girl was walking down the road alone so late at night. She walked until her knees buckled under her and she had to rest. Blood trickled down her legs, but she didn't have the time or energy to deal with it. She was exhausted and didn't want to start walking again, but she knew she had to keep going. She had walked miles before she saw a gas station ahead. It was closed and all the outside lights were tuned off, but she spotted an outdoor telephone booth and ran toward it.

Her sister was married now and had a six-month old son, but Rosanna knew Nancy would help her. She found a dime in her purse, placed it in the phone slot, and dialed her sister's number. Someone picked up the phone after just a few rings and she was relieved that her brother-in-law, Matt, had not answered the phone.

"Nancy, I need your help," she whispered into the phone.

"Rosanna, is that you?" Nancy said. "What are you talking about? Speak louder, I can barely hear you."

"Please come get me. A guy took me to a party and things got out of hand. I'm at an Esso gas station just before the big sign for Haulover Beach."

"What do you mean, things got out of hand? Do Mom and Dad know where you are?"

"Nancy, I'll tell you everything when you get here. Please don't tell Mom and Dad where I am. Call them and tell them I'm going to spend the night at your place." She was talking so fast she was running her words together. "Hurry, Nancy. I'm really scared."

"I'm on my way, Rosanna. Stay at the gas station until you see my car."

Rosanna sank to the ground beside the phone booth and began to sob. Trembling with rage and fear, she prayed Phillip wouldn't find her before her sister arrived. Every part of her body ached and she knew she'd been ripped apart.

Rosanna didn't return to school for several days, and against the advice of her sister's husband, Matt, she didn't go to the police and file charges against Phillip.

"I can't, Matt. I'd die if Mom and Dad found out. Please try and understand."

"Rosanna, you better hope I never see that boy. He belongs in jail, whether your parents get angry with you or not."

"Matt, give her some time to pull herself together. She'll do the right thing," said Nancy.

Rosanna never went to the police and she prayed she would never see Phillip again. She tried hard not to relive the events of Halloween night. When she did return to school, she was afraid she would turn a corner and he would be there. But after several weeks, she realized he was no longer at school and perhaps she was safe.

By January, she knew she was pregnant. At first she was sick with fear and then she began to feel sorry for herself. How could she care for a child? How could she finish school? What about her dreams? What good could come from a child conceived in violence? And, how could she tell her mother she had broken the rules?

When she was several months along, she began to think about the baby and the future. She needed help, and again, went to her sister for advice. Although she had put on a few pounds, she didn't think anyone suspected. That was confirmed when she saw the surprised look on her sister's face. They both knew this kind of news would devastate their parents, and there was no money available to help her with doctor bills or hospital costs. After tears and prayers, Nancy told Rosanna she would help her deliver the baby and, if all went well, they would take the baby to be adopted. Nancy's husband was in the Coast Guard and usually spent six months at sea. He would not be in town when the baby was born or Nancy would not have agreed to this plan.

Hiding the pregnancy from her parents was not the easiest thing to do. But, she worked hard to hold her weight down, and when she did develop a small stomach, she covered it by wearing a loose fitting sweater. Knowing she was going to give her baby up made her keenly aware of the people around her. Every weekday morning when she caught the Route Six bus to school, she began to notice the regulars who rode with her every day. She would look at them and wonder, "Would you make a good parent for my child?" This ritual was helping her prepare for the fact a stranger would be raising her baby. She always sat near the front of the bus by the window and as she walked down the aisle she made sure to say hello to Mrs. Snyder. This kindly, middle-aged woman seemed to represent the perfect mother. But, she ruled her out because she knew Mrs. Snyder had children who were grown. She knew the bus driver's name, and he lived a few blocks from her family. She guessed he lived with his mother because she often saw them out in their yard when she walked to the park. Whenever she stopped to talk with them, Mrs. McDeal would tell her about the flowers and show her any new things she had planted. Almost every day when she got on the bus, she asked Carter how his mother was doing and how her garden was coming along. Carter always smiled and gave her a brief update on what his mother was planting or clipping. Rosanna knew Carter and his mother would make a good family.

She made up her mind to leave for California as soon as things were settled with the baby. She told her parents she had applied for several jobs in Los Angeles and had received two positive responses from companies that wanted her to come in June for interviews. Over her parents protest, she went forward with her plans and made arrangements to stay at the YWCA in Los Angeles until she had enough money to find another place to live. Her teachers wrote reference letters for her at the same time they were encouraging her to remain in Miami. But, she wanted to get as far away as possible from the memories that would always be a part of Miami.

One week after graduation, bad cramps told her she must be going into labor. As planned, she told her mother she was going over to Nancy's for a few days. She explained she wanted to spend some time with her sister before she left for Los Angeles.

A small, delicate little girl was born to Rosanna on June 10, 1956. The baby only weighed 5 pounds, but she had a hardy cry. When she gazed into the face of her child, she knew she would love her forever and giving her up for adoption was going to be one of the hardest things she would ever do. Whenever she thought of strangers raising her baby, she cried.

"Rosanna, it's been over a week and you're getting more and more attached to the baby. It's time to take her to the adoption services at the church. And, I've run out of excuses to tell Mom. She's bugging me about when you're coming home."

"Please," Rosanna begged. "Let me have one more day and I promise I'll take her this evening."

"I know this is hard, Rosanna. But you're only making it harder on yourself."

"You're right. Nancy, she's beautiful, isn't she? I never expected to love her so much."

"She looks just like you. I don't know what her creepy father looks like. But, there's no doubt she comes from our family."

After Nancy left for her shift at the hospital, Rosanna prepared to carry out her plans. She knew Nancy would leave the hospital when her shift ended at 11:00, and would go to the sitter's to pick up her son before she came back to the apartment. That would give Rosanna plenty of time to do what she needed to do. She found a large box in the back of Nancy's closet that was just the right size for her to carry the baby, several bottles, a can of formula, her diapers, and the two little outfits she and Nancy had bought. She sat down at the table and began to write the note she would also include in the box.

"My name is Jocelyn. Please raise me as your own. Love me, care for me, and give me the life that my mother can't afford to give me."

When she was sure she had everything the baby would need, she picked her up, hugged her one last time and left Nancy's apartment. The box wasn't heavy because the baby was so tiny, and she knew she would be able to carry it the distance she needed to walk. After she dropped off the baby, she was going to return to her parents' home, pack her own things, and catch the Greyhound bus for Los Angeles. If she didn't leave Miami in the morning she would never be able to go through with her plan.

Rosanna arrived on 11th Avenue about 9:00 PM. She stood across the street from the house for a long time before she summoned up the courage to do what had to be done. She leaned down and kissed Jocelyn on the forehead, whispered she loved her, and walked to the door of the house. She took a deep breath, placed the box in front of the door and rang the bell. Then she ran as fast as she could toward the end of the block. Just as she reached the streetlight, she turned to see Carter standing in the door with the box in his arms. He was looking up and down the street and she couldn't be sure if he saw her or not. When she saw him go inside and close the door, she blew her daughter one last kiss and thanked God these people would raise her child. She wiped away her tears and turned to walk the four blocks to her parents' house. She knew Jocelyn was safe and would be cared for with love.

Chapter Four

Carter, June 1956

"What's the matter, son? You look like you've seen a ghost. What in the world is in that box?"

Carter walked over to the table and gently placed the box in front of his mother.

"You're not going to believe this." He kept shaking his head. A mixture of surprise and amazement was written on his face. "Someone left this on the front porch."

Gracie looked from her son's face to the box and her mouth fell open. "There's a baby in this box, Carter! Holy Mother of God, it's a real baby." Crossing herself, Gracie continued. "Who would put a baby in a box and leave it on the doorstep?"

But before he could answer her, the baby opened its eyes, looked up at Gracie, and began to cry. "Oh, you poor little thing," she said as she picked up the whimpering bundle. "Carter, look and see what else is in the box. Surely, someone has made a big mistake."

Hurriedly, Carter began to rummage through the items in the box and place them on the table. "Mom, there's bottles, diapers, clothes, and some stuff that must be formula. Oh, wait, there's a note in here, too."

"Well, what does the note say? Read it to me, Carter."

"It says, "My name is Jocelyn. Please raise me as your own. Love me, care for me, and give me the life that my mother can't afford to give me."

"Mom, someone is trying to give us this baby. This has got to be some kind of joke!"

The baby started to cry harder, so Gracie got up and began to walk around the room. She put the baby up on her shoulder and began crooning, "There, there, little one. It's going to be all right." Then she said to Carter, "Before we can think about that, we have got to feed this child. Read the label on that can and see what we have to do to make up a bottle."

Following the directions, Carter made up the formula, filled the bottle and put a pan of water on the stove so he could heat it. While he was waiting for the bottle to warm, he looked over at his mother, who was now cooing softly to the baby. There was a smile on her face and she looked radiant. "Oh, no, she thinks we can keep this baby."

"Mom," he called. "Mom," he called again. But she did not hear him; she was looking too intently into the face of the child.

"Welcome home, Jocelyn. It's just like Mother Mary told me, little one. I've been waiting for you for so long," Gracie whispered.

"Mom, what are you babbling about?"

"Oh, Carter, this little girl was promised to me years ago."

When she looked up, he could see the tears rolling down her cheeks. "We will keep this baby, Carter. God has given us this little one to raise."

"Mom, that's not possible!" He was stunned by her intensity and his voice began to rise. "This is not our baby. Nobody promised you this baby. We have to go to the authorities and get this straightened out. You know we can't just keep her. Someone has to try and find out who she belongs to."

"She belongs to us, Carter," she was calm, yet emphatic. "Her mother wants us to care for her. Isn't that what the note says?"

"Hush little one." Never taking her eyes off the baby, Gracie motioned for Carter to take the bottle from the pan and hand it her. "Drop a little milk on your arm, Carter. Make sure it's not too hot for the baby."

"Okay, Mom. It's too late to do anything tonight, but tomorrow we will have to try and find out what this is all about."

"I'll take care of her, Carter. You go on to bed. I know you have to get up early in the morning. We'll talk about this some more tomorrow. She'll be fine for tonight. I'll finish feeding her and change her. She can sleep in the box tonight, beside my bed. Everything's going to be all right. You'll see."

Heart sinking, Carter went to bed knowing that his mother's "all right," probably wasn't going to be the same as his.

As he climbed into bed, he was haunted by the glimpse of the girl he had seen in the streetlight. Even though he couldn't see her face, he knew that the girl had on her Tuesday dress. He closed his eyes and asked God to have mercy on her and to give her some peace about what she had done. And, he ask God to help him find a way to handle what his mother was planning to do.

Gracie never gave another thought to going to the authorities. She asked Carter to crawl in the attic to bring down the box of baby things, and she spent time preparing the house for a baby. The room that was used for sewing and ironing would be Jocelyn's room as soon as she was old enough to move from the cradle to the crib. Jocelyn would sleep in Carter's cradle under the blanket Mrs. Dillon had made for him, and would wear his beautiful crocheted christening gown. Her vision was coming true. Yes, this was meant to be.

For the next three weeks, Gracie did not leave the house. Carter went to the store, no work was done in the garden, and neither of them went to church. Late at night, after the housework was finished and Jocelyn was fed, Gracie thought about what she would say to Father Sean and her neighbors. How could this baby be explained? Then, it came like a flash. All she had to say was her niece died in childbirth, and she and Carter had agreed to take the baby.

Getting out of bed, she knelt down before the statue of the Virgin Mary on the night stand. She looked up into the face of the saint who had raised her own child under the strangest of circumstances and prayed. "Mother Mary, forgive me for the lie I'm about to tell. As a loving Mother, I know you'll understand what I'm doing. I've never lied to a priest before, but I'll have to tell a lie to Father Sean about this baby, or he'll call the authorities to come and take her away from me. I promise I'll love and protect Jocelyn for the rest of my life. That makes it all right, doesn't it?" When she finished her prayer, she got back in bed unbothered by any premonition of how her lie might impact Carter's or Jocelyn's lives.

The next morning, it was time to introduce Jocelyn to the world. She called Mrs. Dillon at the boarding house and asked if she could come for lunch. Then she picked up the baby and walked over to Mrs. Harvey's, her next door neighbor. If she could tell a believable story to Mrs. Harvey and Mrs. Dillon, then she knew she could tell Father Sean.

Chapter Five

Jocelyn, The Early Years

Jocelyn knew she was a special child because her Nana told her so every day. When she woke up in the morning, Nana was always there to tell her she was beautiful and God had made this day just for her. Jocelyn was a pretty child with softly rounded cheeks, straight brown hair and big, brown eyes. She had been an easy, adaptable, healthy baby, and as a toddler, she was physically strong and mentally alert.

Every day was an adventure that started with a walk with Nana to the church for Mass. Dad had already gone to work by the time she got up, so he never went to Mass with them. She and Nana would hold hands and sing silly songs as they walked.

"Remember, Jocelyn, we are going to God's house. Father Sean will expect you to be very quiet," said Gracie.

"I know, Nana. I will whisper to God and I won't say a word to you or Father Sean until we leave the church. You'll see. I'm a very good girl," replied Jocelyn.

Gracie smiled. She and Carter were doing a good job at raising this little girl. "That's right, sweetheart. You are a very good girl. Your dad and Nana are proud of you."

After church, they returned home to do the chores. It made her feel so grown up when Nana let her help. By the time she was four years old, she was putting the laundry in the washing machine or sweeping the porch. Her favorite chore was helping Nana cook. If Nana was baking a cake she got to lick the bowl and if they were going to have beans for supper, she got to help snap them. When she and Nana walked to the store to buy the groceries, they always stopped in at the Five and Dime to buy a bag of hard candy for their treat. They loved to shop for a special treat for her dad. Sometimes they would buy him a tin of shoe polish or a new box of razor blades. And, Nana always let her give these treats to Dad when he came home for supper.

On grocery days, she would stand by the front window so she could meet him at the door when he came home from driving the bus. "I bet you can't guess what we got you at the store,"

"Did you buy me an elephant today?"

"No, Dad, we don't have room for an elephant. We got you a new tin of shoe polish instead." Then they would laugh.

Her dad was a quiet man and never had much to say, so she usually spent more time with her grandmother than she did with him. But Jocelyn's favorite days were when she got to take a ride on the Route Six bus. At least once a month, she and Nana dressed up in their Sunday clothes and went downtown. They walked two blocks down 11th Avenue to the bus stop on 36th Street where they waited for Dad's big city bus. Nana always gave her the bus token so she could put it in the slot, and Dad always looked at her and said, "How is everything going today, sweetheart? Are you ready to take the best ride in town?" She was so proud her dad drove the bus, and she wanted to tell everyone the bus driver was her father. Nana said that wasn't a good idea, but Carter didn't agree. Every time they got on the bus he would say to anyone who would listen, "You see that pretty little girl with the big brown eyes? That's my daughter." He told Mrs. Snyder, Miss Ruby and Mr. Fitz everything that Jocelyn learned and did.

"She took her first step this morning, Mrs. Snyder."

"She's talking in sentences now, Mr. Fitz."

"She's knows her ABCs, her numbers and her colors, Miss Ruby."

Jocelyn led a happy but isolated life until she was old enough to go to school. Her small circle was complete - she had Dad, her cat, the church, and the adventures and lessons she shared with Nana. And, for her, it was enough.

Jocelyn loved school. Her classroom was bright and inviting; Sister Mary Dolores was welcoming, and she shared this room with 18 other girls. She didn't cry on the first day when Nana left her at the door, although she knew there were tears in Nana's eyes. She was too excited to cry and by the time recess was over she had made friends with Ruthie Thompson. Ruthie was about her same height but she had curly blond hair and blue eyes that were an instant contrast to Jocelyn's dark straight hair and brown eyes.

"I look like my mother," said Ruthie. "Who do you look like?"

Jocelyn was stumped by this question. She never thought about having a mother and she didn't know how to respond to her new friend. She brightened as she thought about it and finally answered, "I look like me."

"No, silly. You have to look like somebody in your family."

"No, I don't. I just have to look like me."

This answer made them laugh and within seconds they moved on to other things. But Jocelyn knew she would ask Nana that question when she went home today.

***

"Oh, Nana, I love school! I love Sister Mary Delores! I like story time and drawing and recess. And, I have a new friend named Ruthie." Jocelyn was so excited she was dancing.

"Slow down, child. Slow down and start at the beginning. Tell me all about your day."

"Well," said Jocelyn, "I have a girlfriend, and her name is Ruthie. Isn't that the best thing you've ever heard?"

"Yes, it is," said Nana. "What do you like about this Ruthie?"

"Oh, Nana, she is so smart, and she likes to color and swing, just like I do. And, we talk at recess, but not in our class because Sister Mary Delores won't let us talk while we are sitting in our seats, except when she calls on us."

"Did you behave for Sister Mary Delores, today?"

"Of course I behave," laughed Jocelyn. "Only the bad girls don't mind the teacher, and I'm not a bad girl."

"No, dear, you are not a bad girl."

"Nana, who do I look like?" questioned Jocelyn.

Gracie stammered and looked at Jocelyn in surprise. "My goodness, Jocelyn, where did that question come from?'

"Ruthie said she looks like her mother and wanted to know who I look like."

"What did you tell her?"

"I told her that I look like me."

"That's exactly right, dear. You look just like you," she said and tried to change the subject.

"Was my mommy pretty?"

"Sweetheart, your mommy was very pretty, just like you."

***

In her six years, Jocelyn had never asked these kinds of questions, so Gracie kept putting off having any conversations about the child's parentage. She and Carter were going to have to talk about this and come up with a plan. But how much truth was Jocelyn ready for and how much was Gracie ready to tell her?

That evening after Jocelyn entertained her father with all the stories of her first day at school and had been tucked into bed, Gracie asked Carter if she could talk to him for a minute.

"Sure, Mom, what's up?"

"A girl in Jocelyn's class asked her who she looked like and poor Jocelyn didn't know how to answer her. She finally told the girl she looked like herself and that seemed to satisfy her for the moment. But on our way home today she asked me the same question. I've been praying all day about what we are going to say to all the questions that will be coming our way now that Jocelyn is out in the world."

"Okay, Mom, you tell me the answers." Carter sighed. He'd been dreading this since the day he found Jocelyn on the doorstep.

"We'll tell her that her mother died when she was born."

Carter shook his head and looked sadly at his mother, "You know you're asking for trouble with that answer, don't you?"

"Do you have a better idea, Carter?"

"Yes, Mom, tell her the truth."

"How do you think it will make her feel to learn some stranger left her on our doorstep? For heaven's sake, Carter, that would be devastating news to Jocelyn. How would she ever explain it to her friends? No, Carter, we can't hurt her that way."

"Don't you think it'll hurt her more to find out, when she's older, that we've lied to her? Don't you think she'll feel betrayed by the people she trusts the most? This isn't a good idea," replied Carter, "and you know it'll come back to haunt us." Little did he know how prophetic his words were or how fate would twist Gracie's plan.

"It's God's plan, Carter. He has shown us the way so far and He will continue to show us the way. I just wanted our stories to be the same. We don't need to confuse her."

"Then why don't you go to the church and ask Father Sean what he thinks we should do? He definitely has God's ear and will add his blessings to your idea if it's the right one."

Gracie knew she couldn't go to Father Sean. The lies she had told him about who Jocelyn was and how she had come to live with them were too big. Too much time had gone by.

She bowed her head and the vision of the Virgin Mary came to her as she had expected. The Mother of God had been so close to her since Jocelyn had been given to her, and she had never shared the story of the Virgin Mary's visit with anyone but Mrs. Dillon and she knew now she would never tell anyone else.

All through school, Gracie and Carter encouraged Jocelyn to study hard and be involved in classes beyond the academic scope.

When Jocelyn was ten years old, they had taken her to her first play at the Allappatah Little Theater. The troop was doing Thornton Wilder's Our Town and Jocelyn was entranced. When they saw how thrilled she was, they made a point of taking her as often as they could afford. After one show she met some teenagers who were helping out back stage and she begged her nana and her dad to let her volunteer in some way at the theater. After much discussion and lots of tears, they decided she could work several hours each week as long as she kept up her studies.

"Dad, I promise I'll get good grades. You'll see."

"I'm going to hold you to it, 'cause the minute I see your studies suffering, it'll be over. Your nana will walk you to the theater and stay there with you. Okay? You're never to go there by yourself."

"Oh, thank you Dad. I understand."

Bright and early on Saturday, she began begging Nana to walk with her to the theater. "Please, Nana, can we go now? Pretty please."

"Child, you're like a dog with an itch. Give me a minute to finish what I'm doing. You know I'm not going to do your talking for you. You're going to have to do this by yourself," stated Nana in a matter of fact tone. "If you want to do this, you'll have to march in there like you know what you're doing and make them glad they let you help."

"I know, Nana. I've practiced my speech and I'm going to tell them I'll do anything to help."

"Now don't get carried away. You've got to tell them your first priority is school, and you can help only when it doesn't interfere with your schoolwork. Your dad wasn't kidding about this, Jocelyn."

There wasn't a trace of hesitation when they arrived at the theater. Jocelyn walked into the theater office with determination and asked a young woman seated behind an old wooden desk if she could speak to the manager.

"Excuse me, did you say you want to see the manager? Is there a problem?" inquired the woman.

"Oh, no ma'am, there's no problem. I want to volunteer to work."

"Really, what do you think you can do to help? Do you have any experience?" the woman looked at Gracie and winked.

Jocelyn's face fell, "No, I don't have any experience. I didn't think about that. But, I'll learn to build sets or make costumes or anything else you want me to do." She was talking so fast she was breathless.

"My goodness, you must have a lot of different talents. What's your name?"

"My name is Jocelyn McDeal, and I love the theater."

"Well, how do you do, Jocelyn? My name is Dottie Bell, and if this theater has a manager, I guess I'm it. Tell me when you're available and I'll put you to work."

Her first job was helping the wardrobe volunteers' hang-up and inventory costumes. She worked under the direction of Mary Ann Moss, a local high school teacher who volunteered as the wardrobe manager. Miss Moss seemed glad to have Jocelyn's assistance and took her under her wing immediately. She helped Jocelyn understand the intricacies of the wardrobe closet and how to catalogue all of the various costumes. "You can see we have quite a collection of costumes, Jocelyn. One side of the closet is for men's clothes and the other is for women. The drawers hold accessories like jewelry, ties, scarves, belts, hats, and some other odds and ends. The shelves at the far end hold the shoes. I've tried to color code things so we can find them easier. You can see the chart I devised hanging on the door. And, I have a nice check-out process, so I can keep track of everything."

Miss Moss was in her late thirties and when she wasn't volunteering at the theater she taught high school English at Notre Dame Academy. When Jocelyn first met her, the woman's stern appearance and autocratic voice seemed frightening, and she wished she had been given another job. But soon, Miss Moss won her over by not treating her like a child, and by giving her more and more little assignments. As a result of the training she received from Miss Moss, Jocelyn quickly learned how to help the actresses choose colors that suited them and styles that were appropriate for the roles they were playing. Although she only saw Miss Moss at the theater, she liked the way the woman treated her and looked forward to the time they spent together in the midst of the skirts, pants, hats, and shoes.

As shy as she usually was with people, Jocelyn found it easy to make friends with everyone from the actors and directors to the stage hands and make-up artists. Although she was eager to learn everything she could about the theater, she liked working in the wardrobe closet. Miss Moss always found time to have a few minutes of conversation with her, no matter where she was working in the theater. The older woman talked to her like she was an adult, taught her the language of theater people, and encouraged her to become more actively involved in the productions.

PART TWO

SHADOWS BLOCK THE LIGHT

"We sow the glebe, we reap the corn,
We build the house where we may rest,
And then, at moments, suddenly,
We look up to the great wide sky,
Inquiring wherefore we were born...
For earnest or for jest?"
Elizabeth Barrett Browning

Chapter Six

Jocelyn 1973-1974

"Ruthie, wait up," yelled Jocelyn, "I'll walk to the bus stop with you if you'll just slow down."

"You'd better start running. You'll make us miss the bus at the rate you're going," Ruthie called over her shoulder. "I have choral practice this morning so I have to catch this early bus." Ever since they started high school, the girls rode the Number Six bus to school. "I'll tell your dad it was your fault if we miss the bus."

Dressed in their school uniforms from Notre Dame Academy, the girls should have looked similar, but Ruthie had added a ribbon to her hair that gave her a cute, sassy look. Jocelyn watched the bright blue ribbon float like a piece of sky above Ruthie's blond curls and felt drab by comparison. She was unaware of the sophisticated beauty lurking behind her long brown hair and dark eyes.

Even though they were opposites in every way, their friendship had lasted since first grade. Ruthie was bouncy, outgoing, smart, and totally in love with boys. Jocelyn was the quiet, studious one who had never had a date. She, however, did have a serious crush on a boy named Mark Sanders, who volunteered at the little theater. Mark, who was a year older, was popular at the theater and was always joking around with everyone. He played the piano and guitar when he wasn't building sets, and she loved to sit on the edge of the stage and listen to him play. She never said more than "hello" to him, but she knew her heart raced whenever he was around, which gave Ruthie a reason to poke fun at her.

"I'll be glad to tell him you like him, Jocelyn," teased Ruthie. "How's he supposed to know you'd go out with him if you never say more than 'Hi' to him?"

"Ruthie, you wouldn't dare. I'd never forgive you if you did."

"Okay, have it your way. But you sure are missing out on all the fun."

This was their senior year, and both of them were taking an academically challenging schedule of classes. Jocelyn didn't have time for the kind of "fun" Ruthie was talking about. Her class schedule was going to overwhelm her if she didn't balance things carefully. Between classes and her extra-curricular activities, Jocelyn knew she wouldn't have time for little theater if she had to worry about dating, too.

***

Wonderful aromas of holiday cooking awakened Jocelyn on Thanksgiving Day. There were the distinct smells of the nutmeg and cinnamon that Nana was using in the pumpkin pie and the pungent sage that flavored the cornbread stuffing. Mouth watering was the way she would describe the feast they would have in a few hours. Reaching over to open the curtains, she groaned at the low hanging clouds. Where's that good ole' Florida sunshine? But, whatever her nana was cooking lifted the gloom of the unseasonal weather that made every corner of her room seem bleak and dreary. Stretching her arms and legs, she crawled back under the covers to sleep a few more hours. Sleeping late is the best part of the holidays. She had talked Nana out of going to church, so she could take advantage of this rare opportunity to sleep late.

Sounds of a crash startled her awake. What was that? She jumped out of bed, grabbed her robe and started down the hall. Her dad wasn't home because he was driving the bus today, so she suspected Nana had dropped something. Please don't let it be the turkey. But all thoughts of dinner left her mind when she walked in the kitchen and saw her grandmother on the floor with a chair pulled over on top of her.

She screamed. "Nana? Nana, what happened? Are you all right?"

There was no response. She threw the chair out of her way and began patting her grandmother on the face. "Nana, wake up, what's wrong?"

Oh, dear God, she's turning blue. Now what do I do? She leaped up and ran for the telephone on the kitchen wall. Emergency numbers were listed on the bulletin board next to the phone, but all she could think to do was dial O. She tried to tell the operator her grandmother had fallen in the kitchen and was not moving but her words were running together as she talked faster and faster.

"Slow down, dear. Tell me exactly what is happening. Is she breathing?"

"Yes, but she's beginning to turn blue, and I can't get her to answer me. Please help me. Send someone right away."

"Give me your name and address. I've got an ambulance ready to go," said the operator. "Please try to calm down. You can't help your grandmother if you panic. Take a few deep breaths and keep talking to me."

Jocelyn gave the dispatcher her name and address and tried to get herself calmed down. She gave yes and no answers to everything the dispatcher asked her as she tried to listen for the sound of the ambulance.

"I'm sorry, but I'm so scared. She doesn't look good and I can't get her to wake up."

She heard the sirens and told the operator she was going to go unlock the front door. She opened the door and ran out into the yard. "Please hurry. Please hurry," she pleaded, as three emergency workers hopped out of the front of the ambulance. They quickly followed her into the kitchen and turned all of their attention to an unresponsive Gracie.

One of the EMTs began asking Jocelyn questions. "Are you the only one home? Is this your grandmother? How long has she been on the floor? Were you in the kitchen when she fell?" She answered each question as succinctly as she could and tried to stop the stream of tears flowing down her cheeks.

"Her name is Gracie McDeal and she is 60 years old." answered Jocelyn. She looked over at the two EMTs working on her grandmother and prayed for a miracle.

Everything was happening too fast. She couldn't think, and she couldn't take her eyes off of her grandmother - an oxygen mask covered her face, an IV needle inserted in her arm, her precious body being lifted on to the gurney. This isn't real, am I dreaming?

Left alone at last, Jocelyn, shaking and bewildered, listened as the sirens died into the grey distance. Looking down, she realized she was still wearing her pajamas.

***

The ride to the hospital was a blur, and later, when she thought about it, she couldn't even remember if she thanked Mr. Thompson. She did remember Ruthie holding her hand and telling her she would come back to the hospital as soon as possible.

"Jocelyn, as soon as dinner is over and I've finished helping mom with the dishes, I'll ride my bike back over and stay with you. Okay? I know your nana will be fine."

Once inside the emergency room, Jocelyn panicked. She stood alone in the middle of a room filled with people; some sat and waited; some paced from one side of the room to the other; some hurried to somewhere else. Bright lights and noise bombarded her. Loud speakers paged doctors, nurses called out patients' names. Where are the EMTs? Where is Nana? She stood in the center of the large, cold room and took a couple of deep breaths to try and calm down. Once she felt steady, she moved toward the reception desk and asked the nurse to help her find her grandmother, Gracie McDeal.

In a few minutes, a young doctor approached Jocelyn and asked her to follow him. He led her down a different hall to an empty glass enclosed waiting room. "My name is Dr. Johnson and I am the doctor who saw your grandmother when the medics brought her in.

Jeanne Moon Farmer

There are a few things I need to talk with you about, but before we start is there anyone else we can call?"

"Why? What's the matter with her?" She felt a sudden chill and wished she had brought her jacket.

"I'll talk with you about her condition, I promise. But I need to know if there is an adult I can call?"

"They've called my dad at work and he'll be here soon."

"Jocelyn, your grandmother is a very sick woman. She has suffered a stroke caused by a brain aneurysm. That's a bulging, weak area in the wall of an artery that supplies blood to the brain. More often than not, a brain aneurysm gives no advanced warning and doesn't have any symptoms we can see. So it usually goes unnoticed. But every now and then, the brain aneurysm ruptures, releasing blood into the skull which causes a stroke. That's what happened with your grandmother."

"But she's going to be all right, isn't she? There are things you can do to help, aren't there?" Jocelyn's panic affected her voice. She could hear the higher pitch, but she couldn't control it. "Please tell me she's going to be fine." She jumped up out of the chair and began wringing her hands. "That's what I need for you to tell me."

The doctor stood up beside her and took one of her hands in his. "I wish I could give you a guarantee that your grandmother will pull through this. But I can't," he said softly. "Right now it's touch and go. And the next 24 hours are critical. We're doing all we can. But I won't lie to you and tell you something I don't know for sure. This is very serious."

***

The hands on the clock didn't appear to be moving. Never before had she been so aware of time and how slowly it moved when you were waiting. She wished her dad would hurry; she really needed his steadying presence. She thought about how much her well-being depended on her family. Her dad and grandmother made her feel safe and protected. Even though her dad wasn't very talkative, in this moment of quiet and concern, she realized deep in her soul he was always there for her. How had she missed knowing it before now?

She was startled awake by a hand on her shoulder and didn't realize she had drifted off to sleep. "Jocelyn! Hey, girl. Wake up," whispered Ruthie. "I couldn't leave you here without company, so my mom told me she could manage at home without me for awhile. Any word yet on your grandmother?"

"Oh, Ruthie! Thanks for coming back! I guess I fell asleep." She became anxious. "I need to go find the nurse to see what's going on."

"Slow down, Jocelyn. If there was any news they would tell you. I thought you might need someone to talk to while you wait."

Appreciation flooded Jocelyn's face. Her friend knew her so well and was always with her when she needed support or comfort. "Thanks, Ruthie, you're right. But waiting is so hard, and my dad should have been here by now. I don't understand why he isn't here."

As the words came out of her mouth, she heard her father's voice calling her name. She looked from Ruthie to the door just as he entered the room. Her father was out of breathe and his disheveled uniform alarmed her. Her dad was always so careful about his appearance.

"Sweetie, are you all right? Hi, Ruthie. I got here as soon as I could. They had to pull me off my route and bring in a sub to finish my run. Sully worked as fast as he could to find someone to take my place. Have you seen your grandmother? Tell me what happened." Carter's worried tone of voice only made her more afraid.

She wanted to cry as soon as she saw her father but managed to sound calm. "I don't know what happened. Nana was in the kitchen working on dinner when I heard a crash. I got up and went straight to the kitchen and I saw her on the floor with one of the kitchen chairs turned over on top of her. I tried to help her get up but she wouldn't open her eyes. That's when I called the operator and asked her to send an ambulance. Ruthie's dad brought me to the hospital. Nana has been with the doctor ever since."

"Have you talked to the doctor?"

"Yes, just for a few minutes. He told me Nana had a stroke and they think it was caused by a brain aneurysm. He said for you to tell the nurse to call him whenever you got here."

"Thanks, I'll do that right now." He looked at his daughter with love and appreciation. "And, Jocelyn, you did the right thing; you made the right calls."

After he left, Ruthie got up and walked over to the chair where Jocelyn was sitting. She placed her hand on Jocelyn's shoulder, but didn't say a word. Right now, words weren't necessary.

Jocelyn and Ruthie watched as a nurse led Carter down the hall. A look of concern passed between them, and an undercurrent of fear made her knees shaky. For the first time since she found her grandmother on the floor, Jocelyn felt like things might not be all right.

"Jocelyn, I passed a chapel on my way into the hospital. Do you think it might be helpful if we went in there and said a prayer for your Nana?"

Thankful for the suggestion and any distraction, she grabbed Ruthie's hand. She told the nurse where they were going and she continued to hold on to Ruthie as they walked out of the waiting room toward the chapel.

The chapel was a small room off the next corridor. There was an altar at one end of the room and a pretty, lighted stained glass window at the other. The room was dimly lit and music was playing softly in the background. When the door was closed, peace and serenity filtered through the space. There was a sense God could hear the whispered prayers being offered up in this oasis. Jocelyn sank down on one of the pews and lifted her eyes to the stained glass window. The colors melted over her as she thought about the look she had seen so many times on her grandmother's face when she gazed at the stained glass windows in her church. *Nana, you're going to be all right, aren't you?*

"Ruthie, what will I do if she doesn't get well? How will I be able to take care of her? She's never sick - she's the one that always takes care of us." She covered her face with her hands. "I'm so scared." In the silence she could almost hear the tears rolling down her cheeks.

"Ruthie, I've got to get back to the waiting room. Something's wrong. I can feel it." Jocelyn jumped up and ran out of the chapel with Ruthie struggling to keep up with her.

When she got to the waiting room, she saw her father slumped in one of the chairs with his head in his hands.

"Dad, what's wrong? Nana's okay, isn't she?"

"Oh, Jocelyn, the situation with Nana is very serious. The doctor is afraid she isn't going to make it through the night. They let me see her for a few minutes, and honey, she doesn't look good. I can't understand how this happened. She's so healthy. I can't remember the last time she was sick."

"Do you think they'll let me see her?" Jocelyn whispered through her tears. "Please, Dad, will you ask if I can see her?"

Without another word, Carter walked out of the room toward the station where the nurse was seated. Jocelyn watched him return and knew by the expression on his face she wasn't going to be allowed to see her grandmother.

"Sorry, Jocelyn, the nurse said they won't let you go in right now. But she said she would ask again later." Carter sat down in a chair across the room from Jocelyn and Ruthie and closed his eyes. After a few minutes, he stood up and mumbled to no one in particular that he was going to go call Father Sean.

Ruthie looked at the clock and jumped up. "Jocelyn, I've got to call my mom. I told her that I'd be back by 4:00, but I can't leave you. The rest of the family will be there at 6:00 and my aunt or somebody will help her. I'll stay here as long as you need me."

Jocelyn stood up and gave Ruthie a hug. "Thank you. You're a great friend, Ruthie. Thank you. But, you go on home. I'll be okay. Really, I'll be okay."

Father Sean joined Jocelyn and Carter and the three of them sat vigil, waiting for some news of Gracie's condition. Words were few, but every now and then, Jocelyn could hear Father Sean praying. Finally, about 9:00 PM, the doctor came back to the waiting room. He told them Gracie was still unstable, but he would let them to go in to see her for a few minutes. All three followed silently down the corridor until they arrived at the door of the Intensive Care Unit. The doctor turned to Jocelyn and Carter and told them they could go in for five minutes. He asked Father Sean if he would stay in the hall with him. Before he let them in, he turned to Jocelyn. "I know this isn't going to be easy for you. Your grandmother is hooked up to a lot of machinery and won't look like the person you are used to seeing. It's not likely she will open her eyes or give you any sign of recognition. But she needs for you to be strong. Do you think you can handle it?"

"Yes, sir. Please let me go in. I need to see her."

Gasping, Jocelyn began to retreat from the room. She wasn't prepared. Her heart beat quickened and she was grateful when her father took her hand.

Her nana, the strength and life force of the family, looked small and helpless in the hospital bed. Her face was distorted and her skin looked grey and swollen. This can't be Nana, my beautiful, sweet Nana. The whine and beeps of the machines made the room sound like something out of a science fiction movie and the harsh reality sucked the air out of the space. Carter reached out with one hand to hold on to the bed railing to steady himself and Jocelyn held tightly to his other hand. His touch helped her quiet the scream she felt building up inside her.

At first there were no words; they stood speechless beside the bed of the woman who made sense of their lives. Jocelyn couldn't comprehend what she was seeing. She couldn't imagine that the silent form in the hospital bed was her grandmother. Finally, Carter gently placed his hand on top of his mother's and softly called out to her. His voice trembled as he begged his mother not to leave. "Mom, please hang on. Don't leave us. We need you. Dear God, please don't take her now. Help her get well."

Father Sean walked into the room and placed his hand on Carter's shoulder. "Carter, the doctor thinks it would be best if I administered Last Rites. We don't know the future, son, and God may have a miracle in mind for our Gracie. This ritual is the only thing in our control right now; everything else is in God's hands.

Jocelyn and Carter stood sentinel, one on each side of the bed, as the priest began to prepare Gracie's soul for death. They lived in a capsule of pain that did not include those who were trying to comfort them and give them hope.

In the early hours of Saturday morning, with her son and granddaughter by her side, Gracie's machines went silent.

***

Jocelyn operated on automatic. Carrying on as Gracie would have expected her to do, she somehow got through the wake and the funeral.

Afterward, all she wanted to do was lie on the bed with the curtains drawn and cry. Her grief was an open pit too steep to crawl out of, no matter how hard she tried. Even with Ruthie's ministering and presence, she felt so alone. All around her there was a stillness. Eye of a hurricane kind of stillness; that deadly, deceitful quiet in the center of the storm. Jocelyn experienced the damage and carnage left in the wake of the first half of the storm and now she waited to see what the second half would bring. Intuitively, she knew the storm was not over and she cowered in her bed waiting. A sense of emptiness hung over the house and colored all her thoughts. What is coming next; why did God single us out for His wrath?

Her bones aching from lack of movement forced her to get up and dress. It had been four days since the funeral and all of her tears had not brought Nana back to her. Her father needed her, but she didn't know if she could deal with his grief while she was still trying to deal with her own fear and pain. She had not been back to school since the Thanksgiving break, and her father had not gone back to work. Somehow, she needed to break through the heaviness. It held her down and prevented her from giving or receiving help. Nana would be ashamed of the way she was acting.

Walking into the kitchen, she expected to see dirty dishes and spoiled food. But to her dismay, the kitchen was spotless. Who had cleaned up the mess left from the unfinished Thanksgiving dinner? Who had done the dishes, and mopped the floor? She certainly didn't remember doing it and couldn't picture anyone else coming in the house to get it done. She opened the refrigerator door and saw foiled casserole dishes stacked up on two shelves, bowls of salad and plates of dessert sat side by side on the other two shelves. Where had all this food come from?

She walked back down the hall to her father's room and knocked quietly on the door. In a few minutes she heard her father walking toward the door and when he opened it she was surprised to see him dressed in his uniform. "Well, well," said Carter. "I see you finally decided to rejoin the world. How are you feeling?"

Jocelyn was stunned. "Have you been to work?" she asked her father.

"Yeah, honey, I went back to work yesterday. I tried not to disturb you because the doctor felt you needed to rest. He gave you some medication to help you sleep. You've been so distraught, we were worried about you."

"You mean the doctor was here at the house and saw me? Are you kidding me? I don't remember any of this."

"No, sweetie, I'm not kidding you. I've been worried about you. But you look better today and I think by the sound of your voice, you're getting back to normal." There was a smile in Carter's voice as he quietly tried to tease his daughter.

"Wow. I feel like I've lost days of my life. I'm sorry, Dad I should have been helping you."

"Hey, I managed. Did you see all the food the neighbors brought to the house? They've all been so kind. Even, Mrs. Adams brought over a cake. She hasn't spoken two words to us in all the years she has lived across the street. And, Mrs. Clements came over and stayed with you yesterday and today while I was at work. We are blessed, Jocelyn."

Anger bubbled up from deep inside Jocelyn and her father was a handy target for her rage. "How can you say we're blessed when

Nana is gone," she blurted out. "Don't you feel anything for Nana? What kind of son are you, anyway?"

Running down the hall, she slammed the bedroom door. Her father must be stunned by her tone of voice and disrespect. Feeling childish and unfair, maybe she needed some kind of counseling to help her get through this.

She stayed in her room the rest of the afternoon and evening. Sometimes punching her pillow or pulling everything out of her dresser drawers, and at other times, throwing her stuffed dog across the room. This was a new feeling. There were no tears, just turmoil and anger. Finally expending all of her energy, she fell across the bed in exhaustion and slept.

Waking to the sound of her father moving around the house, she remembered her actions of the previous day with shame. How could she have behaved so thoughtlessly? He loved Nana as much as she did.

She eased out of bed and walked quietly to the kitchen. Her father sat at the table with his head bent, as though he was in prayer. She tiptoed to her place at the table and sat down. After a few minutes he looked up at her and smiled. What had she done to deserve a father who could look at her and smile after she had treated him so badly?

"Dad, I'm so sorry. I don't know what happened to me yesterday. I never should have said the things I did. I know how much you love Nana. Please forgive me," she begged.

Carter got up and walked around the table to stand beside her. "It's okay, sweetheart. I know you didn't mean what you said. Grief plays some unholy tricks on us, doesn't it? I've got to leave for work, but Mrs. Clements will stop in later to check on you. Let her know if you need something. And, if you feel like it, Ruthie brought over your homework assignments. They're in a folder on the hall table. You might want to try to catch up." Carter squeezed her shoulder, picked up his uniform hat, and walked out the back door. As he turned to close the door, he smiled, "I sure do miss your grandmother's biscuits and jam. She always sweetened me up for the day with her strawberry jam."

Jocelyn vowed she would find a way to keep the biscuits and jam on the table in the future.

Running a house, going to school, studying, and volunteering at the little theater was harder than Jocelyn anticipated and she realized quickly she had taken her grandmother for granted. Without Nana to oversee things, she felt like a master at burning dinner, bleaching the wrong load of laundry, forgetting to buy toilet paper, and using a wet mop on the hardwood floors instead of the dust mop. She could sit down and plan menus, but she was lost when she tried to figure out how much food to buy or whether a melon was ripe. And, she wondered if she was too ignorant to learn. Doing the household tasks had been so much easier when her nana was around to give her directions.

"Okay, Dad, I know Nana spoiled us, but are there some chores that you could do that would make the load lighter?"

"Sure, sweetheart, I'll be glad to help out if you don't mind giving me a refresher course every now and then. I'm fairly useless when it comes to housework. Sad to say, but I depended on your grandmother to take care of me."

"Thank you, dad. I guess that means we're a team. We'll find a way to make it all work." She smiled. "I know I can teach you how to boil water."

"You know, when I was in the army we had cleaning routines."

Jocelyn rolled her eyes and shook her head.

"Really. I'll take care of my uniform and every Saturday I'll clean the bathroom. I'll even do some KP duty on the days when you stay late at school. As long as you don't mind eating hot dogs or grilled cheese, we won't starve."

With the holidays behind them, life became less difficult. Jocelyn went to school and Carter went to work. On Saturday they did house chores, on Sunday they went to church and finished up anything that didn't get done on Saturday. Father Sean, Mrs. Dillon and the ladies from the church checked on them every now and then, but basically they were on their own. Life was the same and yet, it would never be the same again.

"Dad, I miss Nana so much. Sometimes I think I'll never be able to stop crying."

"Me, too. What was that thing your grandmother always said about tears? Oh, yeah, she would look at us and tell us to 'cry once, then don't waste any more tears.' I wonder if she knew how hard it is to do that?"

Father Sean suggested they join one of the prayer groups at the church organized for people who had recently lost a loved one. But, Carter and Jocelyn agreed it would be difficult for them to share their grief with people they didn't know. They were being forced by circumstances to communicate with each other and that was hard enough right now.

They discussed household things, worked together on tasks, and made sure that events were written on the calendar in the kitchen. But, they didn't talk to each other about things that really mattered. Jocelyn had little theater events and outings with Ruthie; he had his bowling league and once a month poker game with some of the other bus drivers. Even with their efforts to be a team, Jocelyn felt like her connection to home had diminished. Her companion and confidant was her grandmother; she never shared on a personal level with her father, and she didn't know how she could start now. Home was a very lonely place for a 17 year old high school senior.

Chapter Seven

January 1974

One afternoon in late January, as Jocelyn studied in the school library, Miss Moss, her English teacher and friend from the theater, approached the table where she was sitting.

"Jocelyn, I hope I'm not interrupting something important, but do you mind if I join you?" asked her teacher.

"No, ma'am. I was just finishing up a report for Social Studies."

"Jocelyn, I noticed on your Senior Survey that you're not planning to attend college. Is that right?"

"Yes, that's correct."

"But why, Jocelyn? You've got good grades, your GPA is a 3.7 and you are one of our best students. What do you want to do in the future? Surely you won't be happy working at Burdines or Jordan Marsh."

"I hadn't given it much thought, Miss Moss. I know Ruthie is planning to go to Florida State; she wants to be a teacher. I don't have the finances to go away to school and besides, I think my dad needs me at home right now. We have talked about me going to the community college for two years and working to save up money to maybe go on to the university, but I haven't really decided what to do."

"Your dad wants what's best for you, don't you think? What if I could help you apply for a scholarship? It's late in the year to be filling out college applications, but you took the SAT in October and did so well, I think colleges in-state would find it hard to turn you down."

"It's nice of you to offer to help me. But, it's pretty much out of the question right now."

"Please give it some serious consideration, and talk it over with your dad before saying no. You're too bright to miss an opportunity to further your education and I think you might be eligible for several scholarships. Will you at least think about it and talk to me later?"

"Okay, I'll think it over, and if I decide this is what I want to do, I'll talk it over with my dad. Thanks, Miss Moss. I'll let you know next week."

Jocelyn didn't tell Miss Moss she had been thinking of college for years. She and Ruthie even planned to be roommates. But, she realized it was just a dream when her father told her there was no money for her to use for college. He asked her to stay home for a year, get a job and save the money she would need for tuition and books. He suggested she could continue to live at home and attend Dade Community College. Once she earned her AA degree, she might be able to go on to the university. Ruthie had cried when Jocelyn told her this news. This plan meant Ruthie would be a junior before Jocelyn made it to Tallahassee.

What if she could win a scholarship? And, get a part time job? Would that be enough for her to persuade her dad to let her go away to school? She was afraid to get excited; she knew better than to count on something before it became a reality.

That evening at dinner she told her dad what had happened with Miss Moss and waited for his reaction. He listened attentively to all she said, and then he put his fork down and sat quietly for a few minutes.

"I didn't know you had your heart set on going away to school, Jocelyn. Money aside, that's a big step for someone who is only seventeen."

"I know dad, but if I could get into FSU, I'd be there with Ruthie. It's not like I would be all alone."

"What do you want to study, Jocelyn? I guess we've never talked about what you want to do with your life. I know you've got the grades to get into the university, but what can you get at the university that you can't start at the community college?"

"I'd really like to teach English. But I'd like to combine that in some way with theater and FSU has a great theater program. I could never be an actor, but I would like to see if I could be a director. That's my dream anyway."

Carter looked sad. "Jocelyn if you leave home in the fall, I would lose you and Nana all in the same year. I'm sorry. That sounded selfish didn't it?" He took a deep breath. "I know at some point you'll be leaving home, but I didn't think it would happen this soon."

"Oh, dad, you can't get rid of me that easy. Going away to school isn't the same as leaving home."

Carter laughed. "I don't want to hold you back. Go ahead and look at your options for a scholarship if that's what you really want."

Jocelyn was elated. She jumped up from the chair and did a little dance around the table.

"Thanks, dad, I can't wait to tell Ruthie and Miss Moss. This is good news!"

"Jocelyn, don't count your chickens before they hatch. As much as you want this, you know it might not pan out for you. All I can promise you is my support. You're out of my league now; my dad had always planned for me to go to college, but it didn't work out for me. I want you to follow your heart. So, go for it and see where it takes you."

She ran to the phone to call Ruthie and she couldn't wait to talk with Miss Moss. Maybe, just maybe, this would work out in her favor.

***

After class the next day, Miss Moss approached her, "Jocelyn, I'll go with you to meet with Sister Mary Lopez, she's the guidance counselor who is in charge of college planning. I know she will help you find some opportunities for scholarships and she can give you all the information you need to apply for college. Have you given any thought to the schools you might like to attend?"

"I really would like to go to Florida State. I want to major in English with a minor in Theater, and FSU has a great theater department. Someday I'd like to be a teacher or a director."

"By the quickness of your answer, it sounds like you've been thinking about this for a long time. You'd be an excellent teacher, but I'm a bit surprised about your interest in directing."

"You know I've worked at the theater since I was ten. I love working back stage and I've been giving some thought to trying my hand at directing."

"That sounds like an interesting plan, Jocelyn. Now let's go to work and try to make your dream come true. I'll talk with Sister Maria Lopez this afternoon and set up a time for us to meet. In the meantime, you need to go to the office and ask for copies of your transcript. We'll need to verify your date of birth with a copy of your birth certificate or your social security card. I'll find out what else you might need to send with the applications. I'm sure the scholarship applications will require pretty much the same information as those for the colleges. I know you have your heart set on FSU, but other schools offer good programs in Fine Arts, too."

"Thanks, Miss Moss. I'll get started looking right away."

It was amazing how quickly her energy changed. For the first time since her grandmother's death, everything in her world looked brighter. For a few minutes she let go of the grief, but it troubled her that she could do it so easily. Then she thought how happy her grandmother would be about her chances to go on to college. She had to take advantage of this opportunity and she could hardly contain her new enthusiasm.

"Hey, dad, will you get my birth certificate for me? I don't know where you keep our important papers. Do I have a social security card?"

Carter stood still and tried to breath. Jocelyn saw the look on his face and thought he looked like he was getting sick. "What's the matter, Dad?'

"Nothing. Nothing's wrong. Why do you need your birth certificate?"

"Miss Moss says I need to verify my birthday with either a birth certificate or my Social Security card. Mrs. Driscoll, in the office, told me I could make the copies on Friday when I go in to pick up the transcripts I ordered. If you'll tell me where they are, I'll go get them."

"I'll have to look for your birth certificate, Jocelyn. Your grandmother took care of those kinds of things. It may take me a while to find it. You don't have a social security card because I didn't think you'd need one until you got a job."

"Okay, but let me know when you have it. Don't I have to have my birth certificate to apply for a Social Security card?" Jocelyn said as she turned toward the kitchen to start preparations for dinner. She'd tell him later that Miss Moss had suggested calling the Bureau of Vital Statistics for a duplicate copy of the certificate.

Chapter Eight

Carter

Closing his bedroom door, Carter sat down on the bed and listened to his heart beating. He had to think straight and figure out what to do, but all he could feel was anxiety. He had pushed the thoughts of Jocelyn's birth so far back in his mind that he sometimes forgot that she wasn't his real daughter. Now all of Gracie's lies were going to catch up with him and he wanted to shout at his mother, "I told you so. Now what do I do? Oh, dear God, now what do I do!" He lay down on the bed and wanted to sleep forever.

Later, he remembered Jocelyn calling him for dinner and he recalled they talked of mundane things. He had no idea how he was going to handle the missing birth certificate. He'd stall Jocelyn somehow until he could figure it out.

A week went by before she asked him again for the birth certificate. "I haven't been able to find it, but I'll keep looking," was all he could think to say.

This back and forth went on for two more weeks, when Jocelyn finally said, "I need the birth certificate next week, Dad. We've got my applications just about ready to put in the mail. There are deadlines for submission and I don't want to miss those. I'm already way behind the other girls at school. Some of them have gotten their acceptance letters."

"Fine, I'll keep looking." He'd run out of time and he wasn't any closer to a solution. If only he could talk to his mother.

Chapter Nine

Jocelyn

She had taken care of as many of the details regarding her scholarship and college entry applications as she could. But, why hadn't she been more curious about her own history? She planned to ask her dad more questions. That evening over dinner, she told her father she had requested duplicate copies of her birth certificate from the Bureau of Vital Statistics. Before he could respond, Jocelyn posed a question, "Dad, how did I get so old without knowing some of the important details of my life? "

"What do you mean, Jocelyn?"

"There are so many things I don't know. You and Nana never told me what hospital I was born in?"

She was so wrapped up in the details of her own life, she didn't notice the blood drain from her father's face, she didn't see his hands begin to shake, and she didn't hear his silent cry of anguish. Even as she cleared the dishes from the table, she was oblivious to the fact he had not spoken and a glaze of fear now covered his eyes. Before she could turn around and ask any more questions, he left the room.

***

Monday dawned like any other day. The sun rose in the east with patterns of red, purple and yellow that made the Miami landscape glow with renewed vitality after a moonless night. The clouds were high and fluffy and the emerging blue of the sky seemed to promise not only good will, but good fortune for those who lived under its umbrella. Carter left for work hours before

Jocelyn headed out the door for school. He was on his second run of the morning by the time she boarded the Route Six bus for the short ride from their house to the stop where she transferred to the bus going north to her school. Like every morning, he smiled at her when the bus door opened and welcomed her aboard as though she was the most important rider on the bus that day. As she started down the aisle to find a seat, he told her he saved the best seat on the bus just for her. At this hour the bus was already crowded with people who were headed to work or school, but she did find a seat. As she looked at the back of her father's head, she thought he seemed distracted; not really himself. He said all the right words, but something was missing.

Ruthie wasn't at the bus stop this morning and Jocelyn wondered if she was sick or whether she had gone in earlier for choral practice. They had not called each other this weekend because Ruthie's family had out-of-town visitors. She needed to talk to Ruthie about all her questions. But, more than that, she needed to talk to her about all the answers she didn't have. Her friend always helped her put things in perspective.

Jocelyn loved to watch the people on the bus, and even those she saw from the window who were walking down busy 36th Street. Miami, in the 1970s, was an exciting city vibrating to the rhythm of the Cuban inhabitants; moving to the tempo of the jazz and gospel sounds of the black community; capitalizing on the energy of the northern transplants; and thriving on the drawl and stability of the southern natives. Jocelyn loved the ethnic changes as the bus moved from neighborhood to neighborhood. This was a bustling and stimulating place to live, confined between the gentle, salty breezes that gusted from the Atlantic Ocean and the steamy, earthy smells that drifted from the Everglades. There was nothing boring about this city.

The school day passed quickly. There was talk of spring break, term papers that were due, her next math test, and the elevated status of being a senior. On her way out of English class, Miss Moss asked her if she received the copies of her birth certificate.

"No, Miss Moss, but I'm sure the packet will be in the mail today. If I counted right, today will make five business days since my request. I'll let you know."

The first thing she did when she got to the house was check the mail box. There were numerous envelopes that looked like bills, a few advertisements, and a standard, white envelope with a return address for the Bureau of Vital Statistics. Puzzled, Jocelyn thought the certificates would be sent in a larger envelope. She rushed inside, put her books on the dining room table and ripped open the envelope.

Dear Miss McDeal,

We are writing in response to your request for

duplicate copies of your birth certificate. We

have searched our archives for a birth record

that matches the information you provided but

have been unable to locate an existing record

for: Jocelyn Marie McDeal, born June 10, 1956

in Dade County, Florida. If additional information

can be provided, please resubmit your request.

Sincerely,

David Campbell

Clerk

"What in the world does this mean? Are they kidding?" She put the letter back in the envelope and laid it on the table. Then, picked it up and read it again. "Wait 'til my dad gets home. He can clear this up in a minute."

***

The moment she heard Carter open the front door she rushed into the dining room and grabbed the envelope. "Dad, you aren't going to believe this! They say there is no record of my birth. What in the world does that mean? I was born here, right? So, they should be able to provide me with a copy of my birth certificate."

Carter stood rooted to the spot. He looked like he'd lost all sense of reality and was being sucked into a deep, dark vortex. Jocelyn grabbed his arm. She thought he could hear her but he didn't seem to understand what she was saying. "Dad, what's the matter? Are you okay? Dad talk to me."

He hung his head and didn't look at her. "Oh, my God, Mom, what have you done?" he said.

"No, dad, it's me Jocelyn. Nana isn't here. Dad, are you okay? You're scaring me." Jocelyn wanted her father to be strong, but at this moment she felt more like a parent than a child.

Looking at her, he whispered, "I'm all right. I think I need to sit down for a minute, the room is spinning. I'm just light headed, that's all."

Sitting down, he put his head against the back of the sofa. He sat that way for several minutes before he lifted his head and looked at Jocelyn. "Now, what were you saying?" he asked.

"I've got a letter from the Bureau of Vital Statistics that says they have no record of my birth. How can that be true?"

"Jocelyn, this has to be a mistake. I'll make some inquiries and we'll get this straightened out. Let me have the letter, please."

"Dad, I'll need to show it to Miss Moss. We'll need to ask for another delay for all of the applications I sent."

"It would be best if you gave me the letter so I can make my inquiries. I'm sure Miss Moss will understand."

"Okay, but I think I should show it to her first." Reluctantly Jocelyn handed the letter to Carter and went back to the kitchen to finish the preparations for dinner.

The next day, she tried to explain what happened to Miss Moss. She was surprised when Miss Moss began asking all sorts of questions about her father and life at home. "I'm sorry, Miss Moss, but I don't understand what all of these questions are about."

"Jocelyn, since we started working on your applications your father's behavior has baffled me, but this turn of events is very troubling."

"Miss Moss, there is nothing wrong at my house. I'll ask my father to call you about all of this. He'll reassure you this is just a clerical error." Jocelyn felt defensive and hurt. She couldn't understand why Miss Moss was trying to imply her father had done something wrong. She knew there were no deep, dark secrets in her family.

Since Nana's death, nothing was going right. Little things were blown out of proportion and nothing she did seemed to make it better. She wanted to curl up in her grandmother's lap and be reassured that her world wasn't falling apart. "Nana, why did you leave me? I need you."

Chapter Ten

Rosanna, Los Angeles, 1974

"Alex, leave your sister alone. She wasn't touching your things. If I have to tell you again, you'll be going to Time Out until dinner," scolded Rosanna. Looking at her children, she wondered if the petty chaos of their childhood would flow into a smoother adolescence, or if it would just be more of the same. Would these years of child-rearing ever end? Did other women experience the same kind of upheaval with their children? But, remembering her own mother gave her the answer to her question.

Her mind wandered back to the day she left Miami. Nineteen years ago and she could still feel the nausea welling up in her throat like it did that summer morning. The nausea returned every time she allowed herself to think about the frightened girl who climbed aboard the Greyhound bus and left everything she knew to find a better life for herself in Los Angeles. How naïve she had been. Today, she had a nice, if not exciting life, with her husband Paul, her eleven year old son, Alex, and her eight year old daughter, Angie. She had a great job as a court reporter in Orange County, California. Court reporting had been a good decision. It had brought her to a good life, not the glamour she had envisioned as a teenager, but a good life.

And, there was Paul - her tall, good looking, gentle Paul. Patiently and persistently, he had courted her until she gave in and went out with him. She giggled at her use of that old fashioned word. But, he had courted her. There wasn't another word to describe it. He brought her little gifts, flowers from the street vendor, and boxes of See's Chocolate. Laughing to herself, she remembered how many months he continued to ask her out, and how long it had taken her to finally say yes. Thank goodness he hadn't given up easily.

Hearing the car pull in the driveway, she brought her thoughts back to reality and ran out to the kitchen to check on the chicken cooking in the crock pot. With her busy schedule she said a small prayer of gratefulness to the kitchen gods for coming up with the idea of the slow cooker. She had put the chicken and vegetables in the pot this morning before she left for court and they should be ready to serve. All that was left to do was to make a salad and call everyone to the table.

"Hey, is anyone at home?" yelled Paul. "Isn't anyone going to bring me my slippers and pipe? How will everyone know I'm the king, if my grateful servants don't spoil me?"

"Dad, you're a dork!" joked Alex. "You don't smoke and nobody crowned you king."

"Ay, now you tell me. You've shattered all my dreams, Alex, my man. What a cruel thing to do to your aging father. And, what in the world is a dork?" Paul teased back. This kind of banter accompanied all the comings and goings of Paul Donovan. He made a joke out of almost everything in life. "No sense worrying about something you have no control over, Rosie baby. Life is too short to waste one minute on sadness or concern. If you make up your mind most of life is silly anyway, you can handle almost anything thrown at you." Sometimes she could go along with his theory, and sometimes she couldn't. She didn't think some of the things in her life could ever be catalogued as silly. But Paul's positive attitude was contagious and it often helped her change the energy of a difficult situation.

Angie came roaring out of the playroom like a bird dog on the hunt. She ran into her dad's open arms and when he swung her up, she gave him a very loud kiss on the cheek. "Hello, baby cakes. At least someone is glad to see me," Paul said as he put his wiggling daughter down.

"Hey, Rosie, my love! What's cooking? It sure smells good in this house." He sang out as he walked into the kitchen and grabbed her around the waist. "My day was way better than silly, how 'bout yours? I've never met so many people who didn't know up from down."

She smiled at her husband, a detective with LAPD, who now had enough seniority to hold down a decent shift. For years he had driven the streets at all hours of the day and night in a squad car, walked a beat on the east side, and sat behind a desk doing paperwork he thought was mindless. It had taken him almost fifteen years to work his way through the ranks and be promoted to detective. She had spent many sleepless nights knowing he was in places where dangerous things happened.

"Have I told you lately how beautiful you are?"

"Okay, Paul, what do you want or, better yet, what have you done? Stop trying to butter me up."

"You are forever the skeptic, Rosie. I don't have an ulterior motive. I just looked at you and thought how lucky I am. What more could I ask for? I've got a beautiful wife and we've got two great kids. We've got a good life, Rosie, and nothing is ever going to change that."

Chapter Eleven

February 1974

"Ah, a quiet evening with the Miami Herald, a bottle of iced cold ale, and my best girl. I needed this tonight. My back hurts and my feet are swollen," lamented Carter.

"Yeah, you're just getting old, Dad. Won't be long before you'll need the hot water bottle instead of a bottle of beer," Jocelyn joked.

Carter laughed and turned his attention back to the newspaper. It was one of those Miami nights when a nice breeze was blowing off the ocean and the air was filled with the fragrance of jasmine and gardenias. It was a siren's song calling to him, and he picked up the paper and moved to the table on the screened porch. It was hard to concentrate because this was a "Gracie" kind of night. He could picture his mother seated in the swing on the porch, watching as night came like a soft blanket being gently pulled up over the city. His grieving was a spot deep within that was still raw and jagged, and most of the time it felt like it was still bleeding. There was so much he needed to talk over with his mother, so many things to ask her advice about. Tonight he was wearing his fear about Jocelyn like a jacket he had outgrown. It was binding his shoulders and putting pressure on his whole body. There was no place for him to hide from this birth certificate issue.

The ringing of the telephone made him jump and the voice on the other end of the line made his gut hurt. A premonition of trouble was delivered with every word.

"Excuse me, Miss Moss, does Jocelyn have a problem at school?

"No, no, I understand. You want me to come for a parent conference to talk about her college applications. When?"

"Well, I could come in tomorrow around 4:00. I don't get off work until 3:30. Would that work?"

"Okay, but why do you want to meet in Father Sean's office?"

"Yes, I see. I'll be there tomorrow at 4:00. Good-bye."

Returning the phone to the cradle, he scratched his head. "That is one strange woman," he mumbled to himself as he turned back to his chair. Instinctively, he dreaded this meeting.

"What was that all about, Dad? What did Miss Moss want?"

"Your teacher wants to talk with me about your college applications. I'm going to meet her tomorrow."

"Am I supposed to be there?"

"No, she said she just wanted to meet with me. Is she always so curt?"

"She does have a way about her. I don't think you should take it seriously. Really, Dad, she's that way with everybody."

"Hey, since I have to be at the school tomorrow afternoon, why don't you wait for me and I'll take you to the Chesapeake for dinner. We haven't been out for dinner in a long time."

"Oh, Dad, that would be great. I can taste those fried shrimp now. You know that's my favorite restaurant."

Carter knew this was a turning point. This was the moment to make things right in his world. But would it make things right in Jocelyn's world? If they'd only told her the truth when she was old enough to understand?

***

Carter felt disheveled by the time he pulled his car into the parking lot at Notre Dame Academy. He had rushed out of the bus barn as soon as he had punched his time card, and he knew he would have to hurry to be on time for his appointment at the school. Wiping the sweat off his forehead, he ran his fingers through his hair in a hasty attempt to look presentable. He wished there had been time to change out of his uniform, but that would have pushed him. As he left the parking lot, he looked back admiringly at his yellow Ford Mustang. No longer a new car, he made every effort to keep it in tiptop condition. He had bought it around the time of Jocelyn's tenth birthday, so his mother wouldn't have to lug grocery bags when she went shopping. He tried, unsuccessfully, to convince his mother she needed to learn to drive. But he didn't win that battle. Last summer, Jocelyn got her driver's permit and would probably have her license soon. He smiled when he thought about her sitting behind the wheel of the sporty little car.

Pushing open the doors of the school, the warm air from the heated building hit him and he wondered why a school building in Miami ever needed heat. Even in February, Miami's temperature was not low enough to be called winter. He hoped Father Sean's office was not going to be stifling hot.

Walking into the administrative office, he saw Father Sean standing at the reception counter talking with someone he presumed to be Miss Moss. "Good afternoon, Father. It's nice to see you."

"It's been awhile since you honored us with your presence, Carter. Maybe I'll see you at Mass this Sunday, too," the priest said with a chuckle. "Come on to my office and we'll get started. My apologies, do you know Miss Moss?"

"No, Father, we've only spoken on the phone," Carter said as he turned to acknowledge the teacher. Miss Moss nodded but did not speak or smile.

When the three of them were seated in Father Sean's office, the priest turned to Carter. "There's a little information that is missing from Jocelyn's college applications. I know you can answer all of Miss Moss's questions and clear this matter in just a few minutes."

The teacher, sitting primly in the chair, was still not smiling. "Mr. McDeal, as you may know I've been assisting Jocelyn with filling out applications for college entry and for scholarships. She is a very bright young woman and I know she won't have any problems obtaining enough scholarship money to ensure she can attend a four-year university. She does have her heart set on going to

FSU, but I've talked with the admissions offices at Barry, an excellent Catholic school, and they are prepared to offer her a scholarship to cover tuition and books."

Miss Moss seemed to be making the point that she, not Carter, had done all of this for Jocelyn. "The issue is her birth certificate and Social Security number. I know you told her you can't locate the birth certificate, but did you know the Bureau of Vital Statistics can't locate it either? And, why haven't you applied for her Social Security card?" Miss Moss's voice was steely and her facial expressions were hard and accusing.

"I appreciate your efforts for Jocelyn, but I don't think it's appropriate for you to be questioning decisions I made for my daughter." Carter felt like she was attacking him with her words and her eyes. He looked at the crucifix hanging on the wall behind Father Sean's desk, and tried to remember that he was supposed to 'love his neighbor.'

"Carter, you know your mother talked with me about the circumstances of Jocelyn's birth. But I'm not at liberty to reveal the conversation unless you give me permission to do so. I'm sure once we explain to Miss Moss, we will be able to obtain a birth certificate for Jocelyn." The priest spoke directly to Carter with a beseeching look on his face.

"As long as Miss Moss understands this discussion is confidential, you have my permission." Carter was interested in hearing this story himself. He wasn't sure he knew exactly what his mother had told the priest.

"Do you understand Mr. McDeal's request for this information to remain confidential?"

"Father, I don't know if that will be possible. Jocelyn will need to use the information to make sure she can obtain her birth certificate," responded Miss Moss.

"Perhaps if I tell you the story, you will understand why it may be difficult to obtain the document. Her father will then do what is necessary without causing harm to Jocelyn. Carter, how much of the story does Jocelyn know?"

"Father Sean, Jocelyn has never discussed this with me. I know she and my mother must have talked, but I was never included in those conversations. To my knowledge, Jocelyn only questioned her birth once when she was a very young child. I always assumed Mother's explanation satisfied my daughter's need to know. Please, go ahead and tell Miss Moss what my mother told you."

The priest turned to the woman waiting impatiently. "Carter's mother, Gracie McDeal, came to me very shortly after Jocelyn's birth to ask my advice about the birth of the child. It seems one of Gracie's nieces, Jocelyn's mother, became pregnant out of wedlock and died giving birth to the child. The niece's mother, Gracie's sister, had died many years before and there was no one to take the infant. Gracie's brother-in-law, the child's grandfather, lived alone and was unable to care for the child, so he called Gracie and Carter to ask them if they would take her. Gracie asked me if I thought she and Carter would be able to make a family for the child and I assured her, with God's help, they would make a fine family. At the time, Gracie told me she had gone up north to bring the child back to Miami. Within a week or so, she brought the baby to me to be christened. To my knowledge, Jocelyn has always considered Gracie to be her grandmother and Carter to be her father."

"That's all well and good, Father." She turned to Carter, "Mr. McDeal, all you need is your cousin's name and the city where Jocelyn was born and you can request her birth certificate." Miss Moss took a notebook and pencil out of her purse to write down the information.

Carter stood up and walked over to the window. "You don't understand, Miss Moss. Jocelyn thinks I'm her father. It would be devastating for her to suddenly find out that's not true."

"Why in the world would she think you are her father? Didn't your mother tell her the story of her birth?"

"The only information I know my mother gave to Jocelyn is her mother died in childbirth. I never questioned my mother's reasons for not sharing the rest of the story with Jocelyn."

"Oh, my. How unfortunate for Jocelyn. But, surely, if you love this young woman as your daughter, Mr. McDeal, you will want her to take advantage of an opportunity to further her education." Single minded in her purpose, Miss Moss pressed on. "I know it will come as a shock to Jocelyn, but if she is given this information in a loving way, the truth will not devastate her." Firmly, she snapped at Carter, "Don't you think you owe your daughter the truth?"

The walls of the room began closing in on Carter. He was sweating profusely and he couldn't separate out the thousands of voices he heard in his head. Jocelyn was a gift from God to his mother, and they had just buried her, the most important person in Jocelyn's life. How could he explain to these people that what they thought was truth, was really a lie?

"Father Sean, I need some time to think this over. I can't make this kind of decision on the spur of the moment. I need to pray about this and determine what I think is best for Jocelyn, for my daughter. Miss Moss, I appreciate your efforts to help, and yes, I want her to have this chance." Carter turned to the priest, "Father, I'll let you know my decision soon. Please pray we do the right thing for Jocelyn and if there is anything to tell Jocelyn, I will be the one to do it," said Carter emphatically as he looked at Miss Moss. "If you will excuse me, I promised to take my daughter out to dinner and she is waiting for me."

Carter got up with as much dignity as he could and walked out of the office. He fought to stop his hands from shaking and did not turn around to see if Father Sean or Miss Moss was following behind him. He needed to reach the front door and leave the building as fast as he could. He hesitated long enough to hear Miss Moss say to Father Sean, "Something isn't right here, Father, and I intend to find out what it is."

"The McDeal's are good people, Miss Moss. Jocelyn was raised in a loving home and Carter is a very good father. Please remember - Jocelyn has just lost her grandmother. Don't make more out of this than is really there. But, no matter what, this is Carter's decision, not yours; not mine."

Father Sean stood in the doorway and his eyes followed Carter to the front door. "Excuse me, Miss Moss. I need to speak with Carter about another matter."

When the priest reached the sidewalk, Carter was slumped over like an old man. "Carter, are you all right?"

"Who is that woman?" Carter lifted his head and looked at the elderly priest. "Why is she doing this to us?" Tension was attacking every cell in his body and he wished the priest would go away and leave him alone.

"Son, pull yourself back together. I'll help you any way I can. Believe me, I didn't know that Gracie had never discussed this with Jocelyn."

"Father, all I can think about is how much that woman is going to hurt my daughter."

"I wish I knew what was going on in her mind. For whatever reason, she has decided that she's going to be Jocelyn's advocate. I'll try to diffuse as much of this as I can, Carter. But you need to have a serious talk with Jocelyn."

"God, help me," Carter whispered, "and, God help Jocelyn."

The dinner conversation that evening was no different than all the other conversations between them, Jocelyn talked and he listened. She went on and on about a movie she and Ruthie had seen on Saturday. She told him about the research she was doing for her history report and how fascinated she was with the French Resistance during the war. She laughed about a lighting snafu that had occurred last week at the little theater. She was so animated when she talked and he loved how she talked as much with her hands as she did with her words. The longer she talked about herself, the longer he had to think about how he was going to answer all her questions.

"Okay, Dad, I've waited long enough. What did Miss Moss want to see you about?"

The taste of the shrimp he was eating turned sour, and he tried to wash it down with a gulp of iced tea. He hesitated a minute before he spoke. "Honey, she wanted to brag on you a little. She wanted to tell me something I already know; you're bright, capable, and sweet. That's all."

Jocelyn blushed, "Did she talk with you about me going on to college?"

"Of course, she thinks that's the best choice for you."

"Did she tell you why I need my birth certificate?"

"Yes, Jocelyn, and we're working on it."

"Great! I knew there was nothing for me to worry about. I had given up on going to a four-year college, but now it's all I can think about. If I get accepted at FSU, Ruthie and I will room together, and I want to do a double major in English and Theater. Wow, as Nana always said, I'm putting the cart before the horse, aren't I?"

More than anything, he wanted to make his daughter's dream come true. He looked at the innocence and trust in her eyes and wondered if his daughter would ever look at him again with those eyes?

Chapter Twelve

Carter

The knock on the door was loud and very insistent. Carter looked over at Jocelyn and asked, "Are you expecting anyone?"

"Maybe it's Ruthie. We talked about studying together. I'll go see who it is."

Jocelyn opened the door to two well dressed women carrying briefcases. "May I help you?" she asked.

"Yes. We're here to see Mr. Carter McDeal," offered one of the women. "May we come in?"

"Hold on and I'll get him. May I tell him your names?"

"Please, just tell him we would like to meet with him for a few minutes. Thank you."

Closing the screened door, Jocelyn walked back into the living room where her father was seated. "It's for you, Dad. I think someone wants to sell you something," Jocelyn shrugged and walked over to the kitchen door. "There are two ladies at the door who look pretty impressive and they called you by name." She laughed and looked over her shoulder, "I don't think they're the Avon ladies."

Carter opened the door and asked the women to come inside. "I'm Carter McDeal. How can I help you?"

He offered the ladies a seat and returned to his chair before one of the women began speaking. "Mr. McDeal, we are from HRS, Health and Rehabilitative Services, and we are here to ask you some questions about your daughter. My name is Rachel Parks and this is

Marilyn Cooper. The young woman who answered the door, is she your daughter?"

"Yes she is, but I don't understand," said Carter. "Has my daughter done something wrong?"

"No, Mr. McDeal. It has been brought to our attention there may be some irregularities regarding Jocelyn's birth. That is her name, correct? And, we just need to get some information from you to clear up the matter," said Mrs. Parks.

"I see," responded Carter guardedly. "And, who asked you to come see me?"

"I'm sorry, Mr. McDeal, but that information is confidential. Now, if you don't mind, we'd like to begin." One social worker opened her briefcase and took out a file while the other opened a notebook and began writing. Carter took a deep breath and hoped he could stay calm during what he thought was going to turn into an inquisition.

"Please ask your daughter to join us, Mr. McDeal," requested Mrs. Parks.

"Is that necessary? I'm sure I can answer your questions." Carter was beginning to feel sick to his stomach and knew his nerves would be jangled even more if Jocelyn was in the room. Mrs. Parks, sitting rigidly before him, made him feel as though she expected him to comply without any further comment from her. So, reluctantly, he stood up and walked toward the back of the house. When he reached the kitchen door he motioned for Jocelyn to follow him.

"What, Dad? Do you need me to help you pick out a new scrub brush?" Jocelyn giggled.

"These women are from HRS and they want to ask us a few questions. I'm sure this will only take a minute."

"What's HRS? Why do they want to talk to me?" she inquired.

"I think HRS deals with health and family issues. That's all I know. Let's see what the ladies have to say."

Jocelyn walked into the living room and took a chair across the room from the sofa where the women were seated. Carter sat down in his recliner but didn't lean back. He sat on the edge of the chair with his hands folded in front of him. He looked like a rabbit poised to take off at the first sign of danger.

"Mr. McDeal, this is very simple. Do you know where Jocelyn's birth certificate can be located? If we could just take a look at it, all of our questions will be answered."

"Mrs. Parks, as I told Father Sean and Miss Moss, I don't have a copy of the document. My mother took care of the paperwork and since her death last fall, I haven't been able to find it."

"Where was Jocelyn born, Mr. McDeal?"

"Jocelyn, there are things your grandmother didn't tell you and I'm sorry you are going to hear about them tonight in front of strangers," Bowing his head, he closed his eyes. His heart was breaking as he thought about the impact his words would have on the beautiful young girl he loved as a daughter. His voice faltered. "I think she was born in Baltimore, Maryland, to my mother's great niece. The young woman, who was not married, died in childbirth, and my mother was her closest kin. When my mom was asked to raise Jocelyn, she was thrilled." His voice got softer and softer as he finished retelling this lie. He raised his head in time to see the tears flowing down Jocelyn's face as she ran out of the room. "Mrs. Parks, Jocelyn needs me. What else can I tell you tonight?"

"Mr. McDeal, there are more questions than answers and we have just begun this investigation. When you have seen to the girl, please come back to the living room. We will wait for you."

Carter walked to Jocelyn's bedroom door and quietly opened it. But, before he could enter the room, Jocelyn screamed, "How could you lie to me? Why didn't you tell me the truth? What else don't I know? Never mind, just go away. I don't want to talk to you now."

Reluctantly, Carter closed the door and walked back to the living room. The air suddenly felt stale and suffocating, and all around him there was a sense of regret.

"Why are you doing this to us? What can be accomplished by tearing what remains of this family apart? My mother died several months ago and Jocelyn and I are still grieving. Why, Mrs. Parks, that's my question for you and the HRS?"

"I'm sorry this has come as such a shock to Jocelyn. I didn't realize she didn't know the story of her birth. I am sorry, Mr. McDeal. But all of this still doesn't help me locate her birth certificate. If you'll give me the name of this great niece, I can make inquiries in the state of Maryland. They will be able to produce the document we need," Mrs. Parks continued without taking a break.

Finally, the other social worker spoke quietly to Carter. "Mr. McDeal, my heart is breaking for you and your daughter. I wish there was another way to handle this issue. And, surely, if we had known she hadn't been told, we could have handled our part in it very differently. Please accept our apologies. If you'll give us the name and the date of Jocelyn's birth, we will leave you to comfort your daughter and try to help her understand what is going on."

"I'm sorry, ladies. But I don't know the name of my mother's great niece. My mother was estranged from her family and rarely spoke of them to me. I don't know my mother's sister's married name. So I can't help you. Please, leave now. Call me to meet you in your office if you need to talk with me anymore. I don't think Jocelyn can take another home visit. I'm sorry, but I've got to try and talk to her." Carter's voice became more insistent as he talked. He wanted these women out of his house.

"We're not at the end of this, Mr. McDeal. I can assure you, there will be more questions," retorted Mrs. Parks as she and Mrs. Cooper gathered up their things and walked to the door. "We will be in touch with you."

Closing the door, Carter leaned heavily on it for a minute to steady his nerves. The shadows descend on him like a rain soaked blanket. He hadn't felt this kind of weight since his buddy, Jack, had fallen dead on top of him in Korea.

"Mom, I can't handle this. What am I supposed to do now? Help me find the words so I won't lose Jocelyn," He begged his mother to hear him.

Tapping on Jocelyn's door, he turned the knob to go into her room. The room was dark, but he saw Jocelyn sitting on the window ledge staring into the night sky. "Jocelyn, you are and always will be my daughter. Nothing can ever change that."

"Right, Mr. McDeal, or whatever I'm supposed to call you now. Something changed tonight, didn't it?" Jocelyn's voice was unbearably loud and he could almost see her anger spewing out from behind clenched teeth. "Who am I?" she lamented. "Who in the world am I?" Her whole body was trembling as the sobs overwhelmed her. "You're not my dad and Gracie's not my grandmother, so who in the world do I belong to? Or, do you even know the answer?"

"Jocelyn, give me a chance to explain. Please."

"You've had years to explain. And you wouldn't be explaining tonight if those women hadn't shown up. Just go away. I don't want to hear anymore tonight."

Despair wrapped around him as he walked slowly to his chair in the living room and fell into it. His agony had just begun.

Although things were very strained between Carter and Jocelyn and communication was very sparse, the routine of their lives continued on for several days before he received a letter to appear at HRS for a meeting. The appointment was scheduled for next Thursday afternoon at 4:00. The bus run would be complete by then so he wouldn't have to ask Sully for time off.

Carter hoped he wouldn't have to tell Jocelyn about the Thursday meeting. It was useless to upset her further. But she saw the envelope in the mailbox and asked him about it at dinner. "What did the letter from HRS have to say?" she asked pointedly. "Are they coming back to the house?"

"No, Jocelyn, they aren't coming back to the house, but they do want a meeting with me next Thursday afternoon. There isn't any more that I can tell them, but we'll see how it goes." He was quiet for a moment, then he said slowly, "Jocelyn, I've been doing some thinking and praying about you going to college. I have an insurance policy my father took out years ago that can be cashed in. If you can find a part time job to help with your living expenses, it would give you most of the money you need. I'm sorry I didn't think about it before."

"Are you trying to bribe me into forgiving you for the lies you and Nana told me? Do you think I won't be angry anymore if you pay for me to go to college?" Her face turned red and her words sounded so brittle he could feel her breaking apart as she spoke.

"A week ago I knew who I was. I used to have a loving grandmother and father, and a mother who died in childbirth. At least that's the story I thought I knew. Who named me by the way?" she tossed the question to Carter like it was a hot potato. Her words were clipped and her tone of voice was less than friendly.

"I can truthfully say your mother and grandmother named you. Your mother named you Jocelyn before she left you, and your grandmother gave you your middle name, Marie, when you were christened."

"You mean Gracie gave me my middle name, don't you? Remember, she's not my grandmother." The sarcasm dripped from her voice as she threw words at Carter. "You can't even tell me my mother's or my grandmother's names. Oh, forget it. This isn't going anywhere and it's just making me angry all over again. I'm going over to Ruthie's."

"What about the money for school? Won't it make a difference? Now you don't have to apply for scholarships." Carter was talking to her back as she headed out the door.

She didn't even bother to turn around, but spoke as if to nobody. "You really don't get it, do you? The money doesn't matter when there isn't a school out there that will accept a person who has no identity. Your money is just another cruel joke."

The sound of the door slamming echoed in Carter's head as he watched Jocelyn walk across the lawn toward the street. He thought about offering to give her a ride to Ruthie's, but decided his words would probably fall on deaf ears. Now he just wanted the HRS meeting to be over with. He wanted his normal life back. He wanted his daughter back.

Chapter Thirteen

Carter

Carter quickly changed out of his uniform and drove downtown to the office where he was to meet with the social workers. He hoped it wasn't going to take long and they could offer some positive suggestions about filing for a birth certificate for Jocelyn.

The HRS office was located in a high-rise building in the heart of downtown. He found a parking spot in the garage across the street and walked into the lobby trying not to feel intimidated by the mere size of the building. He stood in a line of people at the reception desk to get directions to the conference room where the meeting was to be held. After a short wait, the young woman at the desk told him to take the elevator to the tenth floor. The ride in the elevator was too short for Carter to talk himself out of a bad case of nervousness. His stomach was tied in knots. He never felt comfortable in new situations and wished there were some shadows in this building where he could hide. When the elevator door opened, he was surprised to see Miss Moss standing at the secretary's desk. She turned when she heard him approach and, without smiling, walked away.

Carter wondered why she was here and began to feel even more uncomfortable. He was about to ask the secretary directions to the conference room, when one of the social workers who visited the house touched his shoulder and asked him to follow her. Walking down the long corridor with closed doors on each side made him feel claustrophobic. He wondered how people could work here every day. As he passed several doors, he could hear the sounds of people talking, and behind one door, he even heard laughing. Looking at Miss Moss's back as they walked, reminded Carter of all the men whose backs he had stared at when he marched in the army.

Her head was held high, her shoulders were back, and her whole body gave off an aura of stiffness and assuredness. She was a daunting woman who appeared to be in command of every situation, and her mere presence made him feel small and insecure. He wondered if her students felt that way about her. To give himself some comic relief, he imagined her students cowering in fear as she walked amid the classroom desks ready to lop off the head of any poor kid who came to class unprepared. Instead of a pencil, she must carry an ax in her hand. Carter smiled to himself when the words "battle ax" popped into his head. He shook his head to clear the thought just as they reached the conference room.

When they entered the room, Carter was surprised to see so many people. He expected one or maybe two, but now he faced six or eight. "What in the world is going on?" he thought. The other social worker who had been at the meeting at his house was seated at the far end of the table, but when a man stood up to introduce himself to Carter, it didn't appear either of those women were in charge of the meeting. "Mr. McDeal, Miss Moss, I am Donald Hunter, and I supervise the social workers assigned to this case. Won't you be seated," he said. "Let me introduce the others around the table. You both know Rachel Parks and Marilyn Cooper. Next to them are Agnes Smart and Dan Engels from our investigative unit, Detective Todd Madison from the Miami Police Department, and Dale Harper from Child Protection."

Swallowing hard, Carter slowly sank into one of the two empty seats at the end of the table. For a few seconds the silence in the room was almost deafening and even before the questions began, Carter felt like he had walked in on a court martial. He looked over at Miss Moss to see if she was as surprised as he was, but her look of satisfaction let him know she had prior knowledge of the magnitude of this meeting. A slow mounting anger began to replace his earlier confusion. What in the world is going on here?

"Let me begin by saying this is a fact finding meeting, Mr. McDeal. We have been made aware of some irregularities regarding how Miss Jocelyn McDeal came to be a part of your household, but we are sure you can give us answers to clear up all of the inconsistencies that have been reported. No charges have been issued at this time," he began.

Carter jumped to his feet, "What are you talking about? What charges? What is going on here?" Red faced, he could feel rage growing inside. He wanted answers to his questions before this meeting went any further.

"Please sit back down, Mr. McDeal. I just meant that sometimes these types of meetings result in charges being levied, but I'm sure that isn't what will happen today. If you will calm down, I'd like to proceed," stated Mr. Hunter.

As Carter slowly sank into the chair, the man continued, "First, I'd like for you to tell the others in the room the circumstances surrounding the birth of your daughter. Just begin at the beginning and tell us how she came to live with you."

Carter's hands shook and his tongue felt swollen in his mouth. "To my knowledge, Jocelyn was born in Baltimore to my mother's niece. The niece was unmarried and her own mother died years before. My mother's brother-in-law could not care for a child so he asked my mother if she would raise the baby. That's all I know," Carter's voice was choked and the only thing he wanted was for the people in the room to hear this explanation and end the meeting.

"Do you have a name you can give us? Either Jocelyn's mother's or grandmother's name will do," implored Mr. Hunter.

"I don't have those names, Mr. Hunter. I explained that to the social workers."

"But, surely you would know your aunt's name, wouldn't you, Mr. McDeal?"

"No, Mr. Hunter, I don't know her name. My mother talked very little about her family and I was never curious enough to ask her any questions."

"Who brought the baby to Miami? I'm assuming someone brought her here. Isn't that correct?"

Carter felt trapped by his own lack of imagination. He didn't know what to say next, but he knew they were expecting him to give details of how Jocelyn came to Miami. "My mother went to Baltimore to get her."

"How did she go to Baltimore, Mr. McDeal? Did she ride the train or take a bus, or maybe she flew? And, how did she and Jocelyn travel back to Miami? "

"She took the train. My father was with the railroad and she had a pass. She told me she rode the train using her pass."

"Did she go alone or did someone go with her?"

"She went alone."

"Did she pick up the baby at a hospital or from someone's home?"

"I don't know."

"How old was Jocelyn when your mother brought her home to Miami?"

"Maybe a week or so. I don't remember."

"Think about it, Mr. McDeal. When is Jocelyn's birthday and when did she arrive in your home?"

"Her birthday is June 10, 1956 and I don't remember what day they came back from Baltimore."

The questioning went on for almost an hour. New questions, the same questions, questions with no answers. Carter's head was reeling and he could feel a headache creeping up the back of his neck. Everyone around the table seemed to be talking at once and their words were getting more and more blurred. He felt confused and he was beginning to forget what he had said in the beginning of the questioning. Then, all of a sudden the room fell silent and everyone seemed to be staring at him.

Mr. Hunter had a strange look on his face as he asked Carter to repeat the answer he had just given. "Mr. McDeal, please repeat that answer again."

"What answer? I don't remember what I just said. I can't even remember the question," Carter whispered.

"Mr. McDeal, you just told us your mother always wanted a daughter, and Jocelyn was a gift to her. Would you care to explain that statement further? What did you mean; you gave Jocelyn to your mother as a gift? Is that what you just said, Mr. McDeal?" Mr. Hunter's voice was sterner now than Carter remembered it in the beginning of the meeting.

"I don't think that's what I said."

Stumbling over his words, Carter felt the weight of all the lies smashing him like he was a bug on the ground. "Jesus, Mary and Joseph, help me," he intoned out loud.

"Mr. McDeal, I know you must be very tired. Why don't you come with me to the precinct office? We'll get a cup of coffee and chat about this in a quieter atmosphere," Detective Madison said as he took Carter's arm and helped him to his feet. "I'll bring you back to pick up your car later."

"No, I can't do that. Jocelyn will be worried about me. She doesn't know I'm here," Carter heard himself say these words, but he didn't feel connected to them.

"Mr. McDeal, I'll go by the house and take Jocelyn out for dinner. I'll explain you've been detained and will see her later," said Miss Moss. "Jocelyn will be fine; you go on and finish your discussion with the police. Jocelyn will be just fine."

When Carter looked over at Mary Ann Moss, she was smiling at him.

Shadows formed on the streets and buildings as Carter made a silent trip to the precinct in the detective's car. Nothing made sense to him and the throbbing in his head drowned out any thoughts he might have.

Chapter Fourteen

Mary Ann Moss

Turning the corner on to 11th Avenue, Mary Ann Moss smiled when she saw Jocelyn standing at the hedge talking to a neighbor. She considered Jocelyn to be pretty and intelligent; now she hoped the girl was resilient, too. Certainly Mr. McDeal and his mother raised her to be a God-fearing Catholic, but their motives were not pure. She had figured that out the moment she began working with Mr. McDeal. And now, he was going to discover he had to pay for his crime. She had made sure Detective Madison knew all he needed to know to make Mr. McDeal a suspect. Under the circumstances, she already applied with HRS to be made Jocelyn's guardian if criminal charges were brought against Mr. McDeal. Her plan was working better than she imagined and tonight she would gently begin to prepare Jocelyn for her new life as her ward. Jocelyn was only seventeen and would need a new home for a few more years.

Jocelyn stopped talking to Mrs. Harvey when she saw the car pull up in front of her house. She was surprised to see Miss Moss get out and start up the sidewalk toward her. "Miss Moss, what are you doing here?"

"Jocelyn, may I speak with you inside for a moment?"

"Sure. Bye, Mrs. Harvey, and thanks for the oranges. I'll make juice in the morning," Jocelyn waited until Mrs. Harvey was safely inside before she left. When Mrs. Harvey had closed the door behind her, Jocelyn walked over to meet Miss Moss.

"Our neighbor gave me this bag of oranges, and I think there are enough of them for a pitcher of juice. We don't have any orange trees in our yard, but she has so many that she always shares with us. Now, what did you need to talk to me about?"

"Jocelyn, I have something important to discuss with you. May we go inside?"

"Okay, but my dad's not home and I'm sure he would want to hear any news you have about school. Can we wait for him?"

"I've spoken with your father. Let's go inside and I'll tell you all about it."

Jocelyn led her into the house and asked her to take a seat in the living room while she took the bag of oranges to the kitchen. Miss Moss walked over to a table and picked up a photograph of Gracie McDeal.

"What a lovely picture of your grandmother? I remember when you were younger and she would come with you to the little theatre." Miss Moss returned the framed picture to the table and looked around the room. "I love all the antique pieces of furniture in this room. Your grandmother must have had a good eye for quality and workmanship. I'm assuming of course she decorated this room." She took a seat on the sofa.

"That's my favorite picture of Nana. It was taken several years ago," Jocelyn smiled. "Nana was good with design and color, and knowing how to pick just the right piece of furniture. She always found the best bargains."

"I know you are wondering why I'm here, dear. But, your father asked me to come and take you to dinner."

"My father asked you to take me to dinner? Why? Where did you see him and where is he? He's late getting home today," Jocelyn fired off questions in rapid succession and had started twirling a strand of hair around her finger.

"He didn't tell you he had a meeting with HRS?"

"Yes, but I didn't think it would take this long. Were you at the meeting?" Jocelyn frowned. "Why was he meeting with them again? We answered all their questions several weeks ago. Why were you at the meeting?"

"Apparently, they weren't satisfied with some of his answers and they needed more information. They needed for me to explain why we had to find your birth certificate. Your father went to the police department to talk some more with the detective, and he asked me to come and take you to dinner."

"What? Why would he be at the police station?" she said in surprise. "What is going on? I need to get down to the police station, not go out to dinner. Will you take me there?" She stood up and walked over to get her purse.

"There isn't anything you can do at the police station. Let's go eat and I'm sure your father will be here when we return. This is just a routine kind of thing. Don't worry, okay?"

"Have I done something wrong?" Tears welled up in Jocelyn's eyes.

Miss Moss grabbed Jocelyn's shoulders and hugged her, "You did nothing wrong. Get your things and let's go down to Morrison's Cafeteria for dinner. I'm sure you're worrying over nothing."

Chapter Fifteen

Carter

Carter sat across the table from Detective Madison and tried to think through his previous questions and answers. Something he said evidently made the detective want to talk to him at the police station. Somewhere he slipped up and said something that made the police question his story. He wasn't surprised. He'd never been a good liar. His mother could always tell when he was trying to slip something passed her. Now he was caught up in the story she invented, and he didn't know where to go from here. He tried to fill in the gaps, but apparently he wasn't very convincing.

"Would you like a cup of coffee, Carter? I can call you Carter, can't I?" asked the detective.

All of a sudden Carter realized he hadn't eaten dinner and he was hungry. A cup of coffee might hold him over until he could grab a bite to eat. Even though the woman made him uneasy, he was glad Miss Moss offered to take Jocelyn out to eat. At least he didn't have to worry about her right now.

"Yeah, coffee sounds great."

The detective walked over to a table at the far end of the room and filled a styrofoam cup with coffee left over from earlier in the day. Carter could smell it wasn't fresh, but he needed something.

Handing Carter the cup, the detective sat down. "Okay, let's start at the beginning. How did Jocelyn come to live with you and your mother? You can tell me the truth, Carter. You don't have to defend your mother, and you don't have to worry about what the priest will think."

"But I've told you all I know. All of this was taken care of by my mother and unfortunately, she died last November. Jocelyn and I are still trying to get our bearings. We lived in a household where Gracie, my mother, took care of everything. But we're managing. Jocelyn is great about helping with all the household chores and she's learning to cook on her own. We're getting along."

"Why was your mother so reluctant to talk about her family?

"I don't know the particulars. I was told very little about my parents' life in Baltimore. I gathered my mom had it pretty rough before she and my dad ran away to Florida. There were hints every now and then, and I sort of figured out her parents drank pretty heavily and her father was abusive. But, she never came right out and told me this."

"Why would your mother take a child to raise when you were grown and she could take it easy? I know taking care of children is a full time job. I've helped out with my sister's kid and she's a hand full."

"My mother always wanted more children. She never wanted me to be an only child. So, I guess when she saw her chance to raise Jocelyn, she took it."

"Jocelyn wasn't really born in Baltimore, was she, Carter? Wasn't she born right here in Miami?"

"What do you mean?"

"Carter, I think Jocelyn was born somewhere around here and you or your mother sort of borrowed her from her real mother. Isn't that right, Carter? Isn't that the way it really happened?"

"Absolutely not! What are you thinking?" Carter was getting so agitated he almost yelled at the detective.

"Calm down, Carter. Just think back. It is possible that you knew of someone who had a baby they couldn't keep, and you made some kind of arrangement with her? There's no crime in that. Just tell me the truth and we can work this out. Are you trying to protect your mother? She isn't here, Carter. She doesn't need your protection any longer. The truth, Carter. All I need is the truth."

"You are making this up as you go, aren't you Detective Madison?" asked Carter. "You don't believe me, so you are trying to plant words in my mouth. Well, my story is truth. May I go now?"

"Carter, unless you can come up with some proof your story is accurate, then this isn't going to go well for you. Too many people are asking questions. For now, you are free to go. I'll drive you back to your car. But, I'm telling you this isn't over. Your story doesn't add up and right now, I think Jocelyn came to you some way other than what you are telling me. You think about it, Carter. You think about the price you might have to pay for protecting your mother."

Detective Madison stood up and motioned for Carter to follow him. They walked through the police station to the parking garage in silence. As they were about to get in the Detective's car, he turned and spoke to Carter, "What have you got to lose by telling me the truth? Do you have any idea how messy this whole thing might be for you if you don't?"

Carter remained silent, afraid his voice would betray his fear. He didn't speak until they drove up next to his car and he was about to open the door to get out of the detective's car.

"I don't know what you think you know, but one thing is for certain, my mother and I did nothing wrong. We raised a child who had no one and we gave her all the love we could. We didn't do anything wrong."

He closed the door and walked over to his car. He didn't look back as he fumbled in his pocket for the car key. All he wanted to do was get as far away from this man as possible.

"Damn it! When is this going to end?"

He slammed his hands against the steering wheel of his car. The 'damn' came as a surprise. He couldn't remember the last time he had used profanity. He backed out and headed for home. When he passed the Royal Castle on 36th Street, he remembered he hadn't eaten and he pulled into the parking lot. Maybe he would feel better if he had some food in his stomach. When he entered the restaurant, he looked at the clock on the wall. "Good grief, it's 9:00. No wonder I don't have any energy left."

Pulling in his driveway, he noticed there was a car in front of the house. He never thought Miss Moss would stay this long. When he opened the front door, Jocelyn and Miss Moss were sitting at the dining room table surrounded by papers and catalogues. "Hi, sorry I'm late. I didn't think you would still be here, Miss Moss. Jocelyn, have you finished your homework?"

"Yes. I finished hours ago. We were just looking through these catalogues from Barry."

"Hello, Mr. McDeal. You're right. I should have gone home hours ago. But I didn't want to leave Jocelyn until I was sure you would be coming home."

Carter glared at the woman. Being around her felt more and more like he was in enemy territory.

"Good night, then. I'll be on my way. I'll see you in class tomorrow, Jocelyn."

"Miss Moss, forgive my rudeness. Thank you for taking Jocelyn to dinner. I'm glad she didn't have to eat alone." Carter tried to make up for the hostility he felt toward Miss Moss. For Jocelyn's sake, he hoped he sounded sincere.

After Miss Moss closed the door, Jocelyn turned to him and asked, "Can you can tell me what's going on? Are you in some kind of trouble?"

"I don't think so, Jocelyn. There seems to be some confusion I'm sure I can work out. You go on to bed and don't worry. We're okay. Did you and Miss Moss have a nice dinner?"

"Yes, we went to Morrison's and then came back here to talk some more about college. Thanks for asking her to take me to dinner and for sending her to tell me where you were. But, Dad, if you were with the police, don't you think you should tell me why?"

Carter noticed she hadn't said she was worried about him. Was the gap between them beginning to widen? But tonight he was too tired to try and figure out what to do about it.

"They're just trying to help us track down someone in Nana's family who can help us. Good night, Jocelyn," Carter said, and then added out of habit, "Sweet dreams."

Jocelyn called "good night" to him as she walked down the hall toward her bedroom. He noticed that she didn't respond back to him with her usual, "don't let the bugs bite."

The next thing Carter knew it was 4:00 in the morning. The shadows had formed and were blocking the first light of day. There were no chirping birds, and he was probably the only person awake on 11th Avenue. This morning there was no time for memories. The new problems overwhelmed the horrors of Korea and the break-up with Sharon. He stretched out his body and rubbed the sleep from his eyes, this was not the life he imagined. He was deeper in the shadows than ever before, and there didn't seem to be any way light was going to break through.

Chapter Sixteen

Detective Madison

Todd Madison was one of the youngest detectives on the Miami-Dade police force, but he already had a reputation for being aggressive and thorough. He was medium height and weight, but he knew how to use his stature to intimidate anyone he was questioning. He had intimidated Carter McDeal yesterday and it was going to pay off. He pushed back his unruly brown hair and smiled at the report he had just completed.

Earlier that morning he had finished a routine check of the facts presented to him in the McDeal case and wasn't surprised that they didn't add up. But he was unprepared for what he had uncovered. First, the information he could find on Gracie O'Brian McDeal pointed to the fact she didn't have a sister.

Then when he began pulling missing children reports for 1956, one report caught his attention. Of the five children reported missing that year there was an unsolved case of a baby girl who had been abducted from a hospital in June.

Two little facts that would break this case wide open. He knew he had the right man.

That afternoon when Carter was finished with his Route Six run, he would be arrested on a charge of kidnapping and booked into the Dade County jail.

Chapter Seventeen

Father Sean

Father Sean called Miss Moss into his office shortly after 4:00 PM to tell her Carter had been arrested, and before the words were out of his mouth, she picked up the phone on his desk.

"What are you doing, Miss Moss?"

"Father Sean, I must call the HRS office. I applied to be Jocelyn's guardian in the event something like this happened, and I want them to know I will go immediately and take her to my house. They won't have to worry about placing her with a stranger. She can live with me until all of this is cleared up."

Father Sean scoffed. More than ever, he was feeling that this woman was too pleased - too eager at the turn of events impacting the McDeals. He couldn't put his finger on it, but he had to wonder why Miss Moss was so willing to have Jocelyn live with her.

"Aren't you being a bit premature, Miss Moss? Surely, the police will not detain Carter for more than a few hours. We don't even know why he was arrested. And, Jocelyn will want a say in where she goes while her father is detained. I'm going to call Gloria Thompson, Ruthie's mother, to see if Jocelyn can stay with them for a day or so. You know how close she and Ruthie are. I'm sure she'll feel more comfortable staying with her friend."

Miss Moss was indignant, "Well, Father Sean, I don't know what to say. I take it you don't think Jocelyn would feel comfortable with me."

"No, Miss Moss, that isn't what I think at all. I was thinking only about Jocelyn and where she will want to be. I don't think a guardian will be appointed for her under these circumstances. I'll just call Mrs. Thompson and see how that will work out. I only let you know what was happening because you are so closely involved in this situation. Besides, Carter called me to ask if I would take care of arranging a place for Jocelyn to stay. He and I are sure things can be worked out with the Thompson's. That's all Miss Moss. I'll talk to you tomorrow."

After Miss Moss left the office, Father Sean breathed a heavy sigh. "What is going on with that woman?" he couldn't shake his concerns about her. He had known her for years, ever since he moved from Corpus Christi to Notre Dame Academy, and he had never felt uneasy about her before. But the whole McDeal situation wasn't ringing true in his head, and he kept wondering why Miss Moss was spearheading this move against Carter. What did she think was happening in the McDeal house?

He picked up the phone and called Gloria Thompson. "Hello," she said breathlessly.

"Ah, Mrs. Thompson, this is Father Sean. You sound like I caught you at a bad time."

"No, no, Father. I was just coming in from the backyard when the phone rang. I was working in the yard and needed to come in to start dinner. What can I do for you today?"

"I'm calling you for a favor that is very confidential, Mrs. Thompson. I know I can trust you to keep this request as quiet as possible."

"Certainly, Father. How can I help?"

"There's been some misunderstanding, and Carter McDeal has been arrested. I don't know what the charges are, I just know he called to see if I could make some arrangements for Jocelyn."

"Oh, dear. I can't imagine why Carter would be in jail. You're right. There has to be a big understanding. But how can I help?"

"Would it be possible for Jocelyn to stay with your family for a few days - just until this is straightened out?"

"Of course, Father. She is more than welcome here. Ruthie will be thrilled. But, Father, what should I tell everyone, including the girls?"

"Tell the girls the truth, Mrs. Thompson. I don't see any reason to tell anyone outside the family what is going on, do you? And, please assure Jocelyn I'm doing everything I can to help her father."

"Okay, I will. Do I need to go over to her house and pick her up?"

"No, I don't think that's necessary. I'm going to drive over there in the next few minutes to talk with her about what is happening. I'll drive her to your house. Please expect her for dinner, if that's okay."

"You know that's okay, Father. And, won't you stay for dinner yourself?"

"It's nice of you to offer, but I have dinner plans this evening. I'll see you within the hour. And, Mrs. Thompson, thank you for taking Jocelyn. Her father and I appreciate your kindness. Bless you."

Putting down the phone, Father Sean bowed his head in prayer. He prayed his call to Mrs. Thompson was the right thing to do for Jocelyn. Sometimes, as a priest, he knew he had to follow his gut instincts, and in this case, he hoped the Lord agreed.

As he pulled his old sedan up to the McDeal house, he said another prayer that he would know what to say to Jocelyn. He didn't want her to be frightened by the situation, but she needed to know it was serious.

He knocked on the door and hoped Jocelyn would be prompt in answering. Neighbors had a way of suspecting the worst if they saw a priest come to call.

"Hello, Jocelyn. May I come in?"

"Hello, Father, please come in and have a seat. What brings you to our house?"

"Jocelyn, please sit down. There is something I need to tell you."

"Oh, no, Father. What's wrong? Has something happened to my dad?"

"There has been some kind of misunderstanding and your father has been arrested. I don't know the details. He just called me to make arrangements for you this evening."

"My dad has been arrested! There's got to be a big mistake. Why would they arrest him? He's never done anything wrong! He never would!"

"I don't know, Jocelyn. But I want you to know I will do everything I can to help him. In the meantime, I've made arrangements for you to spend a few days with the Thompson's. The family knows this is a confidential matter, so you don't have to worry about people at school asking you a lot of questions. Just pack a few things and I'll drive you over there. They are expecting you for dinner."

"Father? Should I be afraid?" Can I call my dad? I haven't been very nice to him since all of this started about my birth certificate."

"Jocelyn, one thing is for sure. Your father loves you and he is hurting just like you are about all the secrets. Your grandmother thought she was doing the best thing for you by not telling you about your birth. You know she loved you and would never do anything she thought would hurt either you or your father. Give it some time, dear, and you'll see God has a plan. There is something we all need to learn from this situation. He'll show us what it is in His time, not ours."

"Thank you, Father. I'll try not to worry." But, I feel so lost and afraid.

"By the way, Jocelyn, Miss Moss offered for you to stay at her house. Do you see much of her outside of school?"

"Every now and then we work together at the Little Theater, and you know she's been helping me with my college applications. Why do you ask?"

"Oh, no reason, I just wondered if you would feel comfortable staying at her house; but of course, that won't happen since the Thompson's want you to stay with them."

It didn't take Jocelyn long to pack her overnight bag, and soon she and Father Sean were on their way to the Thompson's. When they pulled up in front of the house, Ruthie ran out to the car to help Jocelyn with her things, and Mrs. Thompson asked Father Sean if she could have a few words with him. Ruthie and Jocelyn knew she wanted to talk with him in private, so they went in the house and closed the door. The priest knew they would try to linger by the door and he smiled.

Mrs. Thompson walked over and opened the door. "And, just what did the two of you think you could hear that you don't already know?"

"Mom, we weren't trying to listen to you. We were just moving slow," laughed Ruthie.

"Be careful, Ruthie. You don't want that nose of yours to grow any longer," said her mother.

The priest loved the bantering that went on in this house. Mother and daughter were always teasing and laughing back and forth. Jocelyn was safe with this family, and was as much at home here as she was in her own house. He overheard Jocelyn whisper to Ruthie as he made his way to his car, "Can you believe Miss Moss wants me to stay at her house? That would be my worst nightmare."

"My thoughts exactly." The priest smiled.

Chapter Eighteen

Mary Ann Moss

Mary Ann Moss lived a routine, lonely and uneventful life. She used the theater as her one diversion from school. Hiding from the past sins she could never take to a priest in confession, she imposed her own penance. Withdrawing from friends and any type of activity that had previously brought her joy, she spent her hours working at the school, the church or the theater. Not even Father Sean knew of her life in the Iowa convent.

1973-1974 began like all the other school years, until she looked at her roll book and saw that Jocelyn McDeal was going to be in her third period class. She enjoyed working with the girl at the theater and knew she was going to be one of her star students. Jocelyn was curious, bright, and so well mannered. In conversations with her, she knew Jocelyn wanted to be an English teacher. Mary Ann knew she would have to watch carefully to make sure she didn't show any favoritism to Jocelyn, and she would have to rein in her attraction to the girl. It had been years since she had taken this kind of interest in one of her students. When Jocelyn's grandmother passed away suddenly, and the girl went from bright and curious to dispirited and withdrawn, Mary Ann seized the opportunity to befriend her.

Mary Ann's attraction drew her closer and closer to the girl and she wanted to find a way to let Jocelyn know she could come to her whenever she needed motherly advice. But her attempts to convey concern were met with an absent smile and a nod, and Jocelyn was not open to the overtures she made.

One afternoon Mary Ann overheard Jocelyn talking with Ruthie Thompson about her disappointment in not being able to go away to college. As Mary Ann continued to listen to the conversation, she thought she saw a way to be more of a presence in Jocelyn's life. This time when she approached Jocelyn, she hoped she was offering assistance the girl might welcome.

Mary Ann talked with the school counselor about options for scholarships, she investigated schools that offered good English and theater programs, and she began discussing admission possibilities with her contacts at Barry College. She knew the program at Barry met all of the qualifications she was searching for, and it was located in Miami. If she could get Jocelyn a scholarship, the girl would be in her debt, and over time she could cultivate a relationship with her.

When Mary Ann mentioned this choice to Jocelyn, she was unprepared for the response she received.

"Thank you, Miss Moss. I appreciate your suggestion, but if I do have a chance to go away for school, I really want to go to Florida State. You know Ruthie is going there and we would love to room together. FSU has a great theater program, and I could do a double major with English."

"But, Jocelyn, I'm sure it's highly competitive to get a scholarship to one of the state universities. Please think about the school I've suggested."

"Thanks, Miss Moss."

"I've started a folder for you with scholarship and college applications, but I'm sorry I didn't include applications for the state schools."

"That's all right. I went to the guidance office and picked-up the one I need."

"I'll be happy to work with you on the applications and the essays you will need to write. That is, if you'd like me to?"

"I know you're busy, Miss Moss, but any suggestions you can give me would be great."

"By the way, Jocelyn, you'll need copies of your Social Security card or your birth certificate to go with your applications, and you'll need to request your transcript from the front office."

"Yes, I took care of that on Tuesday. Sorry, Miss Moss, I've got to run or I'll miss my bus. I'll see you tomorrow."

Every time Mary Ann met with Jocelyn, she asked her for the birth certificate or Social Security card, and there was always an excuse. The father said the grandmother took care of all the paperwork at the house and it would take him time to locate it. That was all well and good, but they had deadlines to meet. They were already behind the other college-bound students in submitting the applications, and Mary Ann was becoming concerned they would miss out on some important opportunities. She knew she couldn't badger Jocelyn about this, but she was compelled to press her a little. When several weeks passed, Mary Ann became agitated about Mr. McDeal's reluctance to help and she felt she needed to take some action.

She talked with Father Sean about the issue and asked him to intervene. "Give it some more time, Miss Moss. I'm sure Mr. McDeal will get it to you in time."

When another week went by, she asked Father Sean again to help her, and this time he told her he would set up a meeting with Mr. McDeal to see if there was anything he could do to help. But the meeting did not produce the results she wanted and Mary Ann began to suspect there was more to the story than she was being told. She had more questions than answers, and something about Carter McDeal made her feel unsettled. She couldn't decide if it was his reluctance or his attitude. But whatever it was, it bothered her enough she was losing sleep over it. That night she made up her mind to protect Jocelyn from what she perceived to be an unhealthy home, and she vowed she would discover the truth.

The next morning, Mary Ann called a social worker she knew at HRS and began asking questions about a "what if" situation. The social worker, Rachel Parks, listened attentively to Mary Ann's story, and told her she would visit with the McDeal family to see if she could uncover any irregularities in the household. For the moment, Mary Ann was satisfied. She knew she should tell Father Sean about the conversation with HRS, but the priest's allegiance was with Carter McDeal and he would be upset she had taken this next step.

She began to think about offering Jocelyn a place to live with her – surely she would be better at seeing to the girl's future than the strange and reticent man who was her father. She asked Mrs. Parks to advise her on possible guardianship of Jocelyn should the visit with Carter McDeal produce doubts about his motives and fitness for parenthood.

"Mary Ann, I think you are being a bit premature. Guardianship is possible when it can be proven abuse has occurred or there is some criminal activity in the home. If this girl is 17, she may not need a guardian. We'll cross that bridge if we come to it. You've given me the information I need to make a fact-finding visit to the home." Then, softening her admonition, she said, "if more people were as observant as you, we could help families before major problems occur in the home. Thanks for calling."

Two weeks later, Rachel Parks called Mary Ann to tell her she had made a preliminary visit to the McDeal home. While she couldn't give her any details of the visit, or discuss her recommended course of action, she was listing her as a possible guardian for Jocelyn McDeal. She asked Mary Ann to be present at a conference with Mr. McDeal the following Thursday at the HRS office.

Mary Ann didn't want any real trouble for Carter McDeal. He seemed like a nice man, but he was hiding something. If Mr. McDeal was removed, she would be able to be a bigger part of Jocelyn's life. She smiled when she thought about Jocelyn living with her.

After the meeting with HRS, Mary Ann became even more convinced that Carter McDeal was hiding something. He tripped over his words and didn't have answers for simple questions. She was glad the meeting included an officer from the police department and some of the people from the HRS investigation team. They knew how to proceed in cases like this one, and she expected them to uncover some unsavory facts concerning Jocelyn's birth. But, she was shocked at how quickly everything turned around. She never expected the man would be arrested on the day following the meeting.

She was glad she followed her instincts and prepared for the possibility Jocelyn would need a guardian. When Father Sean came to tell her the news about Mr. McDeal's arrest, she was ready to move Jocelyn to her apartment. Her emotions became raw and jagged as she listened to the priest outline another plan for Jocelyn. She never considered there might be another temporary home for the girl or she wouldn't have a say in the matter. "I'm the one who suspected something was wrong. I can't believe Father Sean has just taken over and is making his own arrangements for Jocelyn. In the morning I'll call HRS and get this straightened out."

The next day, she called Rachel Parks about Jocelyn's placement. She told her about Father Sean's decision to have Jocelyn stay with the Thompson family.

"You understand, Mrs. Parks, Father Sean thinks the Thompson family is an adequate solution for Jocelyn because Ruthie Thompson is the girl's best friend. But, what if Mr. McDeal is detained for more than a few days? The Thompson's have their own children, and I doubt if they have any extra space for Jocelyn. You know I can offer her a room of her own, and I'm located near Notre Dame."

"Miss Moss, I appreciate your call. I know Father Sean has Jocelyn's best interest in mind, and the Thompson's will work well as a temporary solution. However; if Mr. McDeal is accused of a crime, HRS will have the responsibility of ensuring Jocelyn's protection and safety. It's a good thing you had the forethought to request guardianship."

Mary Ann wished she knew what was going on with Mr. McDeal's arrest, but she had to get ready for her next class. She would try to talk with Father Sean after school. She would also call her acquaintance at Barry College. A scholarship for Jocelyn was more important than ever.

Chapter Nineteen

Sharon

The Miami Herald was scattered on the kitchen table when Sharon came down for breakfast, so she knew her youngest son had already left the house. Usually, she and Tommy ate breakfast together before she went to work and he left for school. But this morning she was starting a week's vacation and she had not set her alarm clock. She smiled at the thought of sipping a cup of coffee and reading the paper in silence for a change. She loved Tommy's company, but he was usually exuberant in the morning telling and retelling all the wonderful things he loved about being a senior in high school. In a few short months he would be away in college, and she knew there would be more silence in this house than she could bear.

She poured the coffee and sat down to enjoy the paper at her leisure. The front page was all about the Watergate indictments and President Nixon, so she briefly scanned that section and moved on to local news. The headline for the local news section caught her attention, Local Bus Driver Accused of Kidnapping, so she read on.

"Dear God in heaven," she said, and almost choked on the coffee. "This can't be true!" Sharon knew Carter McDeal, the man accused. In fact, she had once been engaged to him. Continuing to read, she shook her head. "No, no, no! Carter would never do anything like this. They've got the wrong guy. There's no way Carter McDeal has changed enough to do such a thing. He would never kidnap a child."

The last time she saw Carter, fifteen or twenty years ago, she had been visiting the old neighborhood and saw him at the drug store. "That was a strange moment," she recalled. "I thought I was over him, but my heart and body stirred when I saw him." Her reaction had shocked her. "I'm married," she reminded herself, but her body took over and she wanted to reach out and touch him. She had been afraid he wouldn't speak to her; after all, she was the one who had broken their engagement when he was away in Korea. Like a coward she had written him a letter to tell him Jim was pushing her to get married. She was afraid Carter would talk her out of it if she waited to tell him after he returned home.

She and Carter had been so young and so crazy. With the passion of youth, they explored all the facets of love and they learned together the power of touch. She had their life all planned. Right after graduation they would get married; they would live with his mother until they could save enough money to buy a small house in the neighborhood; they would have several kids, and, they would live happily ever after. But Carter ruined that plan by joining the army and getting himself shipped out to Korea. Even all these years later, she could remember how angry she was when he told her he enlisted and expected her to wait for him.

He had given her his mother's engagement ring, and for a year she wore it faithfully. She sat at home on Saturday nights, aching to be touched, to attend all of the dances at the Elks club, and was sure life was passing her by. It was a hard time for her, but she kept herself from getting depressed by dreaming about getting married. She was so certain Carter was the only man for her. When they first started dating, he was so shy and immature, she blamed his mother for sheltering him and keeping him tied to her apron strings. She went out with him the first time because she felt sorry for him, but they had fun and she decided to go out with him again. She had to admit she had been good for Carter. He went from a shy little boy to a man filled with promise in a few short months, and before she knew it, she had fallen in love with him. And, it didn't hurt that he adored her.

One night, after he had been in Korea for more than a year, she and some girlfriends went downtown to a dance at the Bayfront Park Auditorium, and she met Jim. She was dancing with a sailor on leave when a tall, handsome stranger cut in and took her in his arms. "I've been watching you all night," he said. "You sure can dance!"

He told her his name was Jim Bowers, and they danced together the rest of the evening. When Jim asked her for her phone number, she didn't tell him she was engaged. She knew he would ask her out, and she was ready to say yes. She slipped Carter's ring off her finger and never put it back on. Jim was Carter's opposite. He was older and outgoing. He loved to dance. He dressed and looked like a movie star, and he charmed his way into her heart. He said he was going to be rich one day and he promised her a life she never dreamed could be hers. This swept her off her feet and within six months, she married Jim, and broke Carter's heart.

Jim's father owned a construction company, and Jim was one of the project managers. He worked hard, and in a few short years, they had more money than Sharon ever imagined. They bought a spacious home south of Miami in the Cutler Ridge area, and Sharon spent months buying furniture, working with an interior designer, and enjoying a life filled with material things. She drove a new car every two years, had her hair done every week, and had a cleaning lady who came twice a week. She and Jim ate at fine restaurants. They had season tickets to the University of Miami and the Miami Dolphins football games. She even joined a garden club. Life was on a grand scale and Allappatah was more or less forgotten.

Over the years, she and Jim had three sons, Peter, Alan, and Tommy. When Peter was born, Jim gave her a beautiful diamond pendant. When Alan came along, she received a magnificent pair of diamond earrings. And when Tommy was born, the gift was a two karat diamond solitaire engagement ring to replace the half karat ring he had given her when he asked her to marry him. She knew he was working hard to help his father build the business, but she never thought he would work the hours he did. He was gone by 6:00 every morning, and usually didn't get home until after 7:00 in the evening. Most nights he got home in time to kiss the boys good night. On Saturday and Sunday, he played golf. She tried not to complain, and the few times she did, he reminded her he was building their future.

One afternoon, after they had been married for twelve years, she answered a ringing phone and was startled when a woman began shouting at her, "You are married to a scumbag. He is the worst kind of man in the world. You better ask him how many women he has in his life. He loves them and leaves them like they are property for his personal pleasure." And, then the phone line went dead. Hanging up the phone, Sharon decided the woman must have called the wrong number. She put the call out of her head until six weeks later when Jim came home early from work to tell her a paternity suit had been filed against him. "Sharon, I'm telling you this because I want you to hear the truth before you hear the rumors. I am not the father of this woman's baby."

"Jim, is there a chance you could be? Are you having an affair?' the words were out of her mouth before the emotions caught up with her. After she said them, the look on his face told her everything she needed to know. It was like an agonizing kick in the stomach. "Oh, my God. It's true isn't it? You're having an affair?"

"You're wrong, Sharon. This will blow over. Our life will go on just like always. You've got to believe me. You know you're the only woman for me."

Pulling her to him in a passionate embrace, he lifted her head and wiped away her tears. "I love you, sweetheart. Before the boys come home from school, let's go upstairs and I'll show you just how much I love you," he whispered.

She let him lead her to their bedroom, hoping that making love would miraculously erase all of the ugliness.

Sharon decided she had to know what was really going on with her husband, so she hired a private investigator. It didn't take long for him to discover Jim in more than one compromising relationship. Over the next few months, the investigator produced evidence for her that Jim had been involved with many women. Some he had seen only once, but others seemed to have more than his casual attention. There was one woman he met every Thursday at noon at an apartment near his office.

Thanking the investigator, she paid him for his services, and told him she would call again if she ever needed him. She called an attorney and made an appointment for the next morning. When Jim came home for dinner she told him she had a headache and she went to bed.

The next morning she filed for divorce and presented him with a property settlement and custody agreement that came as a complete shock to him. The papers asked him to move out of the house no later than the following Saturday morning. Once the papers were served, she and Tommy went to Orlando to visit the new attraction called Disney World. When they returned on Sunday, Jim's belongings were no longer in the house. She never confronted him and he didn't contest the property or custody agreement. Peter and Alan were grown and living their own lives, but Jim took Tommy to dinner every other Wednesday and on vacation for one week every summer.

Jim agreed to give her the house and a generous alimony and child support check every month. Her new life should have felt strange, but it didn't take her long to realize not much had changed for her or for her sons. Jim had rarely been home before the divorce, so he wasn't really missed now.

Sharon was brought out of her reverie by the sound of a siren coming from somewhere over on the highway. Remembering old hurts wasn't helping and she continued reading the article about Carter. The paper said he was accused of kidnapping a little girl seventeen years ago and was raising her as his own daughter. He had some personality quirks, but he is not a weirdo. As she read on, she found out his mother had died last year, and felt sad. Mrs. McDeal had always been kind to her.

She put the paper down and decided not to squander any more of her vacation time. Since the divorce, she worked part-time with the interior designer who helped her with the house. Year ago, she had discovered her artistic flair and keen sense of design, but had never pursued it because Jim wanted her to stay at home. As soon as the divorce was final, she called her designer and asked to be an apprentice to the design team. To her surprise, they agreed, and today she was being paid to do the work she loved.

Maybe later, she would try to get in touch with Carter, just to see if there was any way she could help him. She didn't know if he would welcome a call from her, but he might surprise her. After all, the article didn't mention a wife.

Chapter Twenty

Carter

"Hey, McDeal, it's your turn to use the phone. You got anybody you wanna call?" the jail attendant called out to Carter as he sat in his cell. "Make it count, man. You don't wanna be in this place any longer than you have to. Between you and me, this ain't exactly the Fontainebleaue."

Carter tried hard to disassociate himself from this place. The noise and commotion of the other inmates assaulted him and he was embarrassed to be locked in a cell in the Dade County jail. He looked up at the man standing on the other side of the bars and asked him to repeat what he said. "I said you can make a phone call if you want to. Hey, man, do you drive one of the city buses? I think I seen you on the bus."

"What? Oh, yeah, I drive the Number Six. Please, I need to call my daughter," Carter responded.

"It ain't none of my business, but if I was you, I'd call my lawyer or somebody who'd make bond. But, like I said, it ain't none of my business. They got a hearing scheduled for you at 9:00 in the morning."

"Oh, my God," Carter exclaimed. "A hearing? What happens then?"

"Mister, you go to the hearing and tell the judge you ain't guilty. You got a lawyer?"

"No, I don't even know a lawyer to call, and I don't have that kind of money."

"That's tough. You best tell that judge you're broke and he needs to appoint a lawyer for you. He gonna set your bond, and you gotta have somebody willing to fork over the money for your release. You don't wanna spend another night in this place."

Unlocking the cell door, the jailer pointed to a telephone on a desk at the end of the row. "It's a collect call, so call somebody who's gonna pay to talk to you. You got ten minutes."

As Carter walked toward the phone, he tried to think of who he could call. Who would have the money to make bond for him? He sat down and stared at the phone for a few seconds, then picked up the receiver and told the operator he wanted to place a call to Bob Sullivan.

"Hello, Carter. Why are you calling me collect from the jail?"

"Sully, I'm in trouble, I need your help."

"What'd you do, Carter? Did you forget to check off something on your checklist?" Sully laughed.

"Sully, this is serious. They're going to charge me with kidnapping Jocelyn." Even as he said it out loud, he couldn't believe it.

"What the hell are you talking about, Carter?" Sully was flabbergasted. "What's going on?"

"Sully, I'm not sure I understand, but they think I kidnapped Jocelyn when she was a baby."

"That's the dumbest thing I've ever heard. What do you need, Carter?"

"The jailer says there is a hearing in the morning and the judge will set bond. God, I hate to ask, Sully, but do you think you could pay the bond? I'll pay you back," Carter pleaded.

"Damn, Carter, how much are you talking about? I've got a little extra money, but I don't have much."

"Sully, I can't answer that until after my hearing. I don't have any idea. I'll pay you back as soon as I can, promise."

"I trust you, Carter. I'll do it if I have enough money. Guess I'd better find a sub for Route Six for tomorrow. You don't think you'll miss more than tomorrow, do you?"

"No, Sully, I'll be back to work day after tomorrow. This whole thing is a big mistake. I'm sure the judge will believe me. And it'll be over."

"Don't think it'll be that easy, Carter. We'll see. You let me know tomorrow what I have to do." Then Sully laughed, "You're the last person in this shop I thought I'd be bailing out of jail. What's this world coming to?"

As he hung up the phone, Carter repeated Sully's question to himself, "What's this world coming to?"

***

The next morning, Carter rode with seven other men in a van the short distance between the jail and the courthouse. All were dressed in the bright orange jumpsuits that were standard issue for inmates. Their feet were shackled and their hands were cuffed behind them. While the others told vulgar jokes, laughed, and made fun of each other, Carter remained silent and withdrawn. Most of them had done this before and he was glad they were ignoring him.

Once in the court room, he sat uncomfortably on a bench and waited to be called before the judge. There was a clock on the wall opposite him and, as he waited, he watched the hands move slowly from one number to the next.

Finally, his case number and name were called, and the bailiff motioned for him to walk to the podium in front of the judge. He stood alone and waited for the judge to address him.

"Carter McDeal, you have been charged with the felony crime of kidnapping a child. How do you plead?"

"Your Honor, I'm not guilty," Carter said in a voice that was louder than he intended. "I'm not guilty."

"Do you have an attorney or do you need the court to appoint one for you?"

"I need for the court to appoint one for me, sir."

"Okay, that will be done. I've set a pre-trial hearing for August 10th and I'm setting your bond at $10,000. One condition of your bond is you are to have no contact with the child, Jocelyn McDeal. Do you understand?"

"She's my daughter, judge. She is about to graduate from high school and she still lives at home."

"Perhaps you didn't hear me, Mr. McDeal. Arrangements will be made for the girl and you are to have no contact with her until this case is settled. Is that clear now?"

"Yes, Your Honor." Carter was stunned and a stronger sense of disbelief and frustration overwhelmed him.

Returning to his place on the long bench, all he could do was wait to be taken back to the jail.

That afternoon, Sully put up the money for his release, and he met his court appointed attorney, Elena Martinez.

He was led to a small conference room and was told to wait there for his lawyer. When she entered the room, his heart sank. She looked like a teenager, not someone who could defend him in a court of law.

At twenty-seven years old, Elena Martinez had been practicing in the Public Defender's office for three years. Dressed smartly in a navy business suit and high heels, she looked taller than five foot two. Her dark hair was cut short and framed her face with soft curls. Carter couldn't help but see she was pretty. He only hoped she was as smart as she looked.

"Hello, Mr. McDeal. My name is Elena Martinez, and I've been appointed to represent you. We have a few months until your first hearing, and I'm hoping in that time you will be able to give me information that will help me prepare a defense. The best case scenario is to get the charges against you dropped. Remember, I'm on your side." Elena spoke so reassuringly that Carter thought maybe she did know what she was doing.

"Miss Martinez, I'm innocent. I didn't do what they say."

145

"Mr. McDeal, why don't we start at the beginning? You just tell me what this is all about. But, I need the truth. That's the only way we're going to prevent you from spending a very long time locked away in prison. Everything you tell me is confidential so you know you can tell me the truth."

After they talked for several hours, the jailer came to tell Carter his bond had posted and he would be released as soon as all the paperwork was completed.

"Mr. McDeal, call my office to set up an appointment as soon as possible. And, try not to worry. I think everything is going to turn out fine. The condition for your bond was absolutely no contact between you and the girl. Make sure you adhere to it." Elena gave him her business card as they walked out of the conference room.

"I'm in serious trouble, right?"

"Mr. McDeal, the charges against you are very serious and I'm not going to lie to you. This is serious enough you could spend the rest of your life in prison. But my job is to make sure that doesn't happen."

That evening, Carter left the jail and walked several blocks to catch the Route Six bus home appreciating freedom for the first time.

Chapter Twenty-one

Elena

Heading back to the office, Elena stopped in a small Cuban cafe for a sandwich. She had missed lunch waiting to meet with her new client, Carter McDeal, and she was starving. When she first read the arrest charge she was convinced the State Attorney would have a hard time substantiating the charges. But, then she talked to her client and had doubts about his innocence. The man acted guilty.

Picking up a copy of the paper, she groaned when she read that more Cuban immigrants had tried to make it to shore in a small boat, but had been turned away. Her family had escaped from Cuba in the early days of the revolution. They had been lucky.

On the morning of January 5, 1959, Elena's father hurried across the courtyard of their house in Havana, and whispered nervously to her mother, "Che Guevara has defeated the troops at Santa Clara and Castro is headed to Havana to take over the city. They are saying Batista has fled the country. Keep the children behind the gates and don't let anyone inside until I return. This is not good for us, Maria, and we may be in danger. Stay inside, away from the courtyard, no matter what you hear. You'll be safe if you do this. I'll be back as soon as I can." She remembered the kiss he gave her mother and the way her mother clung to him until he moved her arms from around him. She remembered staring at the gate for a long time after her father left, wondering what would happen next.

Her father was a handsome man; tall, dark, and imposing. He laughed easily, angered quickly, and loved Cuba with a passion. He was legal counsel in the government of Fulgencio Batista y Zuldivar, who had just been forced to flee the country. She knew her family did not support the revolution, and Fidel Castro would not look favorably on those who opposed him.

Elena was thirteen years old and on that day she was helping her mother prepare for Three Kings Day. But the feast was never eaten, the gifts were not opened, and everything in her world was left behind in Cuba. Her father had awakened her in the early morning hours, and told her to quickly pack her clothes. She could bring one suitcase. "Where are we going, Father? Will we be gone long?"

"Elena, we must hurry. Pack your things and go help your mother and your grandmother with the younger children. We will talk later."

In the middle of the night, they were taken away in a car with the headlights turned off, to a small airport outside the city where they boarded an airplane bound for Miami. There were twenty or thirty other families on the plane; some she recognized; others she had never seen before. No one was smiling. Everyone looked nervous. The only sounds were made in whispers. She and her sisters were told to sit quietly, and she held tightly to their hands as the plane flew mysteriously in the dark of night. Soon she was looking down at the lights of a new city, in a new country she would learn to call home.

At first, life in Miami was different and often, confusing. In Cuba, her family lived in a spacious home with beautiful grounds and a peaceful courtyard. Her mother had household help and her family had financial and social status. In Miami, they lived in a small, cramped, two-bedroom apartment where they did all the household work themselves. For years, her father lived with the hope Castro would be overthrown and they could go home. Every Saturday, he sat in the park with some of the other men who had escaped and they would talk about what life would be like when they were once again in Havana.

By the end of the year, their life seemed more American than Cuban. Both of her parents had found work in an accounting firm and she and her sisters were in school. Her grandmother cared for the apartment and cooked the meals. Slowly they began to recognize that going back to Cuba was no longer an option. Castro was making it more and more difficult. As thousands were immigrating to Florida, the dark cloud of Communism was separating Cuba from its closest neighbors.

Her well-educated parents were forced to work at jobs they were over-qualified for, and they counted every penny before a spending decision was made. All of them, except her grandmother, were enrolled in English as Second Language classes and, as they were immersed in American life, the English language became more comfortable for them. Soon her father went back to school so he could take the Florida Bar exam, and her mother was promoted to a job with more responsibilities and a higher salary. After her father passed the Bar, he found a job in a small law firm dedicated to helping other immigrants navigate the laws of Florida. This gave him back some measure of self esteem, and allowed them to purchase a home big enough to accommodate all of the family. Elena was elated. Even though she shared a room with one of her sisters; she finally had space to call her own.

Just before she left to attend the University of Florida, the family received their American citizenship. Miami, and America, was their new home. When she graduated from Law School, her father wanted her to join his firm, but she knew criminal defense, not immigration law, was what she wanted to practice.

In law school, she met and fell in love with Eric Randall. He was from Ft. Lauderdale and shared her love of criminal defense work. After graduation, they both moved back to the south Florida area where she joined the Public Defender's staff, and Eric joined a large criminal defense firm. She returned to her parent's home, and Eric rented an apartment in one of the new high rise apartment buildings in downtown Miami.

Her beloved grandmother had passed away two years before she moved back to Miami, and both of her sisters were in college, so when she asked her parents if she could move back home, they were pleased. They knew it wasn't a permanent arrangement and she would only be with them for a short while. Over the three years she dated Eric, her family had grown to love him and knew the couple would probably be getting married in the near future.

Since she arrived in Miami in 1959, the Hispanic population had rapidly increased, making Miami a true multi-cultural center. The Cuban influence was everywhere, and she couldn't walk down the street without hearing people talking in Spanish or hearing music with a Latin beat. Her family, like many others, spoke Spanish at home and English when they were out in the world. Every day she saw evidence that being bi-lingual in a city like Miami was very helpful, especially in her new job. Often she was called by other lawyers to translate for their Hispanic clients.

She and Eric often discussed aspects of their cases and used each other as sounding boards when developing trial strategies for new clients. Eric had a quick mind and grasped the nuances of legal issues that went far beyond her text book interpretation of case law. For him, the law was like a game plan played out in the courtroom. Each step of the plan was designed to dismantle the argument of the opponent and to anticipate where gaps in their case might give him the edge. Some days, when her schedule allowed and she knew Eric was arguing a case, she would take a seat in the court room just to watch him. She reminded him of the details involved in case law and he expanded her ability to persuade and cultivate the members of a jury.

Elena loved to be with Eric's family. She found his mother's southern hospitality charming, got excited with his father during football games, and learned quickly that sailing with Eric on Biscayne Bay was a relaxing way to end a stressful workweek. They found more and more ways to enjoy and deepen their relationship, so she was not surprised when Eric asked her to marry him. They set their wedding date for the following June 14, 1975, knowing with their busy schedules they would need a year to plan.

Three days after her engagement, Elena was assigned the Carter McDeal case.

Chapter Twenty-two

Jocelyn

The day Jocelyn's father was released from jail, the judge also signed a court order granting Mary Ann Moss temporary guardianship of her. She had no choice but to move to her teacher's apartment. She was told she had to remove anything she wanted from her own house by 5:00, and she was to have no further contact with her father until after the trial.

"Mrs. Thompson, can they make me do this? I don't see why I have to live with Miss Moss," Jocelyn exclaimed. "That's not fair. They didn't even ask me what I wanted."

"Honey, I don't understand how the court works. All I know is I got a call from this judge's office just before you came in from school. They asked me to take you to your house to get your things, and informed me Miss Moss would pick you up at the house at 5:00. We're as upset as you are."

"Mom, isn't there anything you can do?" questioned Ruthie. "Miss Moss isn't a family friend or anything like that. Why do you think they appointed her Jocelyn's -- what's the word they call her?"

"Her guardian," answered Mrs. Thompson. "It seems Miss Moss applied to be her guardian if anything like this happened. But, you know what; I don't like this at all. Somehow it doesn't seem right. Jocelyn, do you want me to talk to the people at HRS to see if we can get this changed?"

"Do you think you could do that, Mrs. Thompson?"

"It never hurts to ask. I'll see who I have to speak to about this tomorrow. First thing I'll do is call Father Sean. He'll be able to help us. But, we've got to hustle if we're going to get your things and meet Miss Moss. Oh, I feel so sorry for your dad, honey. He must be devastated."

"Why would you feel bad for Carter?" She used his name sarcastically. "He must have done something wrong to get himself in this trouble." Jocelyn was ashamed her father had been arrested and her frustration was beginning to show.

"Jocelyn, you don't really believe that, do you? No matter what, he's your father and he did a pretty fine job of raising you. You can call him Carter if that makes you feel better, but no matter what you call him, he will always be your father. He never did anything inappropriate, did he?"

"No. Never. He wouldn't do that," Jocelyn exclaimed. She was embarrassed Mrs. Thompson would even ask the question.

"Your father is a fine man, Jocelyn. You have almost 18 years of proof that he is a good man. No matter how you came to live with Gracie and Carter, they gave you love. Don't be so harsh in judging your family, sweetheart. Go get your things. We've got to hurry."

As Jocelyn started out of the room, Mrs. Thompson put her head in her hands, "Ruthie, there has to be some mistake. The McDeal's are good people. It hurts me to see them in so much trouble. We will have to do everything we can to show them our support."

They drove to 11th Avenue, and the three of them hurriedly gathered up the items Jocelyn decided she wanted to take from the house.

"Mrs. Thompson, I'll only be gone for a few weeks, right? I don't need to take much with me."

"I don't know how long this will take. But if you need something, Ruthie and I can always come back here and bring it to you. Take your things to the front porch and we'll wait with you until Miss Moss gets here." Mrs. Thompson smiled at Jocelyn and touched her softly on the shoulder.

"Ruthie, grab the bear off my bed, please. I know it's silly, but I think I'll need 'ole Teddy' to help me get through this," said Jocelyn.

As they walked to the porch, Miss Moss was pulling into the driveway. Mrs. Thompson put her arms around Jocelyn and gave her a big hug. "It's going to be okay, honey. Say your prayers, and please don't call your father Carter anymore. Remember, we're here for you, and if it gets too rough at Miss Moss's, you give me a call," she whispered in Jocelyn's ear.

Jocelyn held on to Mrs. Thompson until Miss Moss walked up to the porch.

"Hello Mrs. Thompson, Ruthie. Jocelyn, I see you're ready to go," Miss Moss said briskly. "I'll help you take your things to the car."

Ruthie grabbed Jocelyn and hugged her. "Call me tonight, Jocelyn. And, I'll see you tomorrow at school. I love you."

"Love you, too, Ruthie. I'm okay, really."

All of them helped Jocelyn carry her things to the car. Just as she was about to leave, Mrs. Thompson slipped a ten-dollar bill in Jocelyn's pocket. Jocelyn started to protest, but Mrs. Thompson hushed her, "In case you need it. You never know." And, then she and Ruthie turned and walked to their car.

Miss Moss started the car and began to back out of the driveway. "I know this isn't easy for you, Jocelyn. But it will all work out. You wait and see. I've cleared out the second bedroom at my place for you, and I think you'll be very comfortable. If there is anything you need, just ask."

"Thank you, Miss Moss. I'll try not to be a bother to you."

"It's no bother. I'm so glad I could help. Tonight, we'll sit down and make a grocery list, and we'll talk about how to make living together easier for both of us. Are you okay with that?"

"Sure, that will be fine," Jocelyn replied with more enthusiasm than she felt. All she could think about was how long she might have to stay with her teacher. This is too weird, she thought to herself.

"Have you talked to my dad? Do you know if he's okay?"

"I don't know anything. I'm sure he wouldn't want to talk to me."

"What do you mean? Surely, he'd want to talk to you if he knows I'm going to be staying with you."

"I meant he probably hasn't had time to make any calls. He'll get in touch when he can, I'm sure."

But two days went by without a word from her father, and Jocelyn was beginning to worry. Finally, she asked Miss Moss if she had missed his call.

"Jocelyn, he hasn't called. It's my understanding the court has ordered him to have no contact with you until after the trial."

"A trial? Why is there going to be a trial?" Jocelyn felt panic rising up inside of her.

"My dear, your father has been accused of a very serious crime."

"What are you talking about?"

"Didn't you know, Jocelyn? He's been accused of kidnapping you, and that's very serious, indeed. I'm afraid it might be a long time before you will be able to speak with him."

Jocelyn grabbed her purse and started for the door.

"Where are you going?" Miss Moss rushed toward the door to prevent her from leaving.

"I'm going to see Father Sean. I need to talk to Father Sean."

"Can't it wait until tomorrow? You'll see him at school, and you can make an appointment to talk with him if you need to."

"No, Miss Moss, I'm sorry. I need to see him now." And, she rushed out the door before she could be stopped.

Jocelyn ran the three blocks to the school. Her heart was racing and she was being bombarded by so many conflicting emotions. Did she love her father or did she hate him? Why did she feel so angry? Why did she feel so alone? Where was this God she'd been taught would keep her safe?

She was breathless when she reached the small house behind Notre Dame where Father Sean lived. There were lights on in the front of the house, and she hoped that meant he was there. Her relief was visible when he answered her knock and opened the door.

Father Sean looked at her tear stained face and reached for her hand. "Good evening, Jocelyn. I was wondering how long it would be before you came to see me. Come in and let's see if I can help." His voice was gentle and soothing, and Jocelyn was grateful he was so welcoming.

"Father, can you tell me what's going on? I'm so confused."

"I'll see if I have any answers for you. You ask the questions and I'll see if I can tell you something that will ease your mind."

"What is my father charged with and why do I have to live with Miss Moss? The Thompson's said I could stay there until this misunderstanding is cleared up."

"First, the authorities think they have enough evidence to prove your father kidnapped you when you were born. And, second, apparently Miss Moss petitioned the court and was awarded guardianship over you. But, I think that's only temporary. The one thing that concerns me, Jocelyn, is the fact your father can have no contact with you. I understand Mr. Sullivan posted bail and your dad has probably already been released. But you are not to call him or try to see him."

"You mean he can't even call me? Father, I don't have any money to live on. What am I going to do?"

"You're father has arranged to send you money each week for your personal expenses, and if you need anything extra, you tell me and I'll let him know. Miss Moss has agreed to provide your room and board. So, I think you'll be able to manage. If there is something at the house you need, I'll go to the house and get it for you. This is serious, Jocelyn, and you don't want to do anything that might cause your father to be locked up again."

"Do you believe he's guilty?"

"No, I don't. I've known your father all his life, and this is not something he would do. I think there is more to the story than we know right now, but when we have all the facts, kidnapping won't be one of them."

"Father, I've been so mean to him since all of this started. I'm still angry that I don't know the truth. And, I hurt whenever I think he and my grandmother kept all of this from me. Am I an orphan? Does anyone know where I came from or who I am?

"Dear girl, you are not an orphan. You were blessed with a loving home. Your grandmother and father gave you everything you needed. And, Jocelyn, knowing who you are is not about knowing who gave birth to you. It's about recognizing God gave you a soul and a heart. It's about your beliefs, your values, and your integrity. And it's about being honest with yourself and others. You may never have the answers to your birth questions but that doesn't mean you don't know who you are. Perhaps God is giving you this time so you can look inward and reflect on the things that make you uniquely who you are. And, I promise," he smiled and winked at her, "you will survive Miss Moss."

"Don't get me wrong, Father. Miss Moss has been a big help to me. It's just so awkward when I think I have to live with her for awhile. I don't feel comfortable there. She's my teacher. What will the other girls say when they find out I'm staying at her apartment?"

"Give it a chance, Jocelyn. You've only been there, what, about an hour? Say your prayers, go to confession, complete your plans for college, and try not to think too much about those questions that perhaps have no answers. And, for heaven's sake, this is not the time to worry about what anybody else thinks. You are prepared for all the questions you will be asked, aren't you? This is probably going to be in the Herald tomorrow morning."

Jocelyn hadn't thought about that. What would she say, and how would the others in her class treat her when they found out her father had been in jail? Closing her eyes, she felt bile rising in her throat. It seemed like every moment that passed was worse than the one before.

"Jocelyn, your classmates may have questions, but I know they will support you. I mentioned it because I didn't want you to be blindsided. I wanted you to have some time to think about what you will say."

Standing up, and slowly walking to the door, she felt out of control and fought hard to stifle her emotions. "Thank you, Father. You've given me a lot to think about. Miss Moss is probably worried about me, so I guess I'd better go. And, I'm sorry I barged in on you like this."

"Child, I'm always here for you. Don't hesitate to come and talk to me when you feel troubled. And, one more thing. Pray for your father; try to find some compassion for him. Is there anything you want me to tell your father when I see him?"

"No, Father Sean, I don't have anything to say to him. Well, I guess I'd better go. I don't want Miss Moss going out to search for me. Thanks again."

"Bless you, Jocelyn."

***

Miss Moss had thought of everything - linens, hair spray, books, radio. Her room was painted a soft blue and all the accessories had a touch of blue in them. She had a single bed, a dresser, bookcase, and chair. Her window looked out on the back of the apartment building, and from the second floor she could see trees and sky. I guess I could be living in worse places, but it's not home. I feel like I'll be in trouble if I touch anything.

Jocelyn actually had more time in the morning because she could walk to school from the apartment. She hated sharing the bathroom, so she was glad Miss Moss left for school before she did. They didn't eat breakfast together, but she was expected to be there for dinner every evening. She had to ask permission to use the telephone and never had a real say in the groceries that were bought.

She worked hard to be pleasant, but knew when she left this apartment; she would never eat tuna casserole again. Her routine didn't vary much - school, homework, church, Little Theater. She hated sitting at the kitchen table to do her homework with Miss Moss hovering over her until it was finished. It was like being in the third grade when Nana drilled her on the multiplication tables.

It was hard not to think about her dad. She wondered how he was doing on his own - was he eating right, was he making sure to sort the laundry before he put it in the washer, did he miss her? She was still angry that he had lied to her, but she was worried about all his legal trouble. What if he really had to go to prison?

When things got too bad, she made an appointment during the school day to meet with Father Sean, or she got permission to call Mrs. Thompson. And at lunch every day, Ruthie listened to her vent. She thought it was very unfair that Miss Moss would not let her spend time on the weekend with Ruthie, but she kept reminding herself that the situation was temporary and soon she would be back home.

Chapter Twenty-three

Jocelyn, Summer 1974

Waking up early the morning of graduation, Jocelyn's mind raced. She and Miss Moss had planned out every detail, and, over her objections, Miss Moss even bought her a beautiful white dress to wear under her graduation gown. They shopped for hours, with Jocelyn trying on twenty or thirty dresses before she settled on a white linen sheathe with a scoop neck and cap sleeves. Jocelyn loved the simple lines of the dress and the rich feel of the linen material. When she put on the dress with her new white high heels, she felt grown-up and sophisticated. She decided today she would wear her hair down and keep it out of her face with a small white ribbon that wouldn't interfere with her mortar board.

"Jocelyn, are you awake?" Miss Moss opened her bedroom door and walked over to the side of the bed and touched her face. "We have a lot to do this morning; you better get up."

Jocelyn hated that she had no privacy. The one time she tried to lock her bedroom door, Miss Moss went on for an hour about fire codes and the safety issues of living in an apartment. She agreed not to lock the door again, but asked Miss Moss to knock before she came in the room. Most of the time, Miss Moss forgot this request.

"Yes, I'm on my way to the shower. What time are we supposed to leave for the brunch?"

There were activities planned all day for the seniors and their families. First, there was a brunch in the school cafeteria, followed by a Mass, and the graduation ceremony. She hoped Miss Moss wouldn't mind that she planned for them to sit with Ruthie and the Thompson family. She couldn't figure out why Miss Moss acted so weird around Mrs. Thompson, but today was her day and being with that family was important to her. Mrs. Thompson was a parent figure for her since her father's arrest, even though Miss Moss made it obvious she wasn't happy about it. Jocelyn couldn't imagine what the last few months would have been like if she hadn't had Mrs. Thompson to go to when things got tough at school and people were asking too many questions.

In many ways, Miss Moss was nice to her, but there was something about the woman that made Jocelyn uncomfortable. For one thing there were so many rules! Jocelyn couldn't even go to the little theater without Miss Moss making sure she had something to do there, too. The guardianship ended on her birthday, but she was trapped by the choices she made in order to continue her education. With Miss Moss's help, she received a scholarship to Barry and had been asked to continue living at the apartment as long as she was in school. She was stuck until she could find a job that paid enough to rent her own place.

Jocelyn was hopeful Miss Moss would ease up on her this summer. She wanted to spend as much time with Ruthie as possible since her friend would be leaving for Tallahassee in August. FSU had only offered Jocelyn a partial scholarship that didn't cover the cost of housing, so she had to give up the idea that the two of them would experience college together.

On a tour of Barry's campus, Jocelyn found out she would be able to take the classes needed to combine her love of English and theater. She would be able to ride the bus to the campus and arrange her schedule so she didn't have any classes on Friday. She planned to use the three day weekend to help her get a good part-time job.

"Jocelyn, we're going to be late. Please, hurry!"

"I'm almost ready. Give me five more minutes."

Everything about the day felt special, she laughed and cried with friends, she received her diploma with honors, and she felt a sense of accomplishment and pride. It did make her sad her Nana wasn't there to celebrate with her, and after Mass she lit a candle in remembrance of her grandmother. The support and love her grandmother gave to her as she was growing up made this day possible. For several moments before the graduation ceremony started she looked to see if her father was there. Part of her really wished that he had found a way to attend. But then she remembered how angry she was with him and closed her mind to any further thoughts of whether he was there or not. As she scanned the audience, she was excited to see most of the people she worked with at the little theater were there to cheer her on. She was particularly happy that Mark Sanders was there. She knew that he had graduated the year before from Archbishop Curley High and was now attending Barry. All through high school, she had worked with him at the little theater, they had talked and kidded around but he never seemed interested in being friends with her. Maybe she could change that once she got to Barry.

"Pomp and Circumstances" started playing and all of the senior girls from Notre Dame Academy were lined up waiting to walk down the aisle toward the stage. Even though her senior year was filled with sadness, anger and uncertainty, Jocelyn was proud of getting through it without a total meltdown. She turned to look at the end of the line where Ruthie was standing, and remembered the day in first grade when Ruthie asked to be her friend. As Ruthie smiled and gave her a thumbs-up, Jocelyn prayed the changes that were about to occur in their lives would not change their friendship. Turning back toward the stage, she and the other graduates began taking the next steps toward their future.

***

The week after graduation, Jocelyn got a part-time job in the Miami Public Library, and began reading all of the books on Barry's list of prerequisites for freshman English. The list was extensive but her supervisor at the library allowed her to read any of the assigned books when she wasn't busy. To her relief, her father sent money to help purchase clothes for college. Since she had worn a uniform in Catholic school, her wardrobe was sparse. She planned to spend Saturdays with Ruthie shopping for clothes but it seemed like every Saturday, Miss Moss had something for her to do that took up most of the day. Ruthie postponed shopping for several Saturdays, but finally told her mother she would have to go on without Jocelyn. When Mrs. Thompson realized what was happening, she called Miss Moss and suggested the four of them go together to shop for the girls. Jocelyn was relieved Mrs. Thompson was so persuasive. She and Ruthie would have at least one Saturday together! But, the day was a disaster. Miss Moss didn't want to go to the stores they chose; she criticized the restaurant where they went for lunch; she disagreed with almost every clothes item Jocelyn tried on; and she wanted to go with her to the dressing room.

"Really, Miss Moss," said Mrs. Thompson in exasperation, "I know this must be hard for you. I mean the girls you see in your classes are all wearing school uniforms, so you probably haven't kept up with the fashions of the day. The girls have made some good, conservative choices they can mix and match. None of these outfits are outlandish. Don't you agree? And, they don't need help trying them on."

"Maybe you're right, Mrs. Thompson. But we do need to give our young women guidance. I was just trying to be helpful, that's all."

The haughty tone of Miss Moss's voice could be heard across the aisle of the store, and Jocelyn knew if she took one look at Ruthie she was going to burst out laughing. Also, she knew if Mrs. Thompson hadn't intervened, she would be going to Barry in outfits that closely resembled the uniforms she had worn for twelve years.

When they arrived outside the restaurant at lunchtime, Miss Moss exclaimed, "Mrs. Thompson, this restaurant is much too expensive. I think Jocelyn and I will have to excuse ourselves and eat at home."

"Miss Moss, this is not an extravagant restaurant. And, besides, it's my treat. Surely you won't object to that."

After they were seated, and had looked at the menu, Miss Moss began complaining – her fork was dirty; her water was warm; the air conditioning was hitting the back of her neck. It continued for over an hour before Mrs. Thompson had enough. "Miss Moss, I'm sorry this has been such an unpleasant experience for you. I've tried on several occasions to do something nice for Jocelyn and you have always found a way to keep her from doing anything with Ruthie and me. It's a shame you can't enjoy being in the company of these two extraordinary young women. Next time, I'd appreciate you staying home." Miss Moss did not have a reply.

The summer passed quickly. Jocelyn went to work, talked to Ruthie over the phone, did her summer reading, and tried not to think too much about the trouble her father was in. She missed being at home. There was a rhythm to life in her house that was missing in Miss Moss's apartment. And, she missed her dad. Several times she met with Father Sean, and tried her best to make life with Miss Moss bearable. Once or twice, Mrs. Thompson persuaded Miss Moss to let Jocelyn come to her house for dinner. These occasional visits with the Thompson's reminded Jocelyn that families laughed and enjoyed each other. There were very few laughs at Miss Moss's apartment.

The week before Ruthie left for Tallahassee, Jocelyn asked permission to invite Ruthie to the apartment for dinner.

"I'll pay for everything, and I'll do the cooking and clean-up. I really want to do something special for Ruthie before she leaves." She pulled a strand of her hair and began twirling it around her finger, thinking of all the first days of school she and Ruthie had experienced together. "It's going to be strange to start school without her, but she'll be home for Thanksgiving."

"That sounds very nice, and I just hope Ruthie appreciates all the money you will be spending on this dinner." Miss Moss was silent for several minutes before she responded. "If you're out of the kitchen by 8:00, I suppose it will be all right. May I join you for dinner, or should I plan to eat somewhere else?"

"Oh, Miss Moss, I wasn't trying to exclude you. Of course, I'm counting on you being with us." Jocelyn was proud of herself for her quick save, but she was very disappointed. She had hoped Miss Moss would be thoughtful enough to leave the girls on their own for one evening.

On the day of the dinner, Jocelyn carefully wrapped the gift she was planning to give Ruthie, and when the doorbell rang, she was ready. The three of them tried to keep the conversation going around the dinner table but it was polite and formal until Ruthie started sharing her excitement about school. Jocelyn could always count on her friend to make a dull party lively. Soon, she was laughing at Ruthie's stories, and even noticed Miss Moss smile once or twice. As they were finishing the dessert, she gave Ruthie her gift.

"What is this for, Jocelyn? You make me embarrassed that I don't have a gift for you."

"No, Ruthie, please don't feel that way. Open it and I think you'll understand why I'm giving this to you. Go ahead, open it."

Ruthie was always like a child when it came to presents. She unceremoniously ripped off the paper and tore off the top of the box. Inside was a beautiful leather journal with her first name engraved in gold letters. When she saw it she began to cry.

"Oh, Jocelyn! This is beautiful."

"Since we won't be together at school, I was hoping you would write down some of the things you do. You know, tell me about your classes and your professors, the parties you go to, and all the guys you're going to fall in love with before Christmas," Jocelyn laughed and got up from the table to give her friend a hug.

"Jocelyn that gift looks quite expensive. You worked so hard for your money this summer; I'm surprised you felt you could spend so much. But, I guess it's your money to do with as you please," snapped Miss Moss.

Jocelyn's shoulders dropped and the smile left her face. She was deflated, and for a few minutes she sat wordless at the table. She made up her mind she wasn't going to cry, so she turned to a stunned Ruthie and ask her to help her clear the table.

"That is one mean woman," Ruthie whispered to her. "I love my gift and I promise I'll write all but the juicy stuff for you to read."

This brought a smile to both of their faces, and for the next half hour they busied themselves making the kitchen look spotless. Just as they were finishing, Miss Moss appeared at the door and reminded Jocelyn it was almost 8:00.

"Ruthie, it was nice to see you, and I know you are going to have a wonderful time at FSU. Hopefully, you will remember to study some of the time," Miss Moss said in her sternest teacher voice.

"Miss Moss, I think you're going to be surprised," countered Ruthie. "I plan to graduate with honors." Ruthie winked at Jocelyn as she walked slowly to the door. "Jocelyn, I'll miss you. Knock 'em dead at Barry, and I'll see you in November. One more thing, you and your dad are going to be all right. I just know it." She was looking at Miss Moss's retreating back as she said this. Jocelyn could see Ruthie shooting daggers at Miss Moss with her eyes, and she smiled.

Chapter Twenty-four

Jocelyn, August 1974

Jocelyn hoped the last week of August 1974 would usher in a new life. College was going to change everything, and give her a chance to redefine her shattered identity. Butterflies and nervous energy accompanied her excitement about the first day of class, but she wished her Nana was with her. For the first time in six months, she wished her father was part of this day. He should be going to the parent event, not Miss Moss. Shaking that thought from her mind, she decided not to let her family issues, and the past, spoil her new beginning.

Life at Barry was everything Jocelyn hoped it would be. Classes with students who challenged her thinking, professors who treated her like an adult, and no uniforms! For the first time in her schooling, she felt the thrill of choosing what to wear each day.

Tension between she and Miss Moss was still running high, but she tried her best to ignore the undercurrent of criticism and the woman's attempts to control her choice of clothes, her class schedule, and her study habits.

The third week of school, as she was walking to her Spanish class, she heard someone call her name. When she turned around, Mark Sanders from Little Theater was hurrying to catch up with her.

"Hey, stranger, wait up! Where you headed?"

"Hi, Mark. I've got Spanish class in Lehman Hall."

"That's where I'm going. Do you mind if I walk with you?" Mark was out of breath by the time he caught up with her.

"No, I'd love to have the company. What class do you have in Lehman?"

"Humanities," Mark groaned as he said it. "It's a second year requirement or I'd opt out. It takes up more of my time than any other class. It's interesting, but next year make sure you don't get Sister Angela. She's brutal with the outside assignments."

"Thanks for the tip." She smiled to think they were having a real conversation." Mark, what's your major?"

"I'm trying to manage a double major in very different areas – music and business. My dad made me promise I'd get the business degree just in case music doesn't work out. Music is my thing."

"I'm surprised. You never do anything musical at little theater except play the guitar for the volunteers."

"Right, I strum a little when we have a break, but show tunes are not my style. I play rock and roll – guitar and drums. You ought to come hear my band play some time."

"Wow, are you really in a band? Where do you play?"

"We do a gig on Friday nights at a small club over on the beach. If you really think you'd like to come, I'll give you a call. What's your number?"

"Sure, just let me know when." She wrote the number on a scrap of paper and handed it to him.

"Great, I'll call you," Mark waved to her and headed down the hall of the building.

"Yeah, right," Jocelyn whispered. "I won't hold my breath."

***

That evening, Jocelyn was in her room reading when she heard the phone ring. She started to go to the living room to answer it but figured it probably wasn't for her anyway. She was surprised when Miss Moss called her name.

"Jocelyn, you've got a call," Miss Moss said. "But don't stay on for long. I'm expecting a call in a few minutes."

"Hello." Melting when she heard Mark's voice, she forgot to be angry with Miss Moss. Mark did most of the talking and by the time she hung up the phone she had made plans to ride with one of his friends to the club where his band was playing on Friday evening. "Wow," she thought as she turned to go back to her room.

"Who was calling, Jocelyn? I didn't recognize the voice."

"Uh, what, Miss Moss? I didn't hear what you said."

"I asked who was on the phone."

"It was Mark Sanders. He wants me to go hear his band play this Friday night."

"Of course you said no, didn't you?" Miss Moss stood up and put her hands on her hips.

"Why would I do that? I'd love to go. He's having a friend pick me up around 8:30."

"I don't think so, dear. You're under-aged. They won't let you in a club. You'll have to let him know you can't go."

"Excuse me." Jocelyn felt a tightening across her shoulders. "Are you saying that I can't go?"

"That's exactly what I said, Jocelyn. I don't approve of this."

Jocelyn's face turned red and she stormed down the hall to her room. Miss Moss was no longer her guardian, but she was letting her live in the apartment rent-free. Did that give her the right to say she couldn't go out with Mark? Could Miss Moss really control what she did? The more she thought about it, the angrier she became. She thought back over the summer and all the ways Miss Moss kept her from spending time with Ruthie. She wasn't going to let the woman mess up her chance to see Mark, and she resolved to find a way to leave Miss Moss's apartment as soon as possible.

The next morning, after Miss Moss left for school, Jocelyn telephoned Ruthie's mother.

"Hello, Mrs. Thompson, it's Jocelyn. Have you got a few minutes? I need to ask your advice."

After Jocelyn explained the situation, Mrs. Thompson told her she would give it some thought and get back to her later.

"I have to work at the library until 7:00 tonight, so I should be home by 8:00."

Jocelyn interrupted when Mrs. Thompson began talking about her father.

"It's nice of you to spend time with him, Mrs. Thompson. But, I don't need to know how he's doing."

"Jocelyn, I know you don't agree with me, but I think you're being really hard on your dad. Honey, your anger is only going to hurt you in the long run." Mrs. Thompson paused before she went on. "Sorry, I didn't mean to start preaching. But, I care about you, and can't wait for this mess to be cleared up. Enough said on that subject, I'll call you later."

"Mrs. Thompson, I'm sorry. I didn't mean to upset you. It's all so confusing, and sometimes it hurts so much I don't think I can stand it. He lied to me, and there's a chance he may have stolen me from my real parents. I don't know how to be anything but angry right now."

"I'm trying to understand how you feel Jocelyn. But it's hard. For years I saw the love you shared with your family and it hurts me to see you turn your back on your dad when he needs you."

"Why are you so sure he's innocent?"

"Honey, I've learned there are times when you just have to go with your gut feelings. Your dad is not a criminal; I know that and so do you." Mrs. Thompson was emphatic.

Jocelyn wasn't going to let Mrs. Thompson soften her anger. " Thanks for your help, Mrs. Thompson. I'll talk to you later."

When she got off the phone, she curled up on the sofa and cried. She cried because her Nana was gone. She cried because she didn't understand what was going on with her dad. She cried because she didn't want to be in this apartment any more. She cried because she felt so small and insignificant. And, she cried because it just felt good to let the tears wash it all away for a few minutes.

She walked over to the mirror and looked at her red eyes and puffy face; she wished she could take back all the tears. If she tried to hide the unsightly mess she had made of her face, she would be late to class.

That evening when the phone rang, Jocelyn hurried to answer it. She hoped Mrs. Thompson had thought of a way for her to be able to keep her date with Mark.

"Jocelyn, I've talked it over with Father Sean, and right now we don't think you have any choice but to miss your date on Friday night. Father Sean is going to talk to Miss Moss, and hopefully you won't have to miss out on anything else. And, honey, after your father's trial, you'll be able to go home."

"You're sure there's no way I can go with Mark on Friday? I really wanted to hear his band." Jocelyn wondered why she was the one who always had to compromise. Somehow it didn't seem fair. "Never mind. I sound like I'm whining, don't I?"

"I know you're disappointed, but hang in there. It will get better. I promise."

"Thanks, Mrs. Thompson."

Jocelyn didn't feel like it was going to get better as she dialed Mark's number. She just hoped he'd understand and ask her out again.

When she hung up the phone, she and Mark had agreed to meet on campus the next day for lunch. Jocelyn wanted to kick up her heels and shout! But she wasn't going to give Miss Moss any more ammunition. From now on, she wouldn't mention when she was going to see Mark.

***

As the semester progressed, Jocelyn and Mark met for lunch almost every day. They saw each other at Little Theater and they found time to study together. On the nights Jocelyn worked at the public library, Mark offered to drive her home so she wouldn't have to ride the bus. He always let her out one block from the apartment.

Jocelyn was amazed to discover that she and Mark shared so many interests and enjoyed so many of the same things. They talked about his music, books they loved, places they wanted to see, and people they would like to meet. Their time together was effortless and undemanding so it was very natural when Mark finally kissed her.

They had just gotten into his car when he leaned over and put his arms around her. She turned her face toward him and, before she could say a word, he kissed her. "I've wanted to do that for a long time. I really like you, Jocelyn," Mark whispered in her ear, and then began kissing her again.

Jocelyn didn't know how long the kissing lasted; she just knew she loved the way it felt and she wanted it to go on forever. He finally pulled away from her, "Man, this had better stop before we get carried away. Are you okay with me kissing you? "

"I'm more than okay, Mark. I didn't want you to stop. Did I do something wrong?"

"No, you did everything right. But I know if we don't stop now, I'll never get you home on time. We're going to have to work our time so we can have more than five minutes for kissing. Don't you agree?" Mark laughed and gave her a quick kiss on the cheek.

"Do you really mean that?"

Mark hugged her as tightly as he could across the gear shift, and smiled at her when he replied, "I really, really mean that."

That night when Jocelyn wrote a note to Ruthie, all she could think to say was, "Now I know what you were always talking about. Kissing Mark is wonderful."

Chapter Twenty-five

Mark

Mark loved his life. He had almost everything he wanted - great parents, good looks, success in school, friends, and music. He tried not to let his health issues overshadow all the positives in his life. He made up his mind as a youngster that Type I Diabetes was not going to define him and he did his best to take care of himself. His mom made sure he ate right, and he knew what to do to make sure his insulin levels were balanced. Even though he took his injections every day, he always carried a candy bar in his back pack just in case. Most people he knew had no idea he was diabetic, but his mom insisted he tell his closest friends.

"Ah, Mom, I don't need to tell anybody. I know how to take care of myself."

"Mark, someone needs to know in case you get in trouble. Your dad and I won't always be around, and I don't want you to end up in the hospital. If you don't tell Gary and Eddie, I'll have to."

After some squabbling, he finally told his friends and his mother talked with them about things to do if they ever saw him begin to tremble, sweat profusely, slur his speech, or become glassy eyed. Several times in the high school marching band, he over extended himself and was glad his friend Gary made him sit down and eat the candy bar.

His rock band, The Alter Boys, took up most of his spare time. He was thankful his parents and neighbors didn't object when they practiced in the garage. There were six guys in the band - two guitars, drums, keyboard, a bassist, and one vocalist. He loved filling-in on drums almost as much as he did playing the guitar. But guitar was his passion. The group had been together for seven years and had managed to get a couple of paying gigs in some of the small clubs in the area. They're best job started several months ago when they won the audition to play on Friday nights in a club on South Beach. True, they weren't Eric Clapton, Led Zeplin or Lynyrd Skynyrd, but they were good and the club patrons liked them.

Mark's enthusiasm and outgoing nature made him popular with his peers, and his good manners and integrity endeared him to adults. He played lead guitar, managed the band, and did most of the up front work with agents and club owners. When the band formed, the members were very young and had no trouble staying away from alcohol and drugs and, as they got older, Mark tried to make sure they lived by that rule. One night he saw his best friend, Gary, smoking pot, and told him he would have to leave the band if he did it again.

"We're about music, you idiot. Don't you know how messed up that stuff will make your life? You make the choice, Gary. It's either the band or drugs but not both."

"Don't be a goody two-shoes, Mark. It's not going to hurt me or the music. It'll probably make me a better guitarist."

"If that's your choice, the band will start looking for a new guitarist."

"You're serious, aren't you?"

"This band is going places, Gary. And we don't have time to babysit a druggie. I'm not going to let you or anybody else blow our chances."

Mark was glad the subject never came up again. Word got around to the other band members and Mark could always tell the club owners truthfully his band was clean.

The band and college kept him busy. He hadn't dated much his freshman year, but he knew that would change the morning he spotted Jocelyn McDeal. He'd known her for years through the Little Theater but always thought of her as a kid. Today, he couldn't keep his eyes off of her. "My god, she's beautiful. What have I been missing?" He called to her to wait for him and hoped he could walk with her to class. She had great eyes that reminded him of dark chocolate and he loved the way she smiled. "Man, I'm going to have to get to know her better."

After talking to her, he made up his mind to ask her out, but his attempt to see her was thwarted by the dragon lady.

"Jocelyn, what does Miss Moss have to do with your life? Is she your keeper or something?"

"I'm living at her apartment for the time being, and it's best if I don't make waves. I'm sorry. I really would like to hear your band but it's not going to work out."

"I don't give up easily. Meet me for lunch tomorrow at the campus cafeteria and we'll talk."

Once they started meeting for lunch, he was hooked. He liked her and was determined to find a way to see her more often.

"Mom, I've met this girl, but I'm having trouble getting to see her. It's driving me crazy." Sometimes his mom had good ideas and he hoped she could help.

"Why are you having trouble? Doesn't she want to see you?" asked his mom.

"I think she likes me and wants to see me, but there's some kind of trouble with her father and she's living with a lady who won't let her do much of anything. I've got to figure out a way to see her."

"Don't do anything to cause her trouble, Mark. Is there any way you can study with her or see her on campus?"

"I'm working on it. Mom, I really like her. She's beautiful, smart, and easy to be around. We have fun just talking to each other."

"She sounds wonderful, honey. What's her name?"

"Jocelyn McDeal. I think you'd like her, too."

"McDeal? I used to know a family by that name. Wonder if she's related?"

Chapter Twenty-six

Rosanna, November 1974

On Sunday evenings, Rosanna often called her sister, Nancy, in Florida. They usually spent a half hour or so catching up on the kids, her work, and the latest antics of their husbands. Nancy kept her informed about their parents' health and told her all the ways life in Miami was changing. In turn, Rosanna entertained her sister with the crazy things that often happened in the Los Angeles court room.

California and Florida didn't seem so far apart when they spent time together over the phone. It was so much better than writing letters. They shared the cost of the phone calls by taking turns calling.

"What are you guys planning for Thanksgiving? Mom keeps asking me if you are coming home this year. It's been three years, Rosanna. We don't even know your kids."

"I'd give anything if we could come to Miami this year, especially for Christmas. But our work schedules are crazy and it cost so much for all of us to fly. I'll call Mom and try to explain why we can't make it. The kids really do need to spend time with you all."

"Every year, I think about all of us being together. You wouldn't recognize Mark. He's gotten so tall, and, of course I'm prejudiced, but he is a real looker. And, Rosie, I'd love for you to hear his band. He plays a mean guitar. The kid's got talent."

"Did you tell me he's playing in a club on South Beach, or did I imagine it?"

"Yeah, the band plays on Friday nights. Their making a little money, but mostly they're just having fun."

"Are they good enough for him to think seriously about making this a career?"

"I'm no judge, but I think they're pretty good. His dad keeps reminding him to take his business classes as seriously as he takes his music. We'll see. Hey, did I tell you he has a new girlfriend? I think he may be getting serious about this one. I haven't met her yet but, from all he's told me, she seems like a real nice girl."

"Did he meet her at Barry?"

"Not really. They've both volunteered at little theater for years. I guess it didn't click for them until just recently. She's a freshman at Barry and they've been seeing each other since school started in September. He says she lives with someone who is very strict, so they aren't really dating."

"That must be hard. I can't imagine not being able to date at her age. She's 18 or 19, right?"

"I'm sure she is. Crazy thing is, she used to live in our old neighborhood. Maybe you remember the family. Her dad is the guy who drove the city bus. There's some kind of trouble with the family right now and she doesn't live at home."

As the truth slowly dawned, the color drained from Rosanna's face. Her hands began shaking so badly she almost dropped the phone. Oh, my God, please don't let it be, she thought as she tried to breathe.

"Rosanna, are you listening to me? I've asked you two questions you haven't answered. Are you still there?"

Rosanna tried to find her voice. "I'm sorry; I got distracted by one of the kids. What were you saying?"

"It wasn't anything important. I was just chattering. Sis, I've got to hang up. I'll call next week."

"All right, but before you go, what's this girl's name?"

"Her name is Jocelyn. I think her last name is McDeal. Gotta' go. I'll talk to you soon."

Rosanna sat frozen in a time warp. She hung up the phone without saying good-bye, and knew if she stood up her knees would buckle. Putting her head down on the table, she tried not to think about the beautiful face of her baby girl, her Jocelyn. She tried to forget the terrible emptiness she had felt for so many years. The emptiness that had never been totally filled, not even by the birth of her other children. How was she going to make this right without hurting everybody – her husband and their kids, her sister, and most of all her nephew and her daughter? "Why, this girl, dear God? Of all the girls in the world, why did Mark pick this one?"

Chapter Twenty-seven

Carter, November 1974

The meeting with his attorney was not going well. She kept asking him over and over to start at the beginning and tell her what happened. He had told her Gracie's story until he was worn out.

"Carter, I hate to say it, but there are some missing pieces in this story. I have to have all the pieces if I'm going to be able to defend you with any hope of winning this case," Elena sighed and looked her client in the eyes. "Let's start over. Try to think if there is anything you haven't told me."

"Miss Martinez, I've told you everything I can remember. Going over it again is pointless."

"The police think you are protecting your mother. They think you took Jocelyn to make your mother happy. Could there be some truth to that?"

"I did not take Jocelyn for any reason," Carter's frustration was beginning to show. He stood up and paced the room. Elena didn't try to stop him; she just watched him as he paced.

He was grappling with his conscience and had to figure out a way to tell his attorney what he wasn't telling her. He clenched and unclenched his fists. There had to be a way to tell the real story that was believable. He walked over to the large window of the conference room and placed his hands on the window sill. From the window on the 18th floor, he could see the new high-rise buildings that were helping to change the face of the city and the sun glistening on the ripples of Biscayne Bay. But there was no sound. The symphony of the city had been silenced. For eighteen years, Jocelyn's real story had been silenced, too.

"I love this city. I love to see all the changes. We're becoming more and more like the big cities of the world. New people, new landscape, more traffic, more noise, more troubles. But, I still love it," Carter said as he turned back to face Elena. "I can't imagine living anywhere else. How 'bout you? Do you love Miami?"

"Yes, Carter, I do. It's an exciting place to live. I love the beach and I love the way the breeze always smells of salt. It reminds me of the place where I was born." Carter saw a wistful look cross Elena's face and wondered what her story was. "Have you always lived here, Carter?"

"Born here, raised here, and will probably die here. This is home. How long have you lived here?" Carter was relieved to have the discussion take a new focus. He needed to talk about something other than his case.

"I was born in Cuba but my family came here shortly after Castro took over the country. I was a young girl when the revolution happened. But Miami is home for me now."

"Did your family have to escape from Cuba?"

"Let's just say, we left in the middle of the night. Carter, we need to get back to work. Tell me how you and your mother found out about Jocelyn's birth. Let's go back to who called you and the time frame for the call. I need to develop a timeline of events. Maybe that will help me close up some of the gaps. Let me go find a piece of chart paper. I'll be right back."

After Elena left the room, Carter tried to put a sequence to the events in Gracie's story. When they got it down on paper, maybe he would be able to see it more clearly himself.

"Okay, I think this paper will be good for what we need to do. I'm going to write Jocelyn's birthday in the middle of the page and we can look at the events before and after that date."

Carter watched as Elena began to create the timeline of events Gracie had concocted. He tried to remember what he told Father Sean and the police, but it was all muddled and confusing.

"Miss Martinez, I feel like I'm going around in circles. Do you think it would be possible for me to do this at home? I could take it with me and work on it over the weekend. We could meet again next week to go over it."

"That's not my first choice, Carter. I think we need to do this together." What Elena really meant was she needed to see him go through this process. He knew she was looking for hesitation or confusion, then she would know where to put some pressure on him for more information. He also knew she just didn't trust his story.

"Why don't we at least try to get started today? I'm on your side, Carter. We'll take it slow. You just tell me what you remember as it comes to you and I'll try to help you put it in some kind of chronological order."

Carter felt himself withdrawing. His pulse began to race and he was fighting hard not to hyper-ventilate. The police officer had caught him in a mistake and his attorney would do the same.

"When is Jocelyn's birthday? Let's start there."

"She was born in June of 1956."

"What day was she born?"

"We celebrate her birthday on June 10th. I think she was six days old when my mom brought her home to us."

Elena ignored Carter's last remarks. "When did your mother go to pick her up? Was it when Jocelyn was a day old, a few days old, a few weeks old?"

"Like I said, I think she was six days old. I don't remember. She was very, very tiny when Mom brought her home."

"When did your mother pick her up, Carter?"

"I think it was right after she was born."

"Where did she go to get her?"

"I think she went to Baltimore. Yes, she went to Baltimore."

"From the police report, I see you originally told them Jocelyn's mother was your mother's niece. You said that Jocelyn's grandmother was your mother's sister. Is that right?"

Here we go, Carter thought as he answered, "Yes, that's right." Carter knew she was setting a trap and he couldn't let his guard down.

"But the officer reported your mother didn't have a sister. You need to explain this part to me. I need to know why there are so many discrepancies in your story."

"Miss Martinez, you've got to understand. I'm just retelling my mother's story."

"Carter, why didn't you know your mother didn't have a sister? Even if the family is estranged, I'd think you would know whether you had an aunt or an uncle. Remember, I need all the truth, not the run-around, in order to defend you."

"I don't know what else to tell you. My mother never talked about her family. I wouldn't know any of her relatives if they knocked on my door," Carter tried to explain.

"Okay, we aren't getting anywhere on that subject, so let's move on to something different. Where did your mother have to go to pick up the child?"

"I assume she went to Baltimore. That's where she grew up," Carter was beginning to stammer over his words.

"Your mother didn't tell you where she was going? Carter, I find that hard to believe. You're not helping yourself here, you know. Tell me, do you want to spend a long time in prison? I'm talking anywhere from 25 years to life."

"Of course I don't want to go to prison. Nobody wants to go to prison," Carter was getting agitated. "Oh, my god! Do you think I could be sentenced to life in prison?"

"If you're convicted, it will happen." She leaned across the table and stared into his face. "Tell me the truth, Carter. If I don't know the truth, if I don't know how to fight for you, you aren't going to walk out of that court room a free man. Those are the facts, Carter."

Carter jumped up out of the chair and started for the door like a scared rabbit. "I'm leaving. I can't handle this kind of interrogation."

"Wait, Carter. This isn't an interrogation, and it's nothing compared to what you will face with the state attorney. You need to sit down. We need to come to some kind of decision about the role you want me to play in your defense. We can walk into the courtroom and I can let them eat you alive. Or we can work together in the hope we can win this thing. What's it going to be?"

He had to make a decision about his future. Was he willing to go to prison? The reality gave him a jolt and he walked back to the table with his head hung in resignation.

"Okay, Miss Martinez, are you ready for the truth? 'Cause in all likelihood, you aren't going to believe the truth either."

"Let me be the judge of that, Carter. Now what really happened?"

"Jocelyn was left on our doorstep."

"Oh, Carter, you can do better than that," Elena's face showed her disbelief.

"You wanted truth, and that's it. Jocelyn was in a box that someone left on our doorstep on June 16, 1956. She looked to be about a week old. I thought I caught a glimpse of her mother as she was walking away from our house, but I'm not sure. The box the baby was in had a couple of bottles, some formula, and a note. I wanted to call the authorities but my mother kept putting it off until it didn't seem important any more. That's the truth. Now who is going to believe that?" Carter felt like a weight lifted off of his shoulders and he slumped down in the chair in relief. For the first time in 18 years, he spoke the words that had haunted him every day. He looked toward the sky, and whispered, "I'm sorry, Mom. I don't have a choice anymore."

He turned to face his attorney, "I was never sure exactly what my mother told Father Sean. I heard the story for the first time when I went to his office to meet with Miss Moss about Jocelyn's scholarship application."

"Wow, I almost believe you. I had imagined several scenarios. But, I can truthfully say, this wasn't one of them. Keep going, Carter, tell me more."

"My mother couldn't have any more children, and she wanted a large family. When Jocelyn was left on the doorstep, she took it as a sign from God she was supposed to raise this child. I tried to persuade her differently, but her mind was made up. From that moment, my mother was in control of Jocelyn."

"Did your mother name her?"

"No, her real mother did that. Her name was on the card in the box. Mother gave her the middle name, Marie."

"Carter, do you still have the note?" There was a touch of hope in Elena's voice.

"Yes, my mother kept it in her Missal. I haven't looked at it in years, but I know it's there."

"You said you thought you saw the person who left the baby? Was it someone you knew?"

"I've always thought Jocelyn's mother was a young girl who rode my bus to the vo-tech. And, as Jocelyn gets older, she looks a lot like this girl. I think she was about Jocelyn's age when she had the baby."

"So, you knew the girl was pregnant?"

"No, she didn't let it show. But I remember thinking she had gained some weight."

"If I have her name, I can verify some of the things you've told me. That's a start in the right direction."

"How is Jocelyn going to handle this? What's she going to think when she finds out that her mother left her in a box on our door step? I tried so hard to keep that part from her when all of this started happening. I know my mother told Jocelyn some of the story she made up and it must have satisfied her curiosity. I don't want Jocelyn to turn against her grandmother. She can hate me if she has to, but, how can I save myself at the expense of Jocelyn's security? She's lost so much in such a short time."

"If all of this checks out, Carter, I promise I'll be as sensitive to Jocelyn as I can. What's the girl's name?"

"I know her first name is Rosanna, and her last name might be Russell. I'm not sure. And, I haven't seen her since the night she left Jocelyn."

"You mean she never rode the bus again?"

"Right. I never saw her on the bus again or in the neighborhood. Before she left Jocelyn I'd see her walking in my neighborhood and she always got on the bus at the stop near where I live so I knew she lived close to us. For months after Jocelyn came, I walked around the area looking for her but I wasn't sure which house was hers. Sometimes she would stop for a few minutes at our house if she saw my mom working in her garden. When she got on the bus, she always asked me how my mom was doing. It was strange that I never saw her again."

"Start at the beginning and tell me everything you remember. I want to understand every detail. How did the baby get left on your door step?"

"Like I said, it was the night of June 16th and my mother and I were at home reading. She was in the kitchen and I was in the living room when the door bell rang. It was after dark and we rarely had anybody ring the bell after dark so I went to the door thinking somebody had the wrong house. When I opened the door, no one was there, but I looked down and there was a box on the step. I had the porch light on, so I could see there was a baby in the box. I can tell you, it took me so by surprise I just stood there staring for awhile. Then I began looking up and down the street to see if anyone was around and that's when I saw the girl walking away. When she got to the corner, I could see her a little better because of the street light. I just got a quick glimpse of her 'cause she was walking fast. But I would swear it was Rosanna."

"Okay, then what happened? Did you call to her?"

"No, I didn't. I guess I was too shocked to do anything. In a few minutes, I thought I'd better take the box inside. So I picked it up and took it to the kitchen where Mom was reading a magazine, or maybe the newspaper, I can't remember. I just remember she was sitting at the kitchen table. I put the box on the table and said something to her about not believing what was in the box. It didn't take but a few minutes before Jocelyn began to cry. Mom picked her up, and then I found the note." Carter's voice and facial features softened as he recalled this part of the story. He went back in time and for a few minutes, he was standing in the kitchen looking into the box. "She was a beautiful baby. But she was so tiny! It would have scared me to pick her up but mom knew exactly what to do."

"At that point, how did you know it was a girl?"

"I remember she had on some kind of outfit that was pink. And, when I read the card, it said her name was Jocelyn."

"You need to bring me the note. That is a key piece of evidence in your favor. And, I need to see if I can find this girl. She'd be a woman now and there is no telling where she might be. When you go home tonight, find the note and then write down everything you can remember about Rosanna. I have a deposition in a few minutes but we can meet again tomorrow morning, if that's okay. No, wait, you probably have to work in the morning."

"You know I can't drive my bus any more. They took me off the line and put me behind a desk 'til this is over. It's killing me to sit behind a desk and answer the phones. They put me over in routing so I tell people which bus to ride when they call for information. After all my years of service they say the publicity isn't good for the company and they don't want me out where people can see me," Carter shrugged his shoulders and looked down at the floor as he told Elena about his new work situation. The disappointment and hurt was evident in his tone of voice.

"I'm sorry, Carter. I guess they felt like they had to protect themselves, and you. Let's get together tomorrow afternoon after you get off work. Would that work better for you?"

Carter sipped on a beer as he stared at the scratches in the kitchen table and wondered how they got there. He couldn't remember who made them or what caused them and he really didn't know if he had been aware of them before. Usually, all he saw was the table, not the scratches and nicks that made it unique. It was like the assignment Elena Martinez had given him when she asked him to remember Rosanna. He could remember seeing her but he never paid attention to the details. He thought she was probably around 5'4" but she could have been taller or shorter. He knew she was very thin when she first started riding the bus and he thought she had gained some weight toward the last. But after 18 years, he was having trouble picturing her. He remembered she had brown hair, but he didn't think he ever knew what color her eyes were. He did know that Jocelyn resembled her. He didn't know how accurate his memory was or whether his memory of Rosanna was being distorted by the resemblance he thought he saw in Jocelyn.

Thinking about this made him miss his daughter even more. He could see her dancing around the kitchen as she told him funny stories about her day at school and he could hear the delight in her laughter. Oh, how he loved to hear her laugh. There was a theatrical touch to the way she told her stories. But these thoughts weren't helping him with what he had to do.

Elena had asked him to write it all down and he sighed when he looked at the three things on his list - 5'4, brown hair, skinny. He wasn't giving his attorney much to work with. He was trying hard to remember why Rosanna was going to the vo-tech school; what was she studying to be? He knew how important it was but his thoughts were scattered and he was having a hard time concentrating. "This is pointless," he thought. "I'll have to come back to it later."

Pushing back from the table, Carter walked to his mother's bedroom to search for her Missal. He thought she kept the note from Jocelyn's mother in there but he wasn't sure. He and Jocelyn had been saying for months they needed to go through Gracie's things and clear out her room but they had avoided doing it. He had not gone into this room for months and, when he opened the door, he was overwhelmed by her presence; she was everywhere. The fragrances that were so much a part of her floated on the air and surrounded him: the lilac lotion she always wore, the rose sachets she kept in her lingerie drawer, the leather of the pocketbook still hanging on the back of her chair, the pungent smell of the peppermint candy she kept in a dish on the nightstand. He sat on the edge of her bed to keep from falling down as grief slammed into him. He thought he had finished grieving; but the ache in his heart felt like a lightning strike. He had taken her for granted; he had counted on her always being there. And now, she was gone. She was gone; Jocelyn was gone; and his job was gone. The three things that identified him had vanished and his hiding place in their shadows no longer offered the protection and comfort he depended upon. And he was tired, the kind of tired that assaults your mind and hammers down every part of your body. "No," he thought wearily, "I'm more than tired; I'm nothing."

***

Waking up at 2:00 in the morning, he rubbed his eyes and sat up. He must have curled up on his mother's bed and fallen asleep. But, he couldn't remember why he was in her room. It took a few minutes before he could focus and then, with a sigh of resignation, he remembered. Getting off the bed, he walked over to turn on the light and tried to think about possible places his mother might have kept her Missal. One after another he began pulling out the dresser drawers that contained his mother's clothes and personal items. He was digging under a stack of sweaters when his hand touched a piece of metal. Pulling it out, he was struck by another lightning bolt when he looked down at his mother's engagement ring. Tears rolled down his cheeks as he folded his fingers around the tiny ring and brought his hand up to his heart.

***

Long ago memories of Sharon pushed him further into the melancholy that he had been experiencing all evening. For years and years, he successfully kept her from his thoughts. But, in the early morning hours of what had been a long night, she was there, as real as though she had never gone. He remembered her hair and how he loved to run his fingers through it. He saw her smile, and her eyes, and the body he had wanted so much it was a physical hurt.

187

"Enough," he shouted. "God, why does it still hurt so much? I can't stand it anymore." At that moment, he wanted to curl up in the corner and die. He wanted his life and the trouble he was in to be over. He didn't want to fight this battle anymore. But, then he thought of Jocelyn, and he knew he had to see it through for her sake. He was fighting for Jocelyn's life, not his own, and the thought began to calm him. Gently, he placed the ring back in the drawer and continued his search. When he found what he was looking for, he went back to the kitchen table to finish the list for Miss Martinez before he had to get ready for work.

"You didn't give me a lot to work with, Carter. But, I'll see what I can do. You think she was taking courses to become a court reporter, right?" Elena sat across from Carter and looked at the list he had prepared for her about Rosanna Russell. "This is a start. But you understand that searching for this Rosanna isn't going to be easy?"

She continued to rifle through the pages. "Thank goodness your mother saved the note from Jocelyn's mother. This clearly indicates the child's mother wanted you to have the child. The problem we have is authenticating it. Anyone could have written this note so you better start praying we can find Rosanna."

Elena caught the eye of her client. "Carter McDeal, I keep wondering if you're the quiet, nice guy sitting in front of me, or if you're devious and cunning enough to pull off a kidnapping."

Carter didn't know how to respond and defeat began to crowd out any thought of clearing his name. His own attorney wasn't convinced that he was innocent.

She read the note aloud, stopping at each word to try and discern its meaning: "My name is Jocelyn. Please raise me as your own. Love me, care for me, and give me the life that my mother can't afford to give me."

"Carter, tell me again why you didn't go to the authorities when the baby first came to your house?"

"My mother kept putting it off, saying we'd take care of it in a couple of days. So, I let her take charge. You've got to understand, I usually let her take care of things. She was so much better at it than I am. And, before I knew it, so much time had gone by, it didn't seem as important as it did at first."

"Do you have any idea why she didn't want to go to the authorities? I mean, that would have been an easy solution."

"Think about it, Miss Martinez. What chance would we have to adopt a baby? Here we were - a middle aged woman and her bachelor son. Do you think HRS would have allowed Jocelyn to stay with us? I think mom was afraid she would lose her and she didn't want that to happen."

"Do you think Father Sean really believed her story? Or, was he going along with her?"

"I don't know for sure. But I think he believed her. If you had known Gracie McDeal, I think you would have believed her, too."

Elena looked puzzled. "Okay, Carter, let's talk about the people who can give me a clear picture of you, your mother and Jocelyn. I will need to consider each one carefully, and decide whether they should be called for depositions. Who were your mother's closest friends?"

"My mother wasn't very social. She belonged to a group at the church, and she maintained a long time friendship with Mrs. Dillon, the woman who ran the boarding house where my parents lived when they first came to Miami. Mrs. Dillon's my godmother, in fact. She probably knows a lot more about my mother than I do. And, of course, there is Father Sean. He and my mother were friends, but he may not be able to discuss anything about what he knows. You know, priests have that confidentiality thing,"

"Carter, think. Was there anyone your mother might have confided in? Someone she might have told the truth about Jocelyn?"

"My mom didn't really have friends; Jocelyn and I were pretty much her life. You know, Miss Martinez, now that I think about it, my mom's world was very small. But I don't believe she was ever lonely."

Elena sighed, "Carter, I need Mrs. Dillon's full name, her address, and a phone number where I can call her."

"I can get that for you, and you might want to talk to our next door neighbor, Mrs. Harvey. She and mom were always talking over the hedge. I doubt Mom ever told her anything personal but she might have something to add."

"All right. Put her name on the list. And, Carter, I need the names of people who can testify as character witnesses for you: your friends, your boss, some of the regulars on the bus. Anybody you can think of who has known you since Jocelyn came into your life. And what about Jocelyn? I have so many questions to ask your daughter. How do you think she is going to respond to me?"

"My daughter is angry and hurt. Her world has been turned upside down, and she feels like nothing about her is real. You would probably have a hard time getting any information from her. Is there any way to leave her out of all this?"

"I doubt it, Carter. She will probably be a key witness for the prosecution. But, when they take her deposition, I want to be able to understand a little about her and how you think she will react to the state attorney's questions. The next time we meet, we will talk more in depth about her. But, today I want to talk some more about Gracie. I need to know her story."

Chapter Twenty-eight

Elena

Later that evening, Elena curled up next to Eric on the couch in his apartment and hoped they could spend a few minutes talking about some of the legal issues she was facing with the McDeal case. She would phrase her words carefully to ensure she didn't break client confidentiality but she really needed a sounding board.

"What would you do if your instincts told you a client was telling you the truth, even when everything else pointed to the contrary? Would you spend time investigating a long shot?"

"You know I would. Isn't that what good defense is based on, Elena? You listen, you observe, you go with your gut; and then, you hope you can find some case law to back you up. Why?"

"One of my clients told me a story that sounds like a fairy tale and yet, something about it rings true. But he has lied about so many things; he could be making this story up, too."

"Listen for the gaps. Let him tell the story over and over, until you either catch him in a misstep, or you decide to take a chance on what he's saying." Then Eric laughed, "You know there isn't a guy in jail who admits he's guilty."

"I wish I could talk to you about some of the specifics; because I'm baffled."

"And, I wish we weren't talking at all. I haven't seen you in almost a week, and talking isn't what I had in mind for this evening." When Eric took her in his arms, she forgot all about practicing law. He nuzzled her neck, and began to affectionately nibble on her ear lobe. "You smell delicious. I like that perfume," he whispered as he drew her closer to him. At first, his kisses were teasing and playful, but then they became more impatient and fervent. Both of them were breathing rapidly and the flame of their passion was making it easy for them to leave all reasoning behind. As the heat between them increased, Eric stood up and grabbed her hand, "Come with me to the bedroom, Elena." He pulled her up from the couch and as they walked down the hall, he began to undo the buttons at the back of her dress. He undid each button quickly, letting his hands caress her bare skin as the dress fell away from her body.

"You're getting good at walking and unbuttoning. What else are you good at?" Elena's voice tantalized as she began melting into his warmth. She stepped out of her dress and followed him down the hall eager for more of his touch. He laced his fingers through hers and pushed her gently onto the bed. She hungrily watched him as he undressed; the way his hands moved over his own body heightened her desire for his hands to touch every part of her own. It brought her pleasure to see how much he wanted her, and she opened her arms invitingly as he lay down on the bed beside her. He wrapped his arms around her and pulled her on top of him, his hands expertly removing the panties and bra that kept them apart. Elena experienced sheer joy at the familiarity of his body claiming hers. She felt his fingers dig into her skin and she clung to him with a fierceness that begged him to go deeper and deeper within her.

As her passion ebbed, Elena wondered if her desire for his body would diminish over the years. It seemed like every time he touched her he awakened new feelings that invited her to explore not only her sexuality, but her sensuality. He taught her to appreciate the touch, the taste, the sounds, and the intensity of sex. She loved how her body responded to his and she took as much delight from pleasing him as she did in being pleased. Eric's love encouraged her to give her body to him without reservation or hesitation. She regretted she would have to leave this warm bed and return to her parent's home. Their wedding was still months away, and her family would never understand if she told them she was going to stay the night at Eric's apartment. As she dressed, she looked lovingly at the sleeping face of the man she adored, and smiled. In the afterglow of making love, she felt sated and complete. She leaned over and tenderly kissed his forehead, "Sweet dreams, my love."

Elena sat at her desk surrounded by law books and pondered her next steps in the defense of Carter McDeal. He wasn't what she would call handsome but he was a very nice looking man. He was tall, with a nice build that showed he had taken care of himself. She figured he was in his mid-40s, but she'd have to check the records to be sure. Everything about him suggested his innocence - except he had lied to her and the police. The social workers at HRS couldn't substantiate any sexual abuse, there didn't seem to be anything unsavory in the way Jocelyn had been raised; and she didn't see any evidence Carter was mentally unstable. She also knew that wasn't enough to build a solid defense.

There was something compelling in this story about Rosanna. Her instinct was to believe him. Perhaps her concern was simply a result of his shyness and she prayed she was right. If he was telling her the truth, she knew she needed to find this mysterious woman he claimed was Jocelyn's mother. But she didn't know where to start looking. Then she remembered Carter said the girl went to Lindsey Hopkins Vocational School and was studying to become a court reporter. She looked through her file, and based on the year of Jocelyn's birth, this Rosanna would have graduated in 1956. She called to her secretary and asked her to make some inquiries at the school. "Susan, I need for you to do some checking for me at the vo-tech. I'm looking for someone with the first name of Rosanna, and possible last name of Russell, who graduated in 1956 and was most likely taking a course in court reporting. See if you can find her full name and last known address. If we can find that, I'll decide where to go next.

Several hours later, Susan came back to her with answers. "Okay, I found a Rosanna Jean Russell whose last known address was 2743 NE 17th Avenue. She did graduate from the court reporting program, but they have no records of her taking a job in the Miami area. I checked to see if I could find a Russell at that address but the family must have moved. I also looked to see if anyone by that name ever worked in the courts here and I ran into a dead-end. She could be anywhere in the world, probably married so she has a different name. But, I'll have one of our investigators see if they can track her through her social security number. Even if she's married, they will have her maiden name in those records."

"Great job, Susan. I didn't think you'd be able to find her that easily."

"We haven't found her yet, Elena. All I've done is verify the information you gave me. Let's see where we go from here."

The next day when Carter and Elena met, she tried to take him through each step of the pre-trial procedures. "Depositions will be taken as part of the discovery process. Whenever a deposition is taken, the person is placed under oath and the attorney asks questions about the case. A court reporter will make a record of everything that is said and will later transcribe it into a written report. Once the court reporter has transcribed the questions and answers, a copy is provided to both attorneys. The person being deposed will have an opportunity to review their responses and make corrections to the transcript before the court reporter files the original transcript with the court. This process ensures there are no surprises in the courtroom. It's not exactly like you see it on Perry Mason."

"Who decides who gets called for depositions?"

"Each side will call people they think are important to the case. But, remember, I'll be there when the state attorney takes his depositions and vice versa. Carter, I figure with all that has to be done in this case, we probably won't go to court until March or April at the earliest. Hopefully, that gives us the time we need to find Rosanna."

"I can't imagine how we'll find her. That's like finding a needle in a hay stack," groaned Carter.

"You're right. But in the meantime we can start trying to work a miracle with what we've got. Let's go over this list and think about the information each person might share that would be helpful."

Elena read the names on the list and wondered how she was going to build a case using Mrs. Dillon, Mrs. Harvey, Mrs.

Thompson, Ruthie Thompson, Mrs. Snyder, Miss Ruby, Mr. Fitz, and Sully.

"The prosecution will call Detective Madison, Miss Moss, the social workers, and perhaps, even Father Sean. They will ask for psychological evaluations of Jocelyn and you. They will probably bring in some experts to testify about the psychological profile of men who kidnap children."

"Sounds like they are stacking the deck against me. Do I have any chance at all?"

"Carter, you better start praying that we can find this Rosanna, and that she is willing to corroborate your story."

Chapter Twenty-nine

Sharon and Carter, December 1974

The city put up the holiday lights on Biscayne Boulevard and the store fronts were either decorated with snow scenes or jolly old elves surrounded by palm trees and bright, red poinsettias. Christmas in a tropical city like Miami was a mishmash of wishing for snow and basking in the warm 80 degree temperature that made the city a favorite winter destination for tourists. Sharon finished decorating her Christmas tree and wrapped the last of her gifts. She was disappointed her children were not going to be home for the holidays. This would be the first year she would not have her sons with her on Christmas day and the thought was almost enough to make her want to take down the decorations and return the gifts to the store. She'd known at some point her boys would have their own lives, but she had never really given any thought to the fact they might find those lives far away from Miami. Peter had just gotten married and lived in Portland, Oregon. He would be spending this Christmas with his wife's family. Alan was in the Air Force and was stationed overseas, and Tommy decided to spend his break from college on the ski slopes of Colorado. And, to top it off, her parents had decided to take a 14-day Caribbean cruise the last two weeks of December. True, they invited her to come with them, but at the time they booked the trip, she was still hoping one of the boys would call and say they were coming home.

She could drown her sorrows in a nice bottle of wine but she knew she would pay for that with a killer headache and hangover. So, she put on her running shoes and decided to run from her house to one of the coffee shops in the Coconut Grove village. She could take her mind off herself as she sat at one of the outside tables and watched people passing, sea gulls arguing over little bits of food, and sails flapping on the pleasure boats docked at the marina. There were worse ways to spend an afternoon.

It was a three-mile run from her house to the center of Coconut Grove, and by the time she arrived at the café, her shirt and hair were wringing wet from the humidity. She ordered an iced coffee and found a table in the shade. Was it unseasonably hot, even for Miami, or was she getting too old to run three miles in the heat of the day? At forty-two, maybe she was letting herself get out of shape and she vowed to renew her membership at the gym.

Even in the high humidity, there was always a breeze off the bay and it didn't take long before she cooled off enough to enjoy her outing. She loved living so close to this area the locals called "The Grove." The quaintness of the village had not been destroyed by the new high-rise condominiums. The shops and restaurants were almost all locally owned. Thank goodness, this was not the place for franchises and large chains. Today, as she looked around, she noticed most of the hurricane shutters had been removed from the condo windows, signaling the arrival of the "snow birds." The population in the Grove tripled from November to March because so many people in the north maintained winter homes in the area.

Just as she was about to begin her run back to the house, a city bus rolled down the street in front of her and her thoughts went to Carter. She wondered how he was doing and if anything new had developed in the case against him? She hadn't seen another mention of him in the newspaper and hoped it was a sign a mistake had been made and he was no longer in trouble. Maybe I should give him a call, she thought. But, then she laughed out loud. "What in the world would I say to him after all these years? Hey, Carter, sorry I broke your heart. I see you're in trouble and I thought I could help." She could hear Carter slamming the phone down as he hung up on her.

***

The week before Christmas, as Sharon walked around the women's department at Burdines, she saw him. He was standing in front of a shelf stacked with sweaters. She watched him move his hand gently across the cashmere and then hold up a soft blue V-neck. He turned it from front to back, side to side, and replaced it on the shelf. Her eyes watched him put his hands in his pockets and continue to stare at all the choices, but her heart saw the familiar way he tilted his head and shifted his weight from one foot to the other. He hasn't changed very much at all - how well I remember that stance and those gestures. He looks frustrated and confused and, frankly, so out of place in the women's department. Will he let me make it easier for him?

"Hi, Carter. Are you having trouble deciding the color, the size or the style?"

She watched his body stiffen when he heard her voice. "Remember me?" she asked. "Sharon Bowers. Well it used to be Sharon Peterson." She stood there hoping he would at least say hello. But he just stared at her as though he had never seen her before. "I'm sorry. I thought you were someone I used to know. Won't you excuse me?" She whispered as she turned and started to walk away.

"Sharon." It was not a question. He knew who she was and, as he said it, she thought about how long it had been since she had heard him say her name.

"It is you, isn't it?" She paused for a moment. "Carter McDeal, how are you? It's been a long, long time."

He continued to look at her and didn't say another word. She remembered he was a man of few words but somehow she had expected him to say something. The silence was making her uncomfortable but his silence was what she deserved. "Well, it was nice seeing you. Have a Merry Christmas."

"It's for my daughter," he called after her. "I'm not sure which one she would like. What do you think an 18-year old would like?"

"Tell me a little about her, and maybe I can help you," A warmth ran through her as she walked back to the place where Carter stood. "Is she blond or brunette? Tall or short? What color are her eyes? You really want to pick out something that will enhance her coloring. And, you'll want to look at a style that matches her size. Give me some clues, Carter, and we will be able to select the perfect gift for her. By the way, what's her name?"

"Her name is Jocelyn and she has dark brown hair and brown eyes. She's not as tall as you are, but she is slim like you. Does that help?"

"Okay, that's a start. Let's look at the vivid primary colors first. I bet she looks great in red, vibrant blue, emerald green and, maybe, a lemon-type yellow. I don't think the soft blue you were looking at is the right one for her. Here's one, Carter. Look at this gorgeous electric blue. I think this is my choice for Jocelyn. And she sounds petite so I think the V-neck will look nice on her." Sharon realized she was babbling, talking a mile a minute, and decided to hush before she sounded like a teenager herself. Handing the sweater to Carter, she waited for him to say something.

"I think you're right. This is a good choice. Thanks for your help."

Sharon didn't want the moment to end with the sale of the sweater. For reasons she didn't want to give voice to, she needed to know more about Carter's life. She wanted to talk with him like they used to when they would sit on her family's back porch swing.

"Are you in a hurry, Carter? Maybe we can go across the street and have a cup of coffee? You know I'd really like to talk with you. That is, if you have some time?"

Carter looked like he wanted to run. But he turned to her with a smile, "I've got a few minutes, Sharon. Let me pay for the sweater."

They walked out of the store and crossed the street. Once they were seated in the small café, they sat quietly. Sharon was staring out the window and Carter was staring at his hands. She didn't know where to begin a conversation. The waiter brought the coffee and pie they ordered, and the silence continued. Finally, she looked at Carter and spoke matter-of-factly. "I know you're not going to believe this, but I am truly sorry about the way I handled our break-up. I knew I couldn't face you, and Jim was really pressuring me to break our engagement. My prayer has always been that someday I might have the chance to say this to you."

"Let's not go there, Sharon. It was a long time ago."

"Okay, let's talk about today. Do you still live in the old neighborhood? Where is your wife?"

"Yeah, I'm still in the house on 11th Avenue. I don't have a wife. I never got married."

"Wait a minute. I thought you just bought a sweater for your daughter, didn't you?"

"It's a long story. But, yes, I do have a daughter. How about you? Where is your husband?"

"Oh, I've been divorced for a long time. My ex-husband didn't exactly like just having one woman in his life. But, he did give me three great sons."

"I'm sorry it didn't work out for you."

"Oh, it's okay. After I got over the original shock and knew my boys were going to be all right, I've really enjoyed being single."

The silence returned. She felt the awkwardness and paid more attention to her coffee and pie than she did to him. She didn't want to ask him about what she had read in the paper and she didn't think he would ever initiate the subject. Maybe it was a bad idea to continue trying to make small talk.

After a few minutes, Carter looked at her, and asked, "Where are you living now?"

"I have a small house in Coconut Grove. When the boys lived at home, we had a house in Cutler Ridge. But this year, my youngest son went away to college, and I decided to move to a smaller place. I like living in the Grove. There's always something to do."

"Do you work, Sharon?"

"Some people call it work, Carter. I call it fun. I'm an assistant to an interior designer. I help pick colors, furniture, and accessories for other people's homes. And, you, what are you doing now?"

"I'm with Miami Transit but right now I'm working in routing. Hopefully, soon I'll be back driving, but not now."

Sharon was hoping he would keep talking and tell her about the charges against him. But he didn't seem willing to talk about this part of his life.

"Tell me about your children, Sharon? If they aren't at home, where do they live?"

By the time Sharon told Carter about her sons, he was beginning to look at his watch and she knew it was time to go.

"Carter, this has been nice. I enjoyed talking with you, but I really have to go. I'd like to do this again someday. Here's my card; give me a call." She picked up the bill that had been left on the table, but Carter took it out of her hand. "This one is on me, Sharon. It was nice talking to you."

"Thanks, Carter. I hope to see you soon."

She walked out of the café and wondered if she could emotionally afford to ever see him again.

***

Carter placed the business card on the kitchen table and for the next few days all he could do was pick it up, look at it, and then put it back down. His emotions were vacillating between frustration and fascination. Every time he thought about Sharon, he felt all those feelings he thought he had buried. By Saturday, four days after he had seen her downtown, he walked into the kitchen, picked up the card, and dialed her number. Christmas was in two days, and the thought of spending the day alone was more than he could handle. Maybe he would be able to deal with it if Sharon was there to talk to. When her phone rang, he almost hung up. But before he could do that, she answered.

"Hi, Sharon, it's Carter. I was wondering if you were free for dinner tonight. I know its short notice but if you don't have plans, I'd like to see you."

"Carter, I have an appointment at 3:30, but I could probably meet you somewhere around 6:30. If that's okay? The house I'm working on is in Coral Gables, so I'll be on your side of town."

"Great. Why don't I meet you at the Red Diamond at 6:30?"

"Carter, I can tell you don't get out much. The Red Diamond isn't there anymore. But how about Caffe Vialetto? It's very close to where the Red Diamond used to be and they have great Italian food."

When he hung up the phone, he had to sit down for a few minutes. *Now what have I done?* But, he shook off the thought when he realized he was actually excited about going out on a date with Sharon. *After all, it wasn't like they were in a relationship. This was just a dinner between old friends.*

***

Sharon was surprised and, although she was already dressed for work, she ran back up to her room to change her outfit. *It must mean something that I want to look good when I see him,* she thought. *But, why in the world am I even considering going out with someone who may be facing years in prison? No, I'm not going to think that way. He didn't kidnap that child and he is not going to prison. Besides, this is just dinner between old friends.*

All afternoon, she couldn't keep her mind on her work, and she checked her watch every few minutes. Instead of thinking about the color selection for the living room being redecorated, all she could think about was Carter. He had aged well. There was a bit of gray in his hair, and a few lines in his face, but overall, he looked good. He had stayed slim, and she guessed that he worked out. *Maybe he still rides that old bicycle of his.* She laughed when she remembered how proud he was of it. She also remembered hating that he didn't have a car. There was no place for them to make-out, except the swing on her parent's porch. *Did kids today use the words making-out or heavy petting?* She wondered and laughed. Today's young people seemed so much more advanced and open about sex than she had been. The sixties had changed so many things - and sex was one of them.

She hurriedly finished at the house where she was working, and arrived at the restaurant thirty minutes early. When she got out of her car, Carter was standing at the front of the restaurant. *Perhaps he was anxious, too.* She stood by her car for a minute and looked at him. *This is crazy. I'm a middle-aged mother of three who is having* sexual fantasies about her high school sweetheart. She had to get a grip on herself.

"Hi," he said when he saw her approaching and, as she got closer, he smiled. "You still smell like roses and jasmine. I've always loved your perfume."

"Thanks for remembering, Carter."

"That fragrance kept me going in Korea. I didn't think I'd ever smell it again."

She was touched by his words and so glad she had chosen this perfume for tonight. She didn't remember wearing it as a teenager but, if he did, so much the better.

"Glad you could make it tonight, Sharon. The blue in that dress really is a great color on you."

"Thanks, Carter. I hope you like this restaurant. It's one of my favorites."

When they were younger, Carter's shyness always seemed to disappear when he was with her, and she felt that happening now. Over dinner and dessert, they laughed and talked easily about everything but themselves. The only time the conversation touched on old times was when she asked Carter about Gracie.

"Your mother was always so good to me, Carter. I was never sure she liked me, but she was never unkind. Not even the night I returned the ring. She was a beautiful person, inside and out. I know you must really miss her."

"You know, it's the strangest thing. Sometimes I forget that she's been gone over a year. I turn to tell her something and she's not there. Thanksgiving was really hard this year. But I know from experience that losing someone does get easier."

Sharon knew that he was talking about her and she felt the heat rise in her face. But she was determined not to spoil the evening with regrets and more apologies. Out of the blue, she looked at him and blurted out before she could change her mind, "Carter, what are you doing Christmas day? I'd love for you to come to my house for dinner."

"I couldn't do that. You have your family and they wouldn't appreciate me intruding."

"No, Carter, the boys won't be home this Christmas. I'll be spending the day alone, and it would mean so much if you would spend it with me. That is if you don't have other plans. And, I'd be happy for you to bring your daughter."

"Thanks, Sharon, I'd like that. And, it will just be me." Then Carter whispered, "Jocelyn won't be home for Christmas either."

***

On the drive home, Carter could think more clearly than when he was sitting across from Sharon. He decided that he would call her tomorrow and find a way to politely decline her Christmas invitation. He didn't want her to get caught up in his messy life, and he needed to focus all of his energy on the trial and his defense. For a few minutes, she had helped him forget all of the trouble in his life and he was grateful. But this relationship had to end before it had a chance to begin. When he looked at her across the table at dinner, he forgot how much she hurt him, and all he wanted to do was take her in his arms. But he couldn't get sucked back in. Not now, when his whole world was in jeopardy.

Carter had mailed his gifts to Jocelyn, and hoped he might receive something from her. He hadn't expected a gift but he had hoped for a card. By Christmas Eve, he knew there would be no card and only the invitation from Sharon kept him from feeling depressed. He had really meant to break their Christmas dinner date but he kept putting it off and now it was too late to call her. As he parked the car for midnight Mass, he wondered if he might catch a glimpse of Jocelyn in the church. He thought of her first Christmas, and his mother's insistence they attend this special Mass as a family. His heart skipped a beat to think Jocelyn could actually be sitting somewhere in the sanctuary. He knew he couldn't approach her but the best Christmas gift of all would be a glimpse of her. His eyes searched the dimly lit church but she was not there.

Neither the glorious music nor the candlelight lifted his spirits. He sat through the service without appreciating what he was celebrating. He couldn't find solace in the miracle birth of the Christ child when his own child was lost to him. As he progressed down the aisle after the service, Father Sean tapped him on the shoulder. "How are you holding up, Carter? I've missed seeing you in church."

"I know, Father. But it's really hard to be in this place without my mother and without Jocelyn."

"Son, don't you know God understands what you're going through? He's with you, Carter. Even when you can't find Him; He's still there." The priest rested his arm on Carter's shoulder and pulled a small envelope out of the book he was holding. "This is for you, Carter, Merry Christmas." He handed the envelope to Carter and turned to greet another parishioner.

Carter waited until he was home to open the envelope. He was afraid his emotions would get the best of him no matter what the envelope contained. Pulling out the Christmas card, he closed his eyes and, instead of the picture of the baby in the manger, he saw a baby in a small box. He remembered that night 18 years ago as though it was yesterday. Taking a deep breath, he opened the card. The words Merry Christmas, Dad, were written neatly at the bottom corner of the card in a handwriting that was as familiar to him as his own. And, then his eyes focused on the word Jocelyn. Seeing his daughter's signature was like balm to a wound.

He sat with the card pressed against his heart until his head began to nod. Then he carried it with him to his room and placed it on the nightstand next to his pillow. He wanted to be able to see it when he woke up. As he turned out the light and climbed into bed, he thanked God for this small gift.

Chapter Thirty

Sharon and Carter, Christmas Day 1974

Sharon set the table with the good china and crystal. She used one of her best linen table cloths and arranged two beautiful poinsettias in a Waterford crystal bowl in the center of the table. Planning the menu and cooking a special meal reminded her of countless other dinners she had hosted and she smiled. Hearty aromas of cinnamon, pumpkin, turkey, and sage scented the house. Christmas decorations made her small dining room look like a festive banquet hall. She hadn't gone overboard with decorations this year since she thought she would be the only one home. But she had chosen some of her favorites and created a sense of elegance, not only in the dining room, but throughout the house.

She had run from store to store yesterday morning to purchase the food, select the perfect wine, and find a small token to place under the Christmas tree for Carter. By evening she was so exhausted she missed going to Mass. Her intentions had been good, but her body just wasn't willing. Christmas morning she was startled awake when the phone rang. Looking down, she realized she had slept in her clothes.

"Hello and Merry Christmas," she greeted whoever was on the other end of the line.

"Merry Christmas to you, too. I just realized if I'm supposed to be at your house in a few hours, I need to know your address."

"That's funny! Do you mean I forgot to tell you where I live?"

"Your business card has a Coral Gables address and you said you live in the Grove. If you told me, I can't remember. So, why don't you tell me again?"

"We aren't getting off to a good start today, are we?"

"Oh, I don't know. It might have been fun to ride around the Grove yelling your name," Carter smiled.

"What time is it, by the way?"

"It's 10:00. Did I wake you up?"

"Who sleeps until 10:00 on Christmas morning? Here's my address. Do you have a pencil?"

Two hours later, when Sharon answered the door, Carter stood and stared.

"Oh, dear. I was hoping you wouldn't be able to tell I've been frantically running around the house trying to make up for oversleeping. But, from your expression, I guess it shows."

"No, you look beautiful." Looking boyish, he stammered. "I can't take my eyes off of you."

Her long, red silk dress clung to her curves and made her look sensuous, not sexy. A simple ribbon that matched the color of the dress lifted her blonde curls away from her face and highlighted the sparkling ruby earrings that were her only jewelry. She looked festive and so alive.

"Flattery will get you everywhere, Carter. Thanks for the compliment."

Carter had always thought she was pretty, but today he was mesmerized by her beauty. After a minute, he looked beyond her to the room and its expensive furnishings and he understood Sharon was financially beyond his reach. A city bus driver couldn't afford this house and its furnishings. He would never be able to buy her the clothes or the jewelry she was wearing. If he fantasized about rekindling a romance with her, it was swept away when he walked into this house. He made up his mind to enjoy dinner and then never see her again.

Embarrassed, he handed her the bottle of wine he had so carefully chosen. While the $20 he spent seemed extravagant, he was sure she would look at the label and pity him for making such an inexpensive choice. But, she was gracious and all smiles when she accepted the wine and thanked him for his thoughtfulness. He fought to keep his spirits high hoping his expression didn't reflect his discomfort.

Sharon told him she was serving drinks and hors d'oeuvres in her garden and led him through the French doors. While it didn't look like a winter wonderland, a slight breeze, bright sunshine, and a cloudless blue sky made it the best kind of day Florida offered.

"I thought we could sit out here for a while and enjoy this gorgeous weather. Take a seat and I'll be right back. What can I bring you to drink?"

"Surprise me. Whatever you're drinking will be fine with me." His eyes followed her as she walked back in the house. The small area where he was sitting was breath-taking. The patio was surrounded by lush foliage, and he could see a stone pathway leading to a small fountain. All along the wall that enclosed the yard, small palm trees, flowers, fichus and banyan trees gave the impression of an oasis in the midst of the city. The garden offered a sense of peace and he began to relax.

There was calmness about her and this invitation was helping him get through one of the most difficult days in his life. He had worked hard to look his best for her. Yesterday he had gotten his hair cut, this morning he ran an extra mile, and he had even taken a few minutes to work out with his weights. The yellow v-neck sweater he was wearing showed that his muscles were still toned and his body was strong. Did this kind of preparation mean he really had forgiven her?

She returned with a tray of food that looked like it had been prepared by a five-star chef. Did she go out of her way to make this special for me, or does she treat all of her guests this way? If this was the appetizer, he knew he was going to be awed by the rest of the meal.

After an hour or more in the garden, she led him to the dining room and served one of the best meals he had ever eaten. Every dish was more delicious than the one before and he knew he had consumed enough food to feed the entire city. Together they cleared the table and Sharon told him to take a seat in the living room while she prepared the coffee. "Are you ready for dessert or would you rather wait a while?"

"I don't think I'll be able to eat another bite; even if I waited all night."

"We'll see. I've made a special dessert, but we can wait to enjoy it. Go on in the living room and I'll bring the coffee."

By the time they finished their coffee, the hush of evening was all around them. The Christmas he had dreaded had turned out to be one of the best days he could ever remember. He was grateful to Sharon for making it so memorable but he knew he needed to leave. This was not his world. He knew if he stayed, he would get lost in wanting what he could never have. And, he still hadn't told her about the trial.

"This has been a very special day but it's time for me to head on home," Carter said as he stood up. "I can't thank you enough. And, where did you learn to cook like this? I know your mother didn't teach you."

"You don't have to leave yet, do you? We haven't had dessert. Won't you stay for a while longer? It would be a shame for my efforts to go to waste. Sit back down and I'll just be a few minutes in the kitchen."

Before he had a chance to answer her, she hurried away. He had no choice but to sit back down and wait.

When she brought the dessert dish out, he could tell she had spent time in preparing it. "What do you call this, Sharon? I hope it tastes as good as it looks."

"It's called a Maple Pumpkin Pot Au Crème. That's just a fancy name for custard. I hope you like it? It's one of my favorites."

Carter loved the smooth, velvety texture of the custard and his taste buds were awakened by the combination of maple, pumpkin and spice. Even though his belt had gotten tighter and he felt like he had gained ten pounds in one afternoon, he was glad he had stayed. She was right, it was beyond delicious.

Walking over to the Christmas tree, Sharon picked up a small box wrapped in silver paper and handed it to Carter.

"This is a little something to wish you Merry Christmas and to bring you good luck in the New Year."

"This is too much, Sharon. You shouldn't have done this." Carter was embarrassed again. How did his bottle of wine compare to whatever was in the small box?

"Please open it, Carter. I think you'll like it."

Reluctantly, he opened the gift and gazed at the silver four-leafed clover hanging on a sterling key chain. As he picked it up it turned over and he saw it was engraved. "How in the world did you find the time to have this done?" He held it up to the lamp and read the words, "I believe in you, Carter, 12-25-74."

Appreciation and gratitude flooded over him. She knew about his troubles and she hadn't judged him; she hadn't thought he was a monster. And she hadn't asked him for explanations. Instead she had gone out of her way to let him know she was on his side. He pulled her to him and saw the tears falling down her cheeks. All he could do was hold on to her. He didn't have any words for what he was feeling; he just knew he had desperately needed someone to hold on to and she was there.

Chapter Thirty-one

Christmas Day 1974

Jocelyn jumped out of bed like a two-year old. It was Christmas morning and nothing could dampen her enthusiasm for her favorite holiday. Not even this weird apartment she was forced to call home, or the peculiar woman who seemed determined to control her life. Through the cajoling and sweet-talking of Mrs. Thompson, Miss Moss had finally agreed and she was going to be able to spend most of the day at the Thompson's. Miss Moss would be there, also but Jocelyn was sure she and Ruthie would have plenty of time to catch up on all that had happened in their lives since August. But that wasn't even the best part; Mrs. Thompson and Mrs. Sanders, Mark's mother, had convinced Miss Moss to let her accept an invitation to have dinner with the Sanders family. Mark was going to pick her up at the Thompson's at 5:00, and she would be able to spend an evening with him without having to sneak around or lie about where she had been or how she got home.

Pulling on her robe, she rushed out to the living room. She wanted to be alone when she opened the gift from her dad. This moment didn't belong to Miss Moss. This was Jocelyn's time to pretend life had not changed and she was at home where she belonged. Closing her eyes, she could see her dad sitting on the floor near the Christmas tree handing out the presents and could feel the warmth radiating from her grandmother's smile as she sat in her rocking chair anticipating Jocelyn's delight at Santa's treats. No matter Jocelyn's age, there was always a treat under the tree from Santa Claus. Sitting on the floor next to the tree, she lowered her head and sighed. This morning she needed to remember home for a few minutes.

Two packages under the tree were from her dad, even though one of the tags was signed, "Santa." She opened Santa's box first and hugged her grandmother's rosary beads to her heart. Her dad had written on the card inside the box, "Nana loves you and is always with you." She needed something of her grandmother's to hold on to and her dad had thought to give it to her. "Thank you, Dad," she whispered and carefully laid the beads back in the box.

The gift in the second box from her dad was a luxurious blue cashmere sweater. The color was dazzling, and she knew it would make her come alive when she put it on. Her hand brushed over its softness, and she almost stopped breathing when it occurred to her she had never owned such an expensive article of clothing. Even if her dad was trying to buy back her love with this sweater, she couldn't wait to wear it. Rushing back to her room, Jocelyn tried it on. Looking at herself in the mirror, the magic in the sweater embraced her and she could almost believe she was pretty.

Dinner with the Thompson's was fairly uneventful and she was happy Miss Moss had not caused any problems. Everyone helped get dinner on the table and Jocelyn and Ruthie volunteered to clean up so they could have time together.

"Don't hold out on me, Jocelyn. Tell me everything about Mark. I mean everything."

"Ruthie, you're so funny. You know you don't tell me everything! I will tell you he is wonderful. He's kind and considerate. He's funny and really, really smart. He cares about the same things I care about. And, best of all, I can talk to him about anything."

"He sounds too good to be true. I know he's cute, and you probably enjoy talking to him. But, is talking to him really the best part?" Ruthie teased.

"You're impossible! I'm not telling you anything more."

"Hey, you're the one who told me kissing him was wonderful. I just want to hear all the details of your kissing experience. That's what friends are for."

"Kissing him is wonderful, but it's scary. Ruthie, I don't want to stop with just kissing him. I've never felt like this before. All he has to do is touch me and I'm ready to go to bed with him; that's dangerous."

"Jocelyn, don't do anything stupid. You've only been seeing him for a few months. Wow, you really have it bad. I hate to get personal but are you on the pill?"

"Good grief, Ruthie, you know I'm not."

"Jocelyn, when you feel this strongly about a boy, sometimes things happen. You better think about seeing a doctor and making sure you are protected."

"You're on the pill? You never told me. Ruthie, I wouldn't even know who to go see. I can't walk into our family doctor's office and ask him!"

"Lower your voice, Jocelyn. This isn't a topic I want to discuss with my mother. There are clinics where you can go. Before I go back to school, we better take a little trip downtown."

"Hey, girls, what kind of secrets are you whispering about?" Mrs. Thompson interrupted.

"We're just having a girl talk, Mom. We'll be finished with the dishes in a minute. Do you want us to bring out the desserts?"

"Good idea, Ruthie. I think everyone is ready."

After Mrs. Thompson left the kitchen, Jocelyn turned to Ruthie, "We're Catholic, are you crazy? How do I explain being on the pill?"

"You don't! Think about it, Jocelyn. If there's even a small chance you might have sex with Mark, you better make sure you don't find yourself pregnant. That's the real issue. If you are getting so close sex might just happen one night, you better be ready. That's all I'm saying."

Before she finished with her dessert, Mark rang the door bell. Ruthie welcomed him and introduced him to her family.

"Hi, Mark, it's nice to see you again. I'd like you to meet my mom and dad, my sister Gail, my brother Ben, and my aunt Jen. You know Miss Moss. We were just finishing dessert. Would you like some?"

"Hey Ruthie, how're things at FSU?" He looked around the room. "It's nice to meet all of you. How are things at the little theater, Miss Moss? I'm sorry I haven't been able to help out much this season. I'll pass on dessert, but thank you." He turned to Jocelyn. "Hey, are you ready to go?"

Jocelyn hugged Mrs. Thompson, said good-bye to the others in the room, and told Miss Moss that she would be home by mid-night.

"I'm sorry, Jocelyn. I thought we had an understanding that you would be home by eleven," Miss Moss frowned at Jocelyn as she spoke.

"Miss Moss, it's Christmas. Can't you bend the rule because it's a special day?"

Jocelyn didn't want to make a scene in front of Ruthie's family so she agreed to the curfew. Mrs. Thompson rolled her eyes and shrugged her shoulders. As she hugged Jocelyn good-bye, she whispered, "Remember, it won't be for much longer. Go and have a good time."

Jocelyn looked over at Ruthie, "I'll call you tomorrow."

As she and Mark walked out the door she turned back, "Thompson family, you made this a very special Christmas. Thank you."

Jocelyn had tried not to eat too much at the Thompson's since she would be sitting down to dinner with Mark's family in a few hours. Once they got in the car, Mark turned to her, "That is a killer sweater. You look beautiful."

***

"Hi, sis, how was your Christmas?" Rosanna asked.

"Rosanna, hi. We had a great day. Santa was really good to everyone this year. He even brought me a new dishwasher!"

"Wow. You must have been a very good girl this year. Yeah, we had a nice day, too. But, I sure missed being with you all."

"I know, I missed you, too. Start saving your pennies so you can come home next year. Okay? I met Mark's new girlfriend today, and I like her."

"So you think he's serious about this one?"

"They both act serious. And, she's the first girl he's brought home for us to meet, so that tells me something."

"What's she like, Nancy?"

"Well, she's cute as can be; petite, nice little figure, brown hair, brown eyes. She's very personable. I don't want to make over her too much; you know how kids are? If I say she's great, Mark will probably drop her like a hot potato. Rosanna, I think she's a keeper. I'd like to get to know her better, so I'm planning to invite her to lunch some time soon. But that's enough about us. Tell me about your day."

PART THREE

SHADOWS FADE

A gem cannot be polished without friction,
Nor a man perfected without trials.
Chinese Proverb

Chapter Thirty-two

Depositions, Day One 1975

Carol Snyder had missed seeing Carter on the bus. For years he had helped her go to work with a smile. He often told her funny stories about his daughter, and sometimes even asked her for advice when issues cropped up about raising the child. Many times when the girl was younger, Carol could remember seeing her on the bus with her grandmother, and it was always apparent the child was adored. Why in the world did she have to go to a deposition? What could she possibly tell these lawyers?

Elena Martinez stood in her office doorway and looked at the woman seated in the waiting room. She watched her absently fiddling with her rings, turning them round and round. Then the woman began speaking softly to the young man seated next to her. "This entire meeting is beginning to make me feel uncomfortable. Those lawyers could twist my words and I could end up hurting Carter instead of helping him." The woman looked up at Elena and quickly lowered her head. "Do you think that's Carter's attorney? She sure is pretty, and I bet she's Hispanic. But she looks so young. For Carter's sake, I hope she knows what she's doing. At least she looks friendly." In response to her name being called, she stood and whispered over her shoulder, "Lordy, how long before I can get out of this place?

"Good morning, Mrs. Snyder, I'm Elena Martinez and I represent Carter McDeal. Please take a seat." Elena smiled at her as if to say, We won't bite. Just try to relax. "I'd like you to meet Tom Gorman and Tanya Smith from the state attorney's office, Jackie Gainey, a court reporter who will be recording these proceedings, and Susan Jackson, my assistant. We will try to make this as easy as possible for you, but please understand that once we begin, every word said in this deposition will be entered into the record. Before we start, is there anything I can get you; a cup of coffee or glass of water?"

"No, thank you. I'm fine."

"Then we can begin. Mrs. Snyder, please state your full name and address, tell us where you are employed and how long you've worked there."

"My name is Carol Snyder. I live at 116 NE 65th Street, Hialeah, Florida, and I've worked at the Flagler Street Diner in downtown Miami for about 29 years."

"How long have you known Carter McDeal, and what is your relationship to him?"

She thought about it for a few minutes before she replied, "I've known Carter for about 20 years. He's the man who drives the Route Six bus that I take to work. Or, at least he drove the bus until all this trouble started. Now we have a new driver."

"If he's your bus driver, how do you have a personal relationship with him?"

Mrs. Snyder couldn't keep the irritation out of her voice. She tightened her hands on her pocketbook and answered as clearly as she could.

"I'm the first person on the bus every morning, so I get to pick my seat, and I always sit right behind him. For a couple of blocks, I'm usually the only one on the bus, so we visit a bit before it starts to get busy. Do you want me to tell you what I know about Carter?"

"Perhaps later, Mrs. Snyder. For now, there are some specific questions I'd like for you to answer." Elena looked at her notes. "Did Carter ever mention his daughter Jocelyn to you?"

"Yes, ma'am. We talked a lot about his daughter."

"What kinds of things did you talk about?"

"We talked about everything. When Jocelyn was small we talked about baby things like first steps, first words. We talked about ear aches and scratched knees. When she went to school, he kept me up on her grades, and the things she liked to do. I could tell you all kinds of funny stories about that child. Carter loved to talk about her."

"Did you ever meet Jocelyn's mother, or did Carter ever talk to you about her?"

"Oh, no, Jocelyn's mother died in childbirth."

"How do you know that, Mrs. Snyder?"

"I guess he told me."

"Did you ever meet Jocelyn?"

"When she was younger, she and her grandmother, that's Carter's mother, would ride the bus I took home in the afternoon. Jocelyn loved to go to town, and she loved riding her dad's bus. When she was older, she rode the bus to school, and I'd see her every now and then." Carol smiled at Elena. "She was a pretty little girl with long brown hair and big brown eyes. I can see her now bouncing up the steps of the bus ahead of her grandmother. The child always wore a uniform, so I guess she went to the Catholic school."

"Did you ever see any interaction between Carter and Jocelyn?"

"Of course Carter couldn't give Jocelyn his full attention, 'cause he was driving, but if she got a seat up close to him, they talked." Carol loosened the grip on her pocketbook and Elena thought the woman might be relaxing a little.

"Do you have children, Mrs. Snyder?"

"Yes, ma'am. But they're all grown, and I have seven grandchildren. That's my oldest son out in the waiting room."

"As a mother, Mrs. Snyder, what is your opinion of the father-daughter relationship between Carter and Jocelyn?"

"He adores that girl, and from everything I've seen, that girl adores her dad." She glared at the lawyer. "Carter doesn't deserve all the suspicion he's under right now."

"Do you think Carter is capable of kidnapping Jocelyn?"

"Not in a million years." Her surprise was evident. "That man would never do anything to hurt someone else. And, if he took a child away from her mother, that would be very hurtful, wouldn't it?" Her features hardened and her voice resounded across the room. "No, Miss Martinez, that never happened."

"Thank you, Mrs. Snyder. Tom, do you have any questions for Mrs. Snyder?"

"Yes, a few. Good morning, Mrs. Snyder. Did you ever see Mr. McDeal lose his temper with someone on the bus, or with another driver who may have placed the bus passengers in danger?"

"No, sir, not once. And I can tell you he has had to deal with some pretty ugly folks on that bus. I think some people are just naturally mean and they take it out on everyone they meet. And the bus driver is a good target. But Carter always treated his passengers with kindness and respect; no matter how they treated him."

"Did Mr. McDeal miss work, or was he on the bus most days?" Tom Gorman was an imposing looking man who worked to make the witnesses feel small, not by towering over them, but by using the most arrogant tone of voice that Elena had ever heard. And, he twirled his pencil which annoyed her to no end.

"For all the years I've been riding that bus, Carter was in the driver's seat. That is, up until the time all this mess started about his daughter. Carter is one of the most responsible people I know."

"If you could use only a few words to tell me about Carter, what would they be, Mrs. Snyder?"

She sat quietly for a minute, and then looked Tom Gorman in the eyes, "Carter McDeal is a good man, and anyone who says otherwise doesn't know what they're talking about."

"Thank you, Mrs. Snyder, that's all for today. We appreciate your time."

Elena sighed and hoped her disappointment didn't show. This first deposition had been such a big let-down. The woman hadn't give her any reason to think Carter had kidnapped the child, but it was a shame that nothing meaningful had come during the interview to help her prove it.

Tom Gorman offered her a smug smile,. "Where are you going with these depositions? If this is all you've got, we might as well look at a plea bargain and settle this case right now." He twirled his pencil in her direction.

"In your dreams, Tom. My client is innocent. Remember, you've got to prove him guilty, not me."

"It's your risk, Elena." Tom smirked as he walked out the door and Elena knew he thought he had this case won.

Grabbing an unappetizing sandwich from the tray her assistant had brought into the room, Elena groaned, "Unbelievable that I'm supposed to build a substantial case on the fact that Carter McDeal is a good man?"

At 2:00 the depositions resumed and Susan went to the waiting room to assist Mrs. Dillon to the conference room. The elderly woman walked with a cane, but Elena thought even at 84, she still seemed lively and alert.

"Well dearie, my name is Dolores May Dillon, and I live at the Senior Center next to Annunciation Church in downtown. I don't work anymore, but for forty years I ran a boarding house here in the city."

Elena decided that being in this conference room was the most exciting thing that had happened to the woman in years. If she wasn't careful, Mrs. Dillon would spend hours telling them everything she knew about her friends the McDeals.

"How did you meet the McDeals, and how long ago did you first meet them?"

"Oh, goodness, let me see. I think I first met Edgar and Gracie in 1931. They were newlyweds and rented a room in my house. You know, they were such a lovely couple. So in love and caring about each other. I baked them one of my special coconut cakes the night they got married."

Mrs. Dillon's whole face lit up as she talked about the McDeals and she told the people in the room as much with her hands as she did with her words. She moved the spoon in the bowl as she talked about the cake, and then made a motion like she was sprinkling the coconut on top.

Elena interrupted, "That was nice of you. But please, Mrs. Dillon, just answer the questions."

"I'm sorry, dear. I just have so much to tell you. Where was I? Oh, yes, then in 1932, Carter was born. I've known him all his life."

"Tell me about your relationship with the members of the McDeal family."

"Gracie was my good friend. I loved her like a daughter. And, I'm Carter and Jocelyn's godmother. I helped Gracie raise both of them. She was such a good mother. And, Carter, well, even though he's my godson, I can tell you there's not a better man around. He stepped up after his dad died and took care of his mother."

The woman babbled and Elena tried not to lose patience. She shifted her weight, uncrossed her legs and leaned forward. Time had become a factor. It was almost 3:00 and they weren't close to being finished with Mrs. Dillon. The room seemed stifling and she wondered if the air conditioning was working properly. Perspiration stained her new silk blouse. She felt aggravated that she had spent time on the depositions she had called today. Not one person had given her anything she could use in Carter's defense.

"How did you come to meet Jocelyn?" Elena continued.

"Gracie called me all excited and told me she had a baby she wanted me to meet. You know, Gracie's poor niece died in childbirth, and that's when Gracie and Carter were asked to take care of the baby. Of course, having a baby to care for was like the answer to a prayer for Gracie."

"Was Carter a good father, Mrs. Dillon?"

"If you know Carter, you know he's kind of shy." She smiled when she spoke about her godson. "But when Jocelyn was younger the two of them talked up a blue streak. I don't think I ever heard him talk as much as he did before Jocelyn became a teenager. He always read her bedtime stories, took her for walks, and played with her when he came home from work. After she got older, he wasn't as actively involved I guess, but he was always there for her. That child grew up with a lot of love. I hope that tells you what you want to know, dear."

Elena smiled at Mrs. Dillon, and quietly asked, "Do you think Gracie could have taken this baby from someone other than her great niece? Did she want a baby that badly?"

Mrs. Dillon tapped her cane on the floor and Elena thought she heard the woman asking Gracie to forgive her. "I'm going to tell you a secret. Gracie once had a vision, dear. The Virgin Mary told her she would have a daughter, and Gracie believed if she waited long enough it would happen. If she had been desperate, like you're implying, why would she have waited so long? She wasn't a young woman when Jocelyn was born. No, Miss Martinez, that isn't how Jocelyn came to be with Gracie. How could you even think Gracie would do such a thing?" She shook her head and folded her hands in her lap. "Where do you people come up with these kinds of questions?"

"I guess that's what lawyers do, Mrs. Dillon. We come up with the crazy ideas that we hope will help us uncover the truth." Elena wondered why this woman irritated her so much. "Do you think Carter knew how much his mother wanted a daughter? Do you think he might have taken a baby to make his mother happy?"

"That's ridiculous. You're barking up the wrong tree, Miss Martinez. First of all, Gracie would never share that kind of thing with her son. Second, of course Carter wanted his mother to be happy, but Carter's God-fearing and responsible. It would be a sin for him to take someone's child. It would be an even bigger sin if he did it just to make his mother happy." Mrs. Dillon kept shaking her head. "You know, I tried to imagine the kind of questions you would ask me and I can honestly say that these questions are not at all what I expected." She paused, then added, "Besides, think about it Miss Martinez, Carter's too shy to try and pull off stealing a child."

"Mrs. Dillon, thank you for your time. Tom do you have any questions?"

Tom turned to Mrs. Dillon, "What did you mean, Mrs. Dillon, when you said this was an answer to prayer for Gracie?"

Mrs. Dillon's tone changed from obliging to distrust. "My goodness, you're asking me to remember things that happened a long time ago. Gracie believed that God answers prayers, Mr. Gorman. She'd always wanted a daughter, and now she would have the next best thing to having her own child. She would be raising her great niece. She was happier than I'd seen her since Carter was born. My friend Gracie could have her dark days, you know." She looked over their heads to the window at the end of the room and seemingly folded her hands in prayer.

***

Life at the boarding house was all about the ebb and flow of people who shared space, but lived separate lives. When Gracie did not appear for breakfast three mornings in a row, Mrs. Dillon pulled Edgar aside and asked him point blank if they were expecting a wee one. When he told her they were, she went into action. She made Gracie a cup of hot ginger root tea with a teaspoon of honey and placed several saltine crackers on a saucer. She handed them to Edgar and told him to take them to his wife. When Edgar reported to Mrs. Dillon that this seemed to help, every morning for the next month, she had her remedy ready for Edgar to take to Gracie.

Gracie was treated with special care at the boarding house, she enjoyed the love and attention that she had craved and never received from her own family. Her boss at the Home Dairy allowed her to continue working until the end of the sixth month, but then decided it wasn't proper for her to be waiting on customers in her condition. So, for two months, Gracie was pampered and doted on by Mrs. Dillon and the other boarders. She was learning so much about love from these people that she would be able to share with her child.

On October 2, 1932, Joseph Carter McDeal entered the world at Jackson Memorial Hospital. The proud parents had named him Joseph after Edgar's father, but had decided to call him Carter.

When Carter was first placed in her arms, she knew her reason for living had finally been revealed and she vowed to be the best mother she could be. For the first time, she felt a connection to another human being that denied logic or explanation. Edgar had initiated her into a world of trust and love, but Carter solidified her place in that world.

Carter was taken home to the waiting arms of Mrs. Dillon and the doting care of the other residents. Although he was a colicky baby and didn't sleep through the night for the first few years of his life, his real and adopted family had no complaints. The women of the house cooed over him, cradled him, rocked him, changed him, fed him, and in general, loved him without reserve. The men of the house, including his father, watched over him, protected him and vowed to teach him all the things a boy should know.

Mrs. Dillon and Mr. Bentley were asked to be his godparents and proudly stood with Edgar and Gracie when Carter was christened.

Gracie prayed she would be a good mother and established a routine for her son that would provide him the stable, safe environment she had not experienced. She and Edgar would bring up their child in a world without raised voices, cruelty, and fear.

Several months after her return to work, she was pregnant again and sicker than she had ever been with Carter. Even Mrs. Dillon's ginger tea did not help relieve this morning sickness that had turned into an all-day sickness. After she had missed a week of work, she told her boss she was quitting her job. Now most days, she only got out of bed to take care of her basic needs. Mrs. Dillon and Edgar had to take care of Carter's. For two more weeks, the nausea was relentless. Then one morning when she awoke, the feeling had passed. She was relieved until she sat up in bed and saw she the blood. The bleeding continued for several hours before she miscarried.

Over the next year, this pattern was repeated two more times. Gracie was on a roller coaster of emotions. The joy of finding out she was pregnant would plummet to despair with every miscarriage. Every morning, she left Carter with Mrs. Dillon and walked to the church where she would beg the Virgin Mary to intercede for her and ask God to send her another child. She tried to find comfort, but she did not feel connected to Mary like she had been in Baltimore. There was a growing emptiness nothing seemed to fill.

After the third miscarriage, her bleeding did not stop. She knew she needed to see the doctor. Something was very wrong. Her fears were validated when the doctor told her she would need a hysterectomy. There would be no more children.

Her heart broke and her dreams shattered. First, she would never have the daughter she wanted so badly and second, the money she had saved for a down payment on a house would have to cover of the cost of the surgery.

Gracie's depression did not lessen once she had the surgery and her body began to recover. Edgar and Carter needed her, and Edgar promised her somehow they would find a way to buy a house. For months after the surgery, her life was a grey blur. She went through the motions of living, but inside she felt dead. She no longer found joy in Carter or comfort in Edgar. Her body was recovering, but her spirit had been wounded and she felt lost.

"You've got to give Gracie time to heal," Mrs. Dillon said to Edgar when she saw how worried he was about Gracie. "She's got to finish her grieving. They give widow's at least a year, don't they? Well you've got to do the same for your wife. She'll come around; you'll see."

Gracie's desire to have another child became an obsession and she considered herself a failure. The year passed quickly and Gracie was not getting better. She became more and more withdrawn and despondent. Edgar kept telling her he missed her and Carter needed her. He brought her flowers every now and then and he encouraged her to get out of the house. He even suggested she might like to go back to work. But nothing seemed to reach her. Even though she tried to get back into the rhythm of her life, there was no sparkle in her smile and no light in her eyes. Occasionally, she responded to some silly thing Carter was doing and it gave Edgar hope she might be getting better.

But, to add to Gracie's sadness, Mr. Bentley had a sudden heart attack and was rushed to the hospital. She and Edgar had grown fond of him, and as Carter's godfather, Mr. Bentley had spent countless hours with the child. He played with him, made wooden toys for him to play with, and often entertained the child when Gracie was having one of her dark days. Within a week, he passed away, and Gracie's grief was even heavier.

She continued to spend her mornings at the church. She craved the silence and the familiarity of the rituals that were as much a part of her as her own skin. She convinced herself she was responsible for her father's abuse and this was her punishment. She prayed for forgiveness; she went to confession; and she grew farther away from life than she had ever been. She heard the priest when he told her what had happened to her was her father's sin, not hers, but she didn't know what to do with his words.

On the eve of Carter's third birthday, Gracie cried herself to sleep. She wept silently into her pillow because she knew Edgar had grown weary of her tears. When she finally fell asleep, she slept fitfully and her dreams were chaotic and unsettling. In the middle of the night, she was awakened by something in her dreams that made her afraid. Her heart was beating rapidly and she was afraid something was wrong with Carter. She pulled on her housecoat and walked to the room where he slept. When she entered his room, she realized all was well and her son was sleeping peacefully. The moonlight coming through the window fell on his face and as she listened to his quiet breathing and smelled his baby sweetness, she was suddenly overwhelmed by the love she felt for him. In that moment, she realized that grieving for other children was causing her to miss the wonder and delight of being a mother to this child. She had withheld her love from this child and she was ashamed. She fell on her knees beside Carter's bed and promised she would make amends to him - she would love him with all her heart.

She fell asleep beside Carter's bed and was startled awake by a touch on her shoulder and the sound of someone calling her name. When she opened her eyes no one was there, but she heard the voice again, calling her name. She sat up in the quiet darkness and her eyes were drawn to the moonlight coming through the window.

Then she heard the Virgin Mary saying, "I will give you a daughter and she will come when you are ready."

"Mrs. Dillon, did you hear my question?" Tom had asked her the same question twice with no response.

"Excuse me, I didn't hear you. I was thinking about my friend, Gracie."

"Mrs. Dillon, when did your friend tell you about Jocelyn, and how did she explain the child's presence?"

"Let's see, Jocelyn was a few weeks old and Gracie had just gotten back from going after her. I think she called me to come over to the house. That's the first time I saw the baby. Gracie explained that her sister was dead, her niece died in childbirth, and there was no one to raise the child. So, she and Carter agreed to take her. That's the whole story, Mr. Gorman. Gracie and Carter did what was right and raised that baby."

"Mrs. Dillon, why didn't Carter ever get married?"

"For heaven's sake, that's a strange question to be asking me, young man. Carter would never share this kind of information with me. I do know he was engaged once and got hurt very badly. As shy as he is, I just think he was afraid to put himself in another situation where he could get hurt again. And, after Jocelyn came along, he had a family." Mrs. Dillon picked up her pocketbook and started to stand up. "I don't know anything else. It's time for me to go."

"Are there any other questions for Mrs. Dillon?" Elena waited a few seconds before she turned to the elderly woman and thanked her for her time.

When Mrs. Dillon was gone, Elena laughed out loud. "I guess she told us a thing or two."

"Yeah, she told us Carter is shy and his mother is a saint. That ought to help you win this case." Tom gave her his knowing, sarcastic smile.

Elena hated when the opposition acted like they had won the case before they even got to court. She watched him go down the hall, whistling as he went, and wanted to throw her notebook at his swaggering back.

Chapter Thirty-three

Depositions, Day Two

Today Elena was calling Ruby Bennett, Janell Harvey, Gloria Thompson, and Lawrence Fitz for depositions. The state attorneys, court reporter, and her assistant were all in place when she entered the conference room. "Good morning, everyone. Tom, thank you for being present. Susan, call in Mrs. Bennett, please,"

"Good Morning, Mrs. Bennett. Thank you for coming in so early today. May I get you something to drink?"

"No, ma'am, I had my coffee before my daughter brought me downtown. Thank you anyway." Miss Ruby was almost defiant when she entered the conference room. "You know it was kinda' hard for me to get here today. But, I jus' had to try and hep Mr. Carter."

Elena expressed her thanks to Miss Ruby, introduced the people in the room, and asked her the opening questions.

"My name is Ruby Bennett, and I live with my daughter in North Miami, 615 NE 54th Street. I'm retired, but for 40 years I worked for Mrs. Edward Latimer as her house keeper."

"How do you know Carter McDeal?"

"Mr. Carter drove my bus."

"What can you tell us about him?"

"He treated me fine. I always thanked him for takin' good care of me." She was already tired of these questions and her attention was beginning to wander.

"What do you mean, Mrs. Bennett?"

"Years ago when I got on the bus, Mr. Carter tried to drive slow to give me time to walk to the back of the bus. You know, back then I had to sit at the back of the bus, and he didn't want me to fall. Even when I got to sit wherever I wanted to, he always watched out for me."

The deposition went on with Miss Ruby not adding anything that would benefit Carter's case. All Elena knew for sure was the passengers on Route Six thought highly of the man who drove their bus.

"Thank you, Mrs. Bennett, I know it wasn't easy for you to come downtown today. I appreciate the effort you made to be here."

Miss Ruby rose slowly from the chair and walked to the door. Before she opened it she looked back at Elena and smiled, "Good luck, Miss Martinez. I knows you is gonna do right by Mr. Carter."

"Thank you. I'm certainly going to try my best," Elena responded. As soon as Miss Ruby closed the door behind her, Elena directed Susan to call Janell Harvey into the conference room.

***

"I'm Janell Harvey and I live next door to the McDeal's. They've been my neighbors for almost forty years. I watched Carter and Jocelyn grow up. And, I tell you, they are fine neighbors."

"That's nice for you, isn't it, Mrs. Harvey? Now what can you tell me about the relationship between Carter and Jocelyn?"

"As far as I could see, they had a good relationship. Now, you know, they kept their curtains closed in the evening, so I can't tell you too much about what went on after they closed the curtains, but I can tell you that during the day time, they were a normal family. They laughed a lot, too. I could always hear them laughing."

"Mrs. Harvey, are you telling me you looked in their windows?"

"Of course, dear. How else would I know what was going on over there? Gracie used to talk to me over the fence, but she never shared anything personal. But I looked and listened a lot. Most days I could tell you what they had for breakfast, lunch and dinner."

"That's interesting, Mrs. Harvey. Perhaps you know how Jocelyn came to live with the McDeals."

"That child was Gracie's great niece. Her poor mother died and there was no one in the world to look after her except Gracie and Carter."

"How do you know that, Mrs. Harvey?"

"Well, as I remember it, Gracie told me. I had started to wonder what was going on over there because for several weeks they never opened the curtains, even in the day time. And, I could have sworn I heard a baby crying. I was just about to go over and ask Gracie what was going on when she brought the baby to the fence and told me about her."

"Do you remember how long you heard the crying?"

"I think it was for several weeks. I hadn't seen Gracie anywhere, the curtains were drawn all the time, and the only person I saw coming and going was Carter. But, that crying puzzled me. I heard that baby long before Gracie told me about her."

"Did you think it was strange that Gracie waited to tell you about the baby, Mrs. Harvey?"

"Now that you mention it, Miss Martinez, I guess it was strange that she didn't tell me right away. And, you know what else is strange, she never told me she was leaving town to go get the baby."

"Do you remember anything else?"

"Let me think for a minute." Mrs. Harvey looked like she was deep in thought, then she nodded her head, "No, I can't think of anything else."

"Tom, do you have any questions?" She was hoping this deposition would end soon. There were too many false conclusions that could be drawn from what Mrs. Harvey was saying.

Tom smirked at Elena as if he thought she was digging herself into a deep hole. "No questions at this time."

"My name is Gloria Thompson and I live at 3434 NW 14th Avenue, Miami, and I'm a housewife. I met the McDeal family when my daughter entered first grade and became friends with Jocelyn. I got to know both Gracie and Carter McDeal through the girls' activities, and events at the church."

"What kind of interactions have you had with Carter McDeal?"

"Most of my interaction was with Gracie, but Carter was always there for any school or church event that involved the girls. My daughter loves all the McDeal's, and we all miss Gracie terribly."

"Did your daughter spend much time in the McDeal's home?"

"Those girls spend as much time together as possible. If Jocelyn wasn't at my house, Ruthie was at hers. They had sleepovers at least once a month until Ruthie left for college."

"Did you ever feel uncomfortable about your daughter being around Carter?"

"Absolutely not! And, I'll tell you truthfully, I don't feel uncomfortable even today." She was shocked that Carter's own attorney thought he might be some kind of pervert. "All you have to do is look at Jocelyn to see what kind of household she was raised in. That girl is well adjusted and I trust her father around all of my children."

"Thank you, Mrs. Thompson. Tom, do you have any questions?"

"Yes. Mrs. Thompson, did Jocelyn McDeal ever talk to you about her parents? Did she ever discuss her mother?" Tom asked.

"I always thought it was a bit strange, but Jocelyn never talked to me about her family at all. One time I asked Gracie about Jocelyn's mother, and all she told me was she died in childbirth."

"Mrs. Thompson, were you under the impression that Carter was Jocelyn's father?"

"Yes, I was, Mr. Gorman. I assumed it was Carter's wife who died."

"So, you were never told that Mrs. McDeal's great niece was supposedly Jocelyn's mother?"

"No, sir, I was not. But, I never questioned Gracie again."

"I don't have any additional questions, thank you."

Elena thanked Mrs. Thompson for her time and asked the others in the room to return at 2:00. She walked down the hall with Susan, and hoped the afternoon deposition would produce even a small piece of evidence that would help her build a defense.

***

After lunch, Mr. Fitz was called into the conference room. He was elderly and even though he walked with a cane he held himself erect. He had made a calculated attempt to look distinguished and well educated, so he was dressed in his most expensive suit. After all, he had information that might turn this case around for Carter, and he wanted the attorneys to believe that he was credible.

"My name is Lawrence James Fitz. I live at 3200 Biscayne Boulevard in Miami. I received a bachelor's degree in political science from the University of Virginia and a master's degree in criminal justice from George Washington. My former employer is the Federal Bureau of Investigation." He watched as the people in the room digested this information and sat up straighter in their chairs. This was going to be the most fun he'd had in years.

"What did you do in the FBI, Mr. Fitz?"

"For twenty years I was a special investigator. Then, for twelve years, I worked in the Bureau as an assistant chief-on-assignment to the White House. I'm sorry, but that is all I can tell you about my assignments, Miss Martinez."

"After you retired, you moved to Miami and it's my understanding that you rode the bus to town every week day. Is that correct?"

"Yes, Miss Martinez, that is correct. However, if you need further information about my comings and goings, I'm sure you can obtain an order from the judge." She looked at him with a hint of a smile and he knew she was now looking at him as a witness who might be able to pull the jury to her side of the case.

"I don't think that will be necessary, Mr. Fitz. My main interest is your relationship to my client, Carter McDeal. Can you provide me with some information about that relationship?"

"Our relationship was not of a personal nature, Miss Martinez. From my observations, Mr. McDeal is an excellent bus driver and a genuine human being. That is about the extent of my knowledge regarding the man. However, I have studied all the facts of this case that were available to me, and, in my opinion, to prove his innocence, you need to find the girl's mother. Carter McDeal did not kidnap that child."

"Why are you so sure of that, Mr. Fitz?"

"I am an observer of human behavior. For years that was part of my job, and I am well-trained. I think you will find, at some point, that Jocelyn's mother carefully selected Mr. McDeal and his mother to raise a child she knew she could not care for herself." He tapped his cane on the floor for emphasis.

"Are you basing that on general or specific knowledge, Mr. Fitz? Do you know the identity of Jocelyn's mother?"

"When I heard charges had been brought against, Mr. McDeal, I began to look back through my journals to see if I had recorded anything around the time that Jocelyn was born that might give me a clue to what happened." He had their attention now, even the defense attorney had leaned forward in his chair.

"And did you find anything?"

"I think I found something of interest. There was a young girl who rode the bus every day for several years. She was always on the bus when it got to my stop, so I have no idea where she lived. My interest in her was piqued because she seemed inordinately observant of everything Mr. McDeal said and did. At first I thought she might have a teenager's crush on Mr. McDeal. During the last few months that she rode the bus, I presumed she was pregnant, although she went to great lengths to conceal her condition."

"What made you think she was pregnant?"

"She started wearing a loose fitting jacket, even on days that were extremely warm. It's unusual to see people wearing jackets in Miami in April and May."

"You have this written in a journal?" Elena sounded skeptical.

"Yes, I became a good investigator as a result of keeping journals. I found that writing down my daily observations honed my skills and I continued this after I retired. I made it a practice to never sit down on the bus. By standing and holding on the strap, I could see from the front of the bus to the back. You might say that over the years, I transformed my career into a hobby that keeps my brain active to this day."

"Thank you for sharing that, Mr. Fitz. Your hobby may have given us some very vital information to use in this case."

"I thought that might be true. So I have the journal here in my briefcase. Of course I will need to have it returned once it no longer serves a purpose to this case." He leaned over and unsnapped the clasp on his briefcase. Early in his career, he had observed that good agents knew how to throw off the opposing attorney, and he was calling on those intimidating skills now. He was going for a dramatic effect today, but he was sincere in wanting to help his long-time acquaintance. Slowly he pulled the worn, leather journal from the briefcase and placed it on the table. "Miss Martinez, you do not need to subpoena this journal."

"Mr. Fitz, do you mind if I ask what you plan to do with the journal in conjunction to this case?" Was Miss Martinez afraid he might want to use the journal in a way that would jeopardize her case? If he sold any part of it to the media, it might create some unwanted publicity and questions.

"I have no interest in selling my journal, if that's what you are implying. But I do plan to write a memoir, my dear. I think I have an interesting story to tell."

When Mr. Fitz left the room, Elena held the journal tightly. She looked at Tom Gorman and smiled. "This is getting better, don't you think?"

"Do you really think that journal will be enough to sway the jury? Or do you plan to have Mr. Fitz stand up in court and read it to the jury in his best Shakespearean manner?"

Elena laughed at the defense attorney's attempt to mock her witness. She guessed that for the first time since her depositions began, her opponent saw something that worried him. "We'll see, won't we? You keep giving me such good ideas."

Chapter Thirty-four

Depositions, Day Three

Tom Gorman was anxious to call Detective Madison for his deposition. The man's testimony was going to be pivotal to his case and this deposition might come with a few surprises. The case against Carter McDeal was weak and he needed some new momentum if he was going to convince the jury McDeal was guilty. Elena Martinez and her assistant were seated in the conference room when he walked in. They exchanged pleasantries and talked about the agenda for the day. Madison's deposition was first, and then he was calling Mary Ann Moss. "If everyone is ready, I'll ask the detective to come in."

Todd Madison was introduced to the people in the room and the attorney asked him the first set of questions.

"My name is Michael Todd Madison. I live at 250 Palm Court, Hialeah, Florida. I am a detective for the Miami-Dade County Department of Law Enforcement."

"How are you involved in the case against Carter McDeal?" Questioned the state attorney.

"I first met Mr. McDeal when HRS asked me to attend a meeting with him. The meeting was to gather information regarding the birth of Jocelyn McDeal. A discrepancy had been uncovered in the story being told about her birth and how she came to live with Mr. McDeal and his mother."

"What was the discrepancy?"

"There were no records of her birth. The girl does not have a birth certificate and the Bureau of Vital Statistics has no record of her birth."

"How did Mr. McDeal explain this discrepancy?"

"He said the girl was his mother's great niece. Apparently, his mother's sister died years before, and when the sister's unwed daughter, Mrs. McDeal's niece, died in childbirth, there was no one to care for the child."

"Did that story conflict with the facts of the case as you know them?"

"Yes, my investigation showed Gracie McDeal, Carter's mother, did not have a sister."

"Did you ask Mrs. McDeal to explain?"

"No, that was impossible. Mrs. McDeal passed away last November."

"Did you uncover any other evidence that led to Mr. McDeal's arrest?"

"Yes, I did. When I began looking through the missing children reports for 1956, I found a case reported in June of that year where a baby girl was abducted from a Miami hospital. The case has never been solved."

"Can you tell me the circumstances of the 1956 abduction?"

"It occurred in the nursery at Hialeah Hospital around the time of the 11:00 PM shift change on June 16th. The report states two nurses saw a man lingering in the hallway outside the nursery prior to the shift change. One nurse remembered asking the man to leave because visiting hours were over. Both nurses described the man as white between the ages of 25 and 35. He was approximately 6 feet tall, weighted around 170-180, with dark brown hair. He was wearing some type of uniform."

"Were there any suspects at the time of the kidnapping?"

"No, Mr. Gorman. There were no suspects."

Elena Martinez looked at her notebook and hoped no one detected the disappointment she was feeling at this moment. Detective Madison had just described Carter McDeal.

"Any questions, Miss Martinez?"

"None at this time." Elena watched the detective gather his papers and leave the room. The case against Carter was beginning to tighten.

After a short break, Mary Ann Moss was called in for her deposition.

"My name is Mary Ann Moss. I live at 4770 NE 5th Avenue, Miami, Florida. I teach 12th grade English Literature at Notre Dame Academy. The school has been my employer for sixteen years."

"What is your association with Carter and Jocelyn McDeal?"

"I met Jocelyn and her grandmother, Gracie, seven years ago when Jocelyn volunteered to help at the Little Theater. This year she is one of my students. I became acquainted with Mr. McDeal recently when I began assisting Jocelyn with college and scholarship applications."

"What has your interaction been with Mr. McDeal?"

"I've had very little interaction with him. The applications required verification of Jocelyn's birth and over the period of six weeks, Mr. McDeal was unable to produce the documents. I thought his behavior was odd so I advised Jocelyn to request a duplicate copy of her birth certificate from the Bureau of Vital Statistics."

"What happened when she requested a copy of her birth certificate?"

"She received a letter from the Bureau stating no information was available on her birth. That's when I became very suspicious and asked the school principal, Father Sean, to get involved."

"Did Father Sean share your suspicions?"

"No, he did not! He thought I was over reacting. He has known the McDeal family for many years and assured me Mr. McDeal could clear up the issue. At my insistence, he reluctantly agreed to schedule a meeting with Mr. McDeal."

"What happened at this meeting? Who was in attendance?"

"Father Sean and I met with Mr. McDeal. There was a discussion about Mr. McDeal's mother and how she went to Baltimore to get Jocelyn when she was a few weeks old. Father Sean seemed satisfied with Mr. McDeal's answers, but his story just didn't ring true to me. So I called a social worker I knew and asked her to initiate an HRS investigation."

"And, did HRS think you provided them with a valid cause to initiate an investigation?"

"Yes, they did, and they made a visit to the McDeal house. Perhaps the case would have stopped here, but further questions from me convinced them to call a meeting that included an HRS supervisor, the two social workers who made the home visit, a detective from the police department, Mr. McDeal, and me. The meeting did not go well and resulted in the arrest of Mr. McDeal."

"Will you explain what you mean when you say the meeting did not go well?"

"Mr. McDeal was flustered by all the questions and several different times his answers made no sense at all. He finally confessed Jocelyn was a gift for his mother. That was the truth of the matter. He took the child and gave her to his mother."

"Miss Moss, do you have any proof of that?"

"Why no, but the man admitted that Jocelyn was a gift. What else could he possibly mean?"

"How did you come to be Jocelyn McDeal's guardian?"

"When I first suspected there might be some criminal activity, I petitioned HRS for guardianship."

"Thank you, Miss Moss. I have no further questions. Miss Martinez, do you have questions for Miss Moss?"

"Yes, Mr. Gorman, I do. Miss Moss, you said Jocelyn is one of your students? Correct?"

"Yes, she is. She is one of my brightest students, and she is such a lovely girl."

"But, you have no personal relationship to her. Why would you ask to be her guardian?"

Mary Ann looked as if she had been asked a stupid question. "Really, Miss Martinez, isn't it evident she needs me to protect her. Poor thing, she doesn't have anyone else."

"I have no further questions." Elena felt the icy stare and wondered why the woman was trying to intimidate her. For some reason, Miss Moss was assuming a proprietary responsibility for Jocelyn McDeal, and Elena wondered why.

Chapter Thirty-five

Jocelyn 1975

Father Sean persuaded Jocelyn to voluntarily undergo the psychological evaluation rather than be mandated to do so by a court order. "Jocelyn, my dear, there is nothing to be afraid of. This evaluation will probably only entail answering questions about your feelings for your grandmother and your father before you knew about the circumstances of your birth, how you feel now, and how you were treated at home, Basically, I think they want to show your childhood was happy and normal."

"I'm not afraid of those kinds of questions. But, it scares me I won't have answers to questions about who I am."

"Jocelyn, we've talked about this. You are who you are, no matter what. I know you would like to know more about your biological parents but I don't think that will make a difference in who you are. It will just be an answer to a question. Once you know a name, will it change you?"

"No, Father. I'm just trying to figure out why I feel so resistant to having a psychological evaluation. I'll agree to it without the court order, but I won't like it."

"Good for you. If you need to talk after it's over, you can call me at any time.

***

Sitting across from Dr. Alston, Jocelyn tried to ignore the butterflies in her stomach. All she wanted to do was get this over with and get out of his office.

"Jocelyn, tell me a little about college life and the classes you're taking?"

"I just started second semester of my freshman year, and I'm looking at a double major in English and Theater Arts. I'm on scholarship which is the only way I'm able to be there. I love being at Barry. It's a great school."

"Have you made a lot of friends there?

"Not that many but I do have a few close friends. It's hard to get to know a lot of people when I'm a commuter. If I lived on campus, it might be different."

"Jocelyn, talk to me about your grandmother. What was she like?"

"My grandmother was great. I really miss her."

"What did you like about her?"

"Everything. I thought she was beautiful. She was smart and I can't tell you how much she taught me. When she was alive, we talked about everything. She was funny and loving. She took good care of me."

"Did she ever mistreat you? How were you punished if you misbehaved?"

"Dr. Alston, I was never mistreated by anyone. My grandmother and dad never even spanked me. If I acted out, I was sent to my room."

"How long did you have to stay in your room?"

"It usually only took a few minutes for me to decide I could behave or say I'm sorry. I didn't spend too much time in my room."

"What did your grandmother tell you about your birth?"

"She told me my mother died when I was born. I didn't ask questions and she didn't offer any other information. Maybe I should have been more curious but I wasn't."

"Did you believe Carter was your father?"

"Of course."

"And you thought your mother was his wife?"

"I guess so. I don't remember ever thinking about it. Does that make me strange?"

"I don't think so, Jocelyn. It tells me you felt safe with your family. Now, tell me about your relationship with your father? Did he ever treat you inappropriately?"

"If you're expecting some kind of creepy answer, you're wrong. My dad never mistreated me in any way. I will tell you I wasn't as close to him as I was my grandmother. My dad doesn't talk much but I never doubted he loved me."

"It sounds like you grew up as part of a very loving family. But how did you feel once you found out they hadn't been truthful with you?"

"I was angry and I'm still angry. I was hurt and I can't figure out why they didn't just tell me. What difference would it have made?"

"How did this change your relationship with your dad?"

"One day I hate him and the next, I miss him so much. I wish he could sit down with me and tell me the truth."

"You don't feel like he has told you the truth?"

"No, I don't. There has to be more to the story, and I just hope someday I hear it." Jocelyn pulled on a strand of her hair and began twirling it around her finger.

"This may be a hard question for you to answer, Jocelyn, but do you think your father kidnapped you?"

"I don't know how I came to be a McDeal. But I do know my dad wouldn't have hurt someone so I could be in the family. He would never have taken me from my mother. Never."

"But he hurt you by not telling you the truth, Jocelyn? Doesn't that show you he could have hurt your mother?"

"No, it doesn't. And, if you knew my dad you would understand why I think the way I do. I believe with all my heart my dad did not kidnap me," Jocelyn replied in frustration. "Are we about finished?"

"Just a few more questions. Do you ever see yourself moving back to the house where you grew up?"

"I don't think that will ever happen. I want a place of my own and I'm working so I can move out of Miss Moss's apartment. I think by summer I'll have enough money, especially if I have a roommate." She wondered if this was some kind of trick question. "My reason for not moving back home is about me. It has nothing to do with my dad. I'm ready to be on my own if I can find the money to do it."

"Okay, I understand. Suppose your dad is found guilty. How will that impact you?"

"Dr. Alston, that isn't going to happen. My dad is innocent."

"If your father is found innocent do you see a reconciliation happening?"

"Maybe someday. Only time will tell."

***

"It was the creepiest day of my life, Mark," Jocelyn held the phone close to her mouth so her conversation couldn't be heard by Miss Moss. "The questions Dr. Alston asked me made me angry. It was like he wanted me to say my dad was guilty."

"You don't believe he's guilty, do you?"

"He's guilty of lying to me but there's no way he kidnapped me. If I could just understand why he and Nana didn't tell me the truth when I was little, it would make a big difference. But, the court won't even let me talk to him. It's all so frustrating. Promise me you'll never lie to me, okay?"

"It's crazy, but my mom says she knows your dad. She grew up in your old neighborhood, and remembers your dad from the bus. After my dad got out of the Coast Guard, we moved where we live now. She hasn't seen him in years."

"Does your mom think he's guilty?"

"She says he would never do anything like that. Oh, yeah, before I forget, she wants you to go to lunch with her on Saturday.

My dad and I are going fishing, so she wants some company. Do you think the wicked witch will let you out of her sight for a couple of hours? Mom said she could come and get you."

"That sounds like fun. What time, did she say?

"I think she said noon, but I'll let you know." There was a pause before Mark said, "I hate to, but I've got to study. I'll talk to you tomorrow, and Jocey, try not to let what the doctor said get to you."

Jocelyn couldn't remember when Mark started calling her Jocey, but she liked it. It was one of those intimate little things between them and every time he called her Jocey, she felt safe.

She walked in the kitchen where Miss Moss was making a cup of tea. It was a nice kitchen; one like she hoped to have someday. The wall color was yellow and the curtain on the window over the sink had daisies that matched the wall color perfectly. Jocelyn knew if this was her kitchen, she could make it a happy place.

Miss Moss turned when she walked in, "I'm making chamomile tea. Would you like a cup?"

"Yes, please. Somehow, chamomile helps me sleep. Mark just called and his mother is picking me up at noon on Saturday for lunch. I'll ask her to drop me off at the library before 3:00, so I won't be late for work."

"Jocelyn, don't you think you are too young to be taking this relationship so seriously? You need to be concentrating on your studies instead of running all over creation with this boy and his mother."

"It's just lunch, Miss Moss. I don't think it means I'm getting married any time soon. I really wish you wouldn't worry so much about me," Jocelyn sighed. Sometimes living here wore her out. "If you don't mind, I think I'll take the tea to my room. I've got a lot of reading to do for American Lit before next Monday."

"Before you go, how did the evaluation go? What kind of questions did the doctor ask you?"

Jocelyn got up from the kitchen table and started for the door. She turned back to Miss Moss, "He just wanted to know how I feel about my grandmother and my dad. And, I assured him, that even though they didn't tell me the truth, I love them."

Before Miss Moss could respond or ask her any more questions, she hurried down the hall to her room and closed the door behind her.

Sitting on the end of the bed, Jocelyn wondered why Miss Moss annoyed her so much. She was grateful for all the woman was doing to help her but she didn't like being around her and she definitely didn't like all her rules.

Nothing about today felt good. Dr. Alston made her feel so vulnerable and exposed. She didn't like talking to anybody about her dad, and she especially didn't like talking to someone who was analyzing every word she said.

After reading the same sentence three times, she closed the book and turned on her radio. She changed into her pajamas, propped the pillows against the headboard, and curled up with her cup of tea. It didn't take long for the soft music and the tea to have a calming effect on her. She stopped thinking about all the disappointments of the last ten months; no, it was longer than that, she thought. It all started falling apart the day her grandmother died, sixteen months ago.

She placed the empty cup on the nightstand just as the sultry voice of her favorite singer, Margo, came on the radio and drifted over the room.

"He strummed his guitar just for me,

A song of sunshine and rain.

He sang the words softly

He tried to ease my pain.

Why did you go? Why did you take your song away?

I love you so, I love you so. I wanted you to stay.

His song drifted through the night

I could not hide my heart.

I knew that in the morning light

We would have to part.

Why did you go? Why did you take your song away?

I love you so, I love you so. I wanted you to stay.

All her thoughts turned to Mark, and she allowed herself to get lost in the music.

Chapter Thirty-six

Jocelyn

She was waiting outside when Mrs. Sanders pulled up in front of the apartment because she wasn't in the mood to deal with an interrogation by Miss Moss. It just seemed better for everyone if Mrs. Sanders didn't have to get out of her car and come to the door. Mrs. Sanders was a pretty woman and every time Jocelyn saw her, she was smartly dressed, her hair was perfect, and her fingernails looked like she just finished a manicure. She could see where Mark got his good looks and his nice manners.

"Let's go to the Grove for lunch today, Jocelyn. I know a great café, and today's weather is perfect for sitting outdoors. I like your hair; did you do something different?"

"Thanks, I had it trimmed yesterday. It's shorter than I wanted it, but I'm getting used to it. Lunch in Coconut Grove sounds great. I've never been there to eat before."

They sat at a table in the shade that gave them a good view of the bay and still let them see all the activity going on around them. People were strolling up and down the street, going in and out of the stores, or just gazing in the windows. Jocelyn loved the quaint shops and found herself enjoying the movement all around her. She was glad Mrs. Sanders made this choice.

For an hour they lingered over their lunch and talked about school, Mark, politics, Mark, and any other subject that came to mind. Jocelyn really liked this woman. She was charming and funny. It surprised her to find out Mrs. Sanders had been a nurse. "Oh, I did that for a number of years, but I retired when my husband got out of the Coast Guard. Mark was four-years old when that happened. His dad got a great job that allowed me to stay home.

How about you, Jocelyn, are you planning on a career or do you want to stay at home and raise a family?"

"I'd like to find a way to do both, Mrs. Sanders. I want to teach English, and do something in theater. I haven't got it all figured out but that's where my interests are."

"Goodness, Jocelyn, you sound like my sister. She has a career and kids, and she says she is managing both of them. More power to her and to you, but I don't think I could have done both. Okay, now to what I really want to know." She smiled and Jocelyn thought she could see a twinkle in her eyes. "Tell me why you like my son."

Jocelyn sighed and wondered if she could express Mark in words. "He's great. You raised him right, Mrs. Sanders. He's kind and thoughtful. I can talk to him about anything. And, he is so good looking."

"We seem to like him for the same reasons," she laughed. "He is good looking, isn't he? Do you think your relationship is serious? Oh, never mind, I don't want to push my luck. But let me ask you, has he talked with you about his health?"

Jocelyn put down her fork and thought a minute before she asked, "What do you mean?"

"Uh, oh, I'm in trouble now. Mark should have told you this himself. He has Type I Diabetes, Jocelyn, and you should know how to help him if he ever gets in trouble. I'm going to tell him I told you but I want you to ask him about it the next time you all talk."

"Mrs. Sanders, is this illness serious?"

"It could be, Jocelyn. Mark does a great job managing it, but as close as you are becoming, and as much time as you spend together, he should have told you."

"Wow, you can be sure I'll ask him tonight when he picks me up." She looked at her watch and was surprised so much time had gone by. "I hate to end this wonderful afternoon, Mrs. Sanders, but I have to be at the library by 3:00. I'd appreciate you dropping me off there."

"I can see why Mark thinks you're special. I've had a wonderful time talking with you. I'll ask for the check and we can be on our way." As she was paying the check, her eyes caught a glimpse of a couple who were being seated at a table on the other side of the patio. "Jocelyn, it's been a very long time since I've seen your dad, but I think he just sat down at one of the tables on the other side of the patio. Mark told me you weren't allowed to have contact with him, so this might be a little awkward."

"You must be mistaken. My dad wouldn't be in the Grove," Jocelyn said as she turned to look across the patio. She froze for a second and couldn't believe what she saw. "Oh my god, who is that woman?" She couldn't take her eyes off her father and the woman who sat next to him. She watched as the woman reached over and took his hand, then kissed him on the cheek.

"Mrs. Sanders, I've got to get out of here," panic rose in Jocelyn's voice as she stood up. "Please, we've got to go."

Taking hold of Jocelyn's arm, she steered the girl toward the patio exit. She tried to put her body between Jocelyn and her father in the hope he wouldn't see her but just as they reached the exit he stood up and called out, "Jocelyn! Rosanna! Wait!"

Jocelyn started to hurry, with Mrs. Sanders trying to hold on to her to keep her from stumbling. By the time they reached the car, Jocelyn was sobbing uncontrollably. Mrs. Sanders opened the car door and told Jocelyn to sit down. "I am so sorry, Jocelyn. I never thought something like this would happen. Oh, dear, please try to stop crying," Mrs. Sanders pleaded as she reached into the backseat and handed Jocelyn a box of tissues. "What can I do to help? I'm going to run into the store on the corner and get you something to drink. Try to take a couple of deep breaths. I'll be right back."

Doubled over in the seat of the car, Jocelyn hugged her knees. Her body began to rock back and forth and she wondered if the pain in her stomach was real, or imagined. Why was she reacting this way? Was it because she missed her dad or did it have something to do with seeing him with that woman? It was almost a year since she last saw him and she was surprised at how different he looked. He was supposed to be sitting at home feeling sad and afraid and here he was having lunch with an attractive woman. "He looks better than I've ever seen him; he looks happy." It was all too confusing. In a few minutes the car door opened and Mrs. Sanders placed a damp paper towel on the back of her neck. She brushed the hair away from her face and crooned. "There, there, Jocelyn, it's going to be all right. It's going to be all right."

Her anxiety began to ease as Mrs. Sanders continued to speak and touch her in motherly ways. Was this what it felt like to have a mother, she wondered? Lifting her head, she looked into the sympathetic face of Mark's mother, and wished for a minute she was looking into the face of her own mother. Even though her face was wet from tears, her mouth was so dry it almost hurt. It took several large swallows of water before she could speak. Then she looked over at Mrs. Sanders and said with pain in her voice, "It certainly doesn't look like my dad is sitting home heartbroken that I'm not there. And, who in the world is Rosanna?"

Chapter Thirty-seven

Carter

"I'm telling you, I saw my daughter with Rosanna. They were together at a restaurant in the Grove." Carter called Elena first thing on Monday morning. "They were in the Grove on Saturday."

"Slow down, Carter, are you sure it was Rosanna? You haven't seen her in 18 years. She has to have changed since then. Wait. This is too important to discuss over the phone, can you come to the office this afternoon after you get off work?"

"This can't wait until this afternoon. We've already lost two days we could have used to find her. I'm telling you I saw her and she was with my daughter."

"Carter, my schedule is solid this morning. I can't see you until later today. As soon as you get off work, come to my office. Try and get some work done today, and I'll do the same. See you around 5:00."

After Elena hung up the phone, Carter felt the anxiety return. He was certain he had seen Rosanna with his daughter. Then he thought of the irony. What he had really seen was Rosanna with her daughter. On Saturday, he was beside himself when he looked up and saw the two of them. He wanted to run down the street after them but luckily, Sharon grabbed his arm and reminded him he could go to jail if he took one step closer to his daughter. He tried to shake off her hand as he hastily explained he had just seen Jocelyn's mother. But, Sharon was stronger than she looked and she held on until he got a hold of himself. She was right; of course, he didn't want to go to jail.

All weekend he fretted, he paced, and he worried. How did Jocelyn and Rosanna get together? What had Rosanna told her? Was it really Rosanna? He knew the woman looked a lot like Rosanna, but he hadn't seen her in such a long time. Maybe he was wrong; maybe he simply wanted the woman to be Rosanna. At one point on Sunday afternoon, he even asked Sharon if she thought he was crazy. Sharon assured him he wasn't crazy but she continued to ask him why he thought the woman might be Jocelyn's mother.

"Carter, one sure way of finding out is to get some professional help."

"What are you talking about?"

"We could hire a private investigator."

"I don't have the money to do that!"

"But I do and I know just the right person."

"No, Sharon, I can't let you do that. We'll have to find another way."

Today was going by slowly and every time Carter looked at his watch, only a few more minutes had passed. At one point, after lunch, Sully came over to his desk and glared at him. "What's with you today, McDeal? You're as jumpy as a jack rabbit. You got work to do, so you better settle down. There ain't nothing in your contract that says I can't fire you if you're not doing your work."

As soon as his shift ended, he headed downtown. He knew he was going to be early but he didn't care. If he got there early, maybe Elena could see him sooner than 5:00.

He had been sitting in the waiting room for a few minutes when Elena's secretary, Susan, ask him to go back to her office. When he walked into the office, he was surprised to see she wasn't alone.

"Carter, this is John Avery, one of the investigators on our staff. I asked him to sit in with us this afternoon." Carter walked over and shook hands with the man, then took the empty seat in front of Elena's desk. He would have to tell Sharon she was right about an investigator.

"After you called this morning, I called John and asked him to make some inquiries. We decided to call Father Sean first to see if he had any idea who Jocelyn had lunch with on Saturday. He said he didn't, but he would walk down to Miss Moss's classroom and see if he could discretely ask her where Jocelyn was over the weekend. He called John back about an hour ago with some information." She looked over at John and motioned for him to tell Carter what he had discovered.

"Mr. McDeal, your daughter had lunch on Saturday with her boyfriend's mother. The woman's name is Nancy Sanders. I'm sorry I don't have better news for you but she's not the Rosanna we've been looking for."

"Jocelyn has a boyfriend?"

"Yeah, his name is Mark Sanders. Apparently they met years ago at the little theater, but didn't start dating until she got to Barry. He's a sophomore, majoring in business. But, don't worry, he checks out. I did some research and, from everything I can gather, he's a good kid. Plays in a rock band, but I couldn't uncover any evidence of drugs; not even any alcohol. He makes good grades, lives at home with his parents, and still volunteers at the little theater," said John. "Wish I had more to tell you."

***

"I'm sorry I sent you all on a wild goose chase. I was almost certain the woman was Rosanna." Carter felt his shoulders sag with disappointment and embarrassment. And, now he had to deal with the anxiety of knowing Jocelyn had a boyfriend whose mother looked like Rosanna.

'Thanks, John. I appreciate you jumping on this so quickly. May I see you in the hall for one second? Carter, I'll be back in just a minute."

When they stepped into the hall, Elena looked at John, "What's your take on this? Is he playing with our heads?"

"He seems genuine, but we've been fooled by some of the best. I'll keep on this and see if I can find out something about Nancy Sanders. You never know what might turn up."

"I need all the help I can get on this one, John. We go to trial in a month, and so far, I'm grabbing at straws. Let me know if anything turns up, big or small. It may be the puzzle piece I need to put this case together."

She went back in the office and sat down in the chair next to Carter. "I know how much you wanted this to be real. But, John will keep looking."

"I was so sure." Carter didn't like doubting himself and he sat with his thoughts for a few minutes before he said, "Miss Martinez, everything I told you about Rosanna is true. My mother made up the story about Jocelyn's mother being her niece; I didn't make up the story of Rosanna. You've got to believe me."

"Well, the important thing is to make the jury believe you. Depositions have been going on this week and I've made appointments with everyone on your list. Here's hoping some of the information I've gotten will help turn this case around. By the way, is your evaluation this week?"

"Right, I see Dr. Alston on Wednesday," said Carter quietly. He was dreading having to speak about his private life with a stranger, but willing to do it if it would help his case.

"Good. Jocelyn met with him last week, and I should have his report in a few days."

Looking at her client, Elena let the frown on her face soften. "Carter, I am really working on your behalf. I know things look like they're standing still, but we are moving forward. We'll be ready to go by our court date. Just hold on and you'll get through it."

Carter wished he could believe her.

When Elena met Eric for dinner, she told him how discouraged she was about the McDeal case.

"I don't have anything that's going to help my client. Tom Gorman is going to find a way to use it all against us. If only I could find that mystery woman."

"What are you doing to find her?"

"I've got my investigator trying to locate her. But so far he's come up with a zero. Funny thing though, Carter thought he saw her last weekend. Turned out it wasn't but he was convinced the woman looked like Jocelyn's mother."

"Have you run a check to see if the woman could have a twin?"

"You're a genius! Why didn't I think of that?"

The next morning when Elena arrived at the office, she called her investigator. "John, I need you to run a check on Nancy Sanders. The main thing I want you to find out is whether she has a twin, or maybe a sister. And, make this one a priority. This could just be the info I need."

"Jackpot, Elena!" John Avery was almost shouting when he walked into her office. "The lady has a younger sister, and the sister's name just happens to be Rosanna! Now we've got to see if Mrs. Sanders will help us find her."

Elena sat very still and let the information soak in. Walking over to the window, she looked out toward the changing skyline of the city. Everywhere she looked there was new construction. High rise office and condo buildings were under construction all along the bay front and she watched as the cranes lifted materials to ridiculous heights. She marveled at the changing face of the city she loved. For every new building something had been torn down to make room for it.

As she thought about what John just told her, she hoped what was about to be torn down in Carter and Jocelyn's lives could be rebuilt. The ramifications of John's news might change the whole dynamic of Carter's defense and would definitely alter his daughter's life. "John, do you understand what this means for Jocelyn McDeal?" She turned away from the window and looked at the investigator, "I can't imagine a worse scenario. If Nancy Sanders and Rosanna are sisters, and Rosanna is Jocelyn's mother, then Jocelyn's boyfriend is her first cousin. Oh, dear god in heaven!"

Sitting back down, she thought of ways to deal with this new information. She knew once she informed Carter, she no longer had a legal responsibility in this matter. If Jocelyn and Mark's relationship developed and became serious, Florida was a state that allowed first cousin marriages. But, did she have an ethical or moral responsibility? I try to remain neutral in all my cases, and not get emotionally involved with my clients, but this is different. She wondered if Eric would agree with her.

"John, could you let me have Nancy Sanders' phone number? I've got to call and see if she will agree to meet with me. And, then I've got to talk to Carter."

Dialing the number, Elena listened to the ringing of the phone. Part of her didn't want the woman to answer the call. No matter the outcome, this discussion was going to shatter somebody's world.

"Hello, Mrs. Sanders, my name is Elena Martinez. I was hoping you had a minute to talk with me. I am the defense attorney for Carter McDeal."

"How can I help you, Miss Martinez?"

"I was hoping I could meet with you later this afternoon to discuss a matter of urgency."

"I don't know Carter McDeal. I don't think I can help you."

"Some information has been brought to my attention concerning your son and Jocelyn McDeal that I really need to discuss with you. Could you meet me at the Coffee Zone on Brickell Avenue, in say an hour?"

"You have information about my Mark? Is this some kind of a joke?"

"I assure you this is not a joke, and believe me, if I didn't think this was urgent, I wouldn't be calling you. So, please say you'll meet with me."

***

Elena pulled into the parking lot of the Coffee Zone just as Nancy Sanders stepped from her car. John had given her a good description of the woman so she hurriedly walked toward her and called her name.

"Mrs. Sanders, I'm Elena Martinez. Thank you for meeting me. Let's find a table and order something to drink."

There were three other people seated on one side of the restaurant, so they chose a table on the side of the room that would give them the most privacy. After they ordered their coffee, Elena looked across the table and decided the only way to get through this conversation was to get it over with as soon as possible.

"I am the defense attorney for Carter McDeal and I know your son is dating Jocelyn McDeal. I have so many things to discuss with you that it's hard to know where to start. My first question for you will probably determine everything else. Mrs. Sanders, do you have a sister named Rosanna?"

"As you can imagine, Miss Martinez, I can't see the relevance of your question. What would my sister have to do with the case against this man?"

"Please, if you would answer the question, I think I can make it all relevant."

"Okay, yes, I do have a sister named Rosanna."

"Did your sister give birth to a child in 1956?"

"Why in the world would that make a difference to you or to this case?"

"Mrs. Sanders, I have reason to believe your sister is Jocelyn McDeal's mother."

A stony silence resonated across the table. When the woman finally spoke, her words were clipped and deliberate. "I don't know where you got this idea, but it's not possible. I can't help you." Nancy folded her napkin and placed it on the table. "Now if you'll excuse me, I still have dinner to prepare for my family."

Elena was stunned when Nancy Sanders stood up to leave. The tension between them was evident and her instincts told her the woman was lying. "Mrs. Sanders, there is more at stake here than whether Carter McDeal is convicted for kidnapping."

"Good-bye, Miss Martinez. It was nice meeting you and I wish you good luck with your case."

Chapter Thirty-eight

Rosanna

"I have a few questions for you and I need straight answers. I just had a meeting that has shaken me to the core."

"This must be important if you called me at work. What's going on, Nancy?" Rosanna was very busy, but she could tell by the tone of her sister's voice she needed to take this call and not brush her off.

"I can't remember the last time I was as upset as I am right now. I need the truth, Rosanna and I'm almost afraid to ask the question."

"What in the world are you talking about? Just ask me the question for heaven's sake. I'm in the middle of something and I need to get back to work." Rosanna was becoming impatient with her sister and really needed for this conversation to be over. "Nancy, really, I need to go."

"You need to tell me what happened in 1956. I want to know what you did with the baby!"

The question jolted Rosanna and she took a deep breath. Ever since her sister mentioned Jocelyn's name, she had been expecting this conversation but she still wasn't ready to talk about it. "Why is this coming up after all these years, Nancy? You know what I did!"

"Do I, Rosanna? Do I really know what happened to that child?" Nancy took a breath. "Just a few minutes ago, a woman implied that you are Jocelyn McDeal's mother! And, do you know what that means to my son? Are you listening to me, Rosanna?" Nancy's voice had reached a feverish pitch. The more she talked the more frantic she sounded.

"I can't talk right now. I'll call you later."

Rosanna hung up the phone. Her hands were shaking and the sharp pain of a headache crashed into her head. She had lost sleep ever since Christmas when her sister had first mentioned Jocelyn's name; now she felt trapped by a long ago choice.

Walking to her supervisor's office, Rosanna struggled to speak. "Gail, I've got to go home. I have a serious migraine starting and I need to get home before it really takes hold. I'll see you in the morning, okay?" Not waiting for a reply, she walked back to her desk, grabbed her purse, and left the building.

***

Once she was in her car, she realized she couldn't go home. Thinking about this at home would be impossible and she knew Nancy would be calling her back. Turning the car toward the coast, she kept driving. Her thoughts were jumbled and her body was screaming with tension. Thank goodness the afternoon rush hadn't started and she wasn't caught in a traffic jam. Within a half hour, she reached a small area where she could see the ocean and pulled her car into the parking lot. Turning off the motor, she rested her forehead against the steering wheel. But the extent of her turmoil was so great she knew she had to get out of the car and move around. Perhaps taking a walk would help clear her head. Pulling off her shoes, she locked the car and started walking down the beach.

A cool breeze touched her face and warm sand oozed between her toes. Seagulls squawked overhead and small waves lapped on the shore. Watching the clouds build on the horizon returned her to her senses and the tension in her body began to melt away.

Long ago, she stopped grieving for Jocelyn; stopped missing her every day; and accepted her decision. Once, when she was back in Miami for a visit, she walked past the McDeal's house and watched her child playing in the yard. She heard her laugh, saw her run, and watched Gracie McDeal hug her. Her child, her Jocelyn, was loved and well cared for and she told herself she had acted in Jocelyn's best interest. But now, she had to decide how to handle the storm brewing all around her. She had been praying for a solution that would keep her out of the middle. Mark and Jocelyn would solve the problem by breaking-up; Carter's attorney would find a way to have the charges against him dismissed. She had hoped for the best. Instead she was dealing with the worst.

Later in the evening, when the kids were tucked in, she poured two glasses of wine and asked Paul to join her on the patio. Telling him was going to be hard but she had no choice.

"I have something to tell you that is going to change how you see me and maybe how you feel about me. I was hoping I would never have to tell you, or anyone, but something has happened that I can't ignore."

"What could you possibly tell me that would have that kind of dramatic effect? Did you get fired; did you drop Alex on his head; what?" Paul tried to lighten the mood, but when he saw how serious she was he said, simply, "Just tell me, Rosie."

Looking over at her husband, she studied his face; the sparkle in his eyes; the way his mouth turned up when he smiled. She wanted to remember the way he was looking at her right now. One last time she wanted to see the trust and love, before she destroyed it.

He reached over and took her hand, "Okay, I can see that you're serious. Just start at the beginning and whatever it is, we'll get through it together. I'm listening, Rosanna."

"It was a long time ago," she began in a voice so low, he was having trouble hearing her. "I was 18 years old, and very naïve. I had never really dated before but I was dating a boy I met at school. One night at a beach party, he raped me."

"What the hell! Some boy raped you! My god, Rosanna!" He stopped himself before he lost control. "Okay, give me a minute. I've got to think like a husband, not a policeman." His voice softened and he looked at her with a quizzical expression. "That was a long time ago, why bring it up now?"

"Paul, as a result of that rape, I had a child," she whispered. And, in the silence her whisper sounded like a shout. Paul sat quietly. Then he tipped back his glass and finished his wine in one gulp. Standing up, he started for the sliding glass doors, "I need something stronger to drink."

Tears started to trickle down her face as she looked out at the darkness and wondered if he would come back. A great weariness overcame her and she slumped down in the chair. Then she felt his hand on her shoulder, "Okay, what's next?" was all he said.

"I kept the pregnancy a secret from everyone but Nancy. And a few days after I graduated from school, she helped me deliver a little girl. We agreed I would take the child to Catholic Charities but I couldn't do it. I couldn't let her go to strangers. Even Nancy doesn't know this next part. One night, I wrapped the baby in a blanket, put her in a box and left her on the doorstep of a man and his mother that I knew would take good care of her." Her tears were flowing now but her husband was still holding on to her shoulder. "I saw her once, when I went back in Miami for a visit, and she was healthy," her voice lingered over the words, "and beautiful, and loved." Her tears had stopped and she raised her head to look at her husband. "I know I did the right thing."

Paul walked away from her and sat down. He hunched over in the chair and looked down at the stones of the patio floor. "Why haven't you told me about this before, Rosie? Did you think I loved you so little, it would make a difference?"

"It hurt too much to think about. All those awful months when I was pregnant, I did everything I could to forget what happened to me. I was angry and hurt and afraid. Until I saw her, Paul. When she was born, she was so little and helpless. I was so afraid I would see Phillip when I looked at her, but she didn't look anything like him. She was mine, Paul, and I didn't want to give her up."

"What happened to this Phillip? Did he go to jail? Has he come back to harass you or try to blackmail you?"

"No, Paul, no, nothing like that. He moved away and I've never seen him again. He's not the issue."

"Then what the hell is the issue? What's the rest of this story, Rosanna?" She could hear the change in Paul's voice as he seemed to be bracing himself for even more bad news.

"The man I gave my baby to has been charged with kidnapping her and that's not the worse part. My daughter and my nephew are seriously dating." As the words tumbled out of her mouth, her body began to tremble and, once again, she could no longer hold back the sobs.

"What are you talking about? You've got to be kidding! This sounds like some damn soap opera. You couldn't make it up but Rosie, this is crazy." Paul's voice was laced with anger and he looked at his wife with disbelief. "How do you know all this?"

"Nancy called me and told me Mark has a new girlfriend named Jocelyn McDeal. That's her name, Paul. That's my daughter's name. What am I going to do?"

Paul was silent for a long time before he looked at his wife and replied, "You've got three people who need for you to talk about this. There's a man who might go to prison for the rest of his life and two kids who may have already fallen in love. Geez, Rosanna, in my opinion, you've got more to worry about right now than whether I'm hurt or angry."

There was hurt in Paul's voice, but as he stood up, Rosie could see the policeman in him beginning to take over. "Yes, Rosie, this changes things between us, but I don't think it will destroy us. Maybe there are things I've never told you, either. We'll worry about putting us back together after we find a way to break those young people apart and keep an innocent man out of prison."

Paul walked over and took the seat beside her. "This is nuts, Rosie. I don't know who I feel sorrier for - you or all the people this is about to impact. And, we've got our own kids to think about. Damn."

"Oh, Paul, I'm sorry. I'm so sorry," Rosanna continued to sob. "I didn't mean for anyone to get hurt, and everything's gotten so messed up. Can you ever forgive me for not telling you about this? Will they?"

"Pull yourself together, Rosie and go call your sister. You're going to have to go to Miami. You can't undo all of this over the phone."

"I can't call her, Paul. I don't know what to say."

"Tell her you're coming to Miami and you'll explain everything when you get there."

Rosanna got up and walked to the kitchen. She found a box of tissues and started trying to repair the mess she'd made of her face. Her eyes and cheeks were puffy, her mascara smudged and her whole head felt like it was going to split open. For a few moments, she stared at the phone; then she turned to Paul, "It's after midnight in Miami. I can't call her tonight."

"Pick up the phone, Rosanna, this can't wait another minute!"

Paul's voice wasn't harsh, but it was stern and she knew he was trying to hold back his emotions. Quietly, she asked, "Will you go to Miami with me?"

"I don't know." The weariness in Paul's voice made Rosanna want to start crying again, but instead she picked up the phone and dialed her sister's number.

Chapter Thirty-nine

Rosanna and Nancy, Miami, April 1975

They'd been up all night the night before, and everyone was emotionally wiped out. It started when Rosanna and Paul arrived from California, and Rosanna made her confession. The entire evening had evolved into crying, recriminations, anger, and finally, somewhere around dawn, acceptance. Nancy hadn't realized how angry she was with her sister until she saw her son's reaction. He shattered right in front of her eyes, and her heart broke. They were all in shock, but she had not been prepared for the depth of Mark's feelings for Jocelyn. He kept saying over and over, "I love her. Don't you all understand?"

"You promised me that child would be taken to Catholic Charities if I helped you, Rosanna. You broke your promise," she yelled. "You have certainly made a mess of things. Look around you Rosanna. Everyone in this room is hurting because you didn't keep your promise." She couldn't believe she was shouting at her sister, but the anger kept spilling out of her. Rosanna didn't try to defend herself, she sat on the couch with her head in her hands, and let Nancy vent.

Nancy's husband, Matt, was the only voice of reason in the room, "We have a bad situation here but all this shouting isn't going to make it better. Sit down, Nancy, and get a grip on yourself."

It had gone on like this for hours - Rosanna apologizing, Nancy yelling, Mark pacing around the room, and Paul and Matt trying to keep a handle on the situation.

"What are you going to do about Carter? His trial starts tomorrow and because of you, the man just might go to prison! Don't you think you owe him something for raising your daughter?"

Nancy was still shouting. Her face was contorted with anger and she could feel the tension building across her shoulders. Good grief! Things like this weren't suppose to happen in her family.

Rosanna stood up from the couch and tried to take her sister's hand but Nancy jerked away. "I came back here to do what I can for Carter and for this family. Don't you think I feel bad? Don't you think I want to curl up somewhere and hide? Stop thinking about yourself for a minute and walk in my shoes. How do you think it made me feel to have to tell all of this to Paul? How do you think it makes me feel to see Mark so hurt? I'm hurting, too, Nancy. This isn't all about you!" Now, Rosanna was shouting and sobbing. When her anger was spent, she slumped back on the couch and continued to cry.

Paul put his arm around her and let her cry. He looked at Nancy and Mark and softly pleaded, "Give her a break. She was a kid, for god's sake. She was younger than you, Mark, and she thought she was doing the right thing."

Matt walked over and put his hand on his son's shoulder. Nancy saw a look of understanding pass between father and son and she was able to let go of some of her anger.

"I'm going to put on the coffee." She had to get out of the room so she could calm down. As she reached the kitchen door, she heard Mark say to his aunt, "I can't imagine how Jocelyn is going to deal with this. She's heard so many lies, she might not believe you. And, I hope you all know, I'm not about to walk away from her."

Nancy swung back around to her son, "What do you mean? She's your cousin! The church won't accept this relationship!" She was shouting again.

"Then I'll leave the church!" Mark shouted back at her as he tore out of the room.

She heard his bedroom door slam and wondered if this nightmare would ever end. She sat down on the kitchen chair and forgot all about the coffee.

In a few hours, they were all dressed and ready to head to the courthouse. Their eyes were red and none of them could hide that they hadn't been to sleep. Even with no sleep, Rosanna had a look of determination in her eyes and Mark seemed calmer. Some time in the early hours of the morning, they had decided Nancy would try to approach Carter's attorney before court started. But that plan was derailed when they arrived at the courthouse and were given directions to the wrong courtroom. Thank goodness, when they finally found the right court, Nancy convinced the bailiff to get a note to Miss Martinez.

Chapter Forty

Trial Day, April 1975

The alarm sounded at 4:30 on a dark, rainy morning in April, 1975, just like it had sounded for six mornings of every week for the past twenty years. But this morning the alarm was not reminding Carter to go to the bus barn. Today, the alarm was ringing to remind him the day he dreaded most in life had arrived.

Silencing the alarm, he looked around his room at the shadows cast on the ceiling by a street light on the corner. Every morning the shapes were there; long, dark imaginary blotches that momentarily changed the landscape of his room and usually comforted him. Most days they were like old friends, but not today. Today, they were calling his bluff. They were asking him to decide who he was.

For most of his life he had been content to be part of the shadows, insignificant, lost in the crowd - a man who lived his life in someone else's light. But when he walked into the court room in a couple of hours, he wanted to be strong and brave, more a part of his own light than his shadow.

He was being asked to step out of the shadows and defend himself against the indefensible. He wondered how it was going to feel to be the center of attention in the court room. A year ago he would have cowered in a corner and accepted defeat. But, today he wanted to fight to remain free. He knew Sharon's belief in him made him different. When she came back in his life, he felt the shift. He couldn't describe it, but he could feel it. He wanted to keep Sharon in his life and he wanted to bring his daughter home. Achieving those goals meant walking out of the court room a free man.

When his mother was still alive, he depended on her to know what to do. She would be able to tell his story in a believable way.

She would be able to convince the judge and the jury the accusations against him were absurd, and totally unrealistic. His mother had a knack for making everything turn out all right. But she was gone and at 43 years old, circumstances were forcing him to finally grow up. Taking baby steps out of the shadows felt surprisingly good.

***

Stepping out of the shower, Elena wished she could get back in bed and pull the covers over her head. She was going to court today with nothing but a few character witnesses and a far-fetched story. Eric kept reminding her, a good defense could be built on a persuasive story that created doubt. Last night he tried to encourage her by telling her about cases that had been won with less than she had going for her. It hadn't helped.

She had been so sure Nancy Sanders would cooperate with her. She knew Jocelyn's mother was out there somewhere but time ran out before John Avery could uncover anything about where she might be. Picturing Carter's face, she couldn't remember the exact moment she knew he was telling her the truth. Over the weeks and months of working with him, she had gone from skepticism to belief. Today, standing before the judge and jury, she would say with no doubt that her client was an innocent man. Now, if she only had a way to prove it.

For this court appearance, she wanted to look as professional as possible. Dressed in a dark grey suit, white tailored blouse and black high heels, she checked in the mirror one more time to see whether her make-up or hair needed a touch up. As she was about to leave the house, the phone rang. "I'll get it" she called to her mother, who was in the kitchen. "Hello, Martinez residence."

"Good morning, gorgeous. I just called to wish you luck today."

"You sound chipper this morning, Eric. Thanks for calling."

"How are you doing?"

"You know, it's strange, I'm not nervous. But I'd give anything if I didn't have to do this. I'm as prepared as I can be, given the lack of anything to substantiate my case."

"Go in there like you are ready to win, sweetheart. I'll call you later."

Elena hung up the phone and smiled. She was so lucky to have Eric in her life, and as soon as this trial was over she was going to have time to finalize the plans for their wedding.

"Bye, Mom. I'll see you later. Remember, I'm meeting Eric for dinner so I'll be late."

She started her car and headed for the courthouse. "What will be, will be," she thought, and then added a small prayer she would be able to give Carter the defense he deserved.

***

Mary Ann was hurrying around the apartment making sure she didn't forget anything. She had taken the day off from school so she could attend the trial with Jocelyn. She wanted to be there in case the girl needed consoling when Carter was found guilty. She knew Jocelyn was angry, but never-the-less, for 17 years the man had been her father. There would probably be some kind of emotion when she realized he was going to prison.

All of my efforts to protect her will pay off today, she thought. Jocelyn will finally see I'm the one who didn't stop until the McDeal's deceit was uncovered. She will be grateful to me and then the distance between us will melt away.

Jocelyn hadn't slept well, and this morning she felt tired. She called Mrs. Thompson last night to get advice on what to wear, and they decided a plain, white oxford cloth blouse and black straight skirt was appropriate for court. Mrs. Thompson suggested she wear her hair down, and put on a little face powder. "You don't want to stand out in the crowd today, so conservative is best," Mrs. Thompson offered. "I'll be there for you, honey. Now try to get some sleep."

Mark and Mrs. Thompson would be sitting near her and that gave her some comfort. But, she was surprised Mark hadn't called her. She hadn't worked at the library last night, so she hadn't seen him since lunch yesterday. It wasn't like him not to call but she was sure he would be meeting her in the court room.

She walked to the living room where Miss Moss was waiting for her. "Whenever you're ready, I'm all set to go. I want this whole thing to be over with as soon as possible."

Sharon called Carter early to buoy his spirits. Assuring him she would be in the court room, she asked him to keep the silver four-leaf clover in his pocket. "It's not a good luck charm. It's just to remind you I believe in you and everything's going to be all right."

She believed in him but wasn't so sure the jury would. Carter had no way to prove his innocence and, if the jury didn't pay close attention, they might not see that he projected caring, kindness and integrity. Dressing for him today, she wore her pastel blue silk shirtwaist. She didn't think the dress was special, but every time she wore it he commented on how pretty she looked.

Hiding her anxiety was going to take some work. She never wanted Carter to suspect she had any doubts. If only the investigator had been successful in locating the girl's mother. From what Carter told her, Elena Martinez was a go-getter and had done everything possible. But, Sharon was sorry she hadn't gone ahead and hired her own private investigator. It might have made a difference.

Chapter Forty-one

Court, April 1975

The whispers silenced when the bailiff announced that court was in session. Carter stood up at the defense table to the command, "all rise," and looked down at the suit he had been so proud of last year when he bought it. Dressed in black, he felt like an undertaker, and if the others in the room had this impression of him, it wouldn't be to his advantage.

Waiting for the judge to enter the room, Carter lowered his eyes to the notepad on the table in front of him. Then, like a puppet whose strings had been pulled, his head snapped up and his eyes began searching the gallery. A sea of solemn spectators seemed to ebb and flow before him in a tide of tired, apathetic, even friendly faces.

Jocelyn was sitting out there somewhere and he tried to catch a glimpse of her before he had to direct all of his attention to the proceedings that were about to begin. Sadly he knew when he found his daughter's face in the crowd, she wouldn't make eye contact with him. Even after a year, she was still too angry and hurt for that. But his heart was hungry for a glimpse of her and he continued to scan each row until he saw her. The pain of missing her hit his gut and he took a deep breath.

His eyes soaked in everything about her in the few seconds he had before the judge opened his case. Jocelyn, you look so pretty and so grown up. He had caught a glimpse of her several weeks before at a sidewalk café, but today she seemed taller and much thinner. Her beautiful brown hair had been cut to shoulder length and she had that far-away look in her eyes that he remembered so well. "It's my think about it look, Dad," she once told him. The ache was like the relentless ocean pounding on the shore - every time he thought it had ebbed, it returned with a force strong enough to shake his composure. He regretted all he'd missed in the last year: her birthday, her high school graduation, her first day of college, Thanksgiving, Christmas. Fighting to push his emotions below the surface, he closed his eyes and gritted his teeth against the sadness.

"Please be seated," said the judge, drawing Carter's attention back to the court room, "We are here today to hear evidence in the case of the State of Florida versus Carter McDeal. Is the State ready?"

"Yes, your Honor, the State is ready," said Tom Gorman, the assistant state attorney.

"Is the defense ready?"

"Yes, your Honor, the defense is ready," said Elena Martinez.

"Bailiff, you may seat the jury."

Sweat pooled under Carter's collar as the members of the jury filed into the court room. They were strangers; people who were performing their civic duty and had satisfied some criteria the attorneys established for this case. These strangers would listen to the evidence, render a verdict, and then return to their homes and families, their jobs and friends, and never give another thought to Carter McDeal. He looked at each person and tried to guess by their appearance and demeanor how they would react to what they would hear today. Do any of them have a daughter? What measures would they take to protect her? How will this story fall on their ears and their hearts? But all he saw were the silent, stony faces of the strangers who were about to judge him. Fear caused his chest to tighten and beads of sweat formed on his forehead.

He looked over at his attorney who was shaking her head at him. She had warned him earlier not to look at the jurors and had explained that they would come into the room without emotion. One of his last conversations with her echoed in his ears, and the tension began to ease.

"Carter, it's my job to show the jury the truth of your story. I'm going to win them over. By the time I'm finished, they will doubt your guilt." Elena's voice reassured him. "The burden of proof is with the State of Florida, and we both know they don't have any solid evidence against you."

"Elena, what evidence do you think the state attorney has that will fill in all the loopholes and gaps?" Carter questioned nervously.

"They don't have a solid case, so everything they present will be based on assumptions. But, we can't be complacent about the jury. They look at things revealed in court with a different perspective. I'm carefully building a case that refutes and casts doubt on everything the prosecution will present. Do you trust me?"

She had asked that question several times and he had thought about it from every angle. Trust, he decided, was a difficult concept when you were relying on the skills of another to keep you out of prison. Trust, was perhaps not the right word to describe how he felt about Elena, however he held onto the belief that she would at least fight for him. For the past year, she had followed up on every aspect of his story and had been untiring in her efforts to track down the one other person who knew the truth. Yes, maybe he did trust his attorney when it came to points of law. She might be able to find a way to keep him from going to prison, but he had accepted months ago that he was the only one who would be able to repair the damage done to his relationship with Jocelyn. His daughter had lost trust in him and had turned away. She was like the strangers on the jury, he mused, except she had already returned her verdict as guilty.

He snapped to attention when the judge said to the state attorney, "You may begin your opening statement."

With no control over his life, Carter's reluctant participation in the guessing game that would mold his life, his future, was about up. One decision, made by six jurors, would determine whether he ever had control over his freedom again. Unexpected fury consumed him and he clinched his jaw tighter at the thought that the state attorney would publicly expose him. Tom Gorman, the state attorney, would methodically attempt to turn everyone in the court room against him. He would twist the words as they left the witnesses's mouths, making him look like an idiot. Even worse, an evil idiot. He took a calming breath and attempted to regain his composure. Oh God, Mom, get me out of this mess.

The look on Tom Gorman's face was congenial, but determined, and Carter knew the state attorney would use every trick in the book to make friends with the people seated in the jury box. Carter had wondered for months how Gorman's version of this story was going to unfold. He followed the eyes of the jurors as they turned toward the man who was approaching them. It seemed like they already believed he knew the truth. Will I survive this?

"Ladies and gentlemen of the jury, imagine with me for a few minutes that you are a brand new parent. For nine long months you have anticipated the birth of your child and now the day has arrived when you will meet this little person for the first time."

Cradling a pretend baby, Gorman's tactic worked and Carter felt a sick thud punch at his stomach. The jury, emotional heart strings tugged, instinctively leaned forward in their chairs to get a closer look at the make-believe infant.

"You hear the first cry, that long awaited sound that announces the arrival, and you are told you have a beautiful, healthy daughter. You look into her eyes with love and joy as a nurse places her in your arms. A connection is made between the two of you that will last a life time." Lifting his voice, his head fell forward suddenly, as though for effect. "At least it's supposed to last for a life time." Gorman continued in a whisper, before resuming the rise of his voice. "But, now imagine, if you will, the connection being shattered and broken because someone has decided to take your daughter away from you."

Pausing, the state attorney looked into the eyes of each juror. Carter knew this moment belonged solely to the state attorney and the jury. Gorman kept his back turned away from everyone else in the courtroom as though he was sharing a secret. Placing his hands on the jury box, he leaned toward the jurors in a conspiratorial manner.

"Perhaps she was stolen from her crib in the hospital nursery, or she disappeared when you turned your back for one second while she was sleeping in her carriage. Or you woke up one morning to find that someone had broken into your home and had taken her in the middle of the night. Imagine your pain as you looked into that empty crib or carriage. Imagine the pain caused by that kind of loss. But even harder, imagine the pain of not knowing. There were no answers for you; no one could find your daughter; no one could tell you what happened; no one could give you a happy ending to this story. All you have is a memory, an ache inside you that will never go away. To this day, you walk down the street and see your daughter in the face of every little girl that passes by, and you still ask yourself one constant question. Could that child be mine?

"The years drag on, 18 years in fact, and the day you have waited for finally arrives. You have the chance to look into the face of the person who took your daughter, but you are surprised by what you see. This person doesn't look cruel and heartless. This person doesn't fit the profile of the monster you have imagined. This person looks like any man you might meet on the street, and you are confused.

"I ask you to look at the defendant with the eyes of awareness and don't let yourself be confused or fooled by the facade that you see. Look past his demeanor and his innocent expression and really see him for who and what he is."

Carter tried not to react as Tom Gorman turned to face the defense table and pointed directly at him. The evangelical tone in the state attorney's voice made him shrink down in his chair, and he cringed.

"What you see is a man who willfully took a child away from its mother for his own selfish reasons. The findings that will be presented to you during this trial will show beyond a reasonable doubt that the monster lies just beneath the surface. Beneath the façade that Carter McDeal presents to the public is a man who is capable of, and should be convicted of, kidnapping. Police records will show that a baby reported missing in June of 1956 is most likely the young woman that Carter McDeal claims to be his daughter. This man should be sent to prison, not for the 18 years that he stole from a child's parents, but for the rest of his life."

As the state attorney finished his statement, Carter looked at the jury and saw scorn on the faces of the four women. He noted a small change in the expressions of the two men, and he frowned. The first part of Tom Gorman's job appeared to be successful.

The judge turned toward the other side of the court room and called for the defense attorney to begin her opening statement. Today, Elena, a petite, Cuban fireball of a defense attorney, was Carter's only hope. She was dressed in a tailored suit that drew attention to her nice curves and she wore high heels that added inches to her short stature. In the past Carter had thought her demure, but this morning when she stood in front of the defense table and looked directly at him, he saw a gladiator. The back of his neck began to prickle as all eyes in the court room turned their attention to him. The blood rose in his cheeks. The silence was unnerving and he wished she would just begin her statement. Finally, after someone in the room cleared their throat, he watched her as she began a slow, almost seductive walk to the front of the jury box.

"Good morning, ladies and gentlemen. Today as you begin to hear the case presented against my client, I want you to focus on the law and its relevance to this case. I want you to look with the eyes of knowledge, not the eyes of emotion. This is a case of law, not a soap opera, and, if you look at the findings that will be presented to you by the prosecution from that perspective, you will see they lack substance. The state attorney has based his case upon a suspicion that my client is lying, and on a missing baby report that can not be substantiated. There is no evidence to suggest a crime has been perpetrated, there is only a suspicion. As this case unfolds, you will see, not a monster, but a man who found himself in a perplexing situation, an extraordinary situation to say the least, and out of love, he makes a flawed decision. Jocelyn McDeal was not kidnapped at birth by my client."

When Elena paused, Carter tried to measure the jurors' reactions but there was no sign of emotion on their faces. He watched as Elena took a few steps toward the defense table and wished she would stay on the other side of the room. She stopped and positioned herself at an angle so the jurors could see her face, and then she smiled at him.

"Jocelyn was given, by her mother, to my client, because she knew Carter and his mother would raise her daughter with love. Before Jocelyn was born, her mother searched for a home where she knew her daughter would be safe and well cared for, a place where her daughter would have all the advantages she could not provide for her. And she found all of those things in Carter, and in his mother, Gracie."

He felt self conscious as Elena walked a few steps closer and stood directly in front of the table. She held out her arm in his direction and he struggled to remain expressionless. Her voice was gentle, caressing every word like a mother who was lovingly describing her child.

"Carter is a gentle man who lives a simple life. He drives the Route Six bus for the Miami Transit Company, and every now and then he goes bowling or plays poker with some of the other drivers. He goes to church and he attends Jocelyn's school functions. And, when his mother Gracie was alive, he worked with her in her garden. Eighteen years ago, when Jocelyn's birth mother was pregnant, she made a conscience choice about Carter and Gracie, and decided they represented all the characteristics of a caring family. Without their knowledge, she observed how Carter treated the people who rode his bus, she noted his interaction with his mother, and she studied the care that Gracie gave to her garden. Jocelyn's mother did not abandon her baby; she carefully placed her in a home filled with warmth and love.

"The man you see at the defense table is not a monster and there is no evidence to suggest that he is. Instead, the findings will show that he is a good father, who did his best to provide his daughter with all of the things that her mother wanted for her."

Elena walked with determination back to the jury box and she was no longer soft and gentle. Carter was amazed at the authority and strength he heard in her voice.

"Jocelyn McDeal was not kidnapped. She was a gift, freely given, by a mother who loved her but could not care for her. She was a gift, freely given, to a family who learned to love her, who nurtured her, and who brought her up to be a resilient, smart, and responsible young woman. Jocelyn McDeal was not abused or mistreated, and she was not kidnapped. First, she was wrapped in love by the woman who had to give her up and then, by the family who received her as the greatest gift of their lives."

Carter couldn't gauge the reaction of the jury as Elena returned to her place at the defense table. He had tried to listen to her words and knew she had attempted to change the emotional picture the state attorney had painted, but over and over, all he could hear was the state attorney saying, "he should spend the rest of his life in prison."

"The prosecution may call its first witness," said the judge.

Tom Gorman stood, "The prosecution calls Mr. Robert Sullivan."

The morning sunlight played games on the court room floor. Carter watched as the rays of sun grew brighter and then dimmer as the clouds outside the building moved across the sky. He was glad for this diversion as he wondered what his supervisor was going to say that would help the state's case. He moved his eyes from the floor to the witness stand and waited for Sully to take the oath and begin his testimony.

"My name is Robert Lee Sullivan, but everybody calls me Sully. I live at 4410 NE 27th Avenue in Miami. I'm a supervisor and route manager for the Miami Transit Company. I've worked for the company for 35 years but I'm thinking about retiring in June."

Carter didn't know Sully was going to retire. That would make a big difference at the bus barn. He tried to pay attention as he watched the state attorney approach Sully, but he couldn't get over how nice Sully looked in a suit. He vaguely remembered that his boss was dressed up the day of Gracie's funeral but he didn't want to think about that day. He let go of the thought as the state attorney began his questions. "Mr. Sullivan, please tell the court how long you have known Carter McDeal?"

"Let's see. It's probably been some 20 years. Yeah, I think he's been one of my drivers for about that long. I know he worked for the company before he got to be a driver, but he's been on my roster about that long."

"Can you tell us a little about him, Mr. Sullivan?"

"Sure, but call me Sully. Carter's an odd duck, but he's one of my best drivers. Always there, never gave me any trouble before he got himself arrested last year."

Gorman looked puzzled, "Excuse me. I'm not familiar with the term "odd duck." Will you explain what you mean by that term?"

Sully shifted his weight in the chair and appeared to be struggling to find an answer. "Well, Carter, he stays pretty much to himself. I got some guys at the barn that would knock your brains out if you crossed them, but not Carter. He don't go lookin' for trouble." Sully's expression softened, "For years, the guy rode a bike to work. You know, he lived with his mom 'til she died a year or so ago. And he makes the guys at the bus barn crazy with this checklist that he goes over every time he takes the Number Six out for a run." He shook his head. "The guy's been driving a bus for a hundred years, and he still goes over his checklist. You know, like he don't know his bus or something."

"Why do you think he called you when he was arrested?"

"The guy ain't got no real friends, except maybe for a few of the folks who ride his bus. But, I don't think he would call any of them to get him out of jail, so I guess I'm it for him?"

"Are you saying that he has no friends?"

"I never gave it any thought 'cause he's a pleasant sort. You know, he's shy. Some guys are like that. The only time he joins in with the other guys is when the Yankees are playing ball. He loves them Yanks, and sometimes we have the game on the radio. He used to be on the bowling league, and sometimes he played poker with us. But, he wasn't buddies with the guys."

"Did he ever talk with you about his daughter?"

"What do mean by talk with me? I knew he had a daughter, and every now and then she would come down to the barn for something. But, no, I don't recall him talking to me about her. He's very private about his family."

"Did he ever tell you how his daughter came to live with him?"

"No. I didn't know he had a kid until he comes in and tells me he has to add a dependent to his tax record and insurance. Then one day this little kid appears at the bus barn with Carter's mother. Now that Mrs. McDeal was one fine woman. But she shows up one day with this little kid, and he tells me that's his daughter. I was pretty sure Carter wasn't married 'cause he never claimed a wife as a dependent, so I just guessed he got some gal pregnant and was raising the kid."

"Did that seem out of character for Mr. McDeal?"

"I don't know if I ever thought about it. That was a long time ago. Nah, I'm sure I didn't think about it 'cause it happens sometimes with my guys. Except they don't usually end up raising the kid. They usually just claim them as dependents."

"In your opinion, Mr. Sullivan, is Mr. McDeal capable of kidnapping?

"Objection. The state attorney is calling for a conclusion and leading the witness."

"Over ruled. The state attorney asked for an opinion. Give the court your opinion, Mr. Sullivan," ordered the judge.

"Maybe yes, maybe no. Like I said, he's a strange guy. You never can be sure about the quiet ones. You know what I mean?"

"If it's possible that he's guilty, why did you post his bond?"

"I guess because he asked me to. He'd never asked me for anything before and I wanted to help him out. You know, his mother had just passed away and like I said he ain't got no real friends."

"Thank you, Mr. Sullivan. No further questions."

"Any questions, Miss Martinez?"

"None at this time your Honor."

"The state calls Dr. Benjamin Alston to the stand."

Following the sunbeams filtering into the courtroom, Carter prepared to listen to Dr. Alston's testimony. From his seat at the defense table he could just barely see that more clouds were forming over the city and he prayed for rain. He wanted the rain drops to splash loudly on the windows and the crashes of thunder to beat against the court house walls to drown out these proceedings. The trial had just begun, but he was already tired of the looks of disgust from the jury members and the whispers of curiosity that came from the gallery whenever there was a lull in the proceedings.

The distinct fragrance of pipe smoke hit his nostrils before he saw the man and he was reminded that he liked the spicy tobacco smell of Dr. Alston's office the day of his appointment. It was a surprise that the smoke lingered so strongly on the doctor's clothes. Funny the things one remembered, things that had no relevance. He couldn't remember much of what he said to the doctor, but he could remember what the man's pipe smelled like.

"My name is Dr. Benjamin Alston. My field is psychiatry. I have been in private practice for 19 years and my office is located at 820 Ponce de Leon Boulevard in Coral Gables."

"Dr. Alston, please outline for the court the procedures that are followed when evaluating someone who has been indicted for a crime. But first, would you state your credentials and experience in this area," said the state attorney.

"After completing medical school at the University of Miami and a residency in psychiatry at Duke University, I completed thirty hours of training with the Federal Bureau of Investigation in criminal psychological profiling. This training incorporated both psychological and sociological methodology. Over the years, I have probably created more than fifty profiles for law enforcement agencies across the state of Florida."

Dr. Alston looked toward the jury. "The creation of a criminal psychological profile involves an in-depth study of the accused and the victim, if possible, as well as any psychological and sociological data that is available. Following the protocol established by the FBI, I create the profile using a series of five overlapping stages that closely resemble a medical diagnosis. First, I collect and assess data provided to me by law enforcement and the interviews I conduct with the parties involved. This data usually allows me to reconstruct the situation. If it doesn't, then I know I need more data. Once this is completed, I use the data to formulate a hypothesis which must be tested against the known information. The final step in the process is to report the results. The report includes, but is not limited to, determination of the type of crime committed, the primary intent of the offender, the willingness of the offender to take a criminal risk, and the time and location factors involved in the offense."

"How was the procedure used in this case?"

"I employed the protocol in the evaluation of both Carter McDeal and Jocelyn McDeal."

"Were your interviews conducted voluntarily or were they mandated by the court?"

"Both were conducted voluntarily."

"Can you provide the court with the results of your profiles, beginning with Mr. McDeal?"

Turning to the judge, the psychologist asked to if he might refer to his notes and the judge nodded his agreement. Dr. Alston opened his notebook and continued.

"I met on two occasions with Mr. McDeal. He was born in Miami, raised by working class parents and has never ventured far beyond this geographic location. The one exception is a tour of duty with the army during the Korean conflict. He is an only child, and upon the death of his father when the defendant was ten years old, he assumed responsibility for his mother. He is a high school graduate and has limited his career ambition to driving a bus. He seems satisfied with where he is in life. Mr. McDeal is a high introvert and makes very little effort to develop social interaction with two exceptions – his regular riders on the bus and his former fiancée, Sharon Bowers, with whom he has recently rekindled a friendship. He has very few interests beyond his job and his family.

Mr. McDeal appears to be a man who lives in the shadow of those around him. He has a routine and he seldom varies it. Or, at least that was the case before his mother's death. The dynamics of the family were altered dramatically by her death in November of 1973."

Carter's thoughts raced. He's making a good impression on the jurors. They're taking this in like he wrote the book on who I am. We spent a couple of hours together and now he's an authority on me. What does he know about Korea? What does he know about losing my best friend in a raid by the Chinese? What the hell does he think he knows about how it felt to open a letter from Sharon telling me she's marrying somebody else while I'm stuck in some trench a million miles from home. And, who's shadow does he think I've been living in all these years?

"When matching what I have learned about Mr. McDeal with an FBI profile of a kidnapper, I see several psychological and sociological correlations. First, he is a loner and exhibits a sociological immaturity. He is controlling, in that he has certain expectations for himself and others, and also exhibits many obsessive compulsive traits. His attention to detail and his attraction to patterns indicate that a personality disorder may be present. But the most overt characteristic is his devotion to his mother. He exhibits an unusually high need or desire to please his mother."

"Dr. Alston, in your expert opinion, do you think this desire to please could have driven Carter McDeal to steal a child to make his mother happy."

"I believe that is a distinct possibility."

"And, Jocelyn McDeal, what does your interview tell us about her?"

"I met with Jocelyn on one occasion. Until November, 1973, and the death of her grandmother, Jocelyn appears to have lived a secure life. She believed Carter McDeal was her father; she believed her mother had died in childbirth; and she believed Gracie McDeal was her grandmother. From all indications she has a high intelligence, functions well in social situations, and performs well in school. She is in her freshman year at Barry College on an academic scholarship, and has done very well in her course work for the first semester. Her strongest relationships were her grandmother and a girlfriend named Ruthie. She apparently had a good relationship with her father until the story of her birth began to unravel."

"What happened at that point, Dr. Alston?"

"Jocelyn feels betrayed. She feels her identity was shattered by the truth of her birth, and cannot understand why her grandmother and father would hide this information from her. She is very angry with her father and feels she will never be able to trust him again."

"Did she explain to you why she never questioned the story she was told about her birth?"

"I think Jocelyn was so secure in her life that she never had reason to doubt."

"Did she indicate to you whether or not she was ever abused or mistreated?"

"As a response to my direct question, she replied, 'absolutely not."

"In your expert opinion, do you believe she was telling the truth?"

"Yes, I do. She does not exhibit any characteristics to suggest otherwise."

"I have no further questions at this time, but would request that this witness be subject to recall," said the state attorney.

"Does the defense have any questions?" asked the judge.

"Yes, your Honor, I do." Elena stood up and walked to the jury box. "Dr. Alston, in your interviews with the defendant, did he at any time exhibit the characteristics of a criminal?"

"I'm not sure that I understand what you mean."

"Would you say that your analysis of Mr. McDeal meets the profile of the criminal mind?"

"All I can say with certainty is Mr. McDeal matches several characteristics that are usually present in a person who is capable of committing a crime such as kidnapping."

She turned quickly to face Dr. Alston, "Would you say that my client's desire to please his mother supersedes his understanding of right and wrong?"

"I saw no indication of that. But, I do know he wanted to make his mother happy."

Carter swallowed his anger against the doctor's suggestion that his relationship with his mother was unnatural. His mother had loved him without reservation or expectations. She had made every effort to ensure that his life was better than her own. He thought of the stories his dad had told him about her unhappy childhood and how his dad had rescued her from a family who cared so little they hadn't even tried to find her after she had run away to Miami. It was his father's words that had guided his actions all these years. "Carter, always treat your mother with respect. She didn't have an easy time growing up and our job is to make sure she's happy."

Elena's voice jolted him out of his reverie. "Dr. Alston, in your expert opinion, does a person's desire to please his mother make him a criminal?"

Hesitating for a few seconds, Alston lowered his voice and answered. "No, Miss Martinez, it does not."

"Thank you, Dr. Alston. No further questions."

Carter closed his eyes. What had he said in his interviews that made Dr. Alston characterize him as a kidnapper. He had never thought of himself as abnormal, but now he had doubts. When did being quiet become a felony? Was being a loner a trait that would single him out for a crime of this magnitude? Dr. Alston's words could convince this jury to find him guilty and the judge could sentence him to life in prison! The thought of life in prison clouded his thinking and he felt the bile rise in his throat. What chance do I have when my only defense is a woman we can't find?

He turned in response to some movement in the gallery and his eyes met those of the tall, grey-haired woman who was seated next to Jocelyn. This was not the woman they needed to find, but it was the woman who was responsible for bringing him to this court room. Can I forgive you for reporting me to the authorities? Maybe someday. But am I willing to forgive you for turning Jocelyn against me? Never, Miss Moss, never! His look hardened against her stare but there was no way to avoid her body language which seemed to be shouting at him, "I'm winning, Carter. All the cards are falling my way."

Ice flowed through his bloodstream and a tremor ran down his spine. Venomous words hissed across his lips, "Miss Moss, no matter what verdict is reached in this trial, I promise you will never win my daughter."

Chapter Forty-two

Court

Jocelyn never expected so many people to be in the court. There were a few people she knew, but most of the spectators were people who just came to see the show. She was glad Miss Moss helped her dodge the reporters on the way inside; she had no intention of telling the world how she felt.

As the proceedings droned on, she tried not to look at her father. When she did look over toward the defense table, her eyes were drawn to the woman sitting in the first row, almost directly behind her father. Again, she wondered who this person was and if she was important in her father's life.

All morning the prosecution called their witnesses, Sully, Detective Madison, Dr. Alston, the social workers, and an expert on kidnapping. Stone-faced, Carter tried his best to keep his emotions under control. Mr. Gorman's argument was compelling and the jury seemed to be caught up in the drama that was being presented. Sitting in the court room, listening to his life being dissected and twisted, was harder than he thought it was going to be. He was embarrassed for his daughter to hear the things being said about him. Even when his attorney began calling her witnesses, his feelings of dread did not disappear.

His spirits lifted when Elena called Mr. Fitz to the stand. Mr. Fitz was actually corroborating his story and the faces of the jury did not seem as menacing as they had earlier in the day. Then Tom Gorman started his cross examination.

"Mr. Fitz, you have told this court you can corroborate Mr. McDeal's story through your journal entries. Is that correct?"

"Yes sir, that is correct."

"You are asking this jury to accept a journal you say you wrote 18 years ago. Is that correct?"

"Mr. Gorman, my journal entries, recorded on the dates I have stated, are valid."

"How do you assure the jury your observations, as you call them, are not biased by your desire to help your friend?"

"Mr. Gorman, I believe the credentials I stated at the beginning, under oath, inform this court of my professionalism. My observations were made through the trained eyes of a career veteran of the Federal Bureau of Investigation."

"No further questions at this time."

All day the prosecution managed to tighten the case against Carter and the picture being presented to the jury was skewed toward a guilty verdict. No matter what Elena did to refute the prosecution's case, he could see that her attempts to cast doubt were not working. Tom Gorman was effectively undermining the testimony of all the witnesses she had called so far.

The state attorney had finished his cross examination of Mr. Fitz when Elena was tapped on the shoulder by the bailiff and handed a note. She read the words, and slipped the note to Carter. After Carter read it, she took his hand and squeezed it, then stood and asked the judge if she could approach the bench.

"Miss Martinez, does this request mean you are not ready to continue calling your witnesses?" asked the judge.

"No, your Honor, I'm ready. But some new evidence has been brought to my attention. In light of that, I'm requesting a fifteen minute recess."

"Mr. Gorman, do you have any objections?"

"No, your Honor," Tom responded and gave her a quizzical look.

When the state attorney did not object, the judge informed the court of the fifteen minute break and instructed the bailiff to escort the jury from the courtroom.

She could feel the judge watching her as she made this highly irregular move and knew he would say something to her later. But, the message contained in the note was enough for her to risk the judge's ire.

Stepping into the corridor, Elena saw several people waiting for her. She recognized Nancy Sanders and knew immediately the woman next to her was Rosanna. Elena could hardly contain her surprise and excitement. This moment was an answer to prayer. Nancy stepped forward and introduced Elena to her sister, Rosanna Donovan, her brother-in-law, Paul Donovan, her husband, Matt, and her son, Mark. When she took Rosanna's hand to shake it, she was surprised that the woman was trembling.

"Let's move over to those chairs and sit down. I only have a minute, but you must have come to help Carter. I need affirmation of that so I can ask the judge to meet me in chambers. You are here to tell the court you are Jocelyn's mother, aren't you? "

"My wife is ready to talk to the judge, and we'll see how it goes from there." Paul spoke on Rosanna's behalf, and turned toward his wife. "This is the easy part, Rosanna. The hard part was last night. You can get through this and we're all here for you."

Standing up, Elena pointed to a conference room. "I think it would be best for all of you to wait in that room over there until I can speak to the judge. He isn't too happy that I requested a recess in the middle of calling my witnesses. He would not like it if we caused a commotion in his court." She nodded to everyone and walked back inside the court room.

Elena asked permission to approach the bench and slowly walked toward the judge. She cleared her throat, looked up, and said, "Your Honor, there has been an unexpected turn of events that warrants the attention of the court. I respectfully request a meeting with you and the state attorney in chambers."

"This had better be an earth shaking event, Miss Martinez. You know this is highly irregular. Mr. Gorman, please approach the bench."

Judge Morris told the state attorney Miss Martinez had requested a meeting in chambers, and then said to the court, "I am extending our recess an additional fifteen minutes. Bailiff, please inform the jury of the extension."

"All rise," the bailiff exclaimed, and the judge and two attorneys walked toward his chambers.

"All right, Miss Martinez. What is going on?" Judge Morris was not pleased with Elena and his tone of voice let her know she better have a good reason for delaying the proceedings.

"Your Honor, as Mr. Gorman was cross examining my last witness, the bailiff passed me a note that a Mrs. Nancy Sanders had just arrived and was insisting she see me immediately. She told him it was an emergency having to do with the case. Reluctantly, after asking her a series of questions, he came and got me. When I walked out in the corridor, Mrs. Sanders was standing there with a woman she introduced as Jocelyn McDeal's mother. Judge, I have known of this woman's existence for several months, but was unsuccessful in locating her. About two weeks ago, I approached Mrs. Sanders about her sister and she was totally uncooperative. I don't know why she changed her mind but she did. I didn't take time to question her because I wanted to stop these proceedings and have the charges dropped against my client."

"Are you saying this woman will testify that she is Jocelyn McDeal's birth mother?"

"Yes, your Honor."

"And, how is her testimony going to impact this case?"

"She will affirm she gave her child to the McDeal's to raise. Carter McDeal did not kidnap Jocelyn. Her mother placed her in a box and left her on his door step."

"She what? I can't wait to hear this story. Tom, are you in agreement this woman should be brought in here for questions?"

"Judge, this is not my call. If this is the way you want to handle it, I have no objections."

"What's her name, Elena?"

"Her name is Rosanna Donovan."

Judge Morris picked up his phone and called the bailiff. "Michael, would you please bring Rosanna Donovan to my chambers. I think she is outside the court room." He turned to Elena, "Where is she?"

"She's in the conference room to the left of the court room."

"Michael, she's in our conference room."

Within minutes, Rosanna Donovan was escorted into the chambers and was being seated in front of Judge Morris. "I understand you have something of importance to tell us, Mrs. Donovan."

"Yes, your Honor, I do. Jocelyn McDeal is my daughter. When she was six days old, I left her on the front door step of Gracie and Carter McDeal's house."

"Mrs. Donovan, are you telling me this case has been on the docket for almost a year and you are just now coming forward with this information? I find that very irresponsible." The judge's surprise had changed to irritation.

"I live in California. When my sister told me of the circumstances several months ago, I was hesitant to come forward because my husband and other children had no knowledge of Jocelyn. However, something else has entered the picture that makes it imperative for me to reveal the truth."

"And, Mrs. Donovan, what is this something else?"

Rosanna took a deep breath, "I found out my daughter, Jocelyn, is dating my sister's son."

"Unbelievable," said the judge, shaking his head.

"I had no choice but to come to Florida and try to unravel all of the problems created by the decision I made years ago."

"Let me ask you this, Mrs. Donovan. Is there anyone who might corroborate your story?"

"Yes, your Honor, my sister, who is a nurse, helped me through my pregnancy and delivered Jocelyn in her apartment. To my knowledge, no one, not even my parents, knew I was pregnant."

"And, the father of the child, where is he?"

"Judge Morris, when I was 18, I was raped by Jocelyn's father. We were dating but I had no intention of developing a sexual relationship with him. After the rape occurred at a beach party, I never saw him again. He never knew I was pregnant." The words were coming out of Rosanna's mouth but there were no emotions attached to them.

"Well, this is quite a story. Mrs. Donovan, do you have any idea how irregular it is for a witness to come forward at the last moment and surprise the court?"

"Yes sir, I do. I'm a court reporter in the California judicial system. I have some knowledge of the procedures. I apologize for the way this is happening, but in the last few days I have had to admit this to my husband and I have had to break my nephew's heart. But none of that compares with having to face my daughter and tell her I gave her away."

"Are you willing to tell this story under oath?"

When Rosanna nodded, the judge turned to the state attorney and the defense attorney, "Under the circumstances, Miss Martinez, you will call Mrs. Donovan as your next witness. You will only need to ask her one question, there will be no redirect. You may then request the charges against your client be dismissed. If there is no objection from the prosecution, then I will dismiss the case. But before we do, I want to meet with Carter McDeal. Then I want Jocelyn McDeal escorted to my chambers. This is not news she should receive in my court room."

The bailiff was summoned again and asked to bring Carter to the judge's chambers.

Looking at Tom Gorman, Elena smiled. "All in a day's work, don't you think? Thanks for being so gracious about this."

"No sense in dragging this one out. Mrs. Donovan and Mrs. Sanders will sign an affidavit and that will be the end of this case. This one is a draw, counselor. Your client is a free man and neither of us won or lost."

"I knew I liked you, Tom."

The door opened and a bewildered Carter was escorted into the room. He was startled when he saw Rosanna. Before a word was said, he looked Rosanna in the eyes and whispered, "Thank you."

"It's over Carter. In just a few minutes, I will move for the prosecution to drop the charges against you and ask the judge to dismiss the case. It's finally over and you will soon be a free man," said Elena.

Carter walked over and knelt down in front of Rosanna. He took her hand, and again whispered, "Thank you. From the bottom of my heart, thank you." Then he stood up with a jolt and looked at the judge, "Oh my god, my daughter is in the courtroom. We can't let her hear this in court. I've got to go and get her." Carter's concern for his daughter swept away the relief he was feeling and he started for the door.

"Slow down Mr. McDeal, you had to be told first. Jocelyn will be brought to my chambers as soon as we go back into the courtroom. I will give Mrs. Donovan a few minutes to meet with her daughter." Then he turned to Rosanna, "Mrs. Donovan, do you want to meet your daughter alone, or do you want your family with you?"

"Thank you, judge. I would like for my husband to be here. But I think it would be difficult on everyone if my sister and nephew were here. After Jocelyn has had time for the shock to wear off, then she and Mark will need some time." She turned to Carter, "I knew you would be a good father and I never meant to cause you all these problems. How can I ever make it up to you?"

"Rosanna, you gave my mother and me the greatest gift of our lives. I always knew she belonged to you but I didn't even know your last name. This past year, when I thought I had lost her forever,

I realized how much Jocelyn means to me. There's no need to apologize to me. Jocelyn is our concern now."

The judge motioned for Carter and the attorneys to return to the court room and told the bailiff to go and get Jocelyn. "Mr. McDeal, before we resume court, do you need to speak to your daughter?"

"If you could give me one moment with her, I think I can soften the shock for her. I would like to be the one to prepare her for this moment."

"Okay. I'll give you a few minutes. Then the bailiff will escort you back to the court room."

Carter walked out in the corridor to wait for his daughter. The word daughter took on new meaning for him and he hoped when this was over, Jocelyn would want him to still be her father. Then he smiled. Jocelyn was his daughter, no matter what anyone said or thought. He closed his eyes and said a prayer of thanks and then he whispered to his mother, "You always told me if I took care of the little things, God would take care of the rest. Mom, it took a team, but that's what just happened here. You were right."

Chapter Forty-three

Jocelyn and Rosanna

Jocelyn was surprised when the bailiff approached her and told her to follow him to the judge's chambers. As she stood up to go with him, Miss Moss stood up to follow. "I'm sorry, ma'am. My directions were to bring only Miss McDeal."

"But I'm her guardian. I need to go with her," Miss Moss was indignant she was being excluded. But, the bailiff assured her, he was following orders, "Please take a seat. I'm sure Miss McDeal will be back out here in a minute."

Reluctantly she returned to her seat, and kept her eyes on Jocelyn until she disappeared behind the door that led to the judge's chambers.

When Jocelyn saw her father standing in the hallway, she got nervous. She thought he wasn't supposed to have contact with her but he seemed to be waiting on her. As soon as they reached him, the bailiff excused himself and left the two of them to stare at one another. Jocelyn was the first to speak, "Okay, what's going on? Why did they bring me back here?"

"Hi, sweetheart. It's great to see you," Carter paused for a moment to look at his daughter. "Jocelyn, you once asked me who you were and I didn't have the answer. Today, when you enter that room, you are going to have your questions answered. Are you ready for the truth?"

"What are you talking about?"

"You know your grandmother loved you, and I love you still, but the person who loves you most in the world is waiting for you in that room. Be gentle with her, Jocelyn. She needs you as much as you need her."

"Dad, who is in that room? You're scaring me."

"There's nothing to be afraid of, Jocelyn. Today you will finally know the truth. I have to go back to court, and you have to go in there. I just hope you'll want to talk with me about it later." Carter walked around Jocelyn and headed back to the court room.

Jocelyn's head was spinning. Who was she really about to meet? Did she really want to know the truth? She opened the door and took a long look at the two people sitting in the room. Now she was really confused.

"Hi, Jocelyn, my name is Paul Donovan and this is my wife, Rosanna. Please come in and take a seat. My wife has a lot to tell you."

Rosanna stayed seated. She knew if she tried to stand up, her legs would give way beneath her. Her palms were sweaty but she knew, for her daughter's sake, she had to get through this with some kind of grace. She raised her head and looked into the face of her beautiful, grown-up daughter. Then she smiled.

"Hello, Jocelyn. As my husband said, my name is Rosanna. I don't know how to make this easy even though I've dreamed of this day for a long, long time. So I'll just say what needs to be said." Folding her hands in her lap, Rosanna looked to Paul for encouragement, and then raising her head to meet her daughter's eyes, she said the words she had been longing to say for 18 years. "Jocelyn, I am your mother."

Jocelyn was speechless. She had often dreamed about what her mother would be like if she had lived but she had never imagined that her mother might be alive. She didn't know what to say or how to act.

The silence grew uncomfortable until Paul walked around his wife and stood in front of Jocelyn, "We know you are probably in shock, but we're hoping someday you will want to know us better. You may think what you've just heard is the hard part of this conversation but unfortunately, there is more you need to know, Jocelyn."

Rosanna knew she had never loved Paul more than she did right now. No matter what happened between them in the future, at this moment, she felt loved and supported in ways she had never experienced before.

Jocelyn found her voice, and spoke quietly, "I can't imagine what you could say that would be more shocking than this. For 18 years, I believed my mother was dead. And, today I'm being told all those years were a lie. What could be more shocking than that?" She pulled a strand of her hair and began to twirl it around her finger.

"Oh, Jocelyn, I'm so sorry. I never meant to hurt you. There is so much I need to tell you. So much I want you to know. And, hopefully we will have time to share those things. But, first, I have to tell you that Nancy Sanders is my sister."

At first Jocelyn sat and stared as though she couldn't comprehend the meaning behind the words. Then it hit her like an explosion.

"No, no, no!" she cried.

Jumping up from the chair, Jocelyn started out of the room. But Paul was faster than she was and he got between her and the door.

"Please don't run away, Jocelyn. Please, come and sit back down, at least until you have calmed down. Please!" Paul was pleading with her, and he was blocking her path. He didn't try to touch her, his voice was soothing, but strong, and this caught Jocelyn's attention and forced her to stand still. "We know how hard this is on you and we can only imagine how you must feel. We won't stop you from leaving, once you have calmed down."

Jocelyn was enraged. She wanted to hit and kick this man and make him move out of her way. But Paul had gone into his 'police crisis' mode and he just kept talking to her with his soothing voice. She crumbled to the floor like a rag doll and buried her head between her knees. She couldn't cry, all she could do was rock back and forth. And, all the time, the man's voice kept soothing her. "Stay with us, Jocelyn. Don't run away. You're not alone. Stay with us." She could hear the words being repeated over and over. The tone was soft, but compelling. His words were drawing her back; he was not letting her go.

Somewhere in this void, this terrible empty place, she heard another voice. It came as a whisper, but she knew the voice and she felt her grandmother's love radiating from the sound, "It's going to be all right, sweetheart. It's going to be better than you ever imagined, even though it will hurt for a long, long time. Your mother loves you as much as I do. Remember that, Jocelyn. Remember that."

Closing her eyes, she wished with all her heart her grandmother was really there beside her. Nana would know how to help her get through this chaos. She would help her live in a world that couldn't include Mark. The hysteria was passing and she stopped rocking. She held her hand up to the man.

Paul reached down and gently pulled Jocelyn to her feet.

She turned to her mother, "I should want to know you, and should want you in my life. But I can't do it now. I can't think about it now. I have been in love with Mark for years, and when he finally noticed me, I thought I was the luckiest girl in the world. In two minutes, you've taken him away from me. All I want to do is get out of here. I don't want to deal with my father, Miss Moss, you. I don't want to deal with anything. Oh great, I just called Carter my father. Is he my father? Oh, dear God, will this ever end? "

Taking over again, Paul continued. "Jocelyn, Carter is your father, just not your biological father, and someday your mother will tell you all the details of your story. But, not today, today you have enough to deal with. Think, Jocelyn, is there anyone we can call to help you? We can't let you leave here alone."

Rosanna's heart broke for her daughter. She wanted to hold out her arms and comfort her, but she knew that now was not the time. She had not been in Jocelyn's life before this moment, and she realized that Jocelyn hadn't fully comprehended that she was in her life now. Naturally, Jocelyn's immediate thoughts were about Mark, and Rosanna was trying not to let that hurt her.

Jocelyn looked at Paul and saw the compassion in his eyes. "Mrs. Thompson is in the court room. Would you find her, please?" She felt numb. Her mind detached from her body and was no longer part of what was happening

Once Paul left the room, she turned to Rosanna, "Did my father know that you were my mother?"

"No, Jocelyn, he didn't know. When we have time, I'll tell you the whole story."

"Did you hurt as much as I'm hurting? I mean when I was born. Obviously Paul isn't my father, so there must have been someone else."

"Yes, I was hurt very badly, so badly I thought I would never let another man in my life. Thank, God, Paul changed that."

The door opened and Mrs. Thompson ran over and hugged Jocelyn to her. "Honey, what can I do?"

"Can I come to your house? Things have gotten really awful and I just need to be with you for a while."

"You know you can." She turned to Rosanna, "I'm Gloria Thompson. My daughter, Ruthie, is Jocelyn's best friend. Please, can someone explain what's going on?"

"Thank you for coming to help her. She's had a rough day. I'm Rosanna Donovan, and I'm Jocelyn's mother."

Mrs. Thompson's mouth fell open and she looked like she was going to say something. "You also need to know I'm Nancy Sanders' sister." There was total silence as Mrs. Thompson processed what Rosanna Donovan was saying.

"Dear God in heaven." Whispered Mrs. Thompson.

"I hope someday, we'll have a chance to talk, but right now I have to go in the court room and say the words that will make Carter McDeal a free man," Rosanna said quietly.

Mrs. Thompson tried to hide her surprise as she turned and nodded to Rosanna. She didn't say anything as she wrapped her arm around Jocelyn and led her from the room. Once they were outside the room, she began to quietly assure Jocelyn everything was going to be all right.

Rosanna felt emotionally and physically drained. "Paul, thank you for being here with me. I could never have gotten through this by myself." She smiled at her husband. "I can't go back to Nancy's. I can't handle any more drama."

"I agree. We don't need to be at Nancy's today. Why don't we head to the beach. We can check into a hotel for a day or two."

"Oh, Paul, thank you. I need to get away so I can get myself back together. Your mom is watching the kids for this whole week so it's not like we have to hurry back to California."

***

Elena was thrilled by the turn of events. The charges against her client had been dropped, the ethical issue of Mark and Jocelyn was, at least out in the open. Now she could begin planning her wedding! She couldn't wait to get back to the office and call Eric. He wasn't going to believe what had happened. But first, she had to talk with Carter.

***

He was standing in the back of the courtroom talking with the people who had come to court to help him out. They were all there, Mrs. Snyder, Mr. Fitz, Miss Ruby, Sully, and Mrs. Dillon. They were hugging and shaking his hand and telling him they knew all along he was innocent. Elena loved happy endings. Well, at least her part of Carter's story had one. She noticed a very attractive woman who appeared to be more than a bystander, standing slightly behind Carter, and she wondered who she was. When she had a chance, she'd ask him.

"Excuse me, I don't want to break up this party, but there are a few things I need to go over with you, Carter. Why don't I wait for you in the corridor?" Then she turned and spoke to the group, "I'm really happy I had the chance to meet you all. Carter is lucky to have you for friends."

She walked out of the courtroom knowing she truly meant what she said. It was a pleasure to meet such genuine people. She sat down on one of the benches and relaxed for the first time in days. In a few moments, Carter and the mystery woman joined her on the bench. The others waved good-bye and walked out of the court house.

"Miss Martinez, I'd like for you to meet my friend, Sharon Bowers. You don't mind if she's here, do you?"

The two women exchanged greetings, and Elena went through some of the paper work they had to deal with. "Call Susan tomorrow, Carter, and set up some time for us to meet in the next few days." She stood up to leave, and extended her hand to him. "I couldn't be happier for you. I know you still have some hard days to live through, but you won't have this hanging over your head ever again and that's a very good thing. Mrs. Bowers, it was nice meeting you."

"Miss Martinez, have you seen Jocelyn? I've been watching for her, but I never saw her come back into the court room. I see Miss Moss over there, but no Jocelyn," Carter inquired.

"The last I was told, she asked to see Mrs. Thompson, and I think they left together. She's had some real shocks today, Carter. Why don't you call the Thompson's later? I'm sure she will know where your daughter is."

As Elena walked away, Mary Ann Moss was approaching Carter. The woman looked agitated and upset. If Elena didn't know better she would say Miss Moss was unhappy Carter had not been convicted. She had never liked the woman, and wondered how much longer Jocelyn would stay at her apartment. Technically, Jocelyn could go home tonight.

"Mr. McDeal, it looks like you were saved by the bell, so to speak." The sarcasm dripped from Mary Ann's voice and it was obvious to those standing around Carter that Miss Moss was not happy with today's outcome. "Have you seen Jocelyn? She never came back to the courtroom and I need to take her home."

"You know, Miss Moss, she left the building with Mrs. Thompson." He turned away.

"Yes, you're right. She's probably at the apartment waiting for me. Mr. McDeal, I don't think you will have any success in convincing Jocelyn to move back to your house. If I were you, I'd give up trying to claim her as your daughter." Spinning on her heels, she hurried toward the exit.

"That woman is wretched!" exclaimed Sharon. "I'll go and move Jocelyn's things myself just to get her away from that woman."

Carter was surprised at the venom he heard in Miss Moss's voice but he wasn't going to let her spoil today's victory. When Carter looked up, Rosanna was walking toward him. "I am sorry for all the trouble I caused. I hope you can forgive me."

"Rosanna, please stop worrying about me. How did it go with Jocelyn?"

"She's devastated." Rosanna looked concerned, but then her expression changed. "You did a good job raising her and I know she's going to be all right."

"Thank you, Rosanna. My mother deserves the credit, not me."

"Jocelyn is having a hard time and I hope someday she will be able to forgive me. Thank goodness she has Mrs. Thompson. She'll know what Jocelyn needs today. Paul and I will be in Miami for several more days. Do you think it would be okay for me to call you before we leave? There's so much I need to explain."

"I'd like that, Rosanna. We have so much to catch up on." He looked at her and smiled, "I forgot to thank you for saving my life today."

Rosanna and Paul started for the door just as Father Sean was coming out of the court room. "Just the people I wanted to see. Rosanna, it has been a long time. This must be your husband?" The priest extended his hand to Paul, "We have some broken hearts to mend, don't we? I've spent a few minutes with Jocelyn, and I saw Mark earlier as he was leaving. I came back to tell all of you they're going to be all right. They're strong young people and they can work through this. Pray for them, love them, and let them find their way."

"Thank you, Father, that's good advice," said Rosanna.

"Jocelyn and Mark know they can come and talk to me at any time, and I hope all of you know I'm here if you need me."

***

Mary Ann threw open the apartment door, and called Jocelyn's name. She looked in the kitchen, and in the bedrooms but the girl was not there. She checked Jocelyn's closet to see if her overnight bag was still there and breathed a sigh of relief when she saw it on the shelf. "Good," she said out loud, "that means she will be home sometime soon."

She made herself lunch, watched some television, graded a set of test papers, and, then started dinner. It was 6:00 in the evening and Jocelyn wasn't there. She went to the phone and dialed the Thompson's number but the phone line was busy. She ate her dinner, took a shower, got ready for bed, and picked up a book to read. It was 8:00 and still, Jocelyn wasn't there. She called the Thompson's again and the line was still busy. At 10:00 she was becoming frantic. She decided she would try the phone one more time and if she didn't get an answer she was going to get dressed and drive to their house. She dialed the number and on the third ring, Mrs. Thompson answered the phone, "Thompson residence."

"This is Mary Ann Moss. Is Jocelyn with you? I'm about worried sick!"

"Miss Moss, I'm so sorry we didn't call. Jocelyn is asleep. I'll ask her to call you tomorrow. Good night."

Mary Ann looked at the phone in dismay. She couldn't believe the woman hung up on her.

PART FOUR

AND SHADOWS LINGER

We shall not cease from exploration
And the end of all our exploring
Will be to arrive where we started
And know the place for the first time.
T. S. Eliot

Chapter Forty-four

End of Court Day

Court was over; Carter was free; and poor Jocelyn was devastated. This was a day like none other and Nancy was glad it was over. Her son was a wreck but, with the help of a sleeping pill, she finally got him to go to sleep. She had apologized to her sister for the way she behaved last night and someday she would have a conversation with Elena Martinez about their meeting at the Coffee Zone. She really wanted the woman to know that all of this was a surprise to her, too. But, Mark was her main concern and her heart was breaking for him. Over dinner he had told her that he was thinking of leaving Miami for awhile - he needed to put some time and space between he and Jocelyn.

The house was finally quiet; Mark and Matt were asleep; Rosanna and Paul were at the beach. Nancy kicked off her shoes, poured herself a glass of wine and tried to relax. She was glad the charges had been dropped against Carter but she worried about Jocelyn. How was the girl dealing with everything? Did she have someone to help her through all this? What was going to happen when Mark and Jocelyn met as cousins? Better yet, how was she going to handle being the girl's aunt? Nancy groaned. One glass of wine isn't going to be enough tonight, I may need the whole bottle.

Mrs. Thompson gave Jocelyn a sleeping pill and called Ruthie on the phone. Then she went out to work in the yard so the girls could talk without her hovering over them. She told Ruthie to ignore the cost of the long-distance call and to talk until she was sure Jocelyn was okay. After forty minutes, Jocelyn walked out in the yard and told her she was going to go in Ruthie's room and lie down. "I'm so tired. Is it all right if I take a nap?"

She let Jocelyn sleep all afternoon and then through the night. She figured sleep would do her more good than food and didn't try to get her up for dinner.

When Jocelyn came to the kitchen table the next morning, she looked miserable. "How are you, sweetie?" Mrs. Thompson gave her a hug and told her to fix herself a cup of coffee while she warmed up her breakfast.

"Talking to Ruthie helped. Thanks for calling her. She'll be home in a few weeks for break and that'll be good." Jocelyn sounded pitiful. "Mrs. Thompson, can you believe all of this? My head hurts trying to think about it. I'm not ready to talk to my dad. I don't know what I'm going to say to Mark. And what more can I possibly say to Rosanna?"

"Thank God, you don't have to do it all at once," Mrs. Thompson tried to put a lighter tone in her voice. She had to find a way to put a positive spin on Jocelyn's dilemma. "When you're ready, you'll find the words. But, you don't have to do it today. I was thinking we might drive over to the beach and take a walk. Are you up for that?"

"I don't have anything to wear"

"Go look in Ruthie's dresser. I'm sure you'll find some old shorts and t-shirts. We don't need to sit in this house and brood. Come on, it'll do you good. And better than that, we won't be here when Miss Moss starts calling."

That was all it took to convince Jocelyn. And, maybe as they walked, Mrs. Thompson could help her figure out what to do next.

They walked for more than an hour. When Mrs. Thompson suggested they go find a place to eat lunch, Jocelyn was actually hungry. The sun was warm, and even though there was a breeze, both of them were feeling the heat. Across the street from the beach were several sandwich shops that catered to beach goers, so they knew they could go inside in shorts and flip-flops.

After they ordered, Jocelyn began to talk. "I need a place to live. There is no way I want to go back to Miss Moss and I don't think I want to go back home. Maybe, if I put a notice up at school, someone will need a roommate. My job at the library doesn't pay enough so I'll have to find one that pays more. And, if I have to quit school, then I'll quit school."

"Slow down, honey. Let's look at options. First, none of us want you to quit school. There has to be a way around that. I'd love for you to live with us. But my three bedroom house is popping at the seams - Ruthie, Janie and Betsy share, Peter and Larry share, and I don't think you want to share with me and Ruthie's dad. But, tell me something. Why don't you want to go home?"

"I've said some pretty awful things to my dad and he knows how angry I've been. Besides, it looks like he has some woman in his life."

Mrs. Thompson laughed, "Jocelyn McDeal, I think you're jealous! Cut your dad some slack, sweetie. He's been alone for a long time. If he's found someone, try and be happy for him."

"I am not jealous! It's just that things have changed and I'd be in his way."

"Before you jump to conclusions, why don't you talk to your dad about all of this? And I guarantee you will never be 'in his way' so get that notion out of your head. In all of this you keep over looking how much your dad loves you."

"Maybe someday I'll talk to him, but not now. And, how am I going to face Mark? Ruthie said to call him, but I'm afraid to."

"You know what? He's probably saying the same thing. Don't you think he's hurting as much as you?"

"How do I start the conversation? Howdy, cousin. Sorry I can't be your girlfriend anymore." The sarcasm and pain were heavy in her voice. Then she softened. "That sounded ugly, didn't it?"

Mrs. Thompson was determined to keep her from falling into depression. "That's a start, but it would probably sound better for you to tell him he's a great guy and you're glad he's in your life – one way or another." She smiled at Jocelyn, "Come on, honey. This pity party is over. You have blessings to count. Instead of looking at yesterday, keep your eyes on tomorrow."

Jocelyn looked at the woman she had always wished was her mother, and smiled.

Chapter Forty-five

Sharon and Carter

After the case had been dismissed, Sharon invited Carter to her house for dinner. "I'll fix you a celebration feast. This is one of the best days of your life and I'd like to celebrate it with you."

"You don't have to ask me twice. I'm absolutely drained and the thought of relaxing in your garden is very appealing. But I'll stop on my way over and get carry-out. I want this to be a celebration for you, too."

"Sounds great. I'll go on and start chilling a bottle of wine. See you at the house."

They sat in the garden until it was almost dark. The day had worn down Carter's emotions and, if he had been asked, he would never have found words to express what it felt like to have the weight of the trial removed. He hadn't realized how heavy the last year and half had been until the judge looked at him and said, "Mr. McDeal, you are free to go. The charges against you have been dropped and this case is dismissed." All his fears of prison vanished with those words. Still, he wondered if he would ever be able to erase the damage caused by those fears.

He didn't feel like talking and let the silence seep into all his wounds. The air was heavy with the fragrance of jasmine mingled with the salt from the ocean. Finally, he said, "Sharon, do you think the salty air can really heal?"

"Maybe it can heal the hurts on the surface, Carter. But I think you're going to need time to heal the deeper ones."

"I couldn't have gotten through this without your friendship. You helped keep me grounded."

"That's what friends do for each other, Carter. I believed in you when you didn't believe in yourself. I figured you needed someone to keep reminding you what a good man you are."

"Thank you." He walked over to the swing where she was sitting and sat down beside her. He held her hand and let the gentle swaying of the swing lull him into a feeling of peace. "There is so much I want to say to you. Maybe someday there will be a right time to say it all. But, right now, all I can say is thank you."

She stopped the motion of the swing and stood up. She held his hand and pulled him to his feet. "Do you know I have waited almost twenty years for you to kiss me again?" She put her arms around him and his lips on hers told her he wanted her as much as she wanted him. "Carter," she whispered, "we have some unfinished business and I can't think of a better time for us to take care of it."

***

Carter woke up happy. He reached over and touched Sharon's arm to make sure he hadn't imagined her or the evening they had shared. After years of dreaming what this moment would be like, she had not disappointed him. He knew he would never get enough of her. Her body was pleasure and sensations and comfort. In some ways, he was glad he was twenty years older because he knew as an over zealous young man, he would never have been able to appreciate and enjoy her the way he did last night. Their love making was slow and sensual and unselfish.

He still couldn't believe the way his life had come together yesterday. His legal worries were over, his belief that Rosanna was Jocelyn's mother had been affirmed, and the words convicted felon no longer had power over him. Sharon's touch had been like a magnet drawing out all his worries and concerns. There was still so much for him to think about - his daughter, Rosanna, his job, Sharon. But the heaviness attached to his thoughts was gone.

It was different waking up in her room. The shadows across her walls were not as comforting as those in his room. Yet, he did like the way the light was diffused by the sheer curtains. Being here last night and this morning was the best part of what Sharon had offered him throughout this ordeal. Sharing her bed showed him how lonely he was at home. With Gracie and Jocelyn gone, the house was too silent, the rooms too empty. As much as he liked being alone, he didn't like being lonely. Sharon offered him a lifeline and he stepped out of the shadows to latch on to it.

Earlier, Sully had told him to take some time off, to give himself a chance to work through all that had happened. He said he could have his bus route back when he was ready to go to work. And then Sully surprised him. "Carter, I've been thinking you might be the man to apply for my job when I retire. You could probably handle it better than the other yokels around here. Anyway, give me a call next week and we'll get you back on the schedule. Glad things worked out."

Sometimes Sully was a man of few words, but these few words could change Carter's life. He was relieved he would be able to drive again, but he wanted things to die down some before he got back on the bus. People would recognize him from the pictures in the paper and on TV and he didn't want to talk about the trial with anyone he didn't know. In fact, he didn't want to talk about it with anyone he knew. He had accepted the well wishes from his friends in the courtroom yesterday; now he was ready to forget it.

There was one issue he couldn't forget about. How was he going to reach Jocelyn? When he saw Father Sean yesterday, the priest advised him to stand back and let Jocelyn come to him when she was ready. But he wanted to tell her he missed her and wanted her to come home. He wanted her to get to know Sharon. He wanted to be there to help her forge a relationship with her mother. He wanted to see for himself that she was getting the help she might need. From the moment of Gracie's death, their lives had been upside down. So many things had happened to each of them. He wanted to understand her relationship with Mark Sanders. Were they casual dating or were they serious? How was she dealing with the new twist that Mark was her cousin?

His thoughts were interrupted when Sharon turned over and snuggled up against him. "My schedule is open today. Is there anything you'd like to do?" Carter kissed her. "You mean besides staying in this bed all day?" She giggled.

"Are you inviting me to spend some more time in this bed?"

"Carter, I'd be happy if we stayed here all day and all night, too. I think I could become addicted to you very quickly."

"I'd say we have a plan. If we do decide to get out of bed, I'd like to sit on your patio and listen to the birds for awhile." Carter stretched and sat up. "My head has been so messed up this past year I can't remember if I've stopped long enough to hear a bird sing. Later, I'd like to talk about the one thing I haven't been able to think about for the past year - the future. I want you to help me figure out how to get my daughter back and I want to talk about us. But first things first."

Smiling, he took her in his arms.

Much later, as they sat on the patio enjoying a glass of wine and the sunset, Sharon suggested he invite Jocelyn to dinner. "Maybe she will go to dinner with you. I don't think you need to put pressure on her, but I do think you have to reach out to her. This isn't going to be repaired overnight so don't give up. Every time you reach out to her, you'll be letting her know she's important to you. She'll come around."

"I'll give it a try. If she agrees, will you go with me?"

"Not this time. She's going to need some time to get used to me. When she's ready, I would love to get to know her."

"What about us, Sharon? Where are we going with this relationship? You have to know I don't want to let you go. But I can't match your lifestyle and that bothers me."

"Carter, let's just enjoy what we've got. Now that you're out from under the pressure of the trial, you may find you don't need me as much."

He walked over to her and took her hand, "I will always need you in my life. As long as you're willing to put up with me, I'll be here."

"Good, Carter, 'cause I'm not going anywhere."

Chapter Forty-six

Jocelyn

Jocelyn returned to the apartment and faced the wrath of Miss Moss. "How could you be so inconsiderate? You just went off and left me at the court house. I didn't know where you were or what was going on," Miss Moss shouted.

"I'm sorry, Miss Moss. Yesterday wasn't the best day of my life. I should have told you I was leaving, I'm sorry."

"Well, did you come to get your things, or what?"

"I was hoping I could stay for a while longer. I haven't decided what I'm going to do."

Mary Ann calmed down, "You're not leaving?"

"I'd like to stay, if that's okay?"

"My goodness, you know it's okay. I was afraid you would be leaving me."

"Not yet, Miss Moss." Escaping to her room, Jocelyn closed the door. She hoped she would be leaving here sooner rather than later.

She decided to return to school the next day. It was never going to be easy to face people's questions so she might as well just do it. She was afraid if she stayed out longer, she wouldn't be able to pass her final exams. The sooner she got back to a normal routine, the better. If she ran into Mark, she'd deal with it. But, tonight she needed to study, and work on a paper that was due on Monday.

Two days later, Mark called and asked her to meet him at the corner. He said he really needed to talk to her. Just hearing his voice created warmth and excitement, and she longed to see him. But she knew how much it was going to hurt. What am I going to say to him? Her emotions were all mixed up as she left the apartment.

When she got to the corner, he motioned for her to get in the car. "Mark, can we go for a drive?" she said without looking at him. He didn't respond but started the car and pulled out in the street.

After an uncomfortable few minutes, he asked, "Are you okay?"

"No, but I'm better than I was. How 'bout you?"

"I'm hurting, Jocey. This is a crock - and we got caught in the middle of it. I'm not as angry as I was but I'm not good with any of this. Is it all right if I pull over? I can't drive and talk about this at the same time."

He pulled into a parking lot, turned off the motor, and looked at her, "I've never told you this, but I love you. I love you enough to go against our family and the church. But, we need for some time to pass. Everyone here has our future planned; and it's not together. I figured out I can't stay here, Jocelyn. I've got to get away."

Tears were running down her face. "I love you, too. You can't leave school, Mark," her voice was rising.

"I can't stay! If you love me, you'll try to understand."

"But, what will you do? You can't just run away."

"I'm not stupid, Jocey. A month or so ago, an agent called me with an offer, and I turned it down. Yesterday I called him back and the offer was still out there. I took it, Jocelyn, and I leave on Sunday."

"Where are you going? What are you going to do?

"I'm going to be a back-up guitar for Margo. I'm going on tour. They offered me some real money."

"Margo, the singer? Wow! How did that happen?"

"Somebody heard the band, made some inquiries, and called our agent. I went in to play for her front man and they offered me the gig. At the time, I wasn't ready. So I didn't mention it to you. Like I said, I called back and I'm going on the road. I'm joining the tour in

New Orleans. My folks aren't too happy with me right now but they'll get over it."

"That kind of settles things for us, doesn't it?"

"The next time we get together we may be able to think more rationally about us and our future. Right now, I need to get away from you and my family. You need time to get used to all the changes and if I'm in Miami, I won't be able to stay away from you. I'm trying to give us a chance, Jocey. We've both got a lot to think about. I'll call you so make sure you always have a number where I can reach you."

"Guess this is good-bye." Jocelyn sounded so forlorn.

"It's not good-bye, Jocey. It's time-out. I'm not ready to give you up."

They sat quietly for awhile, lost in their own thoughts and pain. "You know I trust you more than anyone right now and it's going to be hard on me whether you stay or go. Oh, Mark, I need you and I don't want you to go."

When he didn't answer her, she turned to look at him. "Oh, my god, Mark, what's wrong?"

He was staring at the ceiling of the car, his hands were trembling, and sweat was pouring off of him. She pulled on his arm and started shaking him but he didn't respond. Don't panic! Don't panic! then she remembered the conversation with his mother. Where was his backpack? Where would he keep his emergency stash of candy? She searched the glove compartment, the back seat, the door pockets. No candy bars, no canned soda, nothing. She kept calling his name but there was no change.

She opened the car door and started running to the store at the end of the block. "You've got to help me, please," she yelled at the clerk. "My boyfriend is diabetic and he's in trouble."

"Where is he?"

"He's in his car down the street. I need a candy bar or juice or a cola, but I don't have any money."

"Whoa, how am I going to help if you don't have any money, young lady?"

"If you don't trust that I'll pay you back, then call an ambulance," Jocelyn was frantic. "Please do something! Hurry."

The clerk realized she was serious and grabbed a carton of orange juice. He yelled to someone in the back of the store that there was an emergency, grabbed Jocelyn's hand, and ran with her down the street.

When they got to the car, Mark had not moved. The clerk opened the carton and held Mark's head as he forced the juice into his mouth. "Come on, buddy. Take a drink of the juice. That's it, keep swallowing. Come on, one more sip. You're doing great. One more sip. Take another sip."

After a few minutes, Mark began to rally and Jocelyn hoped the crisis was over. The clerk kept insisting that Mark drink more of the juice until he noticed color returning to Mark's face. "Wow, kid. You gave us a scare. Did you take your insulin today? Bet you were thinking about this pretty little lady and forgot, right?" Mark nodded his head. "You're lucky your girlfriend was around."

"Mark, are you okay?" Jocelyn was beginning to calm down. "You scared me. Thank goodness your mother told me what could happen to you."

"I'm okay. Thanks mister. Thanks Jocey." Mark's voice was weak, but he was starting to look like himself again. "I've got a bad headache. Jocey, do you think you can drive me home?"

"Sure. We'll work it out. Do you have a dollar so I can pay for the juice?" She turned to the clerk, "Thank you so much for your help. I was scared to death."

"Hey, the juice is on me. My mom is diabetic, so I knew to grab the juice when I realized you were for real. You guys take care."

Jocelyn thanked the store clerk again and told him how grateful she was that he knew what to do. "Mark, if you're feeling better, slide over and I'll drive you home."

When they got to Mark's house and Nancy was sure her son was not in crisis, she told Jocelyn she would drive her home.

"Wait, Mom. I need a few minutes with Jocelyn."

"Okay. Jocelyn, I'll wait for you in the car."

Mark reached over and took her in his arms. "I love you. I'll let you know how to get in touch with me as soon as I get to New Orleans." He kissed her gently and held her to him. "I wasn't going to say anything, but you know your mother did what she thought was best for you. Give her a chance to tell you her story." He laughed a sarcastic laugh, "Funny isn't it, I've known your mother all my life. She's really great, and you'll like Paul when you get to know him. And, Jocelyn, think about it. You got lucky with your grandmother and father." He kissed her again. "It'll take time but I know someday we'll be together. I'll talk to you soon."

"Take care of yourself and remember I'm waiting for you. You're in my heart, Mark, and I love you."

Jocelyn walked out the door and was surprised that she felt comfortable with Mark's decision. She would miss him but she knew he was coming back and that's what counted.

"Mrs. Sanders, thank goodness you told me about Mark. He scared me, but I knew what was going on so I could get him help."

"I guess with all that's been going on he got a little careless with his blood sugar. It concerns me that he's going on tour but I've got to trust him."

"He took me by surprise with the tour thing."

"His father's furious about school but I know why Mark needs to get away. Jocelyn, we need to talk about us."

"What do you mean, Mrs. Sanders?"

"I'm not Mrs. Sanders anymore. I'm your Aunt Nancy and we've got to learn how to be together in our new roles."

Jocelyn looked out the car window at the lights of the city. She turned and took a good, long look at her mother's sister. "God certainly has a sense of humor, doesn't He?"

When she returned from school the next afternoon, Miss Moss was waiting for her. "You're mother called and wants you to give her a call back. She says she's leaving for California in the morning and needs to talk to you. I left the number next to the phone."

"Please don't call her my mother. I don't feel like she's my mother, but I'll call and see what she wants." Picking up the phone, Jocelyn dialed the familiar number for Mark's house.

When Rosanna came to the phone, she asked Jocelyn to meet her for dinner that evening. "Rosanna, I'll tell you the truth. I had decided not to see you but Mark asked me to give you a chance. Against my better judgment I'll see you tonight. Where would you like to meet?"

She listened to Rosanna's suggestion, "Yes, I know where it is. It's on the bus route so it's convenient. I'll see you at 6:30."

Two in one week. Could she handle Rosanna on top of what she had gone through with Mark the previous afternoon? But, she didn't have too many options since Rosanna was leaving town. She sighed as she thought; "Now all I need is for my dad to call."

She turned to Miss Moss, "I'm going to meet her for dinner." Then she added, "This is a week for the books. Mark is leaving town on Sunday; Rosanna is leaving tomorrow; and everyone thinks I'm going to be able to pick up the pieces of my life. What a joke."

Jocelyn dressed for dinner and told Miss Moss not to wait up for her. "How are you planning to get home, Jocelyn? I don't like to think of you on the bus so late. Don't you want me to come and get you?"

"Thanks for offering, but I'll be okay. I don't think I'll be late." Before Miss Moss could argue with her, she hurried out the door.

Rosanna and Paul were waiting outside the restaurant for her when she arrived. The greetings were formal and the first few minutes of conversation were very stilted. At first, Paul carried most of the conversation and Rosanna and Jocelyn sat and listened. All at once, Rosanna took over, "Jocelyn, I know you don't have a place in your life for us, but I really don't want to lose you again."

"You never lost me. You gave me away. Remember?" Jocelyn didn't realize how harsh her voice sounded.

"You're right, I did give you away. But at the time, my options were very limited. I had no way to care for you. It was either Catholic Charities and an adoption by strangers, or the McDeal's and the life I carefully chose for you. I knew your grandmother and father would love you and take good care of you. That was my priority," she stopped and looked at her daughter hoping to see some kind of thawing in Jocelyn's icy expression. But, she didn't see any evidence that was happening. "I've heard all the details of the terrible way this all unfolded and how many lies you were told, and I'm sorry. I know my apologies don't change anything but I want you to know how I feel."

"We want you to meet your brother and sister, and hope someday you'll consider us part of your family," Paul's voice was imploring. "Give us a chance. No, better yet, give yourself the chance to be involved with your mother. She's a neat lady and I think you'll really like her if you get to know her better."

Jocelyn smiled at Paul. "You are very convincing, Paul. All I can promise right now is I won't close the door. You've got to give me some time." She turned to her mother, "Rosanna, I'd like it if you would call me every now and then. That's a start, isn't it?"

"Thank you, Jocelyn. That's a very good start," she sighed. Now the hard question. "How are you handling Mark's decision? His folks aren't doing too well, but they'll come around. I hope you can understand why he wants to leave."

"I don't understand much about my life right now. We'll just have to see what the future brings. Going on tour with Margo is great for his music. She's the hometown girl who made it big. It's not a bad choice for his career. And it's not over between us, Rosanna, if that's what you mean."

"You are amazing, Jocelyn. You've had a lot dumped on you this past year but you're holding up better than the rest of us," Paul complimented Jocelyn, and then turned to his wife. "And, you're doing better, too. The days at the beach were good for you."

They had finished their dinner and exchanged phone numbers and addresses, when Jocelyn looked at her mother and asked, "Why did you name me 'Jocelyn'? I've never met anyone else with my name, and I'm curious."

Rosanna smiled at her daughter, "It means 'light hearted,' and that was my wish for you. That you, and your life, would be light hearted."

Jocelyn was surprised when she let her mother give her a hug as they were saying good-bye. With time, maybe she would learn to love her. She already knew she liked her. And, after all these years, she could finally tell Ruthie who she looked like.

"Wait, Jocelyn. How are you getting home?" Paul asked.

"I'm riding the bus. I'll be fine. Remember, I'm a bus driver's daughter."

"Bus driver's daughter or not, it's late and this is Miami. It's not safe for you to be riding alone at this hour. We'll take you home." Paul laughed. "Do I sound like a step-father, or what?"

Chapter Forty-seven

Jocelyn

Dear Jocey,

You would have loved New Orleans. There was so much to see and do, but we were only there for three days. Right now, we are on the road to Dallas, then on to Austin, and Albuquerque. I don't know where we go from there. Margo travels in a big, luxurious bus, and we follow behind in a couple of vans. She's a trip; sometimes she can be really nice and fun to be around, and other times she is demanding and mean. I've already seen a side of her that isn't good. So far, I haven't done anything to make her mad and I want to keep it that way. Booze and drugs are everywhere. Some of the guys in the band are heavy users. But I mostly hang out with a guy named Pete who thinks more like I do. We're both good with a couple of beers.

The music is great and the crowds love her. I've never seen anything like it. Everywhere she goes there are mobs of people, and they think I'm great just because I'm with her.

I miss you. I know you will be taking finals in a few weeks, so study hard and stay out of trouble (I'm kidding). I'll call you when I can. If you'd like to write me, here's an address where the band gets mail. Make sure you put this code after my name on the envelope so they'll know its personal mail: M5X52

PO Box 1844, Miami, FL 33139

Funny, isn't it? But someone in Miami gets the mail to us no matter where we are.

I love you.

Mark

The highlight of her week was knowing that Mark kept his promise about writing to her. Studying was going well, her term papers were turned in and she was looking forward to summer. Ruthie would be home in a few weeks and, no matter what, she was going to spend as much time with her as possible. No one replied to her notice about needing a roommate but she wasn't giving up. Something would turn up sooner or later.

Right now things were manageable with Miss Moss. She knew she wasn't giving the woman anything to complain about; all she did was go to school, study, and go to work. Aside from missing Mark, life was feeling more normal.

She was caught off guard when Miss Moss said her father called. She hadn't talked to him since the day of the trial and had convinced herself he was enjoying being free of her. "Did he say what he wanted?"

"Now, Jocelyn, you know you're father wouldn't share that with me. I'm sure he hates me." Miss Moss almost sounded remorseful for initiating the problems Carter had lived through. But Jocelyn knew better. She was convinced Miss Moss still didn't believe Rosanna was her mother.

"I'm sure he doesn't hate you. It must be something important if he called."

"Maybe; maybe not. You won't know unless you call him back. But, if I were you, I'd ignore the call."

Miss Moss knew how to be mean and most of the time Jocelyn let her barks and sarcasm go by unnoticed. That last remark sounded like a challenge, so Jocelyn picked up the phone and dialed her home number. Even though she hadn't called the number in almost a year, it felt right. Her father answered quickly. "Hi Dad, it's me. Miss Moss said you called." Carter asked her a few polite questions about school, and then asked if she would have dinner with him on Saturday. "You name the place, and I'll meet you there, Jocelyn."

"Sorry, but I'm busy on Saturday," she lied.

"Okay, then we can meet on Sunday. Why don't I meet you after Mass and we'll go to that Italian restaurant down the block from the church."

"You really are persistent, aren't you?"

"If you'd rather not, I understand. Good-bye, Jocelyn."

"Wait, Dad, Sunday lunch won't work, but I could meet you some time in the afternoon. I'll be working at the library until 3:00, so why don't I meet you in Bayfront Park. We don't need to meet for dinner."

"Okay, why don't I wait for you on the steps of the library?"

"That's a good idea. I'll see you then."

She knew she had to get this meeting over with. Her feelings for her dad were like picking the petals off a daisy: I love my dad, I'm mad at my dad, I love my dad, I'm mad at my dad. One by one she was making peace with all the players in her life and her dad might as well be next. She couldn't figure out why she was being so resistant.

On Sunday, Jocelyn finished her work at the circulation desk and headed for the door. Her dad would already be there waiting for her. He was so predictable. And, sure enough, when she walked out the door, he was standing on the steps watching the pigeons.

"Hi, Dad," she said as she walked up behind him.

"Hi, sweetheart, it's good to see you. Let's take a walk and find a bench in the shade. Is that okay with you?"

Everything about him was familiar but she sensed a difference. She couldn't put her finger on it but something had changed. She didn't recognize the clothes he was wearing and it surprised her to think he had finally caught up with the fashions of the 70s. His hair was styled the same as always but she would bet someone other than the corner barber had cut it. Her dad was a nice looking man and she'd never even noticed.

"I've been standing on my feet all day, and it would feel great to sit down."

They walked along in silence. He hadn't tried to hug her and she was glad and sad at the same time. Was this meeting a bad idea? They seemed so uncomfortable with each other; it would probably be a very short meeting. "There's an empty bench over near the water, and it's got a little bit of shade. We got lucky," she said and walked ahead of him to claim the bench.

After they sat down, there was more silence. She stared at the bay, the fishing boats, and the people passing by. Was he waiting for her to break the silence? "What did you want to talk about?"

"I wanted to see how you're doing, see if there was anything you needed. I thought you might tell me about Barry and the classes you're taking. I guess I just wanted to spend some time with you."

"I'm holding on, if that's what you mean. I love Barry and I'm getting my freshman requirements out of the way. Next semester I'll be able to take some of the classes in my major, and that'll be more interesting. That's about it."

She knew she wasn't making this easy. Her dad was not very good at small talk, and she could tell he was trying so hard to think of things to say.

"Let's get this over with, Dad. If you want to know whether I'm coming home, the answer is no. I know I've got to move out of Miss Moss's. She's driving me crazy, but I'm not coming back to 11th Avenue." She saw the hurt in his eyes, but she meant what she said.

"I'm sorry about that, Jocelyn. I just want you to know the door is always open, and I miss you."

"Who is that woman, Dad?" Jocelyn demanded.

He looked startled by the intensity in her voice, and he studied her for a few minutes before he answered, "Someday I'd like for you to meet her, Jocelyn. Her name is Sharon Bowers, and a very long time ago I was engaged to her."

"You were engaged? I never knew about that." She was stunned, and then wondered how many other things she didn't know about her dad. "When were you engaged?"

"I guess I was about your age when I asked her to marry me. Then I went off to war, and she married someone else."

"If she's married to someone else, why is she hanging around you?"

"She's divorced now and we happened to run in to each other before Christmas. In fact, it was the day I bought your sweater. She helped me pick it out."

"I knew someone helped you but I never thought it was someone you were dating." She giggled to think her dad was dating at his age. "You are going out with her, aren't you?"

"Yes, you might call it that. She's very special to me."

"Wait, she dumped you for another guy twenty years or so ago; now you think she's special. Didn't she break your heart?"

"Jocelyn, sometimes love doesn't just go away because someone else wants it to. I realized when I saw her again that I had never stopped loving her. It wasn't hard to forgive her after that."

She looked at her dad and decided she didn't really know much about how he felt, or the hurts he had experienced. She always assumed he was single because he was shy and never put himself out there to meet anyone. There was a long silence before she turned to him and asked, "Are you planning to marry her?"

"Not any time soon. It's complicated."

"How so?"

"Well, for one thing, she has a lot more money than I do. For another thing, she has kids that need to be considered. And, for another thing, I would never marry her without your approval."

"She has children? How old are they?"

"Oh, I think they are probably a few years older than you. There are three boys. One's married, one's in the military, and the other is in college. None of them live at home."

"You wouldn't marry her if I didn't approve. Is that what you just said?"

"Jocelyn, you're my family. You're all the family I have. Your opinion matters to me." He looked at her with a serious expression, and she suddenly realized two things: she was his only family and he really cared what she thought.

"Dad, how do we get back to a place where we are family? I don't know how to do that right now. Sometimes I think you and Nana and Rosanna conspired against me. I know, I know, that's not true. But your decisions make me feel like you threw me off a cliff."

"All of us, in our own way, were trying to protect you. But I'm the bad guy in all of it, Jocelyn. I should never have gone along with your grandmother. I should have gone through the legal channels, but your grandmother was so afraid they would come and take you away from us. And, after awhile, it didn't seem important. You had become our family. Someday, if it's not too late, I'd like to make it legal. When, and if you're ready, I'd like to adopt you."

Jocelyn watched the fishing boats returning to the docks. She watched as the fish were unloaded and the tired, sun-burned fishermen gathered their gear. This took her mind off the conversation and gave her an excuse to stop talking. She didn't know what else to say to her father and she wondered if she was too old to be adopted.

"Oh, before I forget it, here's your house key. Now that the restrictions have been lifted, you can have it back. Hang on to it, just in case you ever need it or want to come home."

"Thanks. I'll keep that in mind. I need to go; I've got tons of studying to do. After finals are over, maybe you can take me to meet Sharon. No promises, we'll see how it goes, okay?"

"We'll see how it goes. Do you want a ride?"

"No, thanks, I'll take the bus." She stood up and headed to the bus stop on Biscayne Boulevard. "See you, dad," she called over her shoulder.

Chapter Forty-eight

Sharon and Carter

"How was your time with Jocelyn?" Sharon asked that night. "Was she open to anything you had to say?"

"You know, I think she was. She's not ready to come home, but she didn't slam a door in my face."

"Do you think she's handling things well? You know with all she's been through, she might need to see a counselor."

"Maybe I should ask Father Sean to see her. He would know if she needed to see someone. I'll give him a call tomorrow."

"That's a good idea. Did you have a chance to talk to her about Mark?"

"Not really. But she sure wanted to know about you. It seems silly, but I almost got the feeling she's jealous of you."

Sharon laughed, "I'm not surprised. She's had you all to herself for 18 years; now she thinks she might have to share you with someone else. I understand completely and that's the reason we'll take it slow. We have four kids who will need to adjust to our relationship."

Holding her close, Carter enjoyed the touch of his skin on hers and imagined all the places on her body that he would like to touch. After all the years of self-imposed celibacy, he was hungry for anything she would give to him. Sharon was a good teacher; she had guided him to ecstasy as she opened her heart and her body to him. She knew where to touch him, and how to stir his passion to a fevered pitch.

"Let's not talk about the kids anymore. Talk to me about how much you like our loving, and all the things you want to do with me right now," he whispered in her ear. His mouth covered hers; his hands reached to caress her breasts; and his senses came alive to her touch, her taste, her wetness. He wanted to get lost in her and she was more than eager to let him. As their bodies began to move as one, Carter knew she was all he would ever need or want.

They made love, slept and made love again. There were so many wasted years to make up for.

Chapter Forty-nine

Jocelyn

Dear Mark,

It sounds like you are learning to adjust to life on the road…but don't start enjoying it too much! I miss you more than you can imagine.

I took your advice and had dinner with Rosanna and Paul. You're right, they are people I should probably try to get to know better. I even found myself laughing at some of Paul's jokes, so that must be a good sign. They want me to plan a trip to California to meet their children, but I'm not ready for that step. Rosanna says she will call me and she told me she is sorry for all the years she has missed with me. It's all too strange for me to deal with right now and I don't think I will ever be able to call her my mother.

It got even stranger when I met with my dad. He met me after work on Sunday and we sat in Bayfront Park for an hour or so. We talked….can you believe it….we actually had a conversation. He really wants me to move back home. I don't think I'm angry with him anymore, but I'm not convinced I should go home. (What I really want is a place of my own!)

I asked him about that woman and it turns out he used to be engaged to her. (There is so much I don't know about him.) I think he's in love with her! Any way, he wants me to meet her and says he wants me to give him my approval to move forward with their relationship.

He's different, Mark. Maybe it's being in love that has made him seem more willing to talk. Or maybe it's because he thinks he has to win me back. Whatever the reason, it's the first time in my life that I feel like he is really reaching out to me. I've always felt like he loves me, but we just never connected. When I had Nana I didn't need his connection, too. Maybe I'm like Rosanna, maybe I'm the one who has missed out on having a relationship with him. Do you think it's too late for me to try? And, what if I don't like Sharon? That would be another blow to our relationship.

On a different note, I'm still looking for a new job...one that will pay me enough to move out of this apartment. Miss Moss gets more controlling every day and I can't stand that she is always trying to hug me. She is either fussing at me about something or trying to touch me. Maybe I should move back home.

I can't wait for Ruthie to get home for summer break. If I moved back home, I could spend more time with her. I have really missed her....one more reason to go home!

Mark, I miss you. I miss talking to you....you always give me a different perspective, and you seem to forgive others so much easier than I do. My head knows I should be forgiving, but my heart hasn't caught up yet. I just don't want to hurt anymore.

Tonight, all I want is to be with you....I want you to hold me and tell me everything is going to be all right. And, a few of your kisses would really make me feel better!

Take care of yourself and come home soon.

I love you,

Always yours, Jocey

Chapter Fifty

Carter

Carter drove to the bus barn with excitement. Today he wasn't going to be sitting behind a desk; he was going to be back behind the wheel of the Route Six bus. He parked the car and walked over to the office to punch his time card. When he opened the door, Sully was sitting behind his desk, cigar smoke circling around his head.

"Hey, shut that door, you're letting out my air-conditioning. You think you can remember how to drive that bus? Oh, right, I don't need to worry, you've got your checklist," Sully laughed. "Good to have you back, McDeal. Don't you get out of line again, or I'll have you back on the routing desk before you can snap your finger. Now, you're wasting my time, I got buses to run."

"Good to see things haven't changed, Sully. I'll catch you when I get back this afternoon."

"One more thing, McDeal. Who's that pretty lady that was hanging all over you at court? She must be blind to wanna be seen with the likes of you."

"She's somebody special, Sully. I'd like for you to meet her someday."

Carter closed the door and started across the parking lot toward his bus. There was a bounce in his steps and he found himself whistling as he pulled out his checklist and started his day.

The steering wheel of the bus felt good in his hands as he headed the bus toward Hialeah and the first stop of the day. It was a typical Miami morning and he remembered how much he liked watching the city wake up. It was going to be a beautiful day; he could already see a touch of blue sky and white fluffy clouds. He took a deep breath of the salty air drifting across the land. As the bus moved down 36th Street toward Allappatah, the city was really beginning to wake up. The streets were getting busy with cars, and the noises that could only be heard in a city were growing louder and louder. He smiled; this was his symphony, the music and rhythm of the city he loved and he had missed it.

Mrs. Snyder was the first person to board the bus. A big grin crossed her face when she saw Carter behind the wheel. "Well, look who's back! Sure is good to see you this morning. It's been way too long, and all those other drivers were real grumps."

"It's good to be back, Mrs. Snyder. How're you doing this morning?"

"Carter, I'm fine. But, I've got to tell you my good news. I'm retiring next month, and moving to North Carolina. Never thought I'd leave Miami but my son wants me to move up nearer to him and I'm going to give it a try."

"That's great news, Mrs. Snyder. You might even like North Carolina. I hear it's pretty up there. What city are you moving to?"

"I'll be just outside Charlotte in a little town called Concord. All I can say is its going to be different."

"I've learned different can really be better, Mrs. Snyder. In fact, it can be more than you ever imagined. You know, I've been giving some thought to going back to school, maybe get a degree in business. Maybe I need to do something besides drive the Route Six bus."

"Good for you, Carter. Good for you."

The bus rolled on and the passengers piled in; some with smiles, some with nods, and others who didn't even look awake yet. Carter felt the ghosts of those whose lives had moved on - Rosanna, Miss Ruby, Mr. Fitz, - and he wondered which of his passengers would take their place. One thing was for sure, everyone on this bus had a story and it usually wasn't anything like you thought it would be.

Chapter Fifty-one

Elena

Elena sat down with her mother to go over the guest list one last time; she was going to order the invitations that afternoon and had to have a better idea of how many more people her mother had added to the list. It seemed like every day, her mother thought of someone else who had to be included. "If you add any more people, we'll have to find a bigger church. Between you and Eric's mother, I think we've invited all of south Florida."

"I just don't want to forget anybody. This is a big deal, Elena, and everyone loves a wedding. Stop complaining and start enjoying."

"I'll try. But weddings are a lot of stress. I'll just be glad when it's over."

She and Eric had carefully planned each detail. They had talked over who to include in the wedding party; sorority sisters, fraternity brothers, family members. Just selecting them had been an ordeal. If you asked this one, then you had to ask that one, or somebody's feelings would be hurt. They had gone over his parents' plans for the rehearsal dinner and helped select the menu. They had started their marriage classes at the church, picked the flowers, tasted every possible cake, and finally, selected the invitations. This is like preparing for trial, Elena thought. But, thank goodness, I'll only have to do this once!

They had big dreams. They talked about where they wanted to be in five years. Eric wanted a large family; she'd be happy with two children. She told him she could probably manage two children and continue to practice law. He said he wanted her to quit work when the children started coming. But she balked at that. When he saw she was digging in her heels, he came up with a new idea.

"I think we should go out on our own, start our own firm. We work well together, don't you think."

"You're serious about this idea?"

"Why not? In a few years, you can leave the public defender and we'll both have enough experience to make a go of it. This way, you set your own case load; you can have time for the kids and the law. I think Martin Cannon, in my office, would go with us. Let's think about it after this colossal wedding is over."

"I'm sorry. It has gotten to be a production, hasn't it? Maybe we should have eloped."

"Yeah, I agree. How do think Randall, Randall, and Cannon sounds?"

"I think we need to keep Martinez in the name. That will help us bring in Hispanic clients. Randall, Martinez, and Cannon sounds better. But, let's get back to the wedding. Did you make our airline and hotel reservations? A week in Bermuda! I can't wait!"

Chapter Fifty-two

Jocelyn

As a retired FBI agent, Lawrence Fitz, had the time to do a background search on Mary Ann Moss. There was something about the woman that made the hair on the back of his neck stand up. And, this made him very concerned for Jocelyn McDeal.

He had an eye-opening conversation with a Sister of Mercy who had been in the convent with her in Iowa. The sister had shared with him that after Mary Ann left the convent there was a suspicion that she had stolen some money. The sister also hinted that there might have been an inappropriate relationship between Mary Ann and another novitiate named Margaret.

That was all he needed to convince him that Jocelyn McDeal needed to be removed from her current living situation and he had an idea of how that could be accomplished.

***

Finals were over, and Jocelyn felt good about having her freshman year behind her. Her grades ensured that she would keep her scholarship, and she had pre-registered for all of her sophomore classes. She was still disappointed no one had called her about sharing an apartment and when she talked to the housing administrator, she was put on a waiting list for dorm space.

She spent the first week of summer applying for jobs and was blown away when Mr. Fitz called and offered her one. She had only seen the man a few times, including the day of her father's trial, and she couldn't imagine why he picked her.

"Jocelyn, this is Lawrence Fitz. I'm a friend of your father's. Remember? I used to ride the Route Six bus."

"Yes, Mr. Fitz, I remember you. What can I do for you, sir?"

"My dear, do you have plans for the summer? If not, I have a job to offer you. Your father tells me you are an English major, correct?"

"Yes, I'm an English major, and so far, I don't have a job for the summer. What kind of job, Mr. Fitz?"

"I'm writing my memoir and I need someone to type and edit for me. Do you think you would be interested? I'll pay you $8 dollars an hour and I'll need you to work about six hours per day. No work on the weekends. How does that sound?"

"Wow! That sounds better than great! You're offering me almost double the minimum wage. Mr. Fitz, are you sure you want me to do this? I'm just a student. I don't have any professional editing experience."

"I think you'll do fine, Jocelyn. But, if I see that your spelling is as atrocious as mine, we may have to make other arrangements. When might you be able to begin?"

"Give me your address and I can be there tomorrow. What time do you want me to start?"

Jocelyn got off the phone and danced a little jig. This was great news and $8 an hour was an outrageous amount of money.

"That sounded like a happy call, Jocelyn," Miss Moss said, and smiled at her. "I hope it was good news."

"I've got a job, Miss Moss, a great job that pays well. Why don't I treat you to dinner tonight to celebrate? I'm so excited I can hardly stand it! This is a double wow!"

Surprisingly, she and Miss Moss had a pleasant dinner. Jocelyn told her all about the job offer from Mr. Fitz, and the woman seemed genuinely pleased for her. She even offered to help if Jocelyn had an editing question.

"I've got a couple of books on editing and style I can loan you. They may be helpful. Do you know anything about this Mr. Fitz?"

"He knows my dad. He and his wife live in an apartment on Biscayne Boulevard. I've met him before, but I've never seen his wife."

"Well, it's good his wife will be there. You never know what might happen. I was worried you might be alone with him in that apartment all day."

Poor Miss Moss, Jocelyn thought. She always had to have something to worry about. But, soon, very soon, this job would give Jocelyn the money she needed to find a place of her own. She couldn't wait. Although she was having a somewhat pleasant dinner with Miss Moss, the woman continued to make her uncomfortable. For the last few weeks, Miss Moss seemed to always be right next to her. She tried to hug her, or she had her hand on Jocelyn's arm or back. It was getting creepy and Jocelyn wanted to move as soon as possible.

They finished dinner, walked back to the apartment and watched a show on TV. Then Jocelyn excused herself and went to her room to read and get ready to go to work the next morning. She set her alarm, laid clothes out on her chair, and took her shower. At 10:00, she turned out her light and was soon sound asleep.

Around midnight, Jocelyn awoke with a start. Someone's arms were around her and her breasts were being fondled. She jumped out of the bed and turned on the light. Miss Moss looked startled, and Jocelyn was outraged. "What are you doing in my bed? How dare you touch me like that?"

Miss Moss sat up, "Don't be angry, Jocelyn. I can explain. Just get back in bed and we'll talk. Everything will be fine if you'll just come back to bed."

"You are crazy!" Screaming, Jocelyn ran from the room. Even in the dark, she knew where to place her fingers on the phone to dial the numbers. She kept looking behind her to make sure Miss Moss hadn't followed her. Even though she was in her nightgown, she wasn't going to take time to change. As soon as she made the phone call she was going to leave the apartment.

In a moment, she heard him groggily say, "Hello."

"Dad, come get me! Please, come get me now. I want to come home."

***

Epilogue

Silence punctuated the slamming of the door and a familiar ache of loss stabbed Mary Ann in the stomach when she realized it was over. Reaching across the bed, she touched the warm spot where Jocelyn had been sleeping just moments before and cradled her pillow in her arms. The citrus smell of her shampoo perfumed the pillow and the sheet still carried the heat of her body. In despair, Mary Ann curled her body around the pillow and sobbed. "Margaret, where are you? I can't go through this again."

The heaviness in her body made it hard for her to get out of Jocelyn's bed and open the bathroom cabinet. Swallowing pill after pill, she lay down on the bathroom floor and waited for the final shadow. Carter McDeal had won.

About the Author

Proud to be a native Floridian, Jeanne Moon Farmer has set most of her stories in the diverse cities of this beautiful state. Like her characters, her life has been lived against a background of sandy beaches, palm trees, and unbelievable humidity. And she sees a story behind every hibiscus.

As a wife, mother, daughter, teacher, writer, and friend, she is curious about the threads that bind us to other human beings and searches for significance in the life-dramas that teach us who we are. Her writing reflects the journey of people who have been tried and tested by their own choices -- some are defeated by those choices, while others learn they can rise above the consequences of those choices through forgiveness and love.

Her writing career includes more than twenty years of technical writing in the field of education and one published work of poetry entitled Everything Makes A Difference (co-authored with Dr. Burt Bertram). Her award winning short story, Wheels of Honor, will be published in the Florida Writer's Association 2012 Anthology.

She is a member of the Florida Writer's Association and two critique groups. She holds a degree in English from Florida State University where she studied creative writing with two writers who were profoundly influential, James T. Cox (O'Henry award winner) and Michael Shaara (The Killer Angels). Over the years she has led workshops on technical/grant writing and has honed her skills by attending various conferences and symposiums led by experts in the field of writing.

Joy comes from sharing life with her family - husband, four grown sons, two daughters-in-law - and from having beach sand between her toes.

Her new novel, My Mother's Shadow, will be released in Spring 2013. Read an excerpt at www.familyshadows.com or follow her blog at www.thenextbestseller.org

www.ingramcontent.com/pod-product-compliance
Lightning Source LLC
Chambersburg PA
CBHW031436240626
47154CB00001B/291

9 781938 643002